Spirit
of the
Revolution

by

Debbie Peterson

Spirit of the Revolution

Cover Art by *Angela Anderson*

The Wild Rose Press, Inc.
PO Box 708
Adams Basin, NY 14410-0708
Visit us at www.thewildrosepress.com

Publishing History
First Faery Rose Edition, 2013
Print ISBN 978-1-61217-763-2
Digital ISBN 978-1-61217-764-9

Published in the United States of America

"And—what about you?" Once again, Jo held her breath while she awaited his reply.

Mathias gave her his full attention then. His gaze bore into hers. He sought something, but she couldn't guess. Nonetheless, the look in his eyes at this moment fanned the embers that had settled into her belly. Finally, he spoke.

"I never found anyone special—while in my mortal state," he said.

His answer pleased her. "Oh," however, was all she could think to say in return. Should she add, "Gee, that's too bad" when she truly didn't feel that way? She opted to say nothing more.

"And you?" he asked.

The question caught her off guard. How could she explain what she herself could not? She clasped her hands together, laid them on her lap, and toyed with her fingers. The intensity of Mathias's gaze compelled her to form an answer. "I guess I'm still waiting around to find the unique kind of love my parents shared. I've yet to find it."

Praise for *SPIRIT OF THE REBELLION*

"Civil War ghosts, and ultimate true love create an absolutely enchanting love story. It will have you believing in the magic from the moment you begin reading it. I enjoyed Spirit of the Rebellion, and would very highly recommend it to someone who enjoys a very intelligent book revolving around the aspect of historical romance. You won't regret reading it, I can guarantee it."

~Heather, Sizzling Hot Books

"I cried, I laughed and I fell in love. This wonderful story had it all. This was magical from the beginning until the end."

~Robin, Romancing the Book

"The ending was absolutely amazing; I had hoped for one way and got an even better one."

~Jessica, Wonderland Reviews

"This lovely story captured my attention with its wonderful characters, intense plot, and well written structure. Good ghost romance stories are hard to come by, but this one is a definite keeper!"

~Nikki, Siren Book Reviews

"The romance is heart-wrenching and wonderful and simply toe-curling."

~Englishrose, Clean Romance Review

Dedication

Mom and Dad, this one is for you.
My very own Kay-Kay and Ray.
I love you both so much. Thank you for
all of the love and support, all the days of my life.

And to our beloved Arabian mare,
Lacy Velour 1985-2011.
You are forever immortalized on these pages...

Prologue

Berks County, Pennsylvania
June 16, 1778

A single melodic trill broke the early morning silence. Another chirrup followed the first as Mathias McGregor approached the pasture fence with a saddle hefted over his broad shoulder. In that same instant, the black stallion ceased his grazing. He flung his head upward and turned his neck to face the sound. To the untrained ear, the prolonged warble was naught but the call of a screech owl. Yet, knowing the difference, Beadurinc nickered in response. In obedience born of loyalty and affection, the powerful steed loped across the grassy field to where he waited.

Mathias saddled the horse, mounted up, and then turned his stallion toward the woodland. Once inside the forest, he urged him into a gallop for the need to outrun the dawn. The rustle of dried leaves and the snap of dry, broken twigs accompanied each well-placed hoof. Yet the clamor didn't endanger their journey. Far from disturbing the nocturnal sounds of the forest, they blended in perfect harmony.

Mathias used these elements to his advantage, just as he always used them during this time of uncertainty and war. With calm assurance, he maneuvered through the trees and toward his point of rendezvous. The charred remains of the Van Gelder's barn loomed in the distance. He reined his mount to a halt and slid to the ground. After he dropped the reins, he gave the horse a gentle pat, and left him to graze. The stallion wouldn't wander far.

Mathias's gaze drifted over the landscape, searching for any threat to his current task. Finding nothing amiss, he inched his way forward. He stayed in the darkest shadows as each noiseless footstep brought him ever nearer the rear of the barn. The side door hung precariously on a single hinge, yet he slipped through the entrance without making a sound. He stepped into the obscurity of the darkened corner and waited.

More than once, he took his grandfather's gold pocket watch from its resting place and glanced down at the time. Worry set in as the appointed hour slipped away minute by precious minute. Had something happened to prevent his contact's arrival? Personal danger increased the longer he waited—but perhaps he could spare a few minutes more. Sounds of wagon wheels rolling over the rutted trail ushered in the faint light of dawn. Voices called out to each other as those wagons halted very near the structure. Mathias withdrew his flintlock pistol and cocked the hammer. His left hand rested atop the handle of the large knife tucked inside his wide leather belt.

Footsteps grew louder, two pair, one lighter than the other. He turned his gaze in the direction of the large double doors and held his breath. Shadows cast by the faint light of the rising sun entered the interior first. He could now discern the form of a woman and a child moving along the ground and toward the barn door.

"Mathias?" the woman whispered his name as she entered the structure.

He slowly released his breath, replaced the pistol,

and emerged from the shadows. "Elisabeth, has something happened to Jacob?" he asked in a voice barely audible.

Elisabeth gazed upon her son and shook her head. "No. A few hours ago, the Redcoats asked my husband to accompany them on their march to New York. He couldn't refuse, and he couldn't send word. So, he sent me in his stead. I am to deliver this." She extracted a small scrap of paper from the pocket of her homespun apron. "He would allow me to carry no more than that, I'm afraid."

"You're taking quite a risk meeting me here, whether you carry anything or not." Mathias took hold of the note and tucked it inside the pocket of his vest. "Will you be all right?"

"Yes." She pursed her lips together and then said, "Jacob has charged me with taking the children up north to my father's home. To ensure our safety, he has asked us to stay there until the war ends. We're on our way there now. I bade Willem to ask for a moment of privacy as we approached so none of the servants would suspect my purpose. We must leave now in order to keep it that way."

"Then God speed," Mathias replied.

"Mathias—" Elisabeth placed a hand on his arm to halt his departure. "The information Jacob has acquired is one of great importance. He said you *must* deliver it to General Washington with all haste."

Mathias nodded, made his way to the side door, and left the barn in the same manner in which he entered. He waited for the wagons to pass before he returned to the forest. Beadurinc nickered as he approached, and then sidled up next to his master. Mathias took hold of the reins and drew them over the stallion's head. Before he mounted, he withdrew the note from his pocket and perused the contents. The torn scrap of paper no bigger than an oak leaf simply read, "Time is key" and nothing more. He destroyed the missive in the instant. Without doubt, the message intended for General Washington lay hidden somewhere inside Jacob Weidmann's home. With luck on his side, he could gather his small force of Rangers and conduct their search before the sun climbed much higher.

Less than one hour later Mathias and his four companions rode hard and fast, cutting through the woods toward Weidmann's homestead. Since the Lobsterback army evacuated the area, they didn't expect to encounter any obstructions in regards to this latest mission.

Yet, short of their destination, a large platoon of English soldiers burst through the trees in all directions at once. Mathias reined his mount to a halt. He turned his gaze to his right, to his left, and then behind him in an effort to size up his opponents. Their presence puzzled him until his gaze fell upon Percival Peddelton—one of the Weidmann's most valued and trusted servants. He narrowed his eyes as his gaze drilled into those of the traitorous worm that slithered up a tree seeking refuge.

"That one, right there in the center," Percival said with bravado, as he pointed him out from the safety of his treetop perch. "Mrs. Weidmann gave him something important, and he stuffed it inside his left pocket not one hour ago. I witnessed the whole incident from start to finish. Everyone around these parts knows the McGregors align themselves with the patriots. Whatever she gave him, you can trust it involved our enemy."

The English leader ordered them to dismount. The

Redcoats vastly outnumbered Mathias and his men. That simple fact produced an irritating smirk on the mouth of the officer in charge. The man assumed Mathias and his men would obey his order without hesitation, question, or incident. In return, a single corner of his mouth curved upward. One should never assume. In that same moment, several things happened simultaneously.

"I've a mind to take the lot of them to hell with us, Mathias, starting with that one, right there," bellowed Samuel Fraser. The sound of his voice boomed like thunder as it echoed throughout the forest. The startled soldiers cast each other furtive glances. Then before any member of the Lobsterback army could react to his bold declaration, Sam yanked the pistol out of his belt and with one shot, wiped the smirk from the leader's face.

Just as Sam made his statement, Mathias locked his gaze on Percival Peddelton. He took a small measure of satisfaction when fear replaced the smug expression on the coward's face. With lightning speed, Mathias drew his flintlock in concert with Sam's, and fired. A millisecond later, both Peddelton and the English officer lay dead. Their unexpected deaths set off a haze of musket powder, ball, and shot. Projectiles continued to fly in all directions. As the battle raged, more than half the English platoon fell to the expertise of the five Rangers they intended to capture, torture, and hang.

Their ammunition spent and no time to reload, Mathias and his elite unit made use of every weapon at their disposal. Each Ranger fought bravely for their lives as well as their country. The battle lasted less than fifteen minutes. One by one, each loyal companion fell under a barrage of English gunfire and bayonet that flew from all directions at once.

Then finally, one ball found its target and pierced Mathias McGregor's heart. Slipping away from his mortal frame didn't trouble him and while he witnessed the slow descent of his physical body, he beheld the carnage of the last battle he would ever fight for his beloved nation. The scene yielded a clarity his natural eyes could never have seen.

He had no idea this is what it would feel like to die and the experience amazed him. A brilliant light appeared off to his right. The iridescent beam beckoned him to enter, just as it surely compelled the vast array of dead English soldiers who wandered the grounds looking stunned, lost, and confused. Most of them entered, but some walked away. Mathias stood there in indecision as Sam ambled up from behind and rested an elbow atop his shoulder. Alexander, William, and Jedediah followed, ever loyal in life, now loyal in death.

"Well, I believe this is just about the most extraordinary experience I've ever had," Sam remarked, his tone casual. "Now tell me Mathias, what would you like us to do from here?"

Chapter 1

Present Day Pennsylvania
Late spring

"Okay, Carolyn, I put you on loud speaker so I can set the phone down. Hopefully, you can still hear everything I'm doing." Jo placed her phone on the small antique table left of the sofa. "Right now I'm picking up the very last box. As you already know, it's filled with my most precious things."

"So, dive in and unpack it already," said Carolyn.

"Now you know I can't do that." Jo shook her head as she sat down, placed the box atop her lap, and inched the tape off the cardboard lid centimeter by centimeter.

"Jolena Leigh Michaelsson! What in the world is the matter with you? Why are you removing that tape at a snail's pace? Don't think I can't hear you," Carolyn berated. "Do you or do you not want to be an official resident of your house?"

"You know I do, and you also know anticipation is part of the excitement. I'm supposed to savor this moment, Kay-Kay, you know this," she said using the nickname she gave Carolyn Taylor, well before they discarded their diapers. "If I just 'dive in' as you suggest, this party will end before it begins. Where is the fun in all that?" The exasperated sigh on the other end of the line made Jo laugh.

"Oh, whatever," Carolyn grumbled. "You know this is the very reason I've yet to return to the house. You would surely drive me crazy by *savoring* all of your *special* moments. I mean, get real, girl. What could possibly be so special about taking an hour to plant your last bush or finishing the last section of trim with a one-inch paintbrush? Get on with it, already."

"The excitement, as well as the pleasure, comes in seeing this house restored to its former glory, piece by precious piece. You know, for someone who holds a PhD in anthropology and archeology, you have no imagination or patience whatsoever."

"That's not altogether true, Jo. Just because I didn't want to keep driving out to the house during the restoration, doesn't mean I lack imagination. And patience? How can you say that when a simple dig can take months of excavation one tiny shovel at a time. Well, I'll have you know—"

While Carolyn rambled on, Jo's mind wandered back to the day she stumbled across this place. The journey began as a quest to find the rural farm properties in southeastern Pennsylvania that once belonged to her ancestors. Not that she expected them to look as they did back then, of course. But having a love of world history, family history, and all things antique, she just wanted to see some of the same things they may have seen. Look at the world through their eyes. It really didn't take her long to get lost, and she never did discover the exact location her ancestors lived. But she did find this house.

Despite the shameful neglect, she found the underlying beauty of the homestead amazing. Her vivid imagination conjured the glorious dinner parties and garden luncheons the original owners surely hosted during the late eighteenth century. Something about the house compelled her to explore it, and the faded For Sale sign hanging halfway off the front gate provided permission. After she exited the car, she approached the walkway and took a moment to absorb every detail of the property.

An overgrowth of decayed vines and leaves climbed and twisted in complete disarray over the stone exterior. Massive round pillars held a lovely wrap-around terrace, but the balustrades needed repair. Broken windows needed replacing. The trim needed a miracle. Large, hideous weeds had overtaken the once grand gardens. The former lush lawn had all but disappeared. Add a bit of misty fog, a few creepy ravens, and in its present condition the house would resemble something straight out of a Hollywood horror movie.

She approached the front doors, and found them locked. A search for a hidden key yielded nothing. However, the back door at the rear of the house welcomed her with arms wide open. She peeked inside and stepped over the threshold. This door led into the kitchen, and she gasped in delighted surprise as she took in the old-fashioned charm. The original owners trimmed the large country kitchen with a generous amount of brick on the walls and pine planking on the floor. A wood burning stove still sat on a raised brick platform along the center of the west wall. With a bit of hard work she could restore the kitchen to its former splendor. Thanks to all the lessons from a patient father, she could do a great deal of the labor herself. That would save a ton of money.

She picked her way through scattered debris, dust, and cobwebs to explore the rest of the house. Her mind contrived each room in the original condition. Somehow, she just had to find a way to buy this house and restore it the way she envisioned.

She climbed up the staircase while caressing the hand-carved railing. Jo wandered through each spacious room on the second floor. From the bedroom at the end of the hallway, she strolled out onto the balcony, withdrew her cell phone from her pocket, and called the number on the sign below. The agent said the owner would consider any offer she presented. A true enough statement as the gentleman sold her the property far below the listed price.

Thus began months of hard physical labor, about fifty tubes of analgesic, several boxes of Band-Aids in various shapes and sizes, and more than half her savings. Still, the house turned out better than what she ever imagined.

"Jo? Are you still there?" asked Carolyn, transporting her back to the present.

"Still here and just waiting for you to finish your tirade so I can open the box," she said. "For someone who is in such a big hurry—"

"You haven't even cracked the lid?" wailed Carolyn. "Jo! We don't have all day here. Just because you're on vacation doesn't mean the rest of us are."

"Okay, okay. Box is open and I'm removing the top most treasures, which I wrapped in a generous amount of tissue. Do you hear the paper rustling as I open each individual layer?"

"Jo—"

Jo met the playful warning with laughter. "Oh, yes. I'm looking at the tiny pair of porcelain Cinderella slippers I inherited from my grandmother. Did I ever tell you she received these little blue-and-gold slippers as a wedding gift? Oh, and in the same bundle as the slippers,

I have her elegant white swans with dainty floral motif—ditto the history. Do you remember them?"

"Yes, of course," Carolyn said. "I've always coveted those swans, so if one day you find them missing—"

Jo laughed anew as she arranged the curios on the shelf and then returned to the box. She peeked inside the container. "Okay, I'm now taking out and removing the bubble wrap from around my clock." She took a moment to gaze at the simple beauty of her Delander calendar clock. This walnut clock had passed through at least seven generations of family members. The piece made the arduous trip from the east coast to the west coast and back again. Yet, it remained in perfect condition. Even the silver-and-brass calendar movements adorning both sides of the golden face, still functioned without flaw.

"I don't hear anything—"

"Well, I'm giving the wood a final polish, so what's to hear?" She laughed as Carolyn sighed and muttered under her breath. "Now I'm placing it dead center atop my gorgeous, hand-carved fireplace mantel. I'm setting the time and calendar. I hope you can hear all of this—now giving the pendulum a gentle nudge, closing the face and—it looks perfect. Too bad you aren't here to see if for yourself."

"Aw—don't sound so pathetic. Musicians are only supposed to cry with their music, isn't that right?"

"Good try," Jo countered. "All right, now placing the pictures of family members, generations past and all the way to the present."

While she arranged each of her treasured family heirlooms about the room, Carolyn shared the moment with her. She stayed on the phone until she set her very last Irish pewter goblet on the shelf.

"Well, I guess that's it," Jo said as she brushed the long strands of dark auburn hair off her face and stood back to survey the results. Just as she made the comment, the sun descended below the horizon under a cloud-filled sky. The brilliant colors the duo created cast a warm golden glow through the sparkling windows and into the room.

"All right, I'm officially moved in and the place looks beautiful, even if I do say so myself," she said with a firm nod of her head.

Carolyn met the announcement by blowing a variety of party favor squeakers and applauding for several minutes. "I'm so happy for you. But I want you to know I already miss having you here with me," she said.

"Well then, I guess you'll just have to come out and see the house in all its regal glory. Maybe you could spend some time here. Just think, you could indulge in a little peace and quiet," Jo baited.

"Sounds wonderful. I'll take you up on that offer the first chance I get, too. Listen, I really do have to go now. But thanks so much for sharing your glorious moment with me, and I have a little house-warming gift for you the next time I see you. You're going to love it."

Jo's smile faded as she hung up the phone and took in the wondrous sight of her empty house. Carolyn supported her from the beginning of her purchase and all the way through the arduous renovations. But even her encouragement and enthusiasm couldn't fill the void inside her heart.

Somehow, she arrived smack in the middle of her late twenties, without her knight in shining armor having the decency to show up on his magnificent white charger. Considering her current circumstances, she didn't expect him to make his grand entrance anytime soon either. Therefore, without so much as a "by your leave," she ditched him by the wayside. Well, maybe it took more than an attitude and a snooty lift of her nose. Still, she didn't need a man to make her happy. He simply would've been the icing on the cake she already had.

She had a very satisfying career as a violinist with the world-famous Philadelphia Orchestra, a position she long studied for and worked hard to get. Her career enabled her to travel to many places some only dreamed of going and now enabled her to buy this beautiful home. She could go anywhere she wanted to go and do as she pleased, whenever she pleased. She didn't need to ask anyone's opinion, fret over feelings or conflicting schedules. Life just couldn't get any better, could it?

Just keep telling yourself that, Jo, the tiny voice at the back of her mind taunted. *Maybe one day, you'll believe it.*

A sigh escaped her lips as she shook away the somber thoughts. *Enough of this.* After willfully shifting her mood, she gave her head a little toss and said, "Well, Jo—look at it this way, no one will fuss over how long you're in the shower or crab about how much hot water you use."

"Unless the length of stay is a cause for alarm, of course."

Jo gasped, her mouth dropped and as she spun around to confront the owner of that voice, a hand flew to her heart. Yet, she didn't encounter a soul during the process. No one could've slipped past her either. As she stepped out onto the stone floor of the entryway, she inched her way to the double doors. She took hold of the large round knob and turned it just enough to free the

13

latch. Such an act prepared her in the event she needed to sprint outside. Once outside, she could run screaming down the street.

"Hello? Is someone here? Can I help you?"

No one responded, nor did she hear any sound coming from inside the house. She shook her head and released both the knob and the breath she had held. Her grandfather clock across from the hall tree pointed to the lateness of the hour. She had risen extra early in order to arrive here at dawn determined to finish the house. After the long, arduous hours, fatigue simply set in. Because of that fatigue and the previous reflections of her non-existent knight, she conjured a voice. A magnificent male voice, with a deep, rich timbre and charming accent she couldn't quite place. Mystery solved.

Besides, if anyone snuck into the house, the dog would've sounded the alarm. His ferocious bark would've alerted her immediately. Not to mention, the stone floor echoed when one walked on it, and the massive oak doors creaked when they opened and closed. Old homes just made odd noises. Right? She would have to get accustomed to each one of them or she would find herself jumping all over the place like some nervous ninny.

Just then, the striking of the old iron doorknocker resonated against the metal plate outside. The harsh clank shot through the door, and vibrated against her head. Her hands flew to her mouth. She stifled a scream in the same moment it occurred that the clang simply announced a visitor on the other side of her door. She took a deep calming breath and a moment for composure. Then, she turned around, put a smile on her face, and twisted the knob.

Two couples, both well into middle age, stood a

considerable distance from her doorstep. One of the men, the one with streaks of gray throughout his mousy brown hair, offered her a large basket of fruit. He did so with his arms outstretched and his shoulders kind of hunched over as if he didn't want to budge the placement of his feet. A woman, most likely his wife, drew her brows tight together in disapproval and shooed him forward. The obvious designated spokesman of the group ventured a small, half step closer. And gulped—at least twice.

"Ah! Well, hello there, young lady. We're your neighbors, just down the way," he said, waving a nervous finger in a somewhat northerly direction. "My name is Douglas Parker, this here's my wife Gloria, and this is Richard and Ellen Anderson. They live just a few miles or so down the road and across from us.

"We, uh—well it appears you're all moved in now, what with the moving truck coming the other day. And um—we just wanted to welcome you to the community and let you know we're here if you should ever find you need us." The speech flew out of his mouth with all haste. Douglas then thrust the basket toward her, clearly wanting the whole business finished.

Once again, Jo smiled at her guests, and with a single nod of her head, accepted the offering. The two couples almost made her laugh aloud. They looked so completely opposite each other. The Andersons were fair of complexion, tall and slim, while the Parkers were dark, short, and a bit on the pudgy side.

"Thank you, you're very kind. My name is Jo Michaelsson, and you're right. I just finished unpacking the last of my boxes a few minutes ago. I'm excited to say, I'm officially settled in." She stood back to allow them entrance and swept a hand toward her sitting room.

"Please, won't you come in?"

The look they gave each other all but screamed, "Not on your life, missy! Wild dogs couldn't drag us in there." But, after a deep breath, they followed her inside. Her brows lifted a tad, and she inhaled a breath of her own as she followed these very different people into her sitting room.

The woman named Ellen halted her footsteps just as she crossed the archway. She took a moment to absorb every detail, from the ivory-painted walls, decorative crown moldings, and baseboards, to the warm earth tones Jo used to accent them. The gaze of her guest lingered over the small built-in arched shelf in the corner, littered with porcelain antiques. Her mouth dropped as she studied her antique secretary, tea tables, and chairs, all artfully arranged on the polished hardwood floor.

"Oh, my goodness," the woman finally said. "Look what you've done to this place. This room is just beautiful. I can't ever remember a time when I've seen it looking so grand. *Not* that I have been inside the house overly much, mind you."

While the others bobbed their heads in agreement, Jo beamed with pleasure. "Thank you. I've put many hours of hard work into the place. At times, I wondered if I would ever get finished." She gestured toward the furniture. "Please, sit down and make yourselves comfortable."

They exchanged expressions of sympathy as they gingerly sat on the edge of the sofa. Why they huddled together on the couch while three very comfortable chairs remained empty, escaped all comprehension. In fact, she had difficulty understanding the strangeness of these people all the way around. Why would they feel sorry for her? Did they or did they not just give her a compliment regarding the restoration of the property?

"Is something wrong?" she asked as she gazed from one face to the other.

"Oh. No—no. Well, uh, yes, what I mean to say is..." Gloria stammered, while looking to Ellen for help.

"Oh sweetheart, it's just that—wait a minute. Did you say your name is Jo Michaelsson?" asked Ellen as she sat up a little straighter and placed a hand on her husband's arm.

Jo could literally see that piece of information locking into Ellen's brain. "Yes, I did."

"Do you happen to play with the Philadelphia Orchestra?" she ventured again.

"Yes, I do," she replied.

"Oh my goodness. Then you are Jolena Michaelsson, of course. You know, we attended a concert not too long ago." She turned to her companions with widened eyes and something akin to giddiness. "Remember the big charity performance we attended just before Christmas? She performed as the master violin soloist that evening. Anyone who knows anything about world orchestras knows her name. I must tell you, my dear, I especially loved your arrangement of 'O Holy Night.' You played it so beautifully you had me in tears."

The others turned to stare as if in awe.

Jo shook her head, a bit embarrassed over the fuss she made. "Well, thank you very much. You're very kind."

Her company relaxed a bit after Ellen's revelation, and proceeded to have a somewhat normal conversation. If only their eyes didn't keep darting about as if they expected Jack the Ripper to pop in, the evening might've been a little more pleasant. Gloria's furtive glances finally settled on her antiques, which elicited another gasp of delighted surprise. Better late than never, Jo supposed.

"Oh my. You've done this whole room in antiques. How on earth did you acquire such a collection?" Gloria raised an inquisitive eyebrow. "I mean, you just seem so young to have so many. You must've started this collection when you were just a child."

"Well, I guess you could say I'm one of the fortunate few who descend from a long line of pack rats," Jo replied. "As it so happened, either those pack rats produced very few living heirs, or the surviving siblings simply held no interest in all 'that junk.' Hence, many of the pieces passed to my parents and then on to me. I found a few of them myself along the way."

Questions followed the hesitant acceptance of tea and homemade applesauce cookies. Their inquiries covered everything from the restoration of her house to her career. Eventually, the talk turned to the community and those who lived in it. The fact that Gloria and Ellen were sisters surprised her, for Jo had never seen two people from the same family who seemed so different. Both couples expounded the pros and cons of rural life and gave advice on just about every topic one could possibly think to give. Or at least it seemed so.

Then, after a forever amount of time, the group fell silent. The loud rhythmic tick-tock of the clock made the silence feel even more awkward. Jo struggled for additional conversation, and all the while wished they would just go home. Then, just as she wished it, Richard Anderson jerked forward. He let out a yelp of surprise as he fumbled to find a position to keep from toppling over while hanging on to his cup. His legs wobbled as he shot to his feet. He then grabbed for his wife's ready hand to steady his stance.

"You know, it's late, and we really need to go. We've intruded far longer than we dare—need too, I mean." He gave the others a pleading look as he placed his cup on the tea table. Almost in unison, they rose from the sofa and thrust their hands toward her as if they too, wanted to leave.

"I enjoyed meeting you, Jolena," Gloria said as she gave her hand a brief shake.

"Likewise." She gave a nod and took each offered hand in turn, grateful for their imminent departure.

Gloria hesitated a moment and then cleared her throat. "Um, if you don't mind my asking, dear, is there a Mr. Michaelsson about?"

"No, I'm afraid not." Jo resisted the need to roll her eyes and sigh in exasperation. How she hated that question.

"You're here all by yourself then?" ventured Ellen once again.

"Well, I do have Dakota." She paused as her guests shot each other furtive glances. "Dakota is my dog, and for the past several years he's served as my guard, my companion, and my very dear friend. So, you see, I'm not all alone, after all."

"Oh, of course, but he's just a—" Ellen shook her head as her light brown eyes bore into Jo's deep blue ones. "*Do* be very careful dear. This house? Well, it's…I mean…no one ever stays here very long. Sometimes, it's just a few days at best. Some of the residents have even left belongings behind. Why, they even left food on the table when they…and they never returned to…to…"

Jo drew her brows together. She found it difficult to understand her incoherent babbling, especially when the woman didn't finish her sentences. "Excuse me? I don't know what you—"

"This house is *haunted*—" Gloria blurted the statement as she stepped in front of her sister. "The sounds and the sights that come off this property at times are, are—well they're unholy. That's what they are. No one in this community will step one foot near it for any length of time. I think it such a shame you put in all of this hard work and effort when you're just going to have to turn around and, and—"

Jo had to feign a cough to keep from laughing aloud. Did these people *really* believe in *ghosts* of all things? She hid her smile and attempted to appear a bit more concerned. "Well, I'm sure at one time, given the rundown appearance of the property, one might believe the house—"

"Oh, surely by now you've noticed the strange goings on around here," Ellen interrupted.

"Actually, I haven't seen anything out of the ordinary at all." Jo shrugged as she clasped her hands together and looked into each anxious, incredulous, face.

"Well, I can guarantee you will," Richard said with a firm nod of his head. "It's only a matter of time before something awful happens to you. We've seen it so many times. So, please, you must remain on your guard, especially since you're all alone out here, which I believe is even more—"

"Oh, I'll be careful, I promise," she cut in. "And don't worry, I do have Dakota, and he can be very fierce when he needs to be."

"Just the same," Douglas said as he gripped her hand

and drew it close to his chest. "Our phone numbers are on the card in the basket, we made sure. You can call day or night if you need us. We can, uh, come and pick you up should the need arise."

After thanking them once again for the fruit and their concern, her guests simply nodded and rushed out of the door. Richard whispered something then about icy hands snaking through the cushions and shoving him out of his seat. Jo laughed as she leaned against the closed door. She found it somewhat comical. Still, they had good intentions. Other than a few quirks and a need for a bit of therapy, they seemed like very nice people. Once she cleared her sitting room of empty cups, and cleaned up the kitchen, she opened the back door.

"Come on, Dak," she called. The enormous black-and-tan German shepherd ran to her side and nuzzled his head into her hand as he sought affection.

"So tell me, did you have fun chasing squirrels all over the property today? I bet you really enjoy having all of this space to run in, don't you." She knelt down, gathered him close for a long hard hug, and ran her fingers through his soft coat.

"Well, while you ran about having the time of your life, sir, I had to entertain the neighbors. And guess what? They informed me we have ghosts lurking about the premises." Jo shook her head as she rose to her feet and made her way to the staircase.

"Come on, let's get ready for bed. This day has gone on far too long. I'm tired, and I want to soak in a nice hot bubble bath, complete with candles and soft music."

As she arrived at the first step, she paused, placed her hand on the banister, and looked down at her companion.

"And just so you know? You have guard duty."

Chapter 2

Courtesy of the unseen woman called both Kay-Kay and Carolyn, Mathias finally had the full name of his newest resident. Jolena Leigh Michaelsson. He folded his arms against his chest as he repeated it. The name had a nice ring to it. Finally, they wouldn't need to refer to her as "the girl" anymore.

He waited until Jolena fell into a deep sleep before he ventured into his library, which shared a wall with her bedroom. Over two centuries earlier, he claimed this room as his personal sanctuary. The recent renovations pleased him. Her impressive collection of leather-bound books promised hours of good reading, and the large ornate maple desk would come in handy while he read. She had placed several fascinating instruments on top of it, such as a compass, a sextant, and an astrolabe, to name a few.

He could study the magnificent floor globe, which detailed the current countries of the world, and discover centuries of changes. Behind the desk, she hung a large framed copy of the Declaration of Independence, a document he'd never had the opportunity to read, but could now study in depth. Most especially, he admired her painting of George Washington, entitled Prayer at Valley Forge. The artist truly depicted the spirit of that great and noble man. Jolena also chose this room to house her violin, and he looked forward to hearing her play the thing. Especially after the comments made by the irritating, addlepated neighbors.

She placed a couple of large brown leather chairs in the center of the room facing the fireplace with a small table to separate them. A settee sat against the outermost wall. In front of the chairs and settee, lay small oval rugs.

After he completed his inspection of the library, he headed for the stairs. He wanted to visit the parlor again, and this time, without the disturbance of unwanted guests. The endless chatter of those people could drive even the most patient saint to distraction. He found it a pleasure to rescue the very lovely damsel in distress from their boorish company, and she did look distressed, and then relieved once they vacated the premises.

An instant later, Mathias appeared at the entrance of the downstairs room with a sense of satisfaction. Not just because he ousted the neighbors, but also because the parlor made one feel welcome. The room hadn't accomplished such a feat for quite some time now. Contentment settled into his being as he made his way inside.

"Insufferable bores, the lot of them," Sam thundered beside him. "I didn't think they were ever going to leave. You know, until this evening, their tittle-tattle, and paltry offerings extended no farther than your foyer, and usually no closer than your doorstep. So, could you please tell me why in blazes that had to change now?"

"I don't have an answer for you, Sam." Mathias rubbed a hand against his mouth as he shrugged. "They did stay far longer than they ever dared stay before. Still, it took naught but a gentle nudge to remind them why they prefer the porch."

Sam snorted as he plopped himself on the sofa.

"Gentle indeed, the man almost landed face down on the floor. I wonder if your *nudge* will keep them from coming back, despite their obvious adoration for Jolena."

"I don't know. I suppose we can hope," Mathias replied.

"Or, serve up another reminder, either way. On the plus side, they managed to get us a bit of additional information we've hankered to know. I suppose we could belch out a 'Thank ye kindly' for that. We've learned she plays that fiddle upstairs. And, I'm relieved some miserable cur isn't going to show up on our doorstep expecting a grand welcome after she did all the hard work by herself. Still, there's but one question yet unanswered." Sam cocked one booted foot atop the other. "Did they manage to convince our lady the place is *haunted* or did they not?"

"Nah, I don't think she believes in ghosts," Mathias replied. "Yet."

"Well, that has to change, and soon." Sam stood and at once paced the length of the room with hands clasped behind his back. "The day will come, she'll notice something amiss. Such is inevitable. We can't control every element of our existence forever. A noise or two is bound to come through, especially when we go through our paces."

"I'm aware of that possibility."

"And need I mention everyone is chomping at the bit for an introduction? I mean, how long has it been since we've had the pleasure of such a beguiling woman living underneath our roof?" Sam tilted his gaze upward as he halted his steps. "Let's see, the last one, I believe, was that fine-looking housemaid of your great-great grand nephew. You know—the one with those fetching little dimples. Just what was her name, anyway? Let's see, Margaretha or Margeurite—Maria?"

Mathias blew out a derisive snort and shook his head. "You know very well her name was Margaret, you besotted fool. After all, you were the one who mooned after the girl day and night. You shadowed every step she took, thus making *her* believe in ghosts fast enough. If I recollect correctly, she left shortly after you showed your unsightly face to her though, didn't she?"

Sam merely shrugged, showing no concern over the comment. "If truth be known, 'twas the sight of your ugly face that made her leave. Why, I'd leave myself if you didn't need constant looking after."

"*If* I had allowed her to see my face, lad, I fear she would've mooned after *me*," Mathias countered. "Still, you're right about Jolena. She needs to learn we're here before she happens to catch a sound or shadow. Just the sight of our spiritual form might make her turn tail and run. I don't see the fairness in that after she has gone to all the trouble of making the house livable again."

"Definitely not." Samuel's lips twitched over the remark.

"Want to explain the smirk?" Mathias stepped back and placed an elbow atop the fireplace mantel.

"Oh come on, Mathias, it amuses me the notion of Jolena leaving even troubles you. For the past eight, maybe nine decades, you focus more on evicting the living, than you do anything else. Heaven knows we enjoy that particular sport more than any other, and if I say so himself, we get better at it all the time."

"Yes, well—all of that aside, you have to admit this house needed extensive repair. Now that she's restored the place, she deserves to share in the bounty. So, I think it best for all concerned to introduce myself first. Whether or not she realizes it, she's already responded to my whispered suggestions concerning the work of restoration." Mathias stroked a hand along the length of his jaw as he regarded his companion. "Therefore, she might not find it too much of a shock if I introduce myself in current form."

He need not disclose the fact he revealed himself audibly today. Samuel would jump all over that revelation like flies to stink, and he would never hear the end of it. "Once she accepts my presence, I believe she wouldn't find it at all difficult to meet everyone else."

"If you think it best," Sam replied as he fiddled with the porcelain swans on the shelf. "But again, I wouldn't wait too long. The lads remained on their best behavior while she restored the house just as you requested. That in itself is an extraordinary feat, and I commend you for it. However, I don't know how much longer we can expect them to hold back—"

"Expect who to hold what back?" the voice behind them asked. Mathias and Sam turned toward the other three residents as they popped into the room. Each, with broad grins on their faces, gazed about the finished parlor and nodded their approval.

"Well, Mathias, I must say this room looks even better than it did in our mortality." Alexander stepped over to the secretary and played with the ink well and quill.

"You know, my Aunt Eliza possessed an ivory tea set that looked just like this one," William said. He sidled up next to the small round table, lifted the lid, and peered inside. "Alex is right. The girl has made the parlor feel like home."

"We are home, you dolt." Samuel shook his head, looked heavenward, and rolled his eyes. "Only now we needn't worry about the place falling down around our ears."

"*Jolena* has exceeded all my expectations, Alex," Mathias said. "She's left nothing undone, and the homestead looks better than it ever has before."

"Jolena, you say?" asked Jedediah as he turned toward him. "We finally have her name?"

"Jolena Leigh Michaelsson, to be precise," Sam cut in. "And, it should please you all to know, she plays that fiddle upstairs in Mathias's room. And from all reports, she plays it quite well."

"Then this calls for a celebration." William slapped Alexander on the back. "A toast, Mathias, and be quick about it, man."

Joyful laughter filled the room as a frothy mug of ale suddenly appeared in each hand, each pewter mug filled with a liquid only they could see and taste. They raised their tankards high and waited for him to speak.

"My very good friends—" With a subtle bow, Mathias acknowledged each man in turn. For in truth and deed, one could not find a greater group of friends, breathing or not.

Samuel Fraser stood at his side longer than he had recollection. They were born within a week of each other, lived a stone's throw apart, and shared countless adventures, both good and some not *quite* as good, perhaps. Still, for as long as he held memory Sam watched his back, and by the saints, he'd done the same.

William Ferguson and Alexander Buchanan, both hailing from New Jersey, removed to Pennsylvania with their parents as young lads, no more than seven years of age. He recalled the day he and Sam invited them to join their wild escapades, lest boredom beset them. They accepted the invitation on the spot. To their good credit, they never once uttered a single regret or complaint despite the numerous difficult situations they found themselves in along the way.

Jedediah Gatlin, born of God-fearing, hard-working Virginia folk arrived much later. They took him on board just prior to the war. At that time in their lives, tempers ran high, skirmishes seemed common, and people chose sides. Jedediah did not hesitate to choose theirs. Despite his age, he remained brave, tenacious, and fiercely loyal.

Together they made up a small fraction of the legendary force known as Morgan's Rangers. This army of handpicked men noted for their marksmanship, and extraordinary skills, served under the command of Colonel Daniel Morgan. It pleased Mathias that he and his men completed each assignment with audacity and precision—save one.

"We've shared many adventures together, lads," said Mathias. "May the homestead continue to uphold our chosen pursuits another two hundred years at least."

"Let us not forget the lass," William called out. "We couldn't celebrate now if not for her devotion to this house."

Alexander raised his mug yet again and said, "To Jolena, who restored our home as well as our good nature."

A barrage of toasts and conversation followed as his men continued their celebration. In truth, they hadn't experienced this grand a time in a very long while.

"I think it only fitting to toast Dakota as well," Jedediah said, after the toasts ran out. "He readily accepted our presence and helped liven up the place. Put us all in much better spirits, if you'll pardon the expression."

"Leave it to that pup to draw attention to the dog," Sam hooted, "when the rest of us have our minds firmly planted on that fine-looking woman, upstairs."

His comment solicited another round of raucous laughter, barbs, comments, and exchanges from the men as they continued to commemorate the fine restoration of their home.

****

The clanking of metal against metal, laughter, and a lot of "Hear, hear," slowly wafted up the stairs and intruded into the dreams of Jo Michaelsson. In this dream, she walked in on some kind of party taking place inside her sitting room. A large room made small by some very attractive, well-muscled men who looked as if they enjoyed their celebration. They talked about—about something. She couldn't quite grasp the wisps of memory that still lingered. Let's see—they wore something that just seemed so—so— Hmm. Just what *were* they wearing? She couldn't remember now.

In the vague memory of her dream, the tallest and most attractive man of the group, turned, and met her gaze. Until that moment, none of them paid her any attention. She slowly opened her eyes to make sense of it. All seemed quiet enough. Dakota gazed up at her from his large cedar bed on the floor, his head tilted.

"Everything is okay, sweetheart." She patted him affectionately. "Just another bizarre dream." Jo yawned, turned to her side, and closed her eyes once again. She settled a little more deeply into her covers and drifted off to sleep.

The men grew quiet, knowing their boisterous celebration disturbed the sleep of their guest. Mathias almost laughed aloud. Each of his men held their breath, as if they still had breath to hold.

"We'll have to remember we've a guest we're not purposefully trying to run off this time around and hold down the volume. At least until she meets us," he said in an effort not to disturb her more.

Mathias waited until his companions dispersed before he made his way up the stairs and around to Jo's bedside. He gazed down on her sleeping form. She looked so small in her great big bed. Waves of long hair spilled across the pillow, and her long black lashes hid her lovely blue eyes. Still, she looked as if she slept peacefully enough. He needed that reassurance, and he needed to know their celebration hadn't troubled her overly much. At least that's what he told himself.

But if truth revealed itself, his visit held more than just that. He greatly admired her strength, tenaciousness, and indelible spirit, and he found himself drawn to her like moth to flame. Although he courted personal danger by allowing her to remain underneath his roof, he found he could do naught but stay the course, to whatever end it might lead.

Chapter 3

"Okay, Dak, vacation time is over, I'm afraid," Jo said as Dakota followed her into the kitchen. "I think we've allowed ourselves to get just a little too lazy and fancy free these days. So, *your* job this morning is to go outside and chase those wretched squirrels away from the house. Mine is to head into the library and start working on those new pieces I received this morning—*if* I still remember how to play the violin, that is."

She opened the door and at once Dakota bounded toward the big oak tree in the center of the yard. He did a playful little leap in the air while furiously wagging his tail, then crouched down, and jumped up again as if chasing a bug. A scant moment later, he ran from one end of the property to the other, halted once in the middle, sat down, and then tore off again. His crazy antics made her laugh.

Jo returned to the foyer, swept her package from off the hall tree table, and ascended the stairs. Just as she entered the library, the ceiling fan fluttered a page of the open book atop the desk. Feeling a little bewildered, she picked up her copy of *The Red Badge of Courage*, and stared at it. Strange, she just didn't remember taking it off the shelf. Again. No matter, for the second time this week, she simply put it back where it belonged and turned her attention to her parcel.

After removing the contents from the envelope, Jo

settled into one of the big leather chairs and flipped through each piece of music. A sudden chill coursed through her body. Odd, but this room always seemed so much cooler than the rest of the house. Perhaps a blocked vent needed attention, but not today. Once again, she focused on the music, studying each piece in the order she received it. About three quarters of the way through the stack, she turned a page. Andre Popp's "Love is Blue" met her startled gaze.

For the meaning it held to them personally, her deceased parents favored this song above all others. As she closed her eyes, she could see them dancing, snuggled close in each other's arms, oblivious to anything or anyone else in the room while the song played. They shared a deep and wondrous once-upon-a-time-and-happily-ever-after kind of love and oh, how she missed them. The one—the only—consolation to their passing? They made their final journey together. Coincidentally, they made that trip exactly five years ago today. Perhaps they used this music to say hello. Wiping a tear from her eye, she sniffed as she rose from her seat. She took up her violin and placed the music on her stand. Jo played the piece as if they listened. Perhaps somewhere, they did.

****

Mathias fixed his gaze upon Jolena the moment she entered his domain. His anticipation mounted as she retrieved her violin, nestled it against her chin, and touched bow to string. The enchanting music that followed stirred his soul, for by the saints, she played like an angel.

One by one each of his men, drawn to the beauty of the music, entered the room. Over the next few hours, they remained quiet and attentive. She played piece after piece of music—until the phone rang and ended the pleasure.

The stern look on his face warned against any outward demonstration of discontent or complaint over the unwanted interruption. He cocked his head toward the door and as requested, the lads vacated the room. Once again, he made Jolena the focus of his attention. Her eyes widened and a smile appeared as she yanked the phone from the receiver.

"Nancy Lou! I take it you're finally home. Did you enjoy your Hawaiian vacation?"

"I'll e-mail you some pictures when I get the digitals downloaded. Then you'll see for yourself just how much we enjoyed touring the islands," the woman replied. "Little Mary took to all the traveling as you'd expect. As long as we took her 'bye-bye' by car, boat, or plane, she stayed happy enough. And you should've seen the boys. I found it difficult to get them out of the ocean and convince them to put away the surfboards long enough to see some of the sights we wanted to see."

"That doesn't surprise me in the least."

"Yes, well, on the other hand, Jeannie couldn't stay away from the Polynesian Cultural center in Oahu. I think one young Samoan man in particular caught her attention. He spent a little more time than necessary teaching her how to crack open a coconut. I really couldn't blame the infatuation though. He did have some pretty good pecs, but don't you dare tell Bob I said so."

Jolena laughed over the comment. "Don't worry, I won't.

"So tell me, are you finally settled into your new home? No—wait a minute before you answer that question. I can tell something is wrong, so, out with it,"

Nancy commanded.

"Oh, Nan, buying and restoring this house is the greatest thing I have ever done in my whole life. You should see my garden. The flowers are all in bloom now, and they're just so beautiful. As soon as you can, you need to fly my babies out here for a long visit. You and Bob can come too, if you must." She placed her violin on the desk, and then settled into her chair.

"Oh. Well, thanks for the invite," Nancy retorted.

"Really, I just love it here, and the house turned out even better than what I hoped. The only problem I have is a nest of squirrels or mice living somewhere inside the house. I hear them at times, disturbing things, rattling around and what not, mostly at night. From the corner of my eye I frequently see their shadows, but I haven't discovered their point of entry so I can plug the hole," she added. "I will, though."

"Rodents have invaded your house? Well, of all the—yuck," Nancy sputtered. "Perhaps you ought to call an exterminator. Now tell me, what's wrong?"

"Oh, get real. I'm sure living out here where farmland abounds, an exterminator would only laugh and roll his eyes, don't you think? You get rid of one annoying rodent, and two more scurry in." Jolena bit down on her bottom lip and then added, "You know how it goes. They would probably just tell me to get a cat."

"You could at least give them a try. You've dumped a good chunk of your savings into the place. Therefore, you wouldn't want it infested with nasty creatures. They multiply like you wouldn't believe, they're destructive, and they pee and poop everywhere. Imagine the smell of that mess over time. Now, for the last time, and don't tell me 'nothing' because I can hear it in your voice, what's wrong?"

Jolena combed her fingers through her hair and sighed. "Well, it's because—you reminded me that you didn't get to share in the excitement of my 'Finally, I'm officially moved in party.' And I have to tell you, we missed hearing all of your snide comments while I unpacked my last box. Kay-Kay had to endure my reluctance to set the last goblet on the shelf, all by herself. Without the two of you ganging up on me, things took so much longer than usual, and it drove her crazy."

"Yeah—no. Give it up, Jo. There's something else, I can tell."

She placed a hand to her forehead as she released a lengthy breath. "Look, it truly is nothing for you to worry about. Tender emotions have risen to the top. That's all, I promise. You see, I finally received the music for the motion picture score I told you about a month or so ago, and you'll never guess what they've included in that score."

"So, then just tell me," Nan said.

"Mom and Dad's song. And wouldn't you know, the package arrived just this morning of all days." She breathed out a bit of a laugh as she closed her eyes. "In fact, I was just playing it through for the second time when you called, so now you know the reason I'm a bit weepy."

"Oh, that explains it. I know how you feel, Jo. I miss them too. If it makes you feel any better, we plan to visit the cemetery a little later today. We're going to put some fresh flowers on their graves."

"That's good. Add some for me, will you? You know, you would think their death would get easier to accept as time passes." Jolena dabbed at a tear and sniffed as she grabbed a tissue. "But it just doesn't seem to, does it."

"I'm so sorry for your loss, girl, truly I am."

Nancy said something comforting in return, but Jo didn't key onto it because she could swear that distinctive voice just whispered into her ear again. Her eyes swept over the library with unhurried thoroughness and found nothing out of the ordinary. How very odd. She didn't have a television or stereo in this room. The closest TV and stereo sat in her bedroom, and she'd yet to turn either of them on. In fact, she might not even have plugged them in.

"Jo? Are you still there? Did you here me?"

"Hmm? No—still here. I kind of lost the last thing you said, though," she said.

"I asked you about a convenient time to pack up the family for a visit. What's your schedule like during the summer months? Do you have the week before Labor Day free? The kids start back to school the Tuesday after, so maybe we can fly out then—"

Jo turned her attention away from imaginary voices and focused instead on the chat with her sister. They talked for well over an hour. As their conversation wound down, she said, "Well, Nan, give hugs and kisses to everyone in the family. You can also tell my thoughtless brother to call me every now and again, just to make sure I'm still alive, if for nothing else."

Nancy laughed over the comment. "Don't worry. I'm queen at making Eddie feel guilty, so look for his call. And listen, don't forget to call the exterminator because A, I want your house intact and beautiful when we arrive, and B, you and I both know how scared I am of anything that's furry and scurries."

"I'll call the exterminator, post haste, I promise. I love you and I'll talk to you later. Bye for now." Jo still wore a smile as she hung up the phone.

"You needn't call anyone. There's no vermin in the house."

Jo looked up, yet remained quite still while her hand rested atop the phone. She couldn't possibly have imagined the voice. Not this time. But where in the world did it come from? Once again, her gaze meandered around the room.

Just take a moment and think about the unexplained incidents you have observed. What about the celebration taking place in the parlor? You did witness part of that celebration, did you not? the voice inside her head whispered.

Flashes of memory swirled through her mind and she dismissed them at once. Perhaps she ate something disagreeable that night and it culminated in a most peculiar dream.

There's more to consider, what about the dog—

Dakota's behavior had changed a bit since they settled into the house, both inside and out. His playful actions didn't really look as if he chased something or tried to corner it, they look more like—

He's playing with someone. You've seen the evidence of that. And what about those flashes of motion?

The wandering shadows she saw so often from the corner of her eye were at eye level, not on the floor where she should expect to see squirrels or mice.

The shadows are much larger than any rodent could possibly make, correct? What about the occurrences in the library? Today isn't the first time you found the book out of place.

She had no reason or desire to take that book off the shelf, not unless she walked in her sleep. In her struggle to make sense of her mind muddle, the memory of her first guests crashed into the forefront. Now that she looked back on the visit, Richard looked more as if someone—

Shoved him from behind—

The sofa? Impossible. The sofa sat against the wall and Gloria said the house was—

Haunted.

The word made the hair on the back of her neck rise and goose bumps appear on her skin. She tried to recall everything she had ever read or seen concerning the subject. Jo swallowed hard and shook her head slightly while trying to make sense of this current dilemma.

Television documentaries reported shadows on the walls, and sometimes those interviewed insisted they followed orbs or what not. Shadows, yes; orbs, no. Cold spots throughout the house at various times definitely showed up in the group. She remembered ghost hunters running about old homes, mansions, or castles with some sort of electronic equipment measuring temperature in their quest to find cold spots.

Then she recalled those who professed to hear voices—check that one as a big yes—or seen apparitions. She'd yet to see an apparition, good thing too. Some interviews included people who talked about objects going missing and turning up again later in a place previously searched. She couldn't remember anything like that happening. Objects moving before one's very eye? Nope, unless she wanted to count Richard vaulting from his seat.

Oh, this is just silly. Surely, all of those events were

no more than figments of people's very active imaginations. A large part of the populace enjoyed the sensation of fear, and in turn, they conjured all sorts of unimaginable things in their quest to scare themselves silly. Kind of like people believing in vampires and werewolves, or fairies even—

"Just stop all of this nonsense, Jo," she berated herself aloud. "There are no such things as ghosts."

"Don't be so sure about that," an audible voice said. "For all things are possible, are they not?"

Jo's heart raced as she drew in short, shallow breaths. Bumps appeared on her arms once more. As she sought to rub them away, her eyes traveled around the room, looking for the source of that voice.

"Please, you needn't fear me. My intention is not to frighten or harm you," the voice whispered.

The sudden shiver that coursed throughout her body made Jo clench her teeth, and as she rose from her chair, she placed a hand to her brow.

"I can't believe I'm seriously saying this out loud." She shook her head and cleared her throat. "Look, I can hear you, you know, and I have—several times since I moved into this house. Whoever you are, whatever you are, just—just go ahead and show yourself before I think myself completely mad. Unless of course, you're a spineless coward who enjoys toying with people's sanity and driving them batty—"

"I may be many things, Miss Jolena Leigh Michaelsson." The presence dipped his head and folded his arms across the breadth of his chest. "But I like to think a coward isn't one of them."

Jo just stared at the image that suddenly appeared before her eyes. She didn't know what she expected after her tirade, but surely, she didn't expect this. One minute she found herself ridiculously ranting in the room all by herself, grateful no one could hear her vent. The next moment, to the left of her George Washington at Valley Forge painting stood the man she remembered from her dream.

From the poet-style shirt, form-fitting fringed vest, and leather pants he wore, he could easily have stepped out from the painting. He had shoulder-length dark brown hair, which he tied back at the neck in a queue. Shorter strands of hair framed his face in a most attractive sort of way. His warm brown eyes bore into hers. She didn't detect any animosity from within them. Judging from where his broad shoulders met the top of George Washington's frame, he stood at least six foot four, was much better looking, and—he called her by name.

She had no idea how long they stood across from each other or how long they gazed at each other with such intensity. Mere seconds might've passed or maybe even hours for her brain to accept what her eyes beheld. He looked very solid. If not for the fact he appeared right before her eyes, she would've taken him for a prowler or worse. But ghosts, devoid of their human form, should appear transparent or wispy. Right? Kind of like those cartoon ghosts with that funny-looking tail thing instead of feet.

Did he scare her? Yeah, maybe a little. The thumping of her heart attested to that. But many times in her life she had sensed something truly threatening, something truly evil. She didn't have any of those feelings now. In fact, in a bizarre sort of twist, he made her feel relatively calm. Still, her eyes searched out the door, looking for a means of escape if for nothing more than to think this situation through and try to understand it. She would need to pass by the—by him, in order to leave the room. And go where?

"Won't do you any good, for I'll still be here when you come back, and you know you'd have to come back," her ghost pointed out.

Somewhere in the back of her mind, she appreciated the fact that he stood very still, waiting for her to come to terms with something she didn't understand or believe. Finally, after assessing the truth of his words, she looked him directly in the eye, raised her chin a notch, and tilted her head to one side.

"You are not supposed to be here," she stated with all the conviction she could muster.

Chapter 4

The bold statement elicited a quiet chuckle. "Pray tell, Miss Michaelsson, where then, am I supposed to be? This is my home and has remained thus for a very long while now."

The man remained near the painting and apparently, awaited her response. Man, had she gone stark raving nuts or what? She closed her eyes, inhaled deeply, and slowly released her breath. Jo hoped that when she opened her eyes, he'd be gone. Then she could question the state of her mental health, check into a hospital somewhere, *and* he still stood there. But now, he looked very much amused.

"Miss Jolena?" her ghost prodded.

"Okay." Jo touched the tip of her tongue to her dry lips and said, "You—you should be at the next plane of existence—paradise—spirit realm—heaven—whatever you personally want to call it."

The spirit's shrug accompanied a single shake of his head. "Perhaps heaven is simply found at the location one loves best."

"No. That's not right. The tunnel of light everyone goes on about—you're supposed to go through it, aren't you? Didn't you see it when you—when you passed?"

The bright light seemed a common experience among those who "died" and returned to tell their story. Right? People with a near death experience said the beauty of the light drew them toward it, and once they entered, they had no desire to return to their mortal state.

"I saw it," he said.

"Then why didn't you go through it?" she asked.

"Because I didn't choose to." The tone he used also said, "Case closed, end of subject, move on."

Nevertheless, Jo mulled the comment over. She believed wholeheartedly the gift of choice forever belonged to each soul. Therefore, she supposed, one could choose to stay behind or choose to leave once their mortality ended. The notion made sense in a strange sort of way. But why would anyone want to stay behind? Some unfinished business or a life cut short perhaps. Didn't movie and TV shows point out such a reason? However, her ghost didn't want to pursue the topic any further. *Her* ghost. Her ghost? Wait just a darn minute—

Once again, Jo sat down in a quest to sort the whole thing out. The fact he remained in her presence and witnessed her inner struggle attested to the reality of ghosts. She supposed she could feel grateful she hadn't lost her mind. She peeked over and contemplated the ruggedly handsome man standing across from her, a fact that eased the situation tremendously. If he looked like some diseased zombie from a horror movie, she would've already evacuated the house—probably even the state of Pennsylvania.

A thousand questions swirled around inside her head. Questions like, why did he look so solid, and how could he speak aloud when he had no tangible body and couldn't breathe air? She could even see the stubble on his finely chiseled chin.

"How are you doing that?" she finally blurted out.

"Doing?" Her ghost appeared puzzled over the

question.

"What I mean—" Jo took a deep breath and began again. "I can hear you. I see you as if you're a living, breathing person. You look solid for heaven's sake. How can you *do* that when you have no real body?"

A slight, crooked grin appeared as he shrugged. "Practice, my lady, decade after decade of dedicated practice. I couldn't always express myself in this manner, I assure you."

The deep dimples appearing on either side of his cheeks briefly distracted her line of thinking. *No, don't look at that,* she silently commanded. She needed to stay focused—

Decade after decade did he just say? Just how long had he roamed this house all by himself. Who was he? The spirit had yet to budge from his position. She shook her head and released a short breath. "I find it a little unsettling to have you standing there, not moving a muscle, you know."

Jo laughed a bit as she caught the slight rise of her ghost's eyebrows over the ridiculous comment. "Sorry, please, I would feel much better if you sat down. If—if you can, that is."

The spirit answered with a slight bow of his head, and then complied with her request. Jo found herself staring as he walked, blinked, and sat down as if he still possessed a solid body. Shouldn't ghosts float above the floor, glide, maybe even hover a little? Of course, witnessing a ghost flying through the air would probably scare the tar right out of her, and she could only imagine what it would do to Nancy who freaked over the sight of a hideous bug. Jo settled at once on her sister's upcoming visit. A ghost in the house would cause quite a stir—an unpleasant stir if Bob had anything to say about it. Nancy would probably never come back. She'd bar the kids from coming too.

"Feel free to ask your questions, Jolena, I can see you have them. Above all else, I don't want you to fear me, since I'm assuming neither of us plans to vacate the premises anytime soon," he said.

"Am I the only one who can see and hear you?" she asked.

"At the moment, yes." He settled deeper into the chair without going through the cushions, rested his elbows atop the arms of the chair, and clasped his hands.

Silly thing to say. That much is already obvious. "I mean—I guess what I'm asking is, if anyone else entered this room, could they see you as well?"

"If I wished it," her ghost said.

"Then, if you *wished* it, could I still see and hear you without anyone else in the room knowing it?"

"Yes. You needn't worry about your visitors. I'll make sure they don't see or hear me if that's your desire," he said.

"Just who *are* you? Please. I would like to know." The question encompassed everything at once. Yet, Jo would find satisfaction in knowing his name—thinking of him as "her ghost," unnerved her.

"My name is Mathias McGregor. I am the firstborn son of Adam and Tamar Davies McGregor," he said. "Late of Pennsylvania."

"And, this was your house? You were born here?" Jo had so many questions she didn't know in what order to ask them.

"This *is* my house, yes, meaning my family built the place in my youth. However, this isn't the place of my birth," Mathias replied. "That event took place about one mile north of this location, in a home no longer standing."

"When? When were you born?"

"According to my mother, I entered this world on the fifth day of a very cold December in the year 1747." Then as if anticipating her next question, he added, "And my mortal existence unexpectedly ended the sixteenth day of June in the year 1778."

"Then you *did* live during the time of the Revolutionary War. You *could* easily fit into the time period of this painting then," she said as she pointed first to him and then at the figure of George Washington.

"Yes, I suppose I could have." Mathias nodded as his gaze traveled to the painting. He tilted his head to the side as he studied its subject. "However, I didn't accompany General Washington's army to their encampment at Valley Forge. My assignments took me elsewhere."

Her mouth dropped and as she gasped, she placed a hand over her heart. "You *knew* George Washington?"

"I didn't know him intimately, of course," he said, meeting her gaze. "But I did have the honor of speaking to him on a few occasions when our paths crossed during the war. He's a great man, an admirable man, and we were honored to have served under his leadership."

"Did you serve with one of the Pennsylvania battalions, then?" asked Jo.

"In the early days of the war, I served very briefly with the First Battalion militia. Soon thereafter, Colonel Daniel Morgan recruited me, along with some of my friends, to serve with his army of Rangers. Then toward the end of our lives, Colonel Morgan assigned us to work with Major John Clark," Mathias replied.

"You served as a Ranger? I didn't know the Rangers

even existed during the Revolutionary War." She wondered if the Rangers from his era bore any resemblance to the elite Rangers of today. Perhaps she should do some research. Mathias McGregor, late of Pennsylvania, shrugged in response.

"Is that how you—how you died? Fighting as a Ranger during the War?" she ventured.

Mathias returned a single nod. "Yes. Unfortunately, many good and noble men on both sides of the war lost their lives for what they passionately believed. However, those of us who considered ourselves patriots regarded dying as a necessary evil if men and this country were ever to gain independence and freedom from oppression and tyranny."

The words said with quiet dignity and respect compelled a subject change. They could discuss the war and his part in it, a little later perhaps.

"So, Mathias McGregor, firstborn son of Adam and Tamar Davies McGregor, how many siblings did you take pleasure in bullying around?" She had no idea why such an absurd question popped into her head. Perhaps having a ghost made her a little batty after all.

Mathias chuckled as he leaned forward with his hands still clasped together. "What makes you think I bullied any of my siblings, Miss Michaelsson?"

"Oh, just call it woman's intuition," Jo replied as memories of her brother's merciless teasing, stormed her mind.

Mathias answered each question she asked him. She learned he was of Scottish descent and second-generation born American. He told her he had ten brothers and sisters, none of which he bullied—much. Finally, she learned his father enjoyed success as a merchant, which of course, explained the existence of this beautiful home.

In an effort to avoid the subject of war and death, she sat across from a ghost and casually questioned him about his mortal life and ancestry. She may just as well be conducting some sort of an interview for an historic documentary. At that very moment, she pictured herself sitting primly on an elegant sofa, with notepad and pen in hand. She would adjust her black-framed glasses and say, "So, can you supply me with documentation for the exact dates and locations to each of these events, Mr. McGregor, and would this be a primary or secondary source, sir?"

The whole scenario struck her as funny and it made her laugh. As Mathias assumed a puzzled expression, she laughed all the harder. "I'm sorry." Jo put a hand to her mouth in an attempt to stifle her giggles. "It's not you or your family or anything you said, really. It's just that all of a sudden this whole thing seemed so funny. I mean I'm sitting here talking to a *ghost* about his ancestry, of all things. I'm pretty sure this topic would never be broached with another soul in my same situation."

Mathias smiled broadly, catching her humor. "No?"

She shook her head while seizing control of her mirth. "Nope. Definitely not."

"What then, do you suppose they would choose for a topic of conversation? Curiously, I have never stopped to consider such a thing before," he said.

"Oh, I don't know, something deeply profound and philosophical would be my guess." Jo nibbled at a nail, dropped her hand, and shrugged. "They might ask you about the death experience itself, what happens as you leave your body, and the changes you encountered. Perhaps they might ask about life after death—how it differs from mortality. There are many people who try to prove life does go on, you know. Let's see, I think I remember once on a TV show that featured a supposed haunting—

"This guy ran around from room to room with his tape recorder, asking the ghost why he haunted the place. He asked if the spirit needed help from the living to accomplish a specific task so the entity could cross over to his proper plane. He wanted to make an EVP I think they called it—an electronic voice, something or other. Anyway, the device is supposed to capture the ghost's vocal response to the questions."

"Did he receive an answer?" asked Mathias.

Jo shook her head, crossed a leg over her knee, and began swinging her foot in little circles. "Not that I'm aware of. Apparently ghosts don't like to perform on cue." Horrified over what she just said, Jo's hand flew to her mouth as her wandering foot stopped mid-circle. Mathias simply chuckled in returned. Thankfully, he didn't take offense.

"No, I suppose we don't," he said. "I know we never once considered complying with the wishes of our living guests. To do so seemed a bit beneath our dignity, if you understand my meaning. Especially when they wanted us to *prove* to their visitors, we existed by moving an object or closing a door. We found such a request demeaning."

Mathias shook his head in disgust and looked away briefly before he met her eyes once again. Did he notice her discomfort? For he leaned closer still, and it looked as if he wanted to take hold of her hands. She found herself inching them away.

"What is it?" he asked.

She gave him a side-ways glance. "We?"

"Oh. You needn't fear any of them either. Although they are patiently awaiting your consent, the lads would like to make your acquaintance now. If you think you're ready, that is."

"The lads?" she repeated as her fingers traveled toward her throat. More ghosts lived inside this house? Mathias somehow put her at ease. As absurd as it sounded, he made her feel as if they'd known each their entire lives and simply picked up where they left off. Once the shock of meeting a real ghost rescinded, she discovered she enjoyed his company and conversation. But could she deal with—

"Four of the best men who ever lived on this earth, take my word for it," he said, steadily meeting her gaze. "Together and for a specific purpose, the five of us formed a special unit. These men fell alongside me during our last battle. I believe this is the reason we're all together now. Do you think you're up to meeting them?"

Something tugged at Jo's heart when he mentioned the boys in connection with his final battle. The memory of it seemed a sacred thing. She found herself wanting to meet the men who served and died with Mathias McGregor. However, the words didn't want to hurdle the lump in her throat, so she merely nodded in consent. Then as Mathias rose from his chair, she followed suit. She didn't quite know what she was supposed to do—

"Samuel," Mathias called over his shoulder, though all the while he retained possession of her gaze.

Straight through the bookshelf emerged one of the men from Jo's dream. He wore the same type of Daniel-Boone-backwoods-mountain-man clothing Mathias wore, his light brown hair also tied back in a queue. His hazel eyes danced with mischief and at once, he made her feel comfortable in his presence. He bowed low at the waist in a grandiose sort of way and smiled broadly.

"My very dear lady, I'm so very happy to finally make your acquaintance," he said. He made a play as if to kiss her hand, making several attempts in the process, yet his own hand slipped deliberately through hers. She smiled in response to his antics.

"This buffoon is Samuel Fraser, my greatest friend from clout to breeches," Mathias stated as the corners of his mouth twitched upward. "I think I know more about the man than what his own mother could divulge. So perhaps he ought to take that in consideration before playing the fool?"

"Ah, Mathias—" Samuel chuckled wickedly as he turned his gaze toward him. "Perhaps you might consider the tales that I, in turn, could reveal about you."

Their easy banter, honed over a lifetime and beyond made Jo laugh. She wondered for a brief moment about those tales to which they referred before she said, "Hello, Samuel, it's nice to meet you too."

"William," Mathias called out the name with all haste. To advance past Sam's threat, perhaps?

The ghostly form of William made his way through the door and halted a few paces in front of her. He stood about as tall as Sam did, possessed golden-red hair and gentle green eyes. She could also see a smattering of light freckles across his nose. He revealed a single dimple on one side of his cheek when he smiled.

The ghost dipped his head in greeting and said, "Hello, Jolena, it's nice to meet you."

"Likewise," she said, returning his nod.

"Jolena, this is William Ferguson, and Alexander"— Mathias paused and turned his head toward the wall just as the third ghost entered the room—"this is Alexander Buchanan. I've known these men almost as long I've known Sam, and I can attest to their noble character."

"Hello, Alexander." Jo smiled at the ghost who gave her a friendly wink in return. He had brown wavy hair, a jaw-length mustache, and sky blue eyes.

"Then, to finish up our small group, I'd like to introduce you to Jedediah," said Mathias. Jedediah made his sudden appearance standing beside Sam, and instantly his boyish grin stole her heart.

"This lad is Jedediah Gatlin and don't let the innocent, youthful appearance deceive you in any way. He's as ornery and obstinate as any old codger I've ever met. We think it's the Irish in him," Mathias said, giving her a wink.

A small knot formed in her throat as she gazed at Jedediah. The young blue-eyed blond looked about eighteen, maybe nineteen years of age at best, and it broke her heart to realize he died in battle at such a young and tender age. Nevertheless, he wore a cheerful expression as he stepped toward her and grinned.

"Miss Jolena, I'm so pleased to make your acquaintance," he said. "And I want to thank you for playing your fiddle today. The sound of it did me wonders."

"Hello, Jedediah, and you're welcome. However, I guess I should let you all know that you'll have to bear with me on that. You see, I play with the orchestra for a living and I need to put in a lot of time practicing—" The ghosts didn't allow her to finish her sentence. Protests flew around the room. She laughed as she threw her hands in the air to halt the outcry. "Okay, okay. I get the point. I'm glad you enjoy listening to me play because you're going to hear a lot of it."

Mathias placed a hand on Sam's shoulder and said, "You won't hear a single complaint from any one of us, I guarantee it."

"Hey, Miss Jolena," Jedediah cut in. "Do you know how to play 'Sally in Our Alley'? It's my favorite song."

"I'm not familiar with that title, but let me see what I can find," she replied.

"Well, while you're looking, see about 'The Little Turtle Dove,' my particular favorite," Sam added with a firm nod of his head.

As the requests continued, Jo absorbed the sight of her companions. They were every bit the fine-looking men she saw in her dream. And, she could bring to mind several females who would envy her position, despite the fact these men were dead.

She spent the next few hours getting acquainted with each of them, and it didn't take them any time at all to find a place in her heart. They all made her laugh, but most especially Sam. He possessed a quick wit, which hadn't diminished with time, or perhaps, simply increased because of it. William and Alexander seemed the pranksters. They reminded her so much of her brother, but double the trouble. And Jedediah just wanted to please her. Her maternal instincts swelled, and compelled her to give affection and comfort whether he asked for or needed it.

Finally, she settled her eyes on Mathias. A sigh escaped as she met his questioning gaze from across the room. Something entirely different emanated from the larger than life persona of Mathias McGregor and somehow it filled her with a fervent desire to discover the cause.

Chapter 5

Despite the persistence of Dakota's probing wet nose, Jo snuggled deeper into the warmth of her comforter. Precious little sleep found her during the night, what with all the images of Mathias and the boys dancing around inside her head. So much needed sorting, so much needed reconciling. And really, right now she just wanted to have the ten minutes her alarm clock said she could have. Did she ask too much in wanting those ten minutes?

In answer to the silent question, Dak whimpered urgently and licked at her face. With a sigh of resignation, she tossed back the coverlet and sat up. She turned off the alarm, yawned, and took just a moment to stretch before rising from the bed.

"Okay, okay. I'm up. I'm up. Just give me a minute to remember who and where I am," she said as she donned her robe, made her way to the door, and opened it. Dakota rushed past her and bounded down the stairs.

"Good Morning, Miss Jolena, and don't worry yourself. I'll let the dog out for you," Jedediah called out from somewhere downstairs. "Come on, boy, let's get you outside. You look near to bursting."

"Thank you, Jedediah." From the sound of his voice, Jo guessed he called out from the family room. Ghosts must have very sensitive hearing in order for him to hear the soft rustle of her door all the way up the stairs. But why should that surprise her? As she readied for her morning shower she considered the abilities she had already witnessed. Abilities that truly astounded her. Ghosts could make themselves look like living people, speak out loud, laugh, make jokes, walk through solid objects, and more than likely, a host of other things she'd yet to see.

Jo looked down at the bath towel in her hand. Her gaze then shifted to the glass shower door in her bathroom and back to her towel again. With sudden determination, she tossed her towel on the bed and made her way down the stairs.

As expected, her ghostly friends gathered in the family room. They examined the various components of her customized sound system as if trying to understand the function of each. They all turned and gazed at her as she entered.

"I'm only going to make one rule," she said coming straight to the point. "My bedroom and bathroom is strictly off limits. Everyone understand that?"

Mathias exchanged glances with each of his companions and shrugged. Then, as she turned on her heels and made her way back up the stairs, she caught sight of Sam from the corner of her eye. He waved a hand in dismissal toward her, shook his head, and tsked.

"Women," he muttered and the comment made her laugh.

About forty-five minutes later, she returned dressed in a white tuxedo blouse and black slacks, ready for her day. Since the boys still poked about the stereo as if totally intrigued with the thing, she picked up the remote and turned it on.

"This stereo has a three hundred disk carousel, which

is almost full," she said. "That means it holds hours and hours of music. I have everything from classical to new age already loaded." She explained the function of each button and said, "Does everyone understand how it works?"

William took the remote from her hand and showed her he could follow simple directions. Seconds later, the deep, rhythmic beat of "Smoke on the Water" boomed out of the speakers. Jo laughed at their initial reaction to the song her father used to play so often during her childhood. However, not until William and Alexander got down with the music, in what she could only describe as an eighteenth century boogie to a twentieth century song, did everyone else join in the laughter. Sam laughed so hard at the spectacle they made of themselves, Jo almost expected tears to run down his cheeks. Jed and Mathias weren't far behind in the hilarity of the exhibition, either.

"All right, all right," Jo sputtered as she wiped the tears from her eyes. "I can't take any more of this, so let me show you how to use the remote for the TV, the satellite box, and the Blue-ray machine. I've got lots of must-see movies too."

Once she finished the lessons, Alex bowed his head and said, "Well thanks, Jolena. I believe you've provided us with some new entertainment."

"Indeed." Sam shifted his gaze toward her and nodded. "I hope you'll return shortly to enjoy the day with us."

"Well actually, I won't be back until quite late," she said. "I have a few errands after my work day is over, and then I promised my friend Carolyn I would stop by for a visit. So if you guys don't mind, would you look after Dak for me, while I'm gone?"

"I'd be happy too, Miss Jolena," Jedediah replied.

Jo made her way to the table and picked up her car keys before retrieving her bag and violin. "Thanks, and I guess I'll see you all later this evening. Have fun with the stereo and the television," she said as she slung her bag over her shoulder and headed out the door.

Mathias insisted on accompanying her to her car, to make certain she stayed safe, he said. She couldn't imagine anything adverse befalling her path in broad daylight. Still, she appreciated the gallant gesture as well as his company. He said they'd all anxiously await her return. The comment warmed her from head to toe.

At that moment, she had no idea the day would pass at a snail's pace. She fidgeted and sighed all the way through the rehearsals. Far too many times to count, she lost and found her concentration. At the end of the day, she bolted through the doors ahead of everyone else. From the parking lot of the concert hall, she bounced into her car and drove straight to the library.

After locating all the available books she could find on Morgan's Rangers, and the part they played during the Revolutionary War, she searched for and found one on Major John Clark. Satisfied with her selections, she returned to her car and made the ten minute drive to Carolyn's house.

Jo wanted to see her, not only because they hadn't seen each other since she moved into the house, but also because Kay truly believed in ghosts. Her interest and belief in the supernatural might give her the insight she needed and help her know what to expect in the days ahead. She gave the door a couple of knocks before she stuck her key into the lock and turned the knob. After she let herself in, she headed for the living room.

"Kay-Kay, I'm here," she called out.

"Hey, Jo," said Carolyn as she exited the kitchen, carrying her famous bread dip. "Sit down and make yourself comfortable, girl. I have all kinds of munchies set out, so we can just dive in and eat. As usual, I'm starving half to death, and I have so much to tell you!"

"More drama in the archeological field again?"

"Yes, and you can't believe the idiotic thing Mason's group did this time. They all but ruined an entire dig site. But, we'll discuss that later. First I want to hear about your house now that you've settled into it," Carolyn said as she tucked a piece of her short dark hair behind her ear.

"Speaking about my house, before I forget"—Jo withdrew a key from her pocket and handed it over— "here's the key to my kingdom; guard it well."

"Thank you very much." Carolyn placed it on the shelf, and then settled into the chair opposite her. "So, tell me all about it."

"The house is perfect, Kay-Kay. Having six full acres of lush property makes my surroundings peaceful and quiet. I can play my violin all night long if I want to without worrying about the neighbors. You really are going to have to come out on one of your days off and see the finished product for yourself. Maybe even come and spend the weekend with me sometime? Spending an entire weekend with me might give you some well deserved rest," she baited.

"As if." Carolyn rolled her eyes, lifted a glass to her lips, and took a drink. "When is the last time I had a whole day that I could call my very own? Ray Brennan or one of his cohorts, always has something they want analyzed, cleaned, or preserved. One would think that since Ray hired Paul Sanders, some of the load would shift onto his shoulders. But I've yet to see much difference. Still, I do want to come out and see the transformation of your house. So, maybe one of these days in the not too distant future, I'll show up on your doorstep with overnight bag in hand."

"Said without an ounce of conviction, but, here's hoping anyway." Jo picked up her soda, tilted the glass in Kay's direction, and then took a drink.

Carolyn waved a hand as she retrieved the beautifully wrapped gift on the coffee table and held it out toward her. "Yes, well, in the meantime, here's a little something from me to you. And, if you don't hurry and tear the thing open, I swear I'll do it for you."

Jo laughed as she accepted the gift and placed the box on her lap. She shook her head then and tsked. "This goes against the grain, you know."

"I don't care, so get over it," Carolyn replied.

After Jo drew in a deep breath, she took hold of the paper and ripped it away from the box. Carolyn leaned forward. Her eyes lit up in expectation as Jo lifted the lid. She gasped in surprise as she removed the gorgeous eighteenth-century brass bed warmer from its nest.

"Oh, wow, Kay-Kay." Her fingers traced the intricate etching. "This is perfect. Thank you so much. Where on earth did you find it?"

"Of all places, a garage sale." Carolyn shook her head as she stuffed an olive into her mouth. "I can't believe how cavalier some people are with antiques. Anyway, let me tell you about Mason."

After catching up on all of the gossip and exhausting all the girl-talk, Jo turned to the subject of ghosts. She refrained from telling Carolyn about Mathias and the boys, knowing they chose when and to whom they revealed themselves. Nonetheless, she wanted a better understanding of her situation.

She took another sip of soda and set the glass on the coaster. "So tell me, if one had to do a factual, serious report on ghosts, what kind of information do you think it should contain?"

"One of Nan's kids needing information again?"

"No, but it's something along those lines."

"Well, first of all, despite what *you* believe, I think a report should attest spirits do in fact, exist among us. There are many credible people out there Jo, besides me, who've had experiences. And sometimes those experiences are shared by more than one credible person at a time."

"Methinks you have a recent 'for instance' you're dying to share. So, go ahead and tell me about it." Jo could recite all of Carolyn's personal stories from memory. As a young child in Oregon, she shared her home and communicated with a little boy spirit who continually looked for his mother. Then, she insisted, she encountered many spirits at various archeological sites. Guilt washed over her now, as she recalled the many times she accused Carolyn of hallucinating. After all, she never once caught sight of the little boy ghost herself.

"All right then, I will." Carolyn took a framed photo off the side table and passed into her hands. "Do you remember my friend, Tamara?"

"Yes, I do." Jo met Carolyn's no-nonsense colleague several months earlier. The photo depicted a shot from her recent wedding. "They make a very handsome couple," she said as she handed the photo back.

"Yes, well, that isn't the point. A few weeks before

their big day, they stopped off at the old Methodist Church, there on the outskirts of town, do you remember? We visited it once."

"Yes, I remember the place, it's quite lovely."

"Uh-huh, and that's where they chose to get married. Anyway, they wanted to discuss a few details concerning the ceremony with the minister. They were in his office, discussing those details when this beautiful organ music filtered into the office from the chapel. The minister seemed a bit perplexed because the lady who plays for the congregation left a few days earlier for a two-week vacation.

"Tamara said the woman's ability impressed her, and she wanted to take a moment to compliment her. So, she and Glenn, that's the name of her husband, and the minister walked down the hall and into the chapel. There at the organ, sat a woman dressed in nineteenth-century clothing. They could see the wall right through her spiritual form. She finished the hymn, turned toward them, smiled, and simply disappeared right before their eyes."

"Oh," Jo said, for lack of anything better to say.

"'Oh,' indeed. And that story, my dear, comes from three very respectable and credible people. No one would think to accuse them of mass hysteria, I assure you. Also, let us not forget, the large groups of people who have witnessed and then reported a Gettysburg battle re-enactment only to discover nobody scheduled one. You read accounts such as those in the paper quite often."

"Seriously, Carolyn, do you think ghosts from two entire regiments still fight the Civil War? Do you realize just how many spirits would have to exist on that particular battlefield in order to accomplish such a feat?

Or do you think they go and hang out in the bushes while waiting for the battle to begin yet again?"

Five men remaining in a familiar place seemed reasonable, but entire regiments on a single battlefield, fighting the same battle repeatedly, didn't. What possible good would that do any of them?

"I don't know," she answered with a shrug. "Some men remain very loyal to their commander and would follow him into the very depths of hell and back again if he asked it of them. However, there are those who believe such a display is simply an imprint on time. A residual haunting is what they call it. By definition, this is a scene so traumatic, that it plays again and again. You know, like an old movie rerun."

"Yes, I know about the theory of residual haunting. However, as you said, it's more like a movie. The spirits aren't really there," Jo replied. "But what would compel a spirit to stay around in the first place? Why don't they just pass on to wherever it is, they're supposed to go?"

"From what I've read and or studied, the reasons are varied. Some ghosts died so quickly and unexpectedly, they don't realize they're dead. Then there's guilt about something or other, unfinished business, fear of what's on the other side, like believing they're going to hell on account of past sins. I think that scenario especially applies to those who murdered someone, those who want revenge. The list can go on and on." Carolyn picked up a chip, used it to scoop up a bit of dip, and popped it into her mouth.

"So, what then? You think earthbound ghosts stay here and never, ever cross over? Never find peace?"

"Not at all. I think the majority of ghosts, at least benevolent ghosts, find there way home in time.

Sometimes it takes help from the living, though. Especially if the ghost has unfinished business he or she wants finished. There are murder victims that want justice before they'll cross over. Then there are ghosts who want their bodies found, identified, and buried. Some need to understand and then truly believe, despite all past sins that a merciful God in heaven won't thrust them into a raging inferno the minute they pass through the light. Except of course, for the really bad ones, who probably *are* going to hell for their heinous deeds and deservedly so," she said with a firm nod of her head. "I can't imagine brutal murderers being welcomed into heaven with open arms."

"I see," Jo murmured.

"Sometimes the living can keep a ghost here, as well, you know," Carolyn said as she added some soda to her glass and then slid the bottle toward Jo.

"How would they do that?" she asked.

"Love," Carolyn said. "The spirit loves the person or persons who loved him or her so much they stay behind to help that person deal with the grief of their loss. Despite their own desires to move beyond the light, they feel compelled to stay and give whatever comfort they can provide. Then, once they feel the loved one can finally cope without their assistance, they move on to their destination."

"How very sad," Jo whispered. But at least that one she could understand. Many times over the years since her parents' death, she wished they would've remained behind for a little while or at the very least, visited from time to time. The fact they never once showed themselves to her since the day they passed, gave credence to her belief in the nonexistence of ghosts.

"I guess," Carolyn said as she picked up a carrot stick. "So, any more questions? I can e-mail you some awesome Web sites that have a ton of information, and it would really juice up that report. Some of them even have photographs and EVPs, if you're interested."

"No, I don't have any more questions and yes I'm interested in those Web sites. So please don't forget to send them," Jo replied as she looked down at her watch. "However, it's getting late and since I have a long drive ahead of me, and you have to get up at the crack of dawn, I guess I'd better get going."

After they cleaned up, Carolyn walked her to the door. Jo turned, wrapped her arms around her friend, and gave her a quick hug. "You've given me a lot to think about. Thanks, Kay-Kay."

Carolyn gasped as she stepped back, and clutched at her heart. "Don't tell me, after all of these years, I've *finally* converted you?"

Jo laughed as she made her way out to the porch. "Maybe."

During the drive home, everything Carolyn said swirled around inside her brain in a chaotic mess. She wondered why Mathias and his companions chose to remain. Did they have unfinished business of some kind? Did they fear going to hell? Could she do anything to help them? Better yet, did she really want them to walk out of her life so soon? But what a selfish thought, she chided—

All the troublesome worries fled Jo's mind the minute she crested the hill and looked down at her house. The porch lights shimmered, as did the outside lights on the second floor. She drank in the lights glowing from the windows in her family room, and those lights sang out a welcome.

How very different from the many, many nights she returned home to an empty house or apartment and total darkness. Her gaze meandered over the property and then rested on the solitary soul, pacing along the veranda as if standing guard. Once she turned into the driveway, he halted his footsteps, gave her a courtly bow and the most charming grin she'd seen to date. Her heart skipped a couple of beats, knowing Mathias awaited her.

Chapter 6

"So, Mathias, according to this book—which by the way, is authored by a greatly respected historian— Morgan's Rangers were known as a rowdy, disrespectful, and fiercely independent group of men. The book also states that because of their wild and unruly behavior, Washington wouldn't allow the Rangers to camp close to the main army for fear of the negative impact they'd breed among his own soldiers." That's not all the author said about these honorable, stalwart men. But— "What do you have to say about that assessment? And do remember this book comes complete with sources and documentation."

Mathias turned away from the large library window. He looked at her then, and for the briefest of moments, she glimpsed the Ranger that history revered. She caught her breath and held it as he shrugged off the claim. "Highly exaggerated."

"Oh, come on. Did you or did you not address your commanding officers by their given names as it so states right here on page nineteen, paragraph three?" She held the book aloft and repeatedly tapped the passage.

"Certainly, just as they addressed us by ours. I see no disrespect in that," he countered.

"I suppose anyone else might have been court-martialed," she murmured. "However, did you or did you not simply stand at ease while the regular soldiers stood at full attention when so ordered by their commanding officer?"

"I believe we listened attentively to everything they said; therefore, what possible difference could our stance make in the outcome of things?"

No longer able to withhold her laughter, Jo looked up from the book and said, "Oh, Mathias, it's so easy for me to see you and the boys in this light. In fact, I bet you found yourself in your element."

"I'm assuming from the look of adoring admiration and respect in your eyes, you're giving us a compliment?" He grinned wickedly, leaned toward her, and said, "I humbly accept it."

Jo merely laughed and returned to her book. As she lost herself in the pages, she discovered the impressive history surrounding Morgan's Rangers. Truly, the men earned the respect and esteem they received, despite the playful banter just exchanged between them. Even William Howe, the British general, stated they were the most dangerous regiment in the American army. High praise indeed, coming from one's enemy.

The final chapter began with an historical document. She fixed her gaze on the passage. "Mathias—this book has a letter, originating from General George Washington's headquarters in Middlebrook, dated June 13, 1777, which mentions the Rangers. Do you want me to read it to you?" Then, as she looked up from her book, she found herself surrounded by the rest of the boys. They gazed at her with anticipation.

"Go on then, lass," Sam encouraged as he plopped down on the edge of the desk. "Let's give a listen to what General Washington had to say in his letter."

"All right." Jo returned to the book. "The letter

begins, and I quote—

"'*Sir:*

The Corps of Rangers, newly formed, and under your Command, are to be considered as a Body of Light Infantry and are to Act as such; for which reason they will be exempt from the common duties of the Line. At present, you are to take a Post at Van Veghten Bridge and watch, with very small Scouting Parties (to avoid fatiguing your Men to much, under the present appearance of things) the Enemy's left flank, and particularly in case of any movement of the Enemy you are instantly to fall upon their flanks and gall them as much as possible, taking especial Care not to be surrounded, or have your retreat to the Army cut off.

I have sent for Spears, which I expect shortly to receive and deliver to you, as a Defense against Horse; till you are furnished with these, take care not to be caught in such a situation as to give them any advantage over you. It occurs to me that if you were to dress a Company or two of true Woods Men in the right Indian Style, and let them make the attack accompanied with screaming and yelling as Indians do, it would have very good consequences especially if as little as possible is said, or known of the Matter beforehand.'"

Jo glanced up for a moment and said, "The book goes on to say that just eleven days later, Washington ordered some of his officers and guardsmen to—"

"Meet up with Colonel Morgan's men," Sam finished

for her. "And do all in our power to impede Howe's army there in New Jersey. I remember that order. The suggestion to play Indian calls to mind the battle at Short Hills, doesn't it lads? And the general didn't even have to ask."

The comment ignited the now familiar snickers from her boys. Sam nudged Jedediah and winked. He laughed in return. She put the book down on the desk and sniffed. "Okay, guys, you can't leave me hanging like that," she said. "You have my full attention now, so—tell me about the battle."

Mathias said, "Well, that particular battle ensued because of Howe's desire to draw Washington's forces away from our encampment at Middlebrook. You need to understand the Redcoats greatly outnumbered us at the time. Not only were we smaller in number, most of our men had the barest of necessities. As you can imagine, our armaments for such a battle were sadly lacking. Hence, the reason Washington said he would send us some spears.

"On the other hand, the Redcoats had fine weapons and ample supplies, provided by King George. Therefore, Howe hoped he could force our side out on the open plain. If successful, we would suffer a defeat under his hand that would further demoralize our army."

"Yes, indeed," William cut in. "But of course, Howe's plans didn't dupe General Washington. He countered by sending part of his elite guard and part of our company to harass the enemy and cut off their retreat. At that time we served under Lord Stirling's command and he assigned us the duty of guarding Washington's left flank."

"In going about our duties, our unit happened across

a body of Redcoat grenadiers, resting beside this little stream," Alexander said. "Mathias wanted to round them up before they caused any trouble. So, he had Jedediah smear some mud on his face, arms, and chest, run through the bushes at full speed and whoop it up just as his Indian friends taught him. The tactic worked like a charm."

While the lads laughed over the shared memory, Jo looked at each of them and shook her head in confusion. "Mathias, you had the blue-eyed blond, the fairest among you, play an *Indian?* Wouldn't *you* have been the better choice?"

Mathias shrugged. "Jedediah could handle the job better than all the rest of us put together. Believe me when I tell you, his wicked war cries can scare the darkest devil out of the most seasoned warrior. Trust me. The Redcoats didn't take time to assess his heritage."

"While Jedediah performed his patriotic duty, which you would really need to see in order to fully appreciate," Sam said, "the rest of us laid down ropes about ankle high. When the Lobsterbacks ran for cover, we laid them down flat. The trick is an old one, but one that worked as intended."

"As a result, our eleven men subdued thirty-eight grenadiers, despite their light infantry, which was camped a short distance away," added Jedediah.

"Well, that thunderous 'war dance' you conjured while we did the subduing surely helped our cause. You couldn't see the ground for all the dust you stirred. I've not seen smoke any thicker." Alexander chortled as the memory of that event set off another round of laughter and elbow jabs.

"But, not long after that incident, Howe's infantry attacked and a pretty serious battle commenced," William said. "They forced our army back and subsequently, Lord Stirling ordered a retreat to Middlebrook. Nevertheless, because of Lord Stirling's efforts that day, General Howe feared the strength of our forces. He didn't want to engage us and thus backed off."

"Nonetheless, the old coot boasted a victory," Alex reminded them. "His posturing didn't matter a whit to any of us though. How could we lose a battle that Howe retreated from, as well?"

"Still," Jedediah said, "along with some of Washington's guard, we fought them off long enough to escape with all thirty-eight prisoners still in tow. We made it back to Morgan's field headquarters without a single loss of life or limb on either side. That's quite a feat, all things considered."

"That it is, and I think we need mention here, we made our escape straight through the swamp," Sam said, as his eyes twinkled with mirth. "Mathias, our brave, stalwart leader, led us through the thickest, muddiest swamp I've ever had the displeasure of traipsing through, and why? Not because we needed to, or even because the route proved the safest. No, we trudged through it because Mathias McGregor believed it downright entertaining to get the pretty uniforms of Washington's elite guard, a *little* bit dirty."

"A little bit dirty, you say?" Alexander let loose a snort. "As I remember it, they marched into camp covered in mud from head to foot and that's the truth of it, Jolena. No one could differentiate us from them once we entered the camp at Middlebrook."

"They were none the worse for wear," Mathias said, coming to his own defense. "Besides, Colonel Morgan got a good laugh out of it, did he not?"

"That he did, Mathias," Sam replied, bobbing his head. "That he did. I don't think I ever remember a time before or since, when the man laughed so long or so hard. I'm certain you caused him a moment of cheer on an otherwise trying day."

Jo joined in the laughter as her imagination played the entire scenario out in her mind. She pictured Jedediah playing Indian, while relishing and embellishing the role. Her mind envisioned Mathias, without an outward trace of humor giving away his intentions, leading Washington's elite through the mud. Most certainly, his sportive actions gave him just as much pleasure as it did Morgan. Still, since they were in a talkative mood, she had a few remaining questions.

"I have a few more questions if you don't mind." Jo picked up the volume on Major John Clark and held it up for their inspection. She had devoured this library book after she exhausted all of the ghostly Web sites Carolyn e-mailed. Many of those sites presented some fascinating theories on all the whys and wherefores of spiritual manifestation. Yet, nothing concerning ghostly abilities fed her imagination quite the way this book did when she imagined her boys taking part.

"Mathias, you told me when we first met that Colonel Morgan assigned you all to work under Major John Clark. However, you failed to mention George Washington assigned *him* to gather *intelligence* about the British. This means you all participated in the very dangerous activity of *spying* for and on behalf of your country, right?"

Before Mathias could answer, her recently installed doorbell chimed out a random melody. Dakota jumped to his feet and barked while he raced down the stairs to confront the intruders. Jo abandoned the book to her desk and followed. Her ghostly companions remained a single step behind. Sam swore under his breath as they vacated the stairs and approached the foyer.

"Well if isn't those infuriating neighbors, again," he muttered in irritation. "After you invited them to leave the first time around, Mathias, you think they'd know enough not to return."

Jo took in a sharp breath, halted her steps, and whirled around as she met Mathias's way too innocent gaze. "*You* caused the ruckus my first night here?"

Mathias merely shrugged as if his actions didn't warrant a mention.

She shook her head slightly while she continued her journey toward the door. Just before she opened it, she said, "Then, I'd like to thank you for your timely assistance. I really appreciated it more than you know. But this time, please behave? They already think I've lost my mind."

Douglas and Gloria Parker greeted her with tight lips and furtive glances. A slightly built young man, probably in his early twenties, bearing a bit of resemblance to Douglas, stood beside them.

"Good morning," she sang out in just as pleasant a tone as she could manage.

"Hello, Jolena. How are—how are things going for you, now that you've had the chance to settle in?" Gloria twisted her face into something resembling a smile. "I mean, I truly hope all is going well for you, dear. You *are* all right, aren't you?"

"Yes, I'm fine, thanks and truly, I don't think things could possibly get any better." Jo opened the door a little wider to allow them entrance, even though they clearly wished to stay put. "Please, won't you come in?"

"Oh. No, no, we can't stay, I—" Gloria stammered as she placed a hand over her heart and gulped. "I—we only stopped by to, uh— Oh dear, where are my manners? Jo, I would like to introduce you to my nephew, Owen Parker. He has come down to help us with the harvest, so he'll be living with us for the next three or four months. And, Owen, this is Jolena Michaelsson. She's our master violinist that plays for the Philadelphia Orchestra."

"Hello, Owen, it's nice to meet you." She made brief eye contact with the young man and gave him a smile. In turn, he twisted his head to the side, dropped his gaze, and simply bobbed his head.

Gloria took a deep breath, and said, "I don't know if we mentioned it during our last visit, but as a community we often rally together to help those who are victims of natural disasters. I'm sure you already know the recent earthquake in South America has left thousands of people homeless. So, what we're doing today is gathering any extra blankets you may have, as well as hygiene items you might want to donate to the victims of this disaster.

"Or if you'd like, we're also collecting monetary donations, so we can buy the needed items. There's a cargo plane leaving at the end of the week. If possible, we'd like to make sure it's filled to capacity with the things these people so desperately need to survive and—" Gloria stopped short as she stared passed Jo with a sudden look of horror on her face.

From the direction of her gaze, it seemed she focused on the hall tree. Jo turned and looked at the piece herself, yet didn't see anything out of the ordinary. "Is something wrong?"

"Oh…n-no…I just thought I saw—" Gloria waved a

hand and shook her head. "Probably just a shadow."

"There is a slight breeze today," Jo said as she glanced over at the boys, who shrugged. "The limbs of the trees can create shadows through the windows from time to time. Anyway, I do have some extra blankets I could donate to the cause. Would you like to come in while I gather them? They're in my storage closet, so it might take me a few minutes to get everything together."

"Oh, it's such a lovely day, with the light breeze and all—" Gloria smiled tightly and took a half step backward. "We'll just stand right here and take in the sunshine, if you don't mind?"

"I don't mind at all. Come on, Dak. Let's put you outside for a bit," Jo replied.

"No never mind, Miss Jolena, I'll take him out for you," Jedediah whispered. "Come on, buddy. You're making the neighbors a bit nervous."

Jo dipped her head downward and suppressed a smile by rubbing her lips together. After all, the dog had nothing to do with Gloria's uneasiness.

Mathias elected to stay put as Jo set about her errand. He didn't want to leave the Parkers unattended with the door wide open. Sam stepped forward then and blocked the entryway, just in case they developed a little collective backbone.

"Oh, I hope she hurries," Gloria whispered as she leaned toward her husband's ear. "I don't know why I ever agreed to come to this place. This house is simply horrid."

"Because it's our civic duty," Douglas replied between clenched teeth. "And because if we didn't come, we would chance her finding out about the community effort through other sources. We don't want her to take offense. Ellen would never forgive us, if that happened. After all, she's the *darling* of our community."

"Yes, be that as it may, I'm not going to do this again," snapped Gloria. "They can get someone else to come to this creepy old house or better yet, Ellen can do it herself."

Mathias glanced over at Sam who rolled his eyes in annoyance.

"Bunch of sniveling cowards. And I especially don't like the looks of that sullen young doodle. Just look at him. The boy has a major chip on his shoulder, and his twitchy eyes are all but defiling the place. That's two things that don't bode well," Sam muttered.

"You got that right," Alexander said.

Sam spared them each a mischievous glance, bounced his eyebrows, and then turned toward the offending party. He leaned forward and conjured a lengthy hiss. Catching the spirit of his game, William and Alexander whispered words unintelligible and *almost* inaudible. Mathias stepped back, allowing them greater access.

The startled group turned frightened gazes toward the sounds and peered into the entryway, seeking the place of origin. The boys inched forward. They could hear the erratic thumping of each mortal heart. Just as Gloria dropped her mouth and drew in a deep breath, Jo bounded down the stairs with a box full of blankets. Sam stepped to the side, cast his gaze to the ground, and sighed in disappointment.

Jo gazed briefly at the boys as they stood off to the left allowing her passage. She handed the box to Douglas. His hands trembled as he accepted it and stepped back. In all likelihood, the reason or reasons for that display, stood right beside her.

She tossed the hair away from her face and said, "The bag on top has a check inside to go toward any supplies you may want to buy. I also found some extra hand soap, toothpaste, combs, and brushes, still in their packages. I'm sure they could use those as well. Anytime you need my help with something like this, just give me a call. I'm happy to help."

She tilted her head to the side as Gloria swallowed past the obvious knot in her throat. Yet, the woman said nothing in return. She placed her hand in front of her husband as if to protect, nodded and backed away from the porch. Then, at what she might consider a safe enough distance, Gloria turned, grabbed hold of her husband's elbow, and the three visitors fled to the safety of their car.

Jo leaned against the doorjamb, biding her time until the car disappeared from view. She turned toward her boys then. All of them returned the round-eyed gaze of an innocent child. They overdid it just a little bit. She assumed a stern expression, but failed miserably to carry off the persona when she couldn't stop the corners of her mouth from twitching upward. "Come on now, I believe I asked you all to behave?"

"As I recall," Sam protested, "you told Mathias to behave. And I can testify, on my honor, he complied with your request."

A full-fledged smile burst forth as she replied, "Which means, of course, the rest of you ruffled the feathers of our neighbors, and in broad daylight, no less. All right, but I need you to promise you'll remain on your best behavior during my family's visit. I have a beautiful little niece, and you can't subject her to any of your crazy antics. I wouldn't want her having nightmares on my account."

"Come now, Jolena," Mathias chided. "You should know by now we would never cause undue stress to any member of your family and least of all a little child. I assure you it's not in our nature to trouble a small babe."

"Yes well—" Jo cleared her throat as she walked back inside and shut the door. "If you need to indulge in any 'ghostly activities' you can get them out of your system while I'm gone." The minute the words left her mouth, she held her breath and waited for their response.

Mathias stopped in his tracks and whirled around to face her. "Gone?"

"Yes." She chewed a bit on her bottom lip. A wave of guilt washed over her. "I uh—probably should've mentioned this earlier and really, I have no excuse for the delay, except to tell you that I made every effort to avoid this trip and failed. They just couldn't find anyone to replace me. Anyway, I'm leaving tomorrow afternoon. The entire orchestra is going on our annual summer tour, so we'll—"

"You're leaving *tomorrow*?" Mathias fused his gaze to hers. "For how long?"

"Several weeks, at least through the end of June." She scrunched her shoulders in apology. "A precise date is hard to pinpoint because the publicity and momentum builds. Therefore, sometimes the demand in the final city will hold us over for a day or two. So I can't tell you the exact date of my return."

"What about Dakota?" asked Jedediah.

"Well, I guess that's up to you. I usually let Carolyn watch over him whenever I need to leave, but if you want him to stay here—" Jo allowed her voice trail off. Jed enjoyed having Dakota around, and the dog had developed a genuine affection for Jed in return.

"Don't worry, I can look after him for you," Jed replied.

"Okay." She had trouble meeting Mathias's gaze. He looked so—hurt? She briefly closed her eyes and let out a sigh of self-recrimination. None of the boys seemed happy about her abrupt announcement. She should've given them more notice. Yet, for the life of her, she just couldn't force the announcement passed her lips.

"I'm sorry, really I am. You know, if I could, I would just as soon stay home. Unfortunately, it just isn't possible." Then, as she turned and made her way toward the stairs, Sam said the strangest thing.

"Well, if nothing else, the timing of her trip works to our advantage," he said.

"That it does," said William.

The timing of her trip works to their advantage? What did he mean by that remark? She puzzled over the odd comment all the while she traveled up the stairs and packed for the tour.

Chapter 7

With his hands clasped behind his back, Mathias stood gazing out of his library window and toward the road just visible on the hill. As the minutes passed, a variety of cars and trucks crested that hill. Each time, disappointment washed over him anew as Jolena's car remained elusive. How he missed her. He missed her beautiful smile—he missed their conversations—he missed her very presence.

"I assumed I'd find you up here, pining away," said Sam the moment he popped into the room.

"What makes you think I'm pining away?" Mathias growled without turning around.

"Oh, come on, Mathias." Sam took a seat atop the desk. "How often since Jolena's departure have we found you up here all by yourself, doing naught but staring out the window? I would blame it on our recent pilgrimage knowing how badly you hate the obligatory trek, but—"

"Perhaps I simply like the view," he muttered.

Sam merely nodded as he glanced down at the desk and pointed toward the closed volume laying on top it. "I take it the book is no longer holding your interest?"

Mathias shrugged his indifference over the remark. "I take it the movie is no longer holding yours?" he countered, as at last he turned around to face him.

Sam scoffed and shook his head. "The film is just another one of those awful late night offerings that poorly depict medieval wars between rivaling kingdoms. I mean, you would surely think someone would've taught the actors how to hold a sword a little more realistically. After all, they're engaged in a battle for their lives. The way they portray them wielding the thing, my mother could disarm them without too much effort."

"And what's with all the conversation on the battlefield anyway?" asked Alex as he and the other boys plowed through the walls of the room. "Probably the best way to get killed yourself is to stop fighting your enemy and then tell him, in minute detail, how you're going to kill him before the battle ends. What kind of fool would really do something like that?"

"If an enemy of mine ever blabbered on the battlefield, I'd shut him up in a hurry by using the pointed end of my blade," William added. "I can assure you of that."

"Do you also notice in these movies, while the conversation is taking place, no one else on the entire field of battle attempts to take advantage of two moronic men that are just standing there, making themselves easy targets?" asked Sam. "No one I know would lose such an opportunity to rid themselves of the enemy. In fact, I would dispatch them both for their stupidity. No one needs a soldier like that, be he on your side or not."

"You forget," Jedediah murmured as he leaned down and picked up the ball Dakota placed at his feet. He sent the rubber ball flying down the short hallway, where it bounced off the wall and then bumped down the stairs. "Jolena said the movies are not noted for their accuracy, but only for the entertainment they provide."

"Well, it doesn't entertain if it annoys," Sam retorted as he followed Dakota's determined path.

Mathias chuckled over all the dour comments. Jolena's absence had impacted all of them in different ways, or so it seemed. "Judging from the present mood and tone, lads, I believe we could all use a change of pace. So, how about we all go outside and brush up on some of our skills? Dark clouds are gathering over the horizon and heading this way. With all that heavy moisture in the air, the day looks promising enough for such sport." He cocked his head toward the window.

Sam wiped the corners of his mouth. "That's the best idea we've had in weeks, Mathias."

"You bet it is," Alexander chimed in. "We haven't engaged in any training exercises since Jolena moved into the house. We're probably getting rusty."

"Yes, but that's only because we didn't know how she'd view such activities," Jed reminded them. "We wanted her to get used to *us*, first, remember?"

A mischievous gleam entered William's eyes. "Yes, but Jolena isn't here, now is she?"

"No, she isn't and if you recall, she did say if we needed to indulge in any of our 'ghostly activities,' to do them in her absence," Samuel added.

Scant moments later, they gathered at the southernmost portion of the back property. They made use of this area while conducting their training, both during and after their mortality. This portion of land possessed the perfect blend of open space, hilly terrain, and seclusion. Mathias looked them over. Sam leaned forward on his musket, his pistol, and knife tucked inside his belt where he could grab them at will. Jedediah held a tomahawk in each hand. The other boys seemed equally ready for any command he might issue. He didn't choose to keep them waiting.

"Jed," Mathias called out as he pointed due east of the shrouded sun. "I see a broken branch on that white pine tree. The wind has yet to sever it completely. Take down the last cone pointing north, while leaving the branch intact. The rest of us will keep the thing moving in a northerly direction. Our goal is to keep it in the air. Is everyone ready?"

At his signal, Jedediah sent one of his tomahawks flying. Four shots then sounded off in rapid succession. Mathias called out more targets as the sound of more shots rang out. Each shot coming right atop the one before it. The rich sounds of the booming thunder, mixed with musket and flintlock pistol fire, rumbled throughout the area.

Then as often happened when they put themselves through their paces, they soon garnered the attention of other soldiers, who fought in wars long past. The ghostly army assembled and joined the games. In short order, the sounds, sights, and smells of a full-scale battle echoed in all corners of the valley. While the storm raged, so did the battle. Mathias didn't care a whit that the ominous sounds struck fear into the hearts of the neighbors.

****

Despite the intensity of the summer storm, Jo rolled down the window of her car and inhaled a deep breath of the heady scent. The rain smelled so good, and it only added to the joy of her homecoming. She hoped to arrive within the hour, and the anticipation of seeing Mathias and her boys again filled her heart near to bursting. Just as she envisioned the sweetness of their reunion, the ring of her cell phone intruded. Curiosity took hold as she glanced down at the name on the screen. Ellen? Why would she call her? She turned the volume down on her stereo, touched the call button on her phone, and said, "Hello?"

"Jolena," Ellen whispered. "Are…are you all right, dear?"

"Yes, I'm fine." Ellen sounded terrified and in the background, she could hear persistent knocking on her door. She couldn't imagine the cause of the trouble. "But, are *you* all right?"

"Yes, just a minute." Ellen's footsteps clicked against ceramic tile. A door creaked opened. More footsteps followed a rustling of some kind and then Gloria moaned in the background.

"Have you been listening? Do you hear all of that?" she cried out.

"You'd have to be deaf not to hear it," Ellen snapped. "Those frightful sounds have put me on edge all day."

"But, it's been so long since the last time anything like this has happened. I hoped that maybe because of the restoration of the house—" Gloria's voice quivered as she spoke. "What do you think they're up to? I—I don't ever remember a time when the goings on over there lasted from sunup until almost sundown, and the sounds are driving me insane. What if it doesn't stop this time, what if it just keeps going?"

"No, they always stop," Ellen replied.

"Do you think Jo is there? Should we call to see if she's all right or needs help? What if—what if she can't get out?" asked Gloria. "Only—only Douglas and Richard are still in the city, we would have to go over there by ourselves—and I don't know if I can do that."

"Shush," Ellen commanded. "I have Jo on the phone right now. She's—"

"Ellen," Jo cut in. "What's going on? What are you

guys talking about?"

"The sounds—coming off your property." Ellen gulped several times before she continued. "They sound just awful and I can only imagine the carnage taking place at this very moment. I—I worried that you might be in some kind of trouble or needed help."

"Oh." Jo blew out a relieved sigh. All types of disasters had raced through her mind. Like, maybe her house caught fire, a gas line exploded, or the wicked witch of the west plummeted through her roof. "No, I'm fine. In fact, I'm on my way home now. I just got off the plane a while ago. I am returning from the tour, so—"

"Of course you are. I should've remembered that," Ellen interrupted. "I read all about the tour in the newsletter. But Jolena, dear, I don't think you should go home right now. Stay in the city. Your property just isn't safe right now."

After Ellen made her promise not to do anything stupid, the woman finally hung up. As she released a deep breath, curiosity set in, and she stepped a little harder on the gas pedal. With any luck, she would get home before sunset.

The storm didn't abate during her journey, and the thick, dark clouds made it feel far later than the time indicated on her clock. Jo expected to see some lights emanating from the inside of her house as she arrived. Yet, as she crested the hill the only light she saw, rose up sporadically from the back portion of her property.

After she turned into the drive and parked her car, she hurried into the house. All seemed normal, except she didn't see the boys anywhere. Perhaps they had gathered in the library. She raced up the stairs. Then, just as she stepped onto the landing, the sound of—gunfire?—

entered her ears. She opened the door of the first bedroom and made her way to the back veranda searching for the source. Jo gasped as she absorbed the unbelievable sight at the back of her property. Mathias and her boys, along with many Revolutionary and Civil War soldiers, covered the field. They were engaged in some kind of—battle.

She leaned out against the railing just as far as she possibly could. The army of men aimed their guns and a variety of cannons at each other, but they did so in friendly rivalry. Almost like a modern day football game, but with weapons. Dak made himself the referee, yet no one minded the interference as he raced back and forth across the field, barking his fool head off. Some of the men loaded the cannons, while others loaded their pistols and muskets. Thunderous blasts boomed forth from their weapons, and she wondered how they could accomplish such a feat with nothing but ghostly images. The scene fascinated her no end.

Then all at once, the men rushed the field and engaged in hand-to-hand combat. Some of them used bayonets, while others used knives, tomahawks, or both. One phantom soldier charged toward Mathias with his bayonet thrust forward, intent on skewering his victim. Mathias sidestepped at the last possible moment, took hold of the man's weapon, and while the ghost clung to it, he threw him to the ground. He yanked a wicked-looking knife out of his belt and pointed it at the specter's throat. Just then, Jedediah raced past him, with a tomahawk in each hand. He chased his opponent, threw one tomahawk toward the soldier's chest, pivoted, and tossed the other at the spirit running up behind him, with pistol aimed and ready.

Her Rangers prevailed over each opponent as they

continued this portion of the games, giving credence to their reputation. In all likelihood, the people reporting ghostly re-enactments of various battles actually witnessed this type of *sport*. She wondered what Carolyn would think if she could see it for herself. So much for the residual haunting theory. She could toss that one right out the window along with the other rubbish she'd read.

As the storm ebbed and the clouds moved on, so did many of the soldiers. They disappeared a few at a time until just her boys and a handful of men remained on the field. A spirit, wearing the uniform of a Revolutionary War officer, approached Mathias with one hand extended toward him, and the other tucked behind his back. They shook hands and as the officer spoke, Mathias nodded and said something in return. She would give just about anything to hear what they said to each other at this moment.

After another round of hearty laughter and backslapping, the remaining visitors shook the hands of her boys yet again, and in an instant, disappeared. Mathias finally turned in the direction of the house. With a grin on his face, he bowed, acknowledging her presence. In response to his mere presence, her heart took flight. She returned his smile and rushed down the stairs. By the time she hit the bottom floor, all her ghostly companions had congregated inside the family room. At once, they crowded around her.

"Jolena, my love." Sam nudged past the others and approached her first. In customary fashion, he dropped to one knee, clutched at his heart, and said, "Since the moment of your departure, my heart grieved your loss, and I've found no respite from the pain during your lengthy absence."

"Oh for heaven's sake, get up, Sam." Quiet laughter accompanied the shake of her head. "I haven't been gone *that* long."

"Yet, it seems otherwise." He tossed her a devilish grin as he rose to his feet. "In truth, lass, it's good to have you home. I know I couldn't have lasted much longer without seeing your lovely face."

"Well, then, I'm glad I made it home in time."

"That you did. But, just barely." He winked, ignoring the barbs from his buddies.

Alex elbowed past Sam and rolled his eyes heavenward. "Sam is not the only one who missed you, Jolena. We all did."

"And I missed all of you." Jo cast her gaze over each of them in turn. "You can't believe how much. The layovers tested the limits of my patience."

"Welcome home, Jolena," William said. He gave her a smile and a brief rub on her back.

"Thanks William." Jo shot a glance at Jedediah. Then as she knelt beside Dak, to give her dog the attention he demanded, she said, "Did Dakota give you any trouble?"

"None whatsoever," he replied. "I think it's safe to say, he preferred staying with us over your friend."

"I've no doubt about that. He sure had fun out there today." She stood and gazed at Mathias who had yet to say anything. Nonetheless, the warm look in his eyes told her that had he missed her just as much as she missed him. "I did see both Revolutionary *and* Civil War soldiers out there on the field, right?"

Mathias returned a nod and said, "As well as a few others. They're neighboring souls who come and join us from time to time as we go through our paces."

"You call that—that spectacle, going through your

88

paces?" she gasped as she took in each of their faces. Up until this moment, she believed the phrase meant something like practicing their about faces and forward marches.

"Well, we try to keep our skills honed." He shrugged and glanced briefly at each of his men. "The activity gives us something to do, and you never know when such skills might come in handy."

Jo mulled the comment over and then shook her head. "Just how do you create the sounds of gunfire, cannon explosions, and all the smells?" she asked. The question called to mind Gloria's reference to the "unholy sights and sounds" originating from her *haunted* property. "I mean, the battle looked, sounded, and smelled so real—"

Sam pointed heavenward. "A thunder and lightning storm of this magnitude supplies the necessary energy we need to accomplish something as large as a battle exercise. Anything less is naught but a poor substitute. Enough about us. The subject is boring at best. We'd much rather hear about your tour. Most importantly, we'd like to hear the reason it took you so long to return home. I must confess the delay put us all in such a foul mood. We could barely stand the sight of each other, or ourselves, for that matter—especially Mathias. That man can be such a grouch at times and not at all pleasant to be around."

Chapter 8

Last night, she looked forward to sleeping in her own bed. So why then did sleep escape her? Jo once again turned onto her back, popped her eyes open, and stared at the ceiling. The position remained just as uncomfortable as it did five minutes earlier, and ten minutes before that. She sat up, plumped her pillow, and scrunched down into her covers. Not more than twenty seconds passed before she turned onto her right side, and then switched to her left.

Finally, she rubbed her eyes, sighed in defeat, and tossed her coverlet off to the side. After she slid off the bed, she donned her white cotton robe, and stepped out onto the balcony. Perhaps a bit of fresh air might assist her efforts to fall asleep. Dakota followed close at her heels.

She leaned against the balustrade and gazed out at the sky. Serenity prevailed for as far as the eye could see. The earlier storm had dissipated, and the gentle breeze made for a pleasant night. Stars, made even more brilliant by the recent rain, lit up the sky in spectacular display. She turned around, chose the rocking chair promising the best view, and made herself comfortable. After she closed her eyes, she rocked back and inhaled a deep, cleansing breath.

"I assumed you'd be sound asleep by now," Mathias said. "And having naught but sweet dreams to pass away the night."

"Mathias—" Her eyes flew open the instant he made the comment. She gave him a smile, and as he approached, her heart sang out a welcome. "I'm happy you decided to join me, but—didn't you guys just put on a John Wayne movie?"

"Alex did. I couldn't keep my mind on it though," he said as he settled into the chair next to her, placed one foot against the bottom rail and the other extended outward. "I guess I'm feeling a bit restless."

"Me too. I didn't think it would take me long to fall asleep. But for whatever reason, I'm wide-awake."

"I can't say I'm sorry, for it gives us some time to catch up a bit. You were sorely missed, Jolena Michaelsson," Mathias said. "Sam didn't exaggerate that."

"And I missed you—all of you, you can't believe how much." She paused for a moment as she considered the truth of the statement. Never before had she allowed her concentration to stray while giving a performance. But during the tour, it happened time and again. Most especially when she played the songs Mathias favored. Her Ranger would then step into her mind without need for invitation and remain at her side for the duration of the concert.

The idea extended itself then and she gave voice to it. "You know, next time we go on tour, I might have to take all of you with me. I'll just pack you inside my suitcase and we can take off."

"That might be an interesting alternative." Mathias nodded as he clasped his hands loosely together.

"I have to warn you, though. The beds in the hotel rooms are too soft, too hard, or too lumpy. And most of the time, you'll find the food is too greasy, too spicy, or to bland," she said.

"Ah, don't worry," he countered. "We can make do with the lumpy beds and gag down the food if it becomes necessary."

"Could you?" All of a sudden, the idea didn't sound so absurd. "What I mean is—can you leave the property and go where ever you want to go, no matter the distance?"

Mathias rubbed a hand across his chin and nodded. "I believe so. We've yet to test the theory to the fullest extent possible. We've certainly never traveled the entire breadth of the United States. But in the years following our deaths, the lads visited the homes of their relatives from time to time. Well, they did until they no longer stood on their foundations. Then, a few times during the War Between the States, we traveled quite extensively to assist the Union in their effort to keep this country united. Such is the cause for which we fought and died. Therefore we vowed to do all in our power to keep it the way our founding fathers intended."

Jo's mouth dropped in response to the revelation. "You helped the Union Army? How? Did you gather intelligence from the South and pass it on to the North, or just what?"

"We gathered information on several occasions," Mathias replied. "But we discovered that it's not always easy to get the living to hear us when we speak to them in our spiritual form. And we can't just pop in on the officers and report our findings."

"Why not?"

"First of all, most would run screaming out of their tents at the mere appearance of a ghost."

"But, couldn't you have just walked in, appearing to them as I see you now—as more—mortal looking?"

"No, that wouldn't have worked either. We'd have to adhere to all military protocols. They would ask for our sources of information, the names of our commanding officers and such. And then one always has to worry about physical contact. The pat on the back, a hand extended in friendship or respect. So, no, we couldn't appear solid."

"That makes sense I suppose. Well then—" Jo cleared her throat. "What did you do?"

"During the course of the war, we discovered at various times, plans the Confederate army made to advance on the Union troops. Some of those times, the Union army didn't have the strength of numbers needed to meet them in battle. So, we gathered some of our otherworldly friends, and sort of *convinced* the rebels to take an alternate route to their destination. Thus, we gave the Union army time to strengthen," he said.

"And just *how* did you convince them?" she asked, wanting far more than just that.

"You're not going to let this go, are you?"

"Nope, sorry," she said, giving an apologetic shrug.

"We simply obstructed their path." He chuckled when she sighed in exasperation and then added, "By using some of the skills you witnessed today."

Jo had to laugh as she envisioned some very determined Revolutionary War ghosts impeding the way of the Confederates. "Then what you're telling me is that you purposefully scared the dickens out of the Southern army. Probably even made some of them scream for their mamas and run for home—"

The corners of Mathias's lips twitched over her

comments. "Some of them did, I suppose. Of course, Jed would have to take the credit for most of that, once he started with the war cries."

"That reminds me, I've yet to hear Jed's story concerning the Indians." Her mind skipped to today's "training exercises" and the youngest Ranger's look of deadly concentration as he swung those tomahawks at his opponent. "Care to enlighten me?" she asked.

"I suppose I could start out by telling you that as a Methodist minister, Jedediah's father spent a great deal of time preaching among the Indian people of New Jersey. He, along with his family, lived with them for a couple of years before coming to Pennsylvania," Mathias said. "Jed developed a friendship with several of the lads in the Lenni-Lenape tribe. They made him an honorary brave and taught him all manner of skills, like hunting, fishing, tracking, and of course, the war cries."

"Yet, for all that I think it such a shame that he lost his life, at such a young age," Jo said. "He should've had the opportunity to get married and raise some children. In fact, you all should have."

The notion gave her pause. None of the boys ever mentioned girlfriends, wives, or children. Yet, they might've left a family of their own. They certainly were of an age for such an occurrence. Did they find the subject painful to discuss? Yet, she found the idea of Mathias leaving a wife and children behind difficult to consider. Though, for the life of her, she couldn't fathom why something that happened centuries ago should bother her now. Jo held his gaze before she added, "Or did you?"

"Did any of us ever get married? No, we didn't. And now that you mention it, I don't recall Jed ever talking about anyone in particular prior to his death. That's not to say he didn't have his eye on a couple of young women while he lived. He just didn't take the time to pursue them, given the circumstances of our time. Alexander probably got closer to getting married than anyone else, but unfortunately, his woman died of smallpox before the scheduled 'I do's' could take place."

"Oh, how sad! Tell me about her," Jo said. As she settled a little deeper into her chair and waited for Mathias to continue his narrative. She truly loved hearing him speak. He possessed a wonderful voice, and his unique accent must have been common during his lifetime, at least within his community. After all, she detected the same inflection in Sam's voice.

"Charity Jenkins, daughter of John and Abigail Jenkins, was the youngest member in her family. I remember her being a tiny little thing, big blue eyes and blonde hair, always a bit frail, though. She possessed a sweet, gentle disposition. Everyone loved her. Unfortunately, she and her mother contracted the illness, after nursing some of their afflicted neighbors. They both died within a week or so of each other," Mathias said. "Their deaths devastated everyone, of course. But most especially Alex, as I'm sure you can imagine. I don't think he ever fully recovered from her death."

"And Sam?" she asked, wanting to hurry past the sorrow that filled his eyes. Her question returned his smile.

"I'm not so sure if Sam had lived to the ripe old age of one hundred, he would ever have found one woman in particular to settle down with. Sam loved all the ladies, often and well, but he never lost his heart to any of them."

Soft laughter accompanied her nod. "I can accept the truth of that statement. Samuel Fraser is an outrageous flirt, no doubt about it. So, what about William, did he have anyone special?"

"I'm certain William would've found someone eventually. But during his life, something always precluded him from courting anyone for any length of time. One woman after the other would tire of waiting for him and find someone else. Then the war started," he said as his voice trailed off.

"And—what about you?" Once again, Jo held her breath while she awaited his reply.

Mathias gave her his full attention then. His gaze bore into hers. He sought something, but she couldn't guess. Nonetheless, the look in his eyes at this moment fanned the embers that had settled into her belly. Finally, he spoke.

"I never found anyone special—while in my mortal state," he said.

His answer pleased her. "Oh," however, was all she could think to say in return. Should she add, "Gee, that's too bad" when she truly didn't feel that way? She opted to say nothing more.

"And you?" he asked.

The question caught her off guard. How could she explain what she herself could not? She clasped her hands together, laid them on her lap, and toyed with her fingers. The intensity of Mathias's gaze compelled her to form an answer. "I guess I'm still waiting around to find the unique kind of love my parents shared. I've yet to find it."

He considered that for a moment before he said, "If it isn't too painful, I'd really like to hear about your parents. We've never talked about them."

Jo put a hand to her mouth as countless memories flooded her mind. "Oh, I wished you could've known them, Mathias," she whispered past the lump forming in her throat. "And really, it's such a shame they didn't get the chance to meet you and the boys. I think they would've loved you all. My parents—Edward and Florence Michaelsson—are two of the finest people who ever walked this earth. They had such a deep abiding love for each other and for each of us kids. I just wished they could've stayed with us a little bit longer than they did.

"But—several years ago, a terrible car accident took both their lives. They died almost instantly they say." Jo managed a short, quiet laugh before she added, "And not surprisingly, they were found holding hands. So, believe me when I tell you that for them, they could've asked for nothing finer than to exit this world together."

Mathias understood her sadness. Despite the fact he departed mortal life first, he took great comfort in knowing he could still remain with his family and watch over their daily interactions. During his sojourn, he witnessed their joys, and provided them a semblance of comfort during their moments of sorrow. Even though they remained ignorant of his presence, it hurt when each of them, one by one, left mortality and him behind. And one day, for one reason or another, Jolena would leave him as well. Unfathomable pain accompanied the notion.

"Mathias?"

Her voice cut into his thoughts. The expression on her lovely face verified she understood his mood, even though she couldn't know the cause. She extended a hand toward him, in an obvious desire to provide some kind of comfort. Then seeing the impossibility of her actions, she drew back at the last moment. Would that she didn't have such a restriction.

"Oh, I'm so sorry," she said as she tucked her

wayward hand into her lap.

Mathias responded with a quiet chuckle he hoped masked his torment. He appreciated the intention of her gesture, regardless of outcome. "Nothing to apologize for. I appreciate the fact you cared enough about my feelings to make the offer."

Her discomfiture faded. Curiosity took its place. She carried that same expression when she first learned of his existence.

"You have a question," he said. "Go ahead and ask it."

"Mathias, would I feel anything at all if I touched you—without trying to go through you, that is? I know a spirit lacks solidity. But, while growing up along the coast of Oregon, I had no difficulty feeling the moisture of an early morning fog, Yet, I could still go right through it. I just wondered if I tried not to pierce your form—"

Mathias raised his hand in silent invitation. As he did so, he recalled the times when inadvertently one of his previous tenants walked straight through him, and he could feel the sensation of the passing. Yet, he never stopped to consider whether they could feel anything in return.

Jolena spread her fingers, mirroring them with his. They looked so small in comparison. Nevertheless, he twined his fingers around each one of hers first, and then for several minutes she traced the outline of his entire hand. She presented him with a dazzling smile as she did so.

"I *can* feel you. The sensation is hard to describe, it's kind of like—like soft down feathers when they barely graze the skin, with just a touch of cold—um—crispness. Or maybe the sensation feels more like thin strands of cool silk with a touch of early morning dew. Then there's just a hint of something else I can't quite put my finger on— Oh, I know I'm doing a horrible job of explaining this. But really, there aren't any words *to* describe it. Can you feel me?"

"Yes, I can. But likewise, I have no words to express how it feels when I touch you. I can tell you it's a very pleasant experience." A true enough statement and nothing more needed saying.

She smiled in response to his words and dropped her hand into her lap.

"So," Mathias said, breaking the lengthy silence that followed, "do you have any more questions or experiments you'd like to conduct?"

She studied him for a moment, took in a breath, and then said, "Just one question. I don't know if you remember this or not, but right before I left on tour, Sam said something. I didn't understand what he meant by the comment and it has nagged me every day since."

"Really? What did he say to you?" he asked.

"He didn't say anything to me. I just overheard the comment." She lifted a single shoulder and then said, "His remark had something to do with the timing of my trip. He said it worked to your advantage or something like that. What did he mean?"

Mathias suppressed his surprise. He had no idea she had overheard the remark and he'd rather not reveal the answer if he could help it. Despite his wishes to the contrary, she gazed at him intently, waiting for an explanation. But just then, as if the heavens understood his reluctance, a shooting star blazed across the sky, and he drew her attention toward it.

"Did you see that?" he asked.

Jolena gasped her delight as a second one followed the first. "Yes, I did," she said. "Both of them."

"You know, when we were kids, Sam and I had a neighbor lady who used to insist that every time a shooting star lit up the sky, it indicated that someone had died. She said it was their soul shooting toward heaven— or hell as the case may be," Mathias said, hoping to shift the topic of conversation.

Jolena laughed as she set the rocking chair in a steady, slow motion. "Really? That's funny. When we were kids, we always believed hell was way deep down in the ground somewhere, not up toward heaven. Deep, dark holes used to terrify us for that very reason. Kay and I used to think that if we weren't careful, a devil would surface and yank us in."

Several more shooting stars made their way across the sky, each more vibrant than the one before. All the while, he avoided her previous question by guiding the conversation elsewhere. Finally, Jolena smothered a yawn.

"I'm so sorry, Mathias," she said, "I would love to stay out here with you all night and look at the stars. But I'm finding it very difficult to stay awake now."

"There's no need to apologize," he replied. "Hopefully there will be many such evenings ahead of us."

She looked puzzled by the comment. "What do you mean, *hopefully*?"

"Well, I don't presume to know what your ultimate plans for this house are." He shrugged and folded his arms against his chest.

"Plans? I don't understand."

"Well it seems not everyone keeps a house for an

entire lifetime anymore," he said. "Isn't it possible that one day, you might want to sell this house and move somewhere else?"

"Sell my house? Are you crazy?" She sat upright in her chair and glared. "Why would such a notion even cross your mind? I fell in love with this house the minute I laid eyes on it. As you very well know, I put hours and hours of hard physical labor into restoring it. Part of me is in this house, and now part of this house is in me. No, Mathias, I will never sell it. This is my home, and just so you know, I intend to *die* here. How could you possibly think otherwise?"

Mathias tried very hard not to laugh over her indignation. He lifted a hand to appease her wrath. "All right, I'm sorry. I didn't mean to get you all riled up. I can think of many possibilities for such an event, you know." *Like marriage to some doddering fool*, he muttered inwardly.

"Well, there aren't any circumstances I can think of," she said. "I finally have a place I belong, and I'm staying right here until the day I take my last breath."

Mathias touched his heart as he gave a nod. "I'm relieved you feel that way Miss Michaelsson. However, I truly hope you aren't planning to die anytime soon."

Jolena shook her head and fixed her gaze to his. "No, I'm afraid not. You're just going to have to put up with me for years and years to come. You're going to have to watch me get old and crotchety, and probably even senile in my dotage. People will stop by for a visit and think I've gone quite insane as I carry on the most amazing conversations with my furniture, because by then, I simply won't care what people believe."

Mathias chuckled in response to the imagined scene.

"You? You're going to get old, crotchety, and senile—hmm. Well, in that case, I think I'm going to have to hang around. I certainly wouldn't want to miss the expression on everyone's face when you hold those amazing conversations with your furniture."

Jolena laughed and dipped her head to the side. "Well, let's hope you don't get your first taste of what that's like during Nancy's visit should I forget and speak with you in her presence. After all, my dear sweet sister would probably have me committed."

Chapter 9

"Does everything look all right?" Jo halted just as she stepped past the archway and entered the family room. She took in every detail, looking for something she might've missed.

"There's nothing else that needs doing, I promise you. Everything is immaculate," Sam said yet again. "So stop fussing. Just go upstairs and tidy up a bit before they arrive."

William sent a wink toward Sam and nodded. "That's right, go up now and get yourself all prettied up. Your family hasn't seen you in quite a while. Right? You don't want them to see those dirt smudges on your face and wearing dirty clothes. So, go take your shower and change into something pretty, like that pale blue dress you wore to the summer barbeque. You look very lovely in that one. We can take care of everything else down here while you freshen up a bit."

"Everything else?" asked Jo as she attempted to wipe away smudges that probably didn't exist. "Did I miss something?"

"You're going to want something nice playing on the stereo when they come in aren't you?" He flashed a grin and leaned toward her. "It won't take me but a moment to line up several of our favorite songs. We could have them playing one right after another with no interruptions of any kind, I guarantee it."

"Don't you dare, William Ferguson," Jo gasped, feigning horror. "Despite our upbringing to the contrary, Nancy has never been a fan of Deep Purple or Foreigner, and she would surely think I had lost my mind if "Juke Box Hero" blared from the stereo the minute she walks through the door."

"How about a little bit of the Beatles, then? Everybody likes them, right?" asked Alex. "Maybe we could put on 'Come Together' or perhaps 'Revolution' would be a more appropriate greeting, all things considered."

The comment caused her to giggle. She sat down on the sofa and crossed a leg over her knee, forgetting for the moment the need to take her shower. "You know, it might at that," she said, as her bare foot began swinging in circles.

"We could appear to them then, wearing the cheesiest smiles this side of the Mississippi," Jed added. "Perhaps they might think we're cute instead of scary."

"Not if you don't lose the tomahawks, Jedediah," Sam warned with pointed finger. "Tomahawks and cute just don't go together."

Jo burst out laughing as she conjured the image of Jedediah, smiling from ear to ear while wickedly twirling his weapons of choice. And all the while, they would hear "Revolution" playing in the background. At that moment, she couldn't say the idea didn't tempt her.

"Well, at least we finally got you to laugh," Sam said with a tone of satisfaction.

"Oh, I'm so sorry," she said. "I know I've been wound up pretty tight these past few days, worrying over the house and trying to plan some fun activities. But there's just so much to do and to see around the

Philadelphia area. They're only going to be here one week. I didn't know what to choose, or what they would enjoy the most."

"I think you've chosen well," Mathias said. "Besides, I really don't think it's going to matter what you do, as long as you do it all together."

One hour later, the rented minivan arrived just outside her gate. Nan refused to let Jo pick her family up at the airport, and the wait drove her crazy. So much so, that she paced like a caged animal in front of the sitting room window while awaiting their arrival. As they got out of the vehicle, Jo bounded out of the door, with her boys in close pursuit. With arms outstretched, Jo flew into the open arms of her sister.

"Hello, Nan. Oh, it's so good to see you again!" She proceeded to greet each person with hugs and kisses, taking care to mention each name for the benefit of her ghostly companions. Then standing back, she took in the sight of everyone at once.

A hand covered her mouth as she shook her head in amazement. "Zach and David, I swear you boys have grown at least a foot since the last time I saw you. And Jeannie, my goodness, you've become such a beautiful young woman—"

"You got that right, Jolena. She is a pretty thing, isn't she? Why isn't she married yet?" asked Jedediah as if truly perplexed.

Jo smiled, dropped her arms, and clasped her hands together. "She certainly isn't old enough to consider marriage, for heaven's sake."

Nancy looked puzzled over the odd comment. "Well, of course not, Jo. She isn't even seriously dating anybody—"

She waved a hand in dismissal. "Oh, don't mind me. Just seeing the vast change in the kids is taking its toll, I'm afraid." Jo scooped Mary up in her arms for a hasty change in subject. "And look at you, you precious little thing. You're getting so big. Do you even remember your Auntie Jo, hmm?"

Little Mary giggled, and then pointed at Mathias and waved. "Hi, hi, hi," she babbled.

Jo followed the toddler's gaze as she looked at each ghostly resident, smiled and waved at each in turn. Each of the boys either waved back or blew her kisses, much to her young heart's delight. The display confused her, and she looked to Mathias for an explanation. He simply shrugged.

"Sometimes little children can just see us, Jolena. I have no explanation as to the why of it," he whispered.

Nancy shook her head, shot her gaze heavenward, and sighed in exasperation. "One would think after the long plane ride and the drive here from the airport, our little angel would've had enough 'bye-byes' to last her the rest of the day. Jolena, darling, the outside of your home is even more beautiful than what we could see from pictures alone. Now, hand Mary over to Bob and show us the rest of it. We're so anxious to see all of the details."

After Jo relinquished Mary to her daddy, Mathias made ready to leave so she might have private time with her family, he said. But she shook her head in return and with a subtle wave of her hand, invited them all to follow. They traversed the grounds first. As expected, Nancy fell in love with her bountiful flower garden, but Bob preferred her barn, which housed a plethora of antique farm equipment. Some of those antiques dated back to the eighteenth century and he drooled over them. She then took her family through each room of her house and pointed out the rooms she assigned them. While they settled in, Jo and the boys ambled into the kitchen.

"There were some girls getting *married* at sixteen when I was alive," Jedediah said as he carried a stack of plates to the table. "I don't understand why Jeannie isn't even courting."

"Yes, well, those days are long gone. Girls today wait a great deal longer for marriage than what they used to," Jo replied as she set the bowl of chips and some dip on the table beside the plates.

"Well, does she at least get to speak with the boys her age, or do they keep her locked up inside her bedroom?" asked Alexander.

"Of course, she can speak with boys, you ninny. We don't imprison our children." She turned to retrieve the pitcher of lemonade on the counter. "Unless, of course, they're driving us crazy and they need a time out."

Just as she made the comment, Zachary walked into the kitchen and looked around in bewilderment. "Who're you talking to Aunt Jo?"

Jo's eyes darted downward and with some relief pointed at Dak. "Oh, just the hooligan over there in the corner. I simply reminded him of the need to mind his manners. He can be a nuisance at times."

Her boys laughed and then exited the room before Mary made another appearance. During the meal, the table buzzed with excited chatter as Jo caught up on all the latest events taking place with each family member. In turn, she answered all of their questions concerning her life, having to make a conscious effort not to mention Mathias or the boys. A thing made a little more difficult than what she first anticipated. Somehow, it just didn't feel right to exclude them from conversation.

Despite the difficulty, the next several days passed in a blur. Jo made each moment memorable and fun. They attended a Red Sox baseball game and she found just as much pleasure watching her boys as she did her family. Especially once William and Alex wandered down onto the field, and ran a bit of interference for the home team.

She also took them to visit the Valley Forge National Historical Park and to see the famous Liberty Bell. They toured the Benjamin Franklin Memorial, the Betsy Ross house, and the Declaration House where Thomas Jefferson drafted the Declaration of Independence. Finally, they visited Independence Hall.

Although her family remained unaware, Mathias and the boys accompanied them on each of their outings. She found it touching to witness their depth of emotion while they visited the sights significant to the birth of the United States. They shared many of their recollections with her, and she learned of vital events and conversations that didn't appear in any of the history books she'd ever read. How she wished she could share some of those same things with her family. In fact, she wished she could share many things with her family. Her biggest regret? She couldn't introduce her handsome Ranger to her sister. Unfortunately, she could only wonder what Nancy would think of Mathias.

****

Mathias expelled a sigh of relief as the last full day of the Elliott family vacation neared its conclusion. Although it gave him pleasure to see the joy Jolena's family provided her, he sorely missed their normal routine.

"I think that sums up the tour of Fort Mifflin and we

can be grateful for that," Sam whispered as they wandered toward Jolena's car. "If you want my opinion, that female ghost is creepier than any spirit I've encountered to date. I don't know how the other spirits put up with her. I'm quite certain we would've booted her out a long time ago."

Mathias nodded in full agreement. "Yes, indeed. She does lean toward theatrics if nothing else. No wonder the confederate soldier stays confined to his casement for the most part. I think I would too."

"One must wonder what the tourists would do if they were made privy to all her wicked comments as she followed them about." Sam snickered.

"As Jolena would say, they'd probably scream for their mamas and run for home." Mathias didn't hear Sam's responding chuckle. His focus of attention suddenly shifted to the conversation between Nancy and Jolena. He stopped dead in his tracks.

"I'm so sorry to see this vacation come to an end," Nancy had said as they strolled away from the building. "I had no idea so much history existed in Philadelphia. Well, what I mean is, significant historical places still standing that we could actually see and experience for ourselves."

Jolena smiled and turned her gaze toward the fort. "I know what you mean. But we've only just scratched the surface. There's still so much to see and so much to do. I didn't even know where to begin."

Nan shook her head and as she shifted Mary's position in her arms, she said, "Time is key, says the old family motto, and you have adhered to it most admirably. We've had so many amazing experiences this week."

Mathias stared at Jolena's sister.

"What is it?" asked Sam as he followed his gaze.

"Did you hear what Nancy just said?" In response to his question, Sam shook his head. Yet, before he could say anything else, Jeannie made an abrupt turn toward Jolena.

"I want to ride home with Aunt Jo," she said.

The girl almost walked straight through Sam. He had to pivot and step backward to avoid the collision, thereby interrupting any further conversation he and Sam might've had. Probably just as well. Sam would probably accuse him of grasping at straws. Nancy's comment probably held no meaning to them personally. How could it?

"That's fine by me," Jolena said.

She met his gaze then and the brief smile she gave him faded away as a look of consternation filled her beautiful eyes. She raised a questioning brow.

Mathias shook his head. "It's nothing," he whispered, hoping to reassure her.

Nevertheless, all the way home and all through the night Nancy's comment remained ever present in his mind. How did that particular phrase become a Michaelsson family motto? An *old* family motto, according to Nancy, but how old? As old as the fragment of paper Elisabeth Weidmann handed him over two centuries earlier? No—surely not. He had no reason to entertain such a ridiculous notion. Nonetheless, he couldn't banish the thing from his mind.

The following morning proved hectic as each member of the Elliott family raced to eat their breakfast and take a quick shower. They inspected the house from top to bottom to ensure they collected and loaded all their belongings into their vehicle. They accounted for each treasured souvenir and memento of their stay, including the foul ball, which Zack *miraculously* caught during the last out of the ninth inning. Finally, they made ready to leave for the airport. Mathias followed them outside with a sense of relief.

"All right, everyone," Nancy said as she raised her camera to eye level. "One more shot in front of the old oak tree."

"Oh, come on," Jo grumbled. "You know you've taken at least a million pictures already, Nan. I can't believe you want more when time is so short."

"There's always time for one more picture. Mom even said so, if you'll recall," Nancy said as she clicked away. "One more time, smile everyone—"

"You'll have no one to thank but yourself when the plane leaves without you," Jo countered.

"Fine, fine." Nancy waved her off. "I'm finished. However, after you receive your printed copy of all my pictures, I'll expect your apology."

At last, the family gathered around the van and began their tearful goodbyes. Mathias ambled toward Jolena.

"Thank you so much for all of the wonderful memories, Jo," Nancy said as she embraced her sister one last time. "We've had so much fun together and we've seen so many wonderful places. The baseball game remains a highlight and it's something we'll never forget."

"Well, I'm happy you enjoyed your stay. I really loved having you all here." Jo sniffed as she dabbed at her tears. "I only wished you could stay longer."

"I know, so do I. But I want you to know how much we appreciate everything you did for us. I think you gave the kids a greater understanding of our nation's history and at the same time, kept them well entertained. Time *is* key and I believe we've used this time in the best possible way."

"I'm happy you think so. Maybe it will prompt you to hurry back. There's a lot more to see, you know. As I told you yesterday, we've only just brushed the surface."

"We will. But I believe it's your turn to visit *us* first, so we can return the favor?"

Time is key. Time is key. Jo and her sister continued their conversation while the taunting phrase swirled inside his mind. He could still see the urgency in Elisabeth Weidmann's eyes as she handed him the note penned by Jacob.

What if one of Jo's ancestors gleaned that particular phrase from the Weidmann family, and they in turn, passed it down to their descendants? No, he didn't need to entertain such an absurd idea. Or did he? Although he didn't know anyone with the Michaelsson name, save Jolena, she said some of her ancestors lived somewhere in this area. Could that unnamed ancestor have also worked with Jacob? For nothing more than peace of mind, he needed the answer.

He looked up then as little Mary's babble grew increasingly louder in an attempt to gain his attention. The little cherub had grown quite attached to him during her stay and he had to admit she captured a portion of his heart as well. She smiled broadly and waved her pudgy little hand vigorously in his direction.

"Bye-bye, 'Thias, bye-bye, 'Thias, bye-bye," she cooed.

"Bye-bye, lovely little Mary," Mathias replied. He blew her a kiss and she blew him several in return.

Nancy looked at Jo and then shrugged. "I'm not sure

what she means by all of that—but I will call you the minute we get home so you know we made it safely, okay?" With that, she hurried into the van and as Bob started the engine, they all waved one last time. Mathias waited just until the van crested the hill before he took hold of Jolena's shoulders and turned her body toward him.

"Jolena, listen to me," he said as his eyes bore into hers. "Nancy said the phrase 'time is key' is your old family motto. Do you happen to know where it originated? Is it remotely possible it began with your ancestors who lived here in this area? This is really important, so please think about it before you give me an answer."

Chapter 10

Jolena stared back with something akin to bewilderment. "I'm not really sure, Mathias. Why do you ask?"

"Does it have a special meaning attached to it?" he prodded. "Think hard on that before you answer."

"Oh, I don't know. We've always taken it to mean time is the key to life. How we use that time matters. You know, so there are no regrets later on," she said. "Mathias, please tell me what's wrong."

He released his hold on her shoulders and stepped back. Did the failure over his uncompleted assignment weigh so heavily, he now attempted to make something out of nothing? Anyone could put together that same phrase, not just Jacob Weidmann. Besides, what possible difference could it make to anyone now? Nothing could change the course of history or change the fate he and his men suffered. He shook his head. "Never mind, it's probably nothing. I'm sure it's just an impossible—"

"Just tell me, Mathias, please," Jolena said, cutting off the remainder of his statement.

Simple coincidence could explain the entire situation. Nonetheless, something inside nagged him and that indeterminate feeling bade him continue searching all possibilities until those possibilities no longer existed. "Let's take this conversation into the house before someone happens by and thinks you're having a very serious conversation all by yourself, shall we?"

Once they entered the family room, Jolena kicked off her shoes and sat down on the sofa. She drew her legs up onto the cushion and waited for him to speak. He turned and faced the fireplace, with one hand resting on the mantel. Jolena waited for some sort of explanation and as the seconds ticked by, her patience waned. He could see that. Yet, he just didn't know where to begin this complicated story. Finally, he made his decision. If nothing else, she would learn the details of his death, whether she wished it or not. He turned around to face her.

"Not too long ago, you asked about our dealings with Major John Clark. I've not taken the opportunity to address your questions, until now," he said. "I'll begin by telling you we accomplished a handful of assignments for Major Clark in the few months we served under his command, all of them successfully, save one. Our final mission is the one I want to tell you about now."

The bewilderment in her eyes faded. Dread took its place. She shook her head against the sudden comprehension that flooded into her mind. "Mathias, I'm not sure I can just sit here and listen while you tell me about—about—" Her words stopped short as her hand covered her mouth.

"The event passed well before you were born, Jolena. You needn't be so concerned. I don't know if at the end of my tale, you can answer my questions or not, but I want you to hear this story, nonetheless." Mathias walked toward the window and gazed through the glass. He always liked this view. The lush trees and surrounding farmland made one feel at peace. He turned around to face her once again.

115

"Through the normal channels, John Clark informed me he had set up a meeting with one of my contacts. We were to meet just before daybreak at a place not too far from here. If we rode through the woods, we could arrive at our designated destination in about twenty minutes or so. Anyway, I showed up at our place of rendezvous first. There in the remains of an old burned-out barn, I waited well past the appointed time of our meeting. In the business in which we found ourselves, anything short of promptness, usually meant disaster. Just as I made the decision to leave, the wife of my contact entered the barn. She said she acted on behalf of her husband, who couldn't keep the appointment.

"That same morning, he asked her to take the children north. She would stay with her father until the war concluded. He also asked her to stop long enough to meet with me. So no one would cast any suspicions over her errand, she escorted her young son inside the barn on the pretense he needed privacy. She informed me the Redcoats required Jacob's services and had taken him along on an unexpected march toward New York. For this reason, he couldn't meet with me personally.

"I should probably stop here and tell you we considered this man, a doctor by trade, as one of our staunchest allies. By leading the English to believe he remained loyal to England, by taking care of their sick and their wounded—giving them beds to sleep in and food to eat, he gained the trust of the highest ranking officers living under his roof. Therefore, they made no effort to keep their conversations secret, including those which they should never have uttered in his presence."

Mathias walked across the room and sat in the large chair opposite her. He wanted to study her eyes for the slightest bit of recognition she might reveal as he continued the tale. "This man repeatedly risked his life to send every shred of information he could glean to General Washington. One cannot measure the service he gave his country. Inside the barn, Elisabeth tucked a note written on a small scrap of paper into my hand. She told me Jacob would allow her to carry no more than that. Elisabeth told me that a message critical to the General and our cause, needed delivery with all haste. After she left, I broke the seal on the note and read it. Jolena, the note simply said, 'time is key.'"

He noted her growing apprehension, yet she remained silent, and for that, he gave his gratitude. "After destroying the note and scattering the small bits of paper to a northerly wind, I raced back and gathered the lads as quickly as I could. At the time, finding Alex and William at Sam's house did naught but aid our goal. I've often wondered since that day, if I found the boys scattered in various places, would things have turned out differently. Not that it matters now, of course. After the four of us stopped off at Jed's place and collected him, we rode off toward the doctor's house."

Mathias stood up and paced the floor as he recalled the memory he relived more often than he desired. "In our haste, we drove our horses to their limit. The woods were the shortest and most direct path. Within two miles or so of the doctor's home, a goodly number of Redcoats emerged from the forest and made all haste to surround us. At first, it didn't make sense to see them there. Elisabeth told me the entire army left well before daybreak. She said they had marched toward New York—the opposite direction. Then I saw him and all of the pieces fell into place."

"Saw *him*?" asked Jolena, her confusion obvious.

"One of the doctor's most *loyal* servants," Mathias spat. "A man by the name of Percival Peddelton. Jacob literally rescued this man from the grip of death. Years earlier, he found him off the side of the road, badly injured. He took him into his home without reservation, nursed him back to health, and gave him a place to stay. After he recovered, the doctor supplied him with a job and paid him very good wages for the services he rendered his family.

"Despite all this, Peddelton pointed me out to the commanding officer as the man they sought. He assured him I carried something in my pocket the English army needed to retrieve. Something Elisabeth Weidmann had given me earlier."

Jolena's eyes widened and her mouth dropped as he made the comment. Nevertheless, he wanted to finish the narrative without interruption. He would quiz her at the end of his tale. "The traitorous dog had his pistol trained on me as if that cold piece of steel could protect him from my wrath. The officer in charge ordered us to abandon our weapons and step forward. Sam let me know he targeted the officer. The other lads signaled the targets they had chosen as well. I picked Peddelton. I wanted to see to it personally that he could never again endanger the Weidmann family with his foul mouth." Mathias sat down next to Jolena on the sofa and leaned toward her. He captured her gaze and held it. Tears filled her expressive eyes, yet he needed to finish the story.

"Months earlier, the five of us made a pact. We would never allow the English to take us captive. We had knowledge of things our enemies should never know, and we vowed never to give them the opportunity to extract that information. The fact is, as you have read for yourself, Morgan chose only skilled marksmen for his army of Rangers. That day, none of us missed our targets. Once we emptied our firearms, we fought with all other weapons at our collective disposal. None of us fell quickly or easily during the ensuing battle, not even our horses." Mathias shook his head and gazed upward as he recalled the memory.

"Outnumbered and surrounded, the surviving Redcoats could continue reloading their weapons while we could not. Alexander fell first, followed by Jedediah and then William. Samuel fell in his effort to take down the man who trained his freshly loaded musket on me. At that point, I fought alone, but not for long. Despite the carnage of the battle, and the fact we could see our bloodied bodies lying on the ground, we also discovered we could still see each other. Somehow, there in the forest, we remained together.

"At the time, we could do naught but watch as the remaining English soldiers searched my body, looking for something of importance or material wealth. They of course, found nothing. They searched the bodies of all the lads and again, found nothing. They even searched through the tack on our dead horses. Without troubling themselves further over our bodies, or even the bodies of their own men scattered across the ground, they quit the place. I can only assume they hurried off to rejoin the main body of soldiers on their march to New York."

Mathias chose not to reveal the presence of the brilliant white light she mentioned during their first encounter. None of them wanted to venture a guess as to what fate awaited them on the other side of it, and they discovered they were not compelled to enter it. That day each man personally made his own choice as to his destination. So, they found their way to the McGregor home and made it their haven.

"Mathias?" Tears flowed freely down Jo's cheeks, and try as she might she couldn't get them to stop. Her imagination conjured the sight of her boys lying there on the ground, bloodied and broken, after fighting so bravely against so many. How she wished she could gather him into her arms and just hold him. She wanted to sob into his chest and receive what comfort he could give in return. "I'm so very sorry. I wish—I really wish I could just—"

"Don't cry, Jolena." He cupped her face and used his thumbs to wipe away her tears. "All of this happened a long time ago."

"Did any of you suffer overly long, Mathias? I couldn't bear it if you did—"

"No, Jolena, we didn't suffer. Dry your eyes now. I didn't tell you this story to make you cry," he whispered.

"I know that," Jo said as she struggled for control over her tender emotions. Then suddenly, she remembered what she needed to tell him. "I don't know if there's a relation to this story or not, but Mathias, I know the name Weidmann. I have a set of grandparents, several generations back with that name. I'm not sure my Jacob is married to an Elisabeth right off the top of my head, but I do own a clock that once belonged to Johan Andries Weidmann. Come with me. I'll go check my computer in the library for you and see if anything relative to this situation is in my family genealogical database."

Jo looked up as she wiped at a wayward tear. Mathias disappeared. She found him waiting for her in the library. He had her computer up and running before she entered the room. She activated the program, clicked on her ancestral charts, and searched out the Weidmann family tree. The Michaelssons tied in with the Weidmanns when her fourth great-grandfather, Stephen Michaelsson married the daughter of William Weidmann in Iowa. William was the son of Willem and Anna Hall Weidmann. Jo's mouth dropped as she gazed at the next set of grandparents.

"Look Mathias." She plucked a tissue from the box and sniffed as she pointed toward the highlighted name. "I'm related to the Jacob and Elisabeth Weidmann who *did* live in this county. Do you see? I have them both recorded as being born here in Pennsylvania. I descend through their son Willem. I have a tremendous amount of notes dealing with this family. Give me a minute to see if I can find something that might give you the answers you seek." She turned her attention to absorbing the abundant information dealing with the Weidmann family. After a time, Mathias broke the silence.

"Willem accompanied Elisabeth into the barn that morning, but I think you ought to know—"

"And of course," she said as she looked up from the screen. "Jacob is the son of Johan Andries Weidmann, whose clock is down stairs in the sitting room. We speculate he carried it along with him when he immigrated to America as a young man. After all, he probably couldn't have purchased such an item here at that time in history, could he?"

Mathias waved the comment aside and said, "Jacob's father never lived here. Jacob and Elisabeth emigrated from Germany, along with their two oldest children. Elisabeth's parents and siblings sailed with them, not Jacob's parents. As I recall, the Weidmanns arrived in

121

Pennsylvania shortly after Alexander and his family moved here. So, you see, Jacob and Elisabeth weren't born here, Jolena. They told me themselves they were both born in Baden, Germany."

"That can't be right, Mathias," Jo said, pointing at the dates and places on the computer screen. "These notes say that Johan Andries is buried on the Weidmann farm, and we found an immigration list that shows a very similar name several years prior to the birth of Jacob. The Genealogical Society read and recorded his stone back in 1930. And remember, I have his clock—"

"No, Jolena. You're forgetting how well I know the family. Trust me. Jacob's father never lived here." Mathias stopped short as he gazed into her eyes. "Wait a minute. Time is key; a clock tells time, and you have a clock that belongs to the Weidmann family. Let's go take a look at that clock of yours, shall we?"

Mathias acknowledged the presence of the boys with a single nod the moment they entered the parlor. Jo could literally feel their excitement. Sam fixed his gaze on and stepped closer to her clock.

"I truly don't think there's anything hidden inside, Mathias. I've had it professionally cleaned twice and I know my parents had it done at least once. If Jacob hid something inside it, I'm sure that something is long gone by now."

Despite her misgivings, Jo walked over to the clock and opened the face. The latch on the side allowed the back panel to open so one could clean or repair the mechanism. She clicked the latch and turned the clock around. As the backside of the wooden panel swung open, a crudely etched name and dates appeared on the backside. At once, she found herself surrounded by all her ghostly companions. They wanted a closer look as well.

She pointed at the carving. "Do you see the label? We believe this is proof that my grandfather Johan Andries owned the clock first."

She took a step back as Mathias studied the panel for several moments. His eyes lit up with sudden comprehension. He then turned toward his companions.

"Jacob hid the item we needed to find in his family cemetery," he said the words as if stating a simple fact.

Sam laughed as he slapped Mathias on the back. Soon the room echoed with laughter as the rest of the boys joined in.

"What do you mean?" She gazed at each of their exuberant faces, feeling naught but confusion.

"This label is written in Jacob's hand. As his contact, I have seen examples of his writing many times. If I solved this puzzle correctly, Jacob gave us the clue we needed, when he said, 'time is key,' be that his family motto or not. Such a phrase would set us looking for a timepiece and once we discovered this clock, it wouldn't take us any time at all to open the back panel. In so doing, we would see the note he left for us to find. Don't you see? This carving reads, 'Johan Andries Weidmann 1724, Baden, Germany—1776, Berks, Pennsylvania, Beloved Father,' a common cemetery inscription, should anyone else find it. However, as we were all aware, Jacob's father never sailed to these shores."

"I wonder," Sam said as he scratched at the corner of his mouth, "if the information is still there?"

Mathias shook his head. "I don't know, Sam. But I wouldn't think so. My guess is Jacob learned of our demise from the report of the returning Loyalists. I'm sure he sent someone else to retrieve it. You must remember its importance."

"No—I don't think he did, because I don't believe he could have," Jo said, suddenly excited. "In the notes I have on my computer, I have a copy of an existing letter Elisabeth wrote to one of her granddaughters, years after the war ended. The letter said she assumed her husband died in New York shortly after he left with the British, because he never made contact with her again. No letters, no messages—nothing. He never returned home from the war.

"Mathias, you said yourself one of their servants identified you. Doesn't it make sense he would also betray Jacob to the British army, when he first convinced them to send a company of men after you?" she asked.

"She's probably right about that, Mathias," William said. "In all likelihood, they executed Jacob on the spot and well before we met our own deaths."

"I say we go find out," Jedediah stated.

"How can we do that?" asked Jo. "After all of this time and all of the changes occurring over the centuries, do any of you even know where the Weidmann cemetery is located or even if it still stands?"

"Oh, it's still standing," said Alexander. "The cemetery is located on the property that now belongs to the tedious neighbors a bit north of here. You know, the Parkers."

Jo took in a sharp breath as she stared. "Do you mean to tell me my ancestral grandparents lived on the same property, now owned by Douglas and Gloria?"

"That's right," William said. "And that gives you every right to check it out, doesn't it?"

"Well, I'm up for it," Sam said. "Of course, we'd

need the lass here to go with us. We can accomplish many things on our own accord, but I don't know if we have the skills to dig down into the dirt."

"How about it, Jolena?" Alexander bounced his brows and gave her a nudge. "Are you up for a little adventure?"

"Such an escapade could be fun," William baited.

"I don't know, boys. Just picture the look on their faces when I knock on their door and say something like— "So, you know the ghosts who live at my house? Well they think they might've left something important in your cemetery a couple of centuries back. So, you don't mind if we go and look for it, do you?"

Chapter 11

"We don't have to seek their permission, Jolena," said Sam. "They wouldn't even have to know we're there. The cemetery is quite a distance from the house they live in and to keep our business to ourselves, we should probably go at night, anyway."

"That's true enough," William said. "The original house the Weidmanns lived in hasn't existed since the War Between the States. The new house the family built on the property is nowhere near the location of the original home or the cemetery."

"Yes, but you forget. Jolena would need to climb those rickety fences in order to get there if we go in the back way. I don't know how easy that would be for her to achieve in the dead of night," Alexander reminded them. "Unlike us, she can't simply walk through them."

"I think I'd feel better about it if I asked permission, anyway," Jo replied. "I'm sure when I tell them I've just discovered that some of my ancestors once owned the land and are buried in their cemetery they'd allow me to take pictures of the stones. I can get my camera, my camera bag, and some small tools in case we need to do a little excavation. What do you think of that idea?"

"Are you up for calling them today, so we can get this thing done?" asked Mathias as he recaptured her gaze.

In answer Jo walked into the family room and over to

the phone table. She opened the drawer, retrieved the small card the Parkers left during their first visit, and picked up the receiver.

"Do you really think the article Jacob meant for us to find could still be there after all this time?" Samuel asked while she made her phone call. "Or is this naught but a fool's errand?"

"I don't know, Sam. And I don't know what difference finding it could make to anyone now. It's not as if it has any great importance anymore. We certainly can't deliver it to Washington," Mathias replied. "Still, for my own satisfaction, I would very much like to know what Jacob wanted us to retrieve and transport to the general."

The boys all agreed with the sentiment. Then Jedediah added, "Whatever it may be, it is, in fact, what we died for."

Jo finished her phone call just as Jed made his statement and the comment tugged at the strings of her heart. As she set the receiver back on the cradle, she said, "We're all set. Gloria said I could come over whenever I feel like it. I told her I would arrive just about dusk so I could take infrared pictures of the stones and thus get the best possible photos. I figure going around that time gives us the best chance to keep a low profile."

"What do you mean by 'infrared'?" asked Alex.

"Infrared energy picks up the light we can't see with our natural eyes. So, among other things, infrared technology is used to expose the detail on worn grave stones," she answered. "And Gloria already told me how to get to the cemetery from the main road, so that part is taken care of too. I told her I might carry along some little gardening tools to cut away any grass or weeds hindering my project. However, from what she said, I really don't expect anyone to intrude while we're there. She said she has a touch of the flu and can't make the long walk, but told me to come and help myself."

Just about sunset, Mathias led her down the path toward the cemetery. Along the way, they passed a pasture filled with horses, and despite the urgency of their errand, she just had to stop for a moment to admire them. "Aren't they just beautiful?" she murmured as a gorgeous Arabian sidled up to the fence. The chestnut mare with a bit of flax in her mane and tail demanded some affection and she willingly gave it.

He nodded as he propped an elbow atop the fence and said, "The Parkers do own some nice horseflesh. I have to give them that. Do you ride?"

"Yeah, me and horses go way back. I ride every chance I get." She sighed, turned away from the fence, and continued toward the cemetery. "However, that isn't very often these days, I'm sorry to say."

"You should ask your admirers to lend you one every once in a while," Mathias replied. "I'm sure they wouldn't mind if the famous Jolena Leigh Michaelsson borrowed a horse. If nothing more, the favor would give them boasting rights."

A breath of laughter followed the remark. "You know, maybe one day I might do just that."

Minutes after she made the comment, they arrived at the gate of the Weidmann family cemetery. Even though large trees and thick shrubbery surrounded the entire burial ground, Mathias turned toward the boys and said, "Eyes all around, lads. Despite the seclusion, we need to make sure we protect Jolena while she does us this favor. Don't allow anyone near this location until we've completed our task."

Without need for further command the boys fanned out, each taking a direction. Mathias then approached and opened the heavy wooden gate. All the while, the thing creaked and groaned for lack of use. Jo shifted the camera bag onto her shoulder and stepped through the opening.

The area, larger than what she first imagined, showed signs of neglect. Tall weeds and an overgrowth of foliage threatened to overtake some of the smaller stones. Some lay broken and scattered. Nonetheless, it shouldn't take long to read each inscription if such should become necessary in their quest to find Johan Andries stone. She dug inside the bag, retrieved her camera, and turned it to the infrared setting.

"Mathias, I'll start over here on this side. Call me if you find it first." Row by row, she studied each stone, some which could only be read after squirting them with her water bottle. As she approached the end of the second row, she knelt down and took a picture of a weathered stone memorializing an infant child of Jacob and Elisabeth Weidmann.

"Jolena, it's over here." From the back of the cemetery, Mathias pointed to a crumbling stone about two feet in height and width.

Jo stood up and made her way to his side. "Do you see anything out of the ordinary on the stone itself?" she asked.

"No, it looks as common as any other in this cemetery. I think it might make more sense for Jacob to place the item in the back or on the sides, rather than in front of the grave. That way no one would need an explanation if he got caught digging," he said.

Jo stooped down and traced every inch of the base

with her fingertips. Her grandfather set the stone deep into the earth. She extracted the spade and garden sheers from out of her bag, and then clipped away the overgrowth. She took a few pictures before she began poking into the dirt along the back of the stone, using her spade. Nothing hindered the tool. She then traversed the left side in a tight zigzag pattern and again, found nothing.

"I don't know, Mathias. Maybe what we're looking for is buried deeper than what this spade can go." She brushed a wayward lock of hair from off her face as she held up the tool for his inspection.

"No, I don't think so. He would want easy access so he could come and go quickly. I would think you shouldn't have to dig any deeper than the blade. Come over here, and try the right side."

Jo crawled to the other side of the stone and thrust the spade into the ground using her previous pattern. Finally, the tip of the spade made contact with something hard. She jabbed the blade in a circular pattern in an effort to estimate the size and outline of the barrier.

"Mathias. I think something *is* here and I don't think it's a rock. The object feels smooth and—a little too symmetrical."

The earth surrounding the item soon gave way beneath her fingers. Finally, she unburied the tip of a large iron ring, now rusty and corroded with age. Within minutes, she had uncovered the top of the thing in its entirety. She wiped the back of her hand against her chin and surveyed their discovery.

"I think it's some kind of pot—maybe ceramic or earthenware?" She glanced upward to get his opinion.

"So it seems. Due to the shape and weight of the

container, I don't think we can lift it out or take it with us without a great deal of effort and tools we don't have with us." He pointed toward the ring. "See if you can pry the lid open."

She grabbed hold of the ring with both hands and yanked. Her hands shook with the effort, yet the lid didn't budge from its seat. "The pot doesn't want to give us its secrets easily," she muttered. "And I'm not so sure we can wedge the spade into the tiny seam."

He stooped down beside her. "Let me see if I can help. Are you ready?" Mathias used what ability he possessed to aid the effort. With their combined force, the lid lifted free from the wax that had protected the contents from the elements.

She leaned forward to get a better look inside. "The pot is nearly full. I wonder what the thing on top is."

"I'm not sure," he replied. "Go ahead and take it out."

Jo stuck her hand inside the jar and withdrew an old folded piece of cloth, knowing that one of her ancestral grandfathers placed it there over two hundred years earlier. Other items soon followed. She had an overwhelming need to take a picture of the find.

"Let's make quick work of this, Jolena," he urged as he rose to his feet. "Make sure you take everything out of the container, and we'll assess the contents when we get home."

"All right." She tucked the camera away and then piece by precious piece she removed each item from the container. Once she completed the task, she placed each article inside her camera bag, taking great care as she did so. She didn't want anything damaged or destroyed, least of all the item meant for the boys. "That's everything."

The moment the words left her mouth, the sound of the most horrific, terrifying, ear-piercing scream she ever had the misfortune to hear, shattered the silence. The wail sounded like the cries of a thousand suffering demons. Thunderous footsteps followed, pounding in all directions at once. She couldn't tell the precise direction in which it originated. The precious bag almost hit the ground as she gasped and rose unsteadily to her feet. Instinctively, she tossed the bag over her shoulder and extended a trembling hand toward Mathias. Yet, even as her hand slipped right through him, he somehow righted her steps.

"Not to worry." He chuckled as his hand rested against her back. "You finally got to hear Jedediah's war cries. However, it also means someone is out there and getting close to our position. Hurry now, replace the lid, and cover it over again. We don't want anyone to think you're out here desecrating a grave."

Jo's heart pounded so loud, the sound filled her ears and she trembled from head to foot. Nevertheless, she quickly did as Mathias instructed, and within minutes, she had the vessel reburied.

"Now take some of those dried leaves and brush from under that tree over there and stamp them into the soil we disturbed."

She gathered the thorny debris and tossed the pile onto the gravesite. All the while, Mathias shook his head in silent apology. "I'm sorry, Jolena, I wish I could do this part for you."

Jo glanced up as she tromped the dried brush into the dirt with her booted foot. "I appreciate the fact you care, and that you would if you could. But as you know, this is not the most difficult thing I've ever undertaken."

He muttered something indecipherable in reply. His

tone of voice quashed a request for repetition. Once she finished her task, he moved back and blew a massive amount of dried leaves and brush against the stone bearing her grandfather's name. Within minutes, he had erased all telltale signs of their presence.

"All right," he said, "Let's go."

William and Alexander appeared just as they exited through the gate.

"Sorry for the uproar, but we needed to divert an unwelcome guest," William said, explaining the commotion. "The boy that accompanied the Parkers to our door seemed pretty deep in his cups. We found him stumbling incoherently in this direction. Sam and Jed are now making sure he finds his way home."

"I think we all better find our way home before we run into someone else," Mathias said as he placed a hand underneath her elbow.

A short while later they entered the library. Jo made her way to the desk and placed the bag on top. As she did so, she glanced at Jedediah and wagged a playful finger. "I want you to know, you scared the tar out of me with those wicked war cries of yours, Jedediah. I can see now why Mathias elected you to play the fierce Indian warrior. I probably won't be able to sleep for a week."

Jedediah dipped his head slightly and grinned. "Just trying to be of service any way I can, Miss Jolena."

Jo laughed as she turned her attention to the bag, opened it, and carefully retrieved each item. She first extracted several pieces of very lovely jewelry, which lay at the bottom of the vessel. No doubt, they once belonged to Elisabeth Weidmann, and her grandfather placed them in the pot for safekeeping. Next, she withdrew an old flintlock pistol. The gun looked almost new.

"Careful, Jolena," Mathias warned. "If I know Jacob, the weapon is probably loaded."

"I wonder why my grandfather would bury this pistol anyway. Wouldn't he rather have it out where he could use it?" After taking just a brief moment to admire it, Jo placed it next to the jewelry.

"My guess is he wanted the pistol handy in the event someone discovered him in the act of hiding away his possessions," Mathias replied. "The Redcoats took what they wanted, in the name of King George, of course. And it wouldn't matter whether or not they considered Jacob a friend and ally."

"That doesn't surprise me." Next, Jo retrieved an old leather-bound journal. She slipped her fingers underneath the leather flap and opened the weathered cover. The book contained names and dates of the patients her grandfather cared for, his diagnosis for each one, and the treatment he prescribed. "My grandfather's medical diary. I don't think it has anything to do with your assignment, though," she said.

"No, it doesn't," Mathias replied as he peered over her shoulder. "But I see several names here the English would recognize as patriots. They probably wouldn't have looked too kindly on Jacob for having tended to them, especially considering some of the dates. As you can see right here, these dates coincide with the time Jacob allowed the Tories to live in his house."

Jo closed the ledger with extreme caution and slid it toward the corner of her desk. Next, she extracted her grandfather's well-worn Bible. She used the silk ribbon to open it to the page he marked. "Look, this page lists all of the names and dates of various events for each of his children. And here is the same type of information for

Jacob's parents. You're right, Mathias. They did die in Baden, Germany."

"Probably the information right there is the reason Jacob hid the Bible away in the first place. He wouldn't want the English to see conflicting information concerning the place and date of his father's death."

"At least he seemed thorough in his deception." Jo placed the Bible on top the medical journal before retrieving the next set of documents. She took great care in lifting them out of the bag and spreading them out on the desk.

"Certificates pertaining to his war service," Mathias said as he traced a seal with his fingertip. "Obviously, he would need to conceal any documents showing his loyalty to the patriots."

Jo bit down on her lip as she met his gaze. "I'm sorry Mathias, but these are the last of the documents."

Mathias attempted to mask his disappointment with a shrug, but she could see past the ruse. She sorely wished she could do something about it.

"Perhaps Jacob found the means to retrieve his information and get it to General Washington, after all. That's a good thing and it makes my mind rest easier," he said.

The last item Jo removed from the camera bag was the first item she placed inside it. She situated the heavy folded linen cloth on the desk and layer by layer, revealed its shape. All the while, she held her breath, until at last the cloth lay open to their view.

She drew her brows together. "What do you suppose this is?"

"One of Jacob's aprons," Mathias said. "He used them when he tended his patients."

"I see, and um, I believe the evidence for that is right here," Jo replied, pointing to the brown splatters, still visible. She smoothed out the wrinkles and as she did so, she touched a slight bulge in the area of the left hand pocket. She explored its shape with the tip of her fingers. "Something is in here."

The boys gathered close as Jo coaxed a thick, folded piece of paper out of its hiding place. A wax insignia sealed the contents, keeping the message hidden from view.

"You're looking at Jacob's personal seal," Mathias said, pointing at the emblem.

Suddenly anxious, she turned the paper over. Scrawled across the center, she read aloud the words, "Agent 711." The boys let out a whoop of excitement.

"That's it, Jolena," Mathias said. "We're looking at the missive John Clark assigned us to recover and transport to General George Washington. The information is still here after all these years."

"But what does it mean? What does it refer to?" she asked as she glanced into each of their joyous faces.

"Agent 711 is George Washington's code name," Sam whispered, as if it must remain secret. "He used it in case the enemy intercepted his messages. In this way, no one would know the name of the intended receiver or understand its worth."

"I find all of this so fascinating. I had no idea, until I met you guys that a regiment of Rangers and dangerous spy games existed during the Revolutionary War," she said. "I don't know why it never occurred to me, but somehow it just never did. They never taught those facts in any school I attended."

"Go ahead and open it up, Jolena," William said. "I

think we would all like to finally know what our assignment entailed."

Jo took her letter opener from the desk drawer and millimeter by painstaking millimeter slid the blade underneath the wax. But even as she did so, the brittle paper received a hairline crack next to the seal. She immediately stopped all progress and shook her head. "If I keep going, there is a very real possibility this entire letter will simply fall apart, and then no one will ever know what it says. I don't think we should chance it."

"Then we're no further ahead than when we started," Alex groaned. "I wish we hadn't learned of the letter's existence. I find it more of a torment to have the thing in front us without knowing what it contains, than not having it at all."

"No, that's not true, Alex," Jo replied. "And I simply said *we* shouldn't chance it. However, I know someone who can and will. My friend Carolyn has the ability to preserve this letter *and* reveal its contents to us. Didn't I ever tell you? She does this kind of thing professionally."

"Well then, what are you waiting for?" Samuel slid the phone toward her. "Let's give this friend of yours a call, right now."

"There is one slight problem with that." She paused and fixed her gaze upon Mathias. "Carolyn will want to know how I got all of this stuff. Especially since these things belonged to one of my ancestral grandfathers. What am I going to tell her? She's my best friend, and I don't want to lie to her. I also know you don't want me to reveal your existence to her, either. That being said, I just don't know how else to resolve this, unless I tell her what's going on and have all of you meet each other."

Chapter 12

"To believe one must disclose all one knows in order to consider it truth is a mistake, Jolena," Mathias replied. "We learned a long time ago in the business in which we found ourselves, a person need only be told the information he or she needs to have. There is no untruth in telling your friend a close associate of the Weidmann family, who wishes to remain anonymous, wanted you to take possession of the things rightly belonging to the heirs of your family."

Jo tilted her head to the side and as a slight smile touched a corner of her mouth, she said, "The master spy reveals himself at long last. Of course, you're right. I'll give Carolyn a call right now. She loves this kind of stuff and I know she'll be happy to help."

Early the next morning Jo entered the lab, escorted by Mathias and Sam. Carolyn stood with arms folded beside an empty table. She tapped her toe as they approached.

"Sorry I'm a bit late, Kay, traffic—" Jo explained.

"Good thing you made it when you did," Carolyn said as she donned a pair of white linen gloves. "You wouldn't want me to hunt you down. The results wouldn't be pretty. Now, give me that case, and let's see what you have inside."

With Mathias at her side, Jo placed the case on the table and opened it. Then, just as she dipped her hand inside, Carolyn let out a sharp gasp of dismay. Jo met her horrified gaze and said, "What?"

"Oh, Jo—" wailed Carolyn. "Tell me you didn't touch this stuff with your bare hands."

Jo scrunched her shoulders, knowing her expression smacked of guilt. "I'm sorry. I—guess I just didn't think."

"I can't believe it." She shook her head and with fists clenched, looked heavenward. "I really can't believe it. How many times have I told you? Oil from a person's hands can permanently damage documents as old and frail as the ones you have. Gloves, Jo. You must wear gloves. Now, just—move over."

Jo glanced up at Mathias as Carolyn dived into the case headfirst and extracted the ledger.

"That's Jacob Weidmann's medical journal," she said.

"I must say it's remarkably well preserved considering its age. To tell you the truth, I didn't expect to find your horde in such fair condition." Carolyn opened the cover and ran a gloved finger over the first page. "In fact, my dear, you're really very lucky." She laid the journal on the table, and then retrieved the Bible.

"The family Bible." Jo stated the obvious as Kay simply nodded and then retrieved the remaining documents in one swoop. "The one on top is the letter I told you about, the one I want opened. Those other documents are my grandfather's war records."

The letter penned for George Washington lay face down, with the seal side up. Jo pointed to the seal. "I believe my grandfather wrote this note. As you can see, it has his personal seal here on the back. So, do you think you can open it for me and at the same time keep the letter intact?"

"Of course," Carolyn said.

"Good. I really want to know what it says and share the information with all of Jacob Weidmann's descendants," she replied.

"I can't wait to delve into it myself. However, it's going to take me at least a couple of days, maybe more, depending on what I find when I begin the process. We have to get the level of hydration exact before I can open it without damaging it. But, don't worry. I promise I'll call you often and let you know where we stand. In the meantime, I can get the rest of this stuff in a state of preservation easily enough."

Just then, Carolyn's cell phone rang. She looked down at the screen and sighed. "I'm sorry, but I really need to take this call, Jo. Just give me a few minutes and I'll be right back."

"Sure. No problem, take your time." Jo waited until Carolyn disappeared into her office, before shifting her gaze to Mathias and Sam. "Well, what do you think of her?"

"She seems competent enough," Mathias said. "However, we're really not comfortable leaving the letter here unprotected for an unknown number of days. Sam and I will stay here and watch over things until she's finished with her work."

"Since there are numerous locks on all of the doors and a state-of-the-art alarm system, what you truly mean to say is that you want to see the contents of the letter the minute she opens it." Jo lifted a brow along with her chin, daring them to refute the claim.

"Jacob charged the responsibility of this letter to us, Jolena. Therefore, now that we have it, we can't allow it to leave our possession. And—we really want to be here the minute she opens the letter." Mathias gave her a wink.

"All right. Then I guess I'll see you both when the job is finished."

"You're not coming back to watch the progress?" he asked.

"I don't know if I can. A lot will depend on our individual scheduling," Jo said. Yet before she could finish her sentence, the sound of Carolyn's returning footsteps, echoed down the hallway.

Mathias traced the length of her jaw with a single finger. She drew in a breath as the contact sent a delightful shiver down her spine. "At least try to come back," he whispered.

Unable to finish the conversation, Jo simply nodded.

"Okay, I think we can get started now," Carolyn said. "Want to hang around and watch for a little while?"

Jo finally exhaled as she glanced down at her watch. "I wished I could, Kay, but I have to get to work myself. I'll give you a call when I'm through for the day and see if you're still here. If you are, I'll stop by and see how things are going. That's the best I can do," she said, directing the comment more toward Mathias and Sam, then to Carolyn. They understood, and with a final nod, she exited the door.

****

Mathias and Sam passed the next few days immersed in the tedious process of document preservation. Carolyn labored over Jacob's medical diary first and then his Bible. She placed those items in boxes marked Archival. Carolyn placed all the war documents inside an acid free leather portfolio.

However, the letter remained a mystery. Carolyn finally opened it yesterday but before either of them could read the content, she flipped it over and simultaneously, placed a heavy weight atop it. She left it to sit overnight, locked the lab, and quit the premises. Mathias shook his head in exasperation as they could do naught, but wait for her return.

The morning arrived on schedule, as did Carolyn. As the hours slipped away, she had yet to turn her attention to the letter despite Sam's gentle nagging. He used Sam's impatience to keep him amused while they waited.

"Either the woman is so rattled she can't understand a word I'm saying, or she's choosing to ignore the suggestion," Sam said in an irritated huff.

"More likely, it's because she knows what she's doing and therefore will proceed as she sees fit," Mathias replied.

"Perhaps, but the wait is naught but annoying," Sam muttered. "And where's Jolena? We've not been privy to so much as a phone call between the two of them, and I know she could hurry the girl along."

Mathias had no answer for that. A wave of disappointment washed over him every time the door opened and someone else walked in. Disappointment ensued each time the phone rang, and he didn't hear her voice at the other end. He missed her. Sam nudged him as Carolyn put on a fresh pair of gloves and finally approached the letter.

Anticipation swelled as she removed the weight and then with skillful precision, turned the letter over. Carolyn then placed it on something called plastic sheeting. Her eyes widened in surprise as she read the content for the first time.

"Wow. I wonder what Jo's going to think about this?" she asked herself aloud. Then, after she slipped the sheeting under her camera, she took several photographs, downloaded those images into her computer, printed out the results, and laid them out atop the table.

Unable to see the letter under the camera lens, Mathias nodded toward the copy, and said, "Let's go have a look."

Then, as they stood over the printed copy of the note at long last, they fastened their gaze on Jacob Weidmann's final letter. However, reading it quickly, proved difficult.

"The thing looks hastily written, almost as if Jacob feared someone would find him in the act of writing it," Sam said.

"That it does," Mathias replied. "But look at the date; he must've written this shortly before or after he found out about the march to New York."

While Carolyn busied herself elsewhere, Mathias turned the letter on an angle, slid it closer to the edge of the table, and deciphered the contents.

June 15, 1778

Sir;

It has come to my attention this eve, the erc's have captured and executed thsmcgre one week past. It remains unknown if the said erc's gleaned any pertinent information about the condition or whereabouts of tinker's toy. We therefore find it prudent to change the location of the said contraption with all haste. Consequently, you must cancel scheduled convoy. Updated information and location will follow shortly hereafter.

797

Just as they finished reading the note, the door to Carolyn's lab opened. Mathias turned his attention away from the letter in the hope he'd find Jolena standing there. He wanted so much to share this moment with her.

"Oh, hello, Paul, I didn't expect to see you quite this early." Carolyn glanced down at her watch as she moved Jacob's letter from the camera to the table. "I have the tray for Professor Brennan in the back. I'll go get it boxed up if you'll give me just a minute."

"Take your time. I'm in no hurry," the man named Paul replied.

Mathias fastened his gaze on their visitor. In turn, Paul fixed his gaze on Carolyn while she covered the letter with a linen cloth. She hurried off down the hall and into her office. Paul cast a series of furtive glances down the corridor as he made his way over to the table. He lifted the cover and feasted his eyes on the letter intended for General Washington. Paul's mouth dropped, his eyes widened, and after he shot a glance toward the hall, he turned the document over. The echo of Carolyn's footsteps alerted all of them to her return. Paul placed everything the way he found it and scurried across the room.

"What the devil?" Sam growled.

"I'm not sure." Mathias folded his arms against his chest and studied the man. Despite his outward amiable persona, he detected a bit of malevolence beneath his phony smile.

Carolyn handed him the box and said, "There you go. I have everything identified, logged, and documented. Ray will find everything he needs in the report I faxed over to his office this morning. If he has any questions, just have him give me a call."

"Will do," Paul sang out. He cocked his head toward Jacob's letter and said, "So, what has you so busy today?"

"Oh—" Carolyn cast a brief glance downward and shrugged. "That's just a document that belongs to a friend of mine. She asked me to preserve it before it fell into ruin. The piece is a record pertaining to her family history, that sort of thing."

"Really," Paul replied. He glanced down at the table and spied the printed copies of Jacob's letter. He then placed his box atop those prints. "My keys," he said, patting his pockets. "I don't know what I did with my keys."

"He's holding his keys in his hand. What's he trying to get away with here?" asked Sam as he stepped ever closer to Paul's position.

"Oh, here they are, right here," Paul said as he pretended to withdraw them from his pocket. He picked up the boxed tray along with the top most copy of the letter tucked tightly against the bottom and bid Carolyn a good afternoon.

"We cannot allow that miserable dog to have that," Sam spat.

"No, we can't and we're not going to," Mathias said. "We're going to follow him outside and take it back."

They trailed Paul's footsteps as he took one final look behind him and then exited the door. The man breathed a relieved sigh once the door shut behind him, and with purposeful steps, he headed for the parking lot.

He didn't travel far before Mathias and Sam combined forces and conjured a powerful gust of wind. The icy blast tore at Paul's hair, his clothes, and the box he carried for Professor Brennan. During the fracas, he almost dropped his cargo. Paul gasped as he clutched the box closer to his body. Despite his grip, Sam yanked the stolen photo out of his grasp. Paul gnashed his teeth the moment the copy of Jacob's letter flew upward and out of sight. He jerked the car door open, shoved the box inside, and cast his gaze round about, seeking the document he'd never find. Despite the futile act, the man continued his search in every possible direction, even to the point of looking underneath each car in the parking lot. Once he conceded defeat, he cursed under his breath, and shifted his gaze toward Carolyn's office.

"Do you suppose he's had enough?" asked Sam.

"I don't know," Mathias said, never once taking his eyes off the thief during the exchange. "He's yet to get inside his car. The man is a little more determined than what I gave him credit for."

Paul's shoulders slumped forward. He muttered another curse just as Carolyn walked out of her office. She carried the archival boxes and leather portfolio that held Jacob Weidmann's personal possessions.

"My goodness, Paul," she said as she halted her footsteps. "What are you still doing here? I thought you left well over an hour ago."

"I just ran into an old friend and we did a little bit of catching up," Paul lied. "But I'm leaving now."

"Well, all right then." She smiled and waved. "I guess I'll see you later." Carolyn stood her ground until Paul climbed inside his car and drove away. She then withdrew her cell phone from her pocket.

"Jo? I'm all finished with your documents. Can you meet me for dinner in say, half an hour? Where? You got it. And for heaven's sake, don't keep me waiting."

Mathias looked at Sam and cocked his head toward her car. "I think we better catch that ride."

****

About twenty minutes later, Carolyn entered the

restaurant. Mathias and Sam followed. Each dipped their head in acknowledgment of her presence. Jo spared Sam a glance, and then settled her gaze upon Mathias. She had missed him far more than she thought she would and wanted so much to greet him. Yet, right now, she could do nothing more than return his smile as Carolyn settled into her seat.

Once the waitress disappeared with their order, Carolyn picked up the archival boxes and placed them atop the table. "These boxes hold the medical ledger as well as your family Bible. I know you're excited, and you're going to want to share them with your family. But please, be very careful when you handle them." She fumbled around inside her pocket, and withdrew a handful of gloves, tossed them down on top the boxes, and with a single brow raised, pointedly wagged her head back and forth.

Jo laughed over the dramatic reminder. "Yes, yes. I know, linen gloves, and I promise, I'll wear them before I touch anything."

Carolyn took a sip of water from her glass and nodded. "You better. Latex works just as well. I gave you digital photos of all this stuff, too. They're on the CD inside the portfolio. I suggest you make copies for everyone, instead of playing with the originals anyway. And, a word of caution: don't store the originals in the attic or basement. They need to remain at room temperature. You might even want to rent a safety deposit box at the bank. That's what I'd do if they were mine."

Jo leaned across the table and slid the leather case Carolyn offered toward her. She opened the cover and then thoroughly examined each of the pages. "Everything looks fabulous, Kay-Kay."

"Doesn't it though?" Carolyn batted her eyes and pretended to bask in the glow of her compliment. "I'm only kidding—well, no, I'm really not. But, the grand finale to all of this is your letter." She peered over the top of the book and turned to the last page. After peering in each direction, she leaned forward and whispered, "What you have here is a coded Revolutionary War message, intended for George Washington, himself."

Jo feigned surprise as her hand traveled to her chest and then toyed with the top button on her blouse. "Really? What makes you think that?"

"Agent 711—all historians of the Revolutionary War know George Washington used that code name. I'm guessing either 797 is the code name of your grandfather or he wrote the message in behalf of someone else. I don't know if you truly appreciate what you have here. But this document is worth a tremendous amount of money. There are several museums who would give a pretty penny to get hold of it," she said. "This letter is a very important find, Jo, and in my professional opinion, should be shared with the world."

"You're probably right. But before I do anything like that, I would like to discuss it with my family," she said.

"Well that goes without saying. And of course, such an important decision is not something you need to decide this moment. However, keep in mind; it's not every day one finds an original letter addressed to George Washington. So while you have it in your possession, keep it under lock and key. In fact, I would suggest you guard it with your life," she said as she sat back, thus allowing the waitress to serve their dinner.

Jo and Carolyn spent the next hour discussing the documents and a host of other things while they ate. Yet, the boys wanted to get home and share the letter with everyone else and so did she. She wanted to know if they understood its content. The whole thing seemed such a mystery. Finally, she found the opportunity to make a graceful exit and minutes later, she stood at the back of her car. She tucked the boxes inside her trunk, made her way to the door, and stuck the key inside the lock just as Carolyn honked and waved.

"I didn't think she was ever going to get inside her car," Sam said, as he tracked the progress of her taillights.

"Neither did I. That girl can chatter along with the best of them," Mathias added.

Jo burst out laughing as she took in their bored expressions. "I take it you're both ready to go home then?"

Chapter 13

"You know," Jo said once they merged onto the highway. "I find it hard to believe you were that bored at Carolyn's lab."

Sam snorted and said, "Obviously you've never had the pleasure."

"Can't say that I have. I must admit, all the years Kay and I have known each other, I've never once stood alongside her while she worked. But then again, she has never tagged along with me to rehearsals, either. So, I guess that makes us even."

"Well," Mathias said, "I can assure you, there really isn't much to see."

"How can you say that?" she asked. "The woman takes some unrecognizable artifact buried beneath the ground for centuries. She then transforms it into a recognizable thing of beauty and great worth."

"All well and good," Mathias replied. "But when it comes to preserving a piece of paper, or opening a simple letter, it takes the patience of Job."

Jo shrugged over the dour comments. "I imagine so. But, to tell you the truth, I was a little disappointed when she showed me the content of Jacob's letter. Nothing it says makes any sense to me."

"The message isn't supposed to make sense," Mathias replied. "Such a letter should only be understood by those involved. Should anyone else get their hands on it, the secrets remain protected."

Jo pounced on the comment. Now that she held Mathias captive, he might feel inclined to provide some answers to her many questions. She wasted no time in asking them.

During the remainder of the drive home, Mathias and Sam shared some of the covert activities John Clark assigned them. Some of those missions would've left her quaking in her boots if she had participated. Yet, they took each assignment in stride. Once again, she found herself marveling over the courage and tenacity of Mathias and his team of Rangers. No wonder they left over half the English platoon dead inside that forest before they died themselves.

A twinge of regret swept over her as she crested the hill. And just as she assumed, all the exciting stories abruptly ended once they spied the house in the distance. A few minutes later, she turned into the driveway, turned off the engine, and stepped out of the car.

"I wonder if the lads will have any thoughts or insights concerning Jacob's message," Sam said as they headed for the doorway.

"I don't know. But, I'm sure we can come up with something if we all put our heads together," Mathias replied. "We usually do."

"Hang on just a minute," Jo said as she turned back toward the car. "I forgot to get my stuff. We can't show them the letter unless we have it with us."

Mathias and Sam continued their conversation near the front door as she rounded the back of her vehicle. Then, just as she lifted the lid to her trunk, the sound of rushing footsteps approached. Before she could turn around, someone grabbed her from behind. The assailant placed one arm around her neck and squeezed her throat so tight she couldn't catch her breath or even manage a scream. Terror shot through her as she struggled to free herself. The hot breath against her ear sickened her. His garbled demands carried a harsh and gritty tone.

Just as the man grabbed her, Mathias rushed toward the car. The intensity of his rage sent Jolena's assailant staggering backward. He and Sam exchanged a disgusted glance and then, as if they had discussed it, they lifted the man off his feet and flung his body toward the massive trunk of the oak tree. The impact rendered him unconscious, and he slumped to the ground. Mathias returned to her side in the same moment William and Jed burst through the door, ready for battle.

****

"Did he hurt you?" asked Mathias as he tilted her chin upward and turned it from side to side, checking for any sign of injury to her neck.

After she took a deep breath, she shook her head and said, "No...I'm fine...really. It happened so fast and then you just..." She dropped her gaze and stared at the man's unconscious form while trembling fingers covered her mouth. A shiver coursed throughout her body. She turned toward him, seeking comfort. Mathias sorely wished he could take her into his arms and give her the comfort she sought. He cursed the fates that prevented it. Nonetheless, he gathered her as close to his form as he could manage.

"What happened out here?" asked William.

Sam jerked a thumb in Paul's direction. The expression he wore denoted complete intolerance. "That worthless cur had the audacity to assault Jolena. He intended to forcibly take the things she collected from Carolyn just a few hours ago."

Jolena parted her lips as her eyes widened.

"How do you know?" she asked as she massaged her neck.

"Because this same man visited Carolyn's lab earlier today and pilfered a copy of the letter she had on the table. We made sure he didn't abscond with it, but apparently he doesn't give up his quest easily," Sam raged. "He must've followed us."

"And now he knows where you live," Mathias ground out. "We must remain diligent from this point forward, lads. He'll not touch her again."

"You got that right," Sam said, with a firm nod of his head.

"Why don't we just have Jolena call the sheriff? They could lock this nasty piece of work away for a good long while, I'm sure," said Jedediah as he circled the man.

Jolena shook her head over the suggestion. "How would I explain he's the one who's lying there unconscious, Jedediah, and the only witnesses to his deed are ghosts?"

"You know, she's probably right about that," Alex replied.

"All right," said Mathias. "I'm going to take Jolena inside. I think she's had enough for tonight. I'll give the rest of you the pleasure of escorting Paul off the premises."

"We got it covered," Sam said. "Just see to our lady and we'll take care of the rest."

"What are they going to do with him?" asked Jolena as he escorted her toward the house. "They aren't going to hurt him, are they?"

Mathias chuckled. "Don't worry. He'll live to tell the

tale."

"Wait just a minute, Mathias. I still have to get my things," she reminded him.

Despite the removal of the threat, he refused to leave her side. He placed one hand around her waist, and took possession of the boxes and portfolio with the other. She retrieved her violin and then closed the lid of her trunk. Then as she turned around, her gaze meandered toward the oak tree.

"Let's wait for the lads inside the library, shall we?" he said once he noted the direction of her gaze. Despite his fervent desire to get her inside, she halted their progress just shy of the door. Concern filled her eyes once their gazes locked and held. She raised a hand and rested it lightly against his chest. For her sake, he fought to quell his rage.

She shook her head and with a tsk, dismissed the feeble attempt. "I'm all right, Mathias. He didn't get the chance to hurt me."

"Yes, but he should never have gotten that close," he countered.

Her gaze wandered over to oak tree once again. A look of confusion settled into her features when she found it vacated. "Where did he—"

"Let's go inside, shall we?" he cut in.

"I suppose it best not to ask, anyway." She sighed as they resumed their path. "So tell me, just how do you do that?"

"I'm sorry, do what?" he asked.

"How can you pick up the weight of a grown man and toss it as if it weighed no more than a loaf of bread?" she asked, pointing from her car to the tree. "For that matter, how do you accomplish *all* of the things you manage to accomplish? I just don't understand how that works."

"After our mortal demise, we learned to combine the force of our will along with the ever-present energy that surrounds us to accomplish those things we choose to achieve. It's along the same principal as using the force of thunder and lightning to create a battle exercise," he replied as he opened the door for her. Then indicating the stairway, he continued, "Shall we?"

A short while later, his men returned from their assigned duty and gathered in the library. The enlarged digital copy of Jacob Weidmann's letter sat atop the desk. He read the message aloud twice and then gazed into each of the confused faces.

"Right now, I have only one clue to offer. There's no doubt in my mind but the man captured and executed by the British is my cousin, Thomas McGregor. I'm sure you'll all agree with that conclusion," Mathias stated, pointing at the scrawled "thsmcgre" written by Jacob.

"However, I've no idea as to the reason for it. No one either in or outside the family, ever indicated that Thomas involved himself with the war in any manner." He shrugged. "Any ideas?"

"Now that we're taking the time to look at the thing, I think the 'erc's' are nothing more than a hurried abbreviation for the English Redcoats," said Sam. "If I'm right, then it means any unit or secret organization belonging to the English army might take responsibility for his death. That'll make it even more difficult to discover the reason behind his execution."

"I think you're right, Sam." Mathias nodded as he studied Jacob's scrawl. "But I wonder what 'tinker's toy' is in reference to? Does anyone have any ideas? If we could figure that part out, then perhaps we could figure out the rest of it."

"I don't know. But the thing seemed important enough to change its location in the middle of a scheduled convoy," William said.

"What did Thomas do for a living?" asked Jo. "I mean, he didn't do anything even remotely related to the tinker trade, did he?"

Mathias shook his head. "No. Everyone noted Thomas for his brilliance and not for mundane labor. He often referred to himself as a gentleman farmer. Someone who, as a vast landowner, did nothing more than oversee the business of his lands. I know he traveled quite a bit in conjunction with those holdings. If I'm not mistaken, he inherited some of the ancestral lands in Scotland, the business of which required his presence there on occasion. As far as I could tell, he didn't pay any mind to the war."

"Though possibly, naught but a clever ruse," Sam said. "As you know, many of our staunchest allies pretended neutrality. And as far as tinkers go, Jolena, they were a rare lot in these parts and I don't remember seeing any of them around on a regular basis since before the war began. So, I don't think the term 'tinker's toy' had anything to do with the trade."

"Well then, if Thomas possessed a great deal of wealth, could my grandfather have referred to part of that wealth?" she asked. "Something tangible, such as gold or silver, and he referred to that treasure in code as tinker's toy?"

"Very possible," Mathias said. "However, if that's the case, then I believe he would've needed to sell off some of his lands, either here or in Scotland, to attain something substantial to barter with. Then he would've had to donate whatever he accumulated to the patriot cause."

They discussed the letter long into the night. At the end of the discussion, the true meaning of the note evaded them.

"I have one more idea before we call it a night," Jolena said. "Let's check the Internet and see if there's any mention of a Thomas McGregor from this part of Pennsylvania, connected in any way with the Revolutionary War. Perhaps there's something in recorded history that'll provide the link between your cousin and George Washington."

"Let's give it a try," he said as he circled the desk to stand behind her.

She turned to the keyboard, typed a few key words into the search engine, and hit enter. "Well, your cousin's name, alongside the time period and area, points us to about fifty Web sites. Let me see if any of them look promising," she murmured as she sorted through them one link at a time.

At the end of her search, she leaned back against her chair. "I've only managed to come up with one possibility. There's some kind of volume penned by a T. McGregor, at this museum here," she said pointing to the title on the monitor. "The manuscript is from the time period. However, it isn't digitized yet. That means we'll need to make a trip out there and look at it in person *if* they'll let us see it. Keep in mind there's a good chance the volume has nothing to do with Thomas or what we're looking for and in the end will yield nothing but wasted time."

"The time isn't wasted, Jolena," Mathias said. "The

trip will either prove productive or we can eliminate the book from our list of possibilities. That in itself takes us closer to what we seek."

"All right then, we'll go on my next day off. While we're on this little outing, I think we should also search the land records, and see if Thomas sold anything prior to his death." She tapped her notebook with her pen. "I'm sure we can at least answer that question without difficulty."

"Thomas also owned land in Virginia," Mathias said. "If we're going to research the sale of his property, we'll have to include that area as well as his property in Scotland, if you know a way to do that."

****

Much later that night, as Jolena slept soundly, Mathias entered her bedroom. After her earlier assault and fearing more attempts by the man named Paul, he determined to stand guard over her each night as she slept, whether she willed it or not.

He sat down on the edge of the bed and as he looked down on her lovely face, he recalled the first day she entered his life. The moment she got out of her car and entered his property, she induced feelings difficult to comprehend. Yet, at that time, he never once considered those feelings would lead him to fall in love with her. But fall in love he had. Deeply—and beyond all recall. Despite that love, he couldn't and wouldn't ever tell her that—at least not during her waking hours. She deserved far more than what he, as naught but spirit, could offer.

"Fate hasn't been kind to us, has it, lass?" Mathias whispered to her sleeping form. "Would that you had been born in my century, or I in yours." He gently brushed her hair away from her face. Then, as he caressed the bruises now visible on her neck, he vowed that he would never allow anyone to hurt her again.

What effect would the coming days, months, and years have on their relationship? Would each day bring them closer together? Or would something or someone sever the established bonds and drive them apart. Despite the possible pain of such an occurrence, he renewed his resolve to stay the course, wherever it might lead. He didn't possess the strength to do otherwise.

"Come what may, Jolena Leigh Michaelsson, you will always have my heart." He placed a gentle kiss on her lips, to seal the promise.

Chapter 14

"Hey Kay-Kay, it's just me." Jo leaned forward in her office chair and placed her elbows on the desk. She glanced up at Mathias. He nodded his encouragement.

"Hey yourself, Jo, what's up? Are you calling to tell me just how wonderful I am again?" she asked.

Jo envisioned the cocky smile Carolyn wore on her face at this moment and the image made her laugh. "Absolutely! That's the first and foremost thing on my list of things to do today." She picked up her astrolabe and toyed with the dials. "Truly, Carolyn, I can't thank you enough for all your hard work. Everything turned out beautifully. But, I also have to tell you something else. The news isn't so good, and that's why I'm calling you at such an early hour."

"Oh, no. Did something happen to one of the documents?"

"No, the documents are all fine and safely tucked away for now. I need to tell you, rather, warn you, that someone else knows about them. Last night this person followed me home, with the intention of stealing them." Jo struggled for the best way to explain all this without giving away her boys.

"Are you serious? Tell me what happened."

"Well, after I arrived home, I got out of my car and walked back to my trunk to get my things. Then, from out of nowhere, this man appeared behind me. He grabbed hold of my waist with one arm, put his other arm around my neck, and demanded the boxes. Luckily, some men who live in my community happened to witness the event and hastened to my rescue."

"Well, I'm so grateful for their assistance and you can tell them I said so. What did the man look like, Jo? I'm asking because I remember seeing this guy in the restaurant sitting across from us. He looked us over pretty good. A little too good if you want my opinion, and I wonder if he eavesdropped on our discussion. Do you know who I'm talking about?" she asked. "The tall, dark, and not-so-very-handsome guy?"

"Yes, I remember him. But, I don't think it's the same man. Although I didn't have the chance to see my attacker myself, the description my valiant knight gave didn't fit the one in the restaurant. According to his description, the man stood about five nine, weighed close to one-seventy, had dark blond hair, hazel eyes, and wore silver-framed glasses. His attire consisted of a pair of tan slacks with a dark green polo shirt," Jo said.

"Oh, no. You've got to be kidding me. Jo, that sounds just like Paul Sanders. He stopped by my office yesterday while I—" Carolyn's voice trailed off.

"Kay?"

"Jo, Paul fancies himself an expert on George Washington. This guy is always looking for public attention and recognition. And I left him alone in the lab for a few minutes while I put together some things for Ray. When I returned to the lab, he causally asked me about all the stuff I had strung out all over my tables." Carolyn paused and then the tone of her voice hardened as she said, "I know he read the letter, I just know it. And Jo, he knows what it is. Please tell me you had the police arrest him."

She glanced at Mathias. "No, I'm afraid not. The man just suddenly disappeared—as if someone spirited him away from my presence. And of course, because I have no way of identifying him myself, I didn't even bother with a police report. After all, when they don't have something to go on from the victim—"

"I know, I know—" Carolyn moaned. "Well, be on your guard, Jo. I'm certain our man is Paul Sanders. Yet, without some kind of proof, there isn't a whole lot we can do about it now. Nevertheless, I'm going to delete your file from my computer right this minute—wait just a second—there. I deleted it from the recycle bin as well. Everything is gone as we speak. The CD copy from my archives is going inside my purse, and I'll take it to the bank vault as soon as I go to lunch. I already gave you all the prints I made, so trust me, he won't find anything regarding your documents, should he decide to come looking for them here. Perhaps you ought to make sure he doesn't find anything at your house, either."

"I'm not so worried about that, as I'm of you," Jo replied. "He won't hurt you in an attempt to get the file or the copies, will he? I would never forgive myself if something happened to you or your lab because of me."

"No, he wouldn't do that. We're colleagues, Jo. Right now, his reputation is all he has and he guards it well. I don't think he would risk that or his career by trying to harm me, especially when I could identify him. So please don't worry about me, just take care of you," she said.

Jo found it difficult not to worry some. But as the days passed, she worried less and less about the threat of Paul Sanders and gave more time and energy to solving the puzzle of her grandfather's letter. More often than not, she even dreamed of it at night. Remnants of one such dream teased her memory this very morning as sleep slowly ebbed and consciousness took its place. Perhaps her optimism for their planned outing simply manifested itself in the dream.

After a luxurious stretch from the comfort of her bed, she turned toward her window and found evidence of daylight peeking through the curtains. At the same time, an unexpected knock sounded on her bedroom door. "Yes?"

"Wake up, sleepyhead," Mathias called out. "We're wasting precious daylight."

"You can't waste it when it's not even eight o'clock," she shot back. She emerged from her bed to the sound of his laughter, and hastened through her morning shower. For in truth, she wanted to begin the day just as much as he did.

With one last check in the mirror, she tossed a wayward lock of hair behind her shoulder, smoothed her gray-and-lavender-striped blouse, and brushed a bit of lint off her light gray slacks. She exited her room and raced down the steps. Everything she needed rested on the hall tree table. She picked up her supplies and turned toward Mathias who patiently waited in the foyer.

"Mail's here," Sam called out from the family room.

"Okay, thanks," she replied. "Are you sure you guys don't want to come along?"

"Nope," said Sam as he stepped into the entryway. "We'd rather stay behind and watch over the house. Sanders might decide to come back. And we'll keep Dak company."

She reached down to rub Dakota's ears. "Well, even if

he did, he wouldn't find the letter. We have it hidden well enough," she said.

"Yes, but we don't need him ransacking the house in his quest to find it," Sam replied.

"I guess you're right about that."

"Off with you now." Sam opened the door and stepped back. "I hope your day is productive."

"I hope so too." Jo gave him a smile and turned toward Mathias. "Are you ready?"

"Ready and waiting," he said.

As she stepped onto the porch, the packed mailbox caught her eye and she took a minute to empty it. A thick envelope from Nan sat atop the stack. The promised pictures had finally arrived. After leaving the rest of the mail on the table, she slipped the package atop her notebook and then made her way to the car. She placed her supplies on the console, got inside, and buckled up. A split second later, Mathias appeared in the passenger seat.

"Is that a letter from Nancy?" he asked as he inclined his head toward the package.

"Yep. I think its copies of all the pictures she took during their vacation. We can look at them over lunch if that's agreeable to you."

"That it is. So, where to first?" he asked once they turned onto the main road.

"We'll start with the state archives and see what, if anything, we find there. After all, they are the central depository for all things historic in Pennsylvania and perhaps we'll get lucky and not have to search any further. If not, we'll head out to some of the more promising museums, beginning with the one that has the McGregor manuscript in their collection."

"Sounds good to me," Mathias replied.

"Oh, and there's also a genealogical center that has all kinds of historical records from all over the world. I want to check the place out too. Perhaps we can find Thomas's land records for Pennsylvania, Virginia, and Scotland all at the same time. Not that we couldn't make the drive to Virginia if we needed to. The trip would merely cost us some extra time on another day. However, I'm not sure how easy it would be to get to Scotland and do our research from the British Isles."

"What? You mean you just can't will yourself there?"

"Oh, don't tell me you can do that too," she replied in mock exasperation.

"You know, I truly don't know if the force of my will can take me all the way to Scotland." Mathias gave her a sideways glance and grinned. "Shall I give it a try and see what happens?"

"Don't you dare. It would be just your luck to get stuck somewhere over the Atlantic Ocean and not find your way home." Her smile faded away as she envisioned life without Mathias and it left her feeling empty and cold.

"Looks like autumn has arrived in all her glory," Mathias said, pointing to the colorful trees and the falling leaves along the sides of the road.

Jo shot a glance out the window and nodded. "Yes, it has. Do you realize we're just weeks away from Thanksgiving? I love this time of year; I love the colors and the smells. It also means we're getting close to winter and winter means Christmas, which, by the way, is my favorite holiday of the year. You're all going to help me celebrate it, aren't you?"

"Wouldn't miss it," Mathias replied. "Christmas is a

fine time. You know, over the decades, we've found the changes in celebrations and traditions quite interesting. At least, among the various residents of our house. In my time, Santa Claus, toys, and stockings didn't exist. The notion of cutting down a tree, bringing it inside the house, and throwing odds and ends all over it never once crossed our minds. In fact, Christmas celebrations centered mostly on adults, if one celebrated the day at all. For those who did acknowledge the holiday, they did it with a large feast, singing, and dancing—that sort of thing."

"Well what about the churches? Surely they held services to commemorate the birth of Christ during the time of your mortality," said Jo, suddenly fascinated by the traditions of his era.

"As far as religious services, some of the churches actually forbade any kind of recognition of the day at all. They declared it naught but a Pagan Holiday and would even go so far as to fine their members five shillings a piece, if they were caught having any kind of Christmas celebration.

"However, others did hold services. They would even decorate their churches with a bit of evergreen, garland, and holly, much as they do today, minus the lights, of course. Sadly, at least in my community, we missed out on that delightful tradition with the mistletoe."

Jo couldn't say she was sorry to hear it.

About three hours later, they walked out the door and down the steps of the State Archive building. Despite the help of a very knowledgeable employee, they found nothing in the vast accumulation of books and manuscripts concerning Thomas McGregor, or anything remotely connected to something called tinker's toy.

They stopped next at the genealogical center and as

luck would have it, the facility carried the land records they needed for both Pennsylvania and Virginia on microfiche. Despite a thorough search, they couldn't find any indication Thomas McGregor ever sold anything prior to his death.

Jo then searched the probate records for the state of Pennsylvania. The file they found for Thomas recorded he died intestate the same month and year Mathias died, just as he surmised from Jacob's letter. The record indicated the heirs of Thomas McGregor received an equal portion of all his property and earthly goods. They couldn't eliminate his lands in Scotland as the source of tinker's toy, since the library didn't carry those particular records and the probate file didn't mention ownership of anything outside the United States.

"Just let me get a copy of the probate record for my file and we can leave," Jo murmured just loud enough for Mathias to hear. "I'm starving."

After they left the center, she drove to the nearest fast food restaurant in an effort to save some time. They still had several more stops on their list of things to do. "Can I get you anything?" She asked the question without a trace of humor as she waited in line at the drive-through. No easy feat, that.

He studied the menu for a minute and said, "Let's see, you can make mine a double with cheese, some onion rings, and the strawberry shake looks pretty good too."

A smile finally appeared as she ordered her food, and then made her way to the park just across the street.

"Let's sit at that table over there, in the far corner," she said, once they parked and exited the car.

"I'm right behind you," Mathias replied.

While she ate her meal, Jo opened the package and perused the bundle of pictures. She placed the photos close to Mathias so he could see them too. As she picked up a napkin to wipe away the last of her hamburger, she stared down at the picture, now laying on top of the pile. The sharp intake of breath that followed made her choke a bit on the last remnants of her sandwich. She coughed and sputtered before taking a long drink of her juice.

Mathias leaned toward her. "Are you all right?"

She could only nod and while trying to catch her breath, picked up the photo and turned it to face him.

His face took on the same look of surprise hers must surely hold.

"How is such a thing possible?" he asked as he studied the thing.

"I don't know. But it's a great shot of you and Sam by the Liberty Bell. You guys look like those war re-enactors. Look, here is another one, and another." The number of pictures that included her ghostly companions amazed her. They looked just as solid in the photos as they did when they projected themselves to her. She and Mathias looked at each other for a moment. "I wonder if it puzzled Nan to see all of you touring the same historical places we visited and on the same days."

"Perhaps she would think it naught but coincidence," Mathias replied. "Are any of us in any of the photos taken at home?"

Jo gasped as she considered the consequences of that occurrence. "I don't know, let me look." She thumbed through the entire stack and placed the pictures in which Mathias and the boys appeared in a separate pile.

"Nope, you're not in any of them, thank goodness," she said. She picked up the photos and began counting.

"Now that I have them separated, we only have—let's see—fifteen, sixteen, seventeen pictures total in which you boys appear. So, considering just how many photos Nan sent, that's not that big of a percentage. Perhaps she won't even notice. She focuses more on family faces, anyway—"

****

Jo's mind centered on the impossible pictures as they arrived at the museum holding the McGregor manuscript they hoped to read. Casting the photos aside for the moment, she sought out a curator among the crowd of visitors, opened her notebook, and showed him the title and number copied from their Web site.

"I wonder if you could show me the location of this item you have listed in your inventory as, um, catalog number SPC5525108. I would really like to read it if I can, because it deals with an ancestor," Jo said.

"I'm sorry, madam," the curator replied, raising his nose just a little higher than necessary. "That particular manuscript is part of our Special Collections department and we keep them locked away from the public. Only those who have the highest professional credentials are allowed to handle such items and even then, only rarely."

"Oh, really?" Jo put a hand to her hip as her temper flared. She didn't much care for his attitude and she *hated* it when someone called her "madam."

"It's all right, Jolena." Mathias placed a hand at her waist and said, "We don't want to antagonize the man because we need to stay here just a little while longer. So, just look around at all of the displays and enjoy them while we're here. While you're busy perusing them, I'll help myself to the Special Collections section, since I'm quite certain I have the necessary credentials to handle

169

such items. Don't worry, I'll be right back."

Jo took in a deep breath and smiled sweetly at the suddenly confused curator. "I understand, sir. In that case, I'll just look around at your lovely displays then." She turned away without waiting for a response while Mathias disappeared through one of the doors at the back. Seconds later, he reappeared and shrugged.

"Bathroom—"

Jo almost laughed aloud. She found another display to peruse as Mathias disappeared through the wall once more. In fact, she found several interesting displays to study while she patiently waited. She cast several furtive glances toward the wall, and worried over his lengthy absence. Suddenly, he stood next to her.

"Follow me." Mathias led her toward the back and around to the left side of the building. "I know it took a while, but I found the book, Jolena and we're in luck. The journal did belong to my cousin. I don't know if it contains anything we need or not, but I'm going to slide it through the bottom of the door and place it inside your notebook. You need to kneel down, put your notebook and bag on the floor just as close to the door as you can get them. Then I want you to look through the literature right there while I complete the maneuver," he said pointing to the pamphlet display.

As Mathias disappeared once more, Jo stooped down and inched her things toward the opening under the door. Seconds later, the curator made his way toward her. Her heart thumped wildly as he approached. But, he couldn't possibly know what they—

"Excuse me, madam—" He withdrew a large ring of keys from out of his pocket.

Jo followed his gaze from the keys to her belongings

on the floor. "Oh, of course. I'm so sorry." She replaced the pamphlet she clutched in her hand, and all the while hoped Mathias had already placed the journal inside her notebook. If not, the snobbish curator might just catch sight of the thing sliding underneath the door all by itself. She then turned around and gathered her possessions as slowly as she dared. Once gathered, she stood up to allow him entrance.

"All right." Mathias gave her a wink as he walked through the wall just next to the door the curator entered. "We have everything we need. Let's go home."

Just then, a yelp and a sudden commotion sounded from the other side of the wall. She could hear the tell-tale sounds of several heavy objects crashing to the floor and scattering in complete disorder across the tile. She shifted her gaze to Mathias.

"Not to worry. Our benevolent curator has a little mess to clean up in there." He gave her a wink and said, "I thought a little bit of hard work might lower his nose a notch or two and take away some of that arrogant sass he's so fond of dishing out. So—let's go home, shall we?"

Chapter 15

Laughter announced the return from their quest. Jo clutched the precious notebook to her chest as she and Mathias raced into the foyer. Then in a play of grand exaggeration, she locked the door, turned the deadbolt, whirled around, and gazed at each of the boys. They all stood looking at her as if she had quite lost her mind, which in turn, made her laugh even harder.

"Shh." She placed her finger to her lips. "We have absconded with stolen booty and it must remain secret."

"You found something?" asked Sam as he followed Jo and Mathias into the family room. The other boys trailed a step behind.

"Indeed, we have, Sam," Mathias replied. "We have in our possession Thomas McGregor's personal journal. I've yet to convince Jolena, and believe me I've tried, that this manuscript rightly belongs to the McGregor family. Therefore, we have simply returned it to a rightful member of the family. Besides, I don't think anyone really cares. They had the thing buried beneath layers of dust and junk. From all appearances, no one has looked at this book in decades and I don't think it's scheduled for display anytime soon."

Jo made her way to the sofa, dropped her bag beside it, and sat down. Once she found a comfortable position, she retrieved the journal from inside her notebook and placed it on her lap. She stared at the thing for several seconds in indecision.

Finally, she shook her head slightly and tsked, "Carolyn would kill me if she could see me now, but the gloves are all upstairs and I just can't wait." She took a deep breath and opened the cover. All the while, she made sure the delicate pages made very little contact with her bare fingertips.

"In case any of you wondered, it says here, a very lovely lady, by the name of Shirley Hendrickson donated the journal to a representative of the museum in the year 1909. She presented the book to a Mr. George Bond in Lancaster. And I can't thank her enough for her generosity. Anyway, Thomas begins this journal from Scotland on March 17, 1773 and in this first entry, he records his thoughts about the trip. He says—

"'I very much enjoyed my visit with James and Anna Watt. As always, they remain gracious and hospitable hosts. James and I enjoyed our scholarly conversations and learned much from each other. But now, alas, it's time to go home where such conversations are a rarity.'"

Jo caught the tip of the next page with her fingernail and turned it over. "Who are James and Anna Watt?"

"James Watt is the man who married my father's cousin, Anna McGregor. My father corresponded with them a few times, as I remember. I believe they lived in Glasgow much of that time," Mathias replied. "We considered it a grand event to get a letter from Scotland."

"I bet." Jo used the tip of her fingernail to blaze a path down the page. "Let's see, the next several entries are merely day to day observations of his voyage back to the States. They encountered a rough storm and he records the death of two passengers along the way. As time passed, conditions onboard the ship deteriorated. He says here, toward the end of the voyage, the captain gave them nothing but moldy bread and spoiled cheese to eat. Yuck." She held her hand to her mouth and shivered at the mere suggestion of eating such fare.

"Not uncommon, really," Alex said, "if the lack of wind hindered the journey."

She then turned several more pages in a search for something significant to their quest. "So far, most of the notations on these next pages detail family events. He records their baptisms, marriages, and the like. Thomas also records the sponsors and witnesses to each of those events."

"Keep searching," Mathias said as he paced the floor with hands clasped behind his back. "We need to see if there is any mention of the war or any dealings with the patriots."

"I know and I'm looking," she replied.

"And don't forget to look for the sale of his properties," Sam added. "Or for that matter, anything that might indicate an addition to his wealth."

"We can already eliminate his property here in America as being the source," Mathias said. "Jolena found the probate records dealing with his estate after his death and as we concluded, he died about the same time we did. The court documents also show his properties, both here and in Virginia, divided equally between his heirs.

"However, we found no mention of his properties in Scotland in that record. So, that means either he already sold his property there, or the State of Pennsylvania had no jurisdiction over his assets outside of this country."

"Well then, how do we find out if Thomas sold any of his property in Scotland before his death?" asked Sam, directing the question to her.

"I'm going to write a letter to the Scottish archives and ask a genealogist to search the land records during the years the war took place. Then we'll just have to wait and see what they find." She shrugged as she turned a page. "Other than that—"

"I suppose that sounds reasonable enough," Sam replied.

Mathias halted his steps just in front of where she sat. "Anything else in that book?"

"Be patient, I'm still looking. Oh—" She extended a hand toward him without taking her eyes off the page. "Thomas visited the British Isles again. This entry dated August twenty-third of 1775 mentions another trip to Scotland and a second visit with the Watts family. He writes, 'I'm very impressed with James's new shop in Glasgow. The improvement he made to the Newcomen mine pump is most brilliant, indeed.' Whatever that means."

Mathias took a seat beside her. "Well, to give you a little history—early on, James studied to become an instrument maker and after a few setbacks, including the rejections from the Clockmakers Guild, he finally set up a shop at the University there in Glasgow. I believe that transpired with the help of some friends who believed in his talent. So, perhaps in this shop someone put him to work on some kind of mine pump. Of course, my cousin having a like mind would find all his inventions fascinating, I'm sure."

"I've no doubt about that," she said, as she turned several more pages.

"Here's something a little different and it sounds promising given the date." Jo pointed to the entry. "He wrote this July 1, 1777. He says, 'Talked to Joshua Porter. There is progress and I'm much relieved.' Progress on what? Do you think the entry might have anything to do with the cause of the patriots and our letter?"

"Very possible. Joshua and all his kin supported the patriot cause with each breath they took," Mathias said. "But I've no idea what Thomas's dealings with the man would entail. I can't think of anything they shared in common unless it had something to do with farming. But making a connection between progress and farming crops is something that totally escapes me right now. It isn't as if anyone tried any new techniques in the planting or sowing of their produce."

"Still, I think I'll write his name down on our list of possibilities. I don't think it would hurt to do some research on the man and see what we come up with," she said as she took a moment to jot his name in her notebook. She returned to the journal and turned the page. "Oh, here he is again. Only this time we have an additional name, this entry, dated March 7, 1778, says, 'Met up with Porter and Brewster near to Valley Creek. I believe the selected location is an excellent choice for this undertaking. Will begin work immediately.' Do you know someone named Brewster?"

"Matthew Brewster is again, another staunch patriot, but I don't know what they would have in common other than friendship." Mathias glanced at each of the boys, awaiting their input.

Samuel shook his head as he rested an elbow on the mantel and a cheek against his curled fingers. "Joshua owned land near to Valley Creek, so I wouldn't think it out of the ordinary to meet in that location, but for what purpose I have no idea."

"You have to remember, Matthew was a blacksmith by trade," Alexander said. "What would a farmer and a blacksmith together, have to do with your cousin?"

"I don't know." Mathias paused. "Nevertheless, *something* progressed nicely, as stated in the first entry and then they discovered an excellent location, where they could undertake that something as so noted in the second entry. Gut feeling tells me those entries are somehow related to Jacob's letter."

"I think you're right about that," Sam said.

"Could Thomas have bought arms for the patriots and they simply needed a place to hide them, before dispersing them?" asked Jedediah. "That might identify the use of the word 'contraption' in Jacob's letter."

William shook his head. "All things are possible, Jedediah, of course. But I don't see the need for a blacksmith if such were the case, unless they needed his wagons to carry them."

"Still, that's something to consider, William," Mathias replied. "But if Thomas bought a significant amount of weapons, I think it would make more sense to get them out to the men immediately, if even just a few at a time. And if you recall, the date for the entry is March of 1778. That's three months prior to my cousin's execution. If the 'something' is referring to a cache of rifles, surely he would see to it they got into the hands of the patriots. Those men desperately needed them at the time. Therefore, I don't think he would keep them locked up somewhere over a period of several months. That scenario doesn't make any sense at all."

"Unless we're talking cannon instead of muskets and if they suspected the British of spying on them,"

Alexander added. "Perhaps they couldn't find a favorable moment to relocate something of that size and weight."

"Well, if 'progress' is in reference to the acquisition of weapons, either cannon or rifles, couldn't we locate a record somewhere for their purchase? Maybe we could even find a ship manifest which notes the arrival of the shipment to the United States and to whom the shipment belonged," said Jo.

"I think the chances of finding something along those lines are next to impossible." Mathias shrugged. "The countries sympathetic to our cause and willing to sell armament to the patriots, such as Spain and France, took great care in ensuring England didn't discover the act. For this reason, we bought most of our supplies with gold or silver from an undisclosed source and then smuggled them into this country via ships that sailed through Cuba and often times even Haiti before they finally made shore here. We used some pretty crafty gunrunners on many an occasion as well and of course, they never left any kind of trail for anyone to follow."

"Well, don't forget, we might still be looking for the gold or silver, itself," William said. "Perhaps the 'progress' referred to the accumulation of wealth they needed. And if they planned to purchase some kind of armaments, then the knowledge, by necessity, would only include those taking part in the mission."

Jo chewed on a fingernail as she looked down at her notebook. "I'm going to go ahead and add the name of Matthew Brewster to our notebook. I'll see what the genealogical society can find out about either of these men and the part they played during the war. Maybe they can locate a record or two that'll help us narrow down some of the possibilities. And tomorrow, I'll get that letter off to Scotland. With any amount of luck, we'll find out whether or not Thomas sold any of his property there," she said.

"Is there any further mention of either of the men?" asked Mathias, giving a nod toward the book.

Jo read the last of the pages and then lifted her gaze to meet with his. "There is one entry written on May 21, 1778. He writes, 'Almost finished. We are optimistic all will run smoothly and as expected.' The passage sounds like it could easily connect with the other two, but—"

"I'm sure it must," Mathias said. "They all fit together. We just have to make sense of the pieces. Anything else?"

"There are two more entries regarding family matters. The last one, written on May 31, 1778, notes his first grandson's day of birth, and then there's nothing more." Jo closed the book, placed it on the coffee table, and sighed.

Samuel snorted and waved a hand in disdain. "Well, we all know the reason for that, don't we."

The boys discussed the notations of Thomas's journal long into the night and at one point, Jo finally excused herself from their conversation. The events of the day tired her out and she needed some sleep before morning arrived. Once she entered her bedroom, she placed her bag and notebook down on the bedside table. The pictures Nan sent spilled out of the opening. She intended to show the boys the images when she got home, but in the excitement over the journal, she altogether forgot them.

She gathered the photographs and sat down on the edge of her bed. Once again, she looked through them. She took time to study each one, and found them all remarkable. The boys looked just as normal and real as any other living person did.

She isolated her favorite picture of Mathias and put it on top of the stack. He stood very close to her as they entered Fort Mifflin. As they gazed at each other, he gave her that charming grin that always set a swarm of butterflies soaring through her belly. She couldn't have asked the camera to capture anything better.

Nan took some great shots of the other boys as well. She noticed something then. Her boys only appeared in photos of historic significance to the Revolution. Could the emotion of such places produce the miracle she held in her hands?

At that moment, an idea found its way into her mind. The perfect Christmas gift to give her boys sat right in front of her. Something so much better than surprising them with a personal Christmas Eve concert that featured their favorite songs.

At a gallery inside the mall, a rather well known artist possessed the ability to paint people as if they hailed from other eras and cultures. A good friend and colleague in the orchestra hired the artist to paint her husband as a seventeenth-century pirate. The painting turned out exceptionally well. Perhaps she could engage the artist to immortalize her boys on canvas, making them Revolutionary War soldiers, of course. She selected her favorite photos of each and then tucked them into her bag before getting ready for bed. Come the morning she could leave early for work and pay the man a visit. She could hardly wait to see the finished product.

****

Downstairs in the family room, after the discussions finally ended, Sam approached Mathias.

"I didn't want to mention this until Jolena fell asleep. I could see no sense in worrying her over something so trivial," Sam said. "We had an unexpected visitor while you attended your errand today."

Mathias narrowed his eyes. "Not Paul Sanders again."

"No." Sam shook his head. "Not quite that bad. No, the Parker boy finally emerged from his hiding place in the bushes, crossed the road, and tried the front door."

"You don't say." Mathias gazed out the window that faced the street. "Took all of a week for him to gather enough courage huh?"

"I don't think the doodle has any courage," Sam replied. "I think what he has is stupidity. William turned the stereo on, with the volume at full bore. The boy dashed off across the street like a deer with a bobcat on her tail."

"Well, if all he owns is stupidity, then he'll surely return."

Chapter 16

"You look pleased about something." Mathias brushed a length of wind-blown hair away from her face as they stood by the side of her car.

"Well—" Jolena shot him a wide-eyed glance and blushed. She looked down at her bag, clutched it a little tighter, and said, "I have the letter to the Scottish archives ready to mail and you know I'm still excited about finding the journal."

"I see. Do you think you'll arrive home on time?" He caught sight of the Parker boy peering through the bushes. His eyes narrowed as he considered the possible reasons for his daily presence this past week. None of those reasons pleased him.

"I should," Jo replied. "If something happens to cause delay, I'll call and let you know."

"All right, then I'll see you later." Mathias stood away from the open door to allow her entrance into the car. The boy hadn't so much as twitched. "Drive carefully."

"I will." She climbed into the car and started the engine. While she strapped into her seat belt, she said, "Have a good day. Because I plan to."

"Will do." Jolena returned his wave as she drove off. Yet, he maintained his position while keeping his gaze fixed on Owen, who fixed his gaze on Jolena. Sam appeared at his side the moment her car disappeared from view.

"What the devil do you think he's up to?" he asked, as he too focused on the solitary figure, hunched beneath the foliage.

"I think we're about to find out." Mathias nodded toward the bushes just as Owen separated, then inched his way through them.

Owen shot a furtive glance in each direction before he made a dash straight for the house. He looked at the front door and then glanced over to the side of the property.

"I believe the boy is weighing his options," he said.

"Yes, indeed. How far do you think we ought to let him get before we send him on home?" Sam asked as they charted the kid's progress around to the back side of the property.

"I think we'll just go ahead and invite him in," Mathias replied. "And see what it is he's after. Meet me inside. I'm going to follow him around and let him in the back. Get the rest of the boys ready. We'll want to make sure our guest is properly entertained before he leaves us."

Sam's eyes lit up with anticipation. "Yes, good idea. I think it rude to do otherwise."

Mathias accompanied Owen as he climbed over the fence and made a beeline for the door. The boy peeked in each direction before he took some gloves out of his coat pocket. From all appearances, the dog concerned him a bit, but since Dakota barked furiously from the other side of the second fence, he threw caution to the wind and approached the house.

Owen put his gloves on and just as he placed a hand on the knob, Mathias caused a gust of wind to blow it slightly ajar. The boy smiled a bit as he entered, seemingly pleased with the ease of his task. Once inside, he placed his hands on his hips and cast his gaze around the kitchen.

Mathias slammed the door shut. Owen let out a short, almost inaudible scream. He jumped and while in midair turned toward the door and stared. The boy shook his head, took a few deep breaths, and then licked his dry lips before heading toward the hallway.

Mathias met up with Sam near the family room. He raised an eyebrow in question. Mathias shrugged in return. They followed Owen into the room. The boy's eyes lit up at the sight of Jolena's stereo system.

"Awesome," he whispered. He ran his hand appreciatively along the sides and tsked. "I gotta have this."

"Looks like we have a thief, Mathias." Sam sneered.

"I would have to agree, except he has yet to put anything in his pockets," Mathias replied. He stood back as Owen made his way to the small telephone table. Their uninvited guest opened the drawer, and then rifled through the contents. Yet, instead of leaving it a mess, he put everything away exactly as he found it. Owen dropped his head and sighed, then turned around. His gaze ambled over every nook and cranny inside the room.

"What in the blazes is he looking for?" asked Jedediah the moment he and William popped into the room.

"Something valuable, no doubt," Sam replied.

"Well, it seems he's finished in here," Mathias said. Owen exited the family room, and walked toward the parlor. They followed him past the archway. Alexander waited inside the room, with arms folded, guarding

Jolena's smaller antiques.

As Owen cast his gaze around the room, Jedediah circled him, looking him over with contempt. The boy shivered, rubbed his arms, and then made his way to the small secretary. He opened each of the empty drawers in turn and peered inside. Next, Owen examined all of the cubbyholes. He searched the top of the mantel and then looked under her clock. Still, he had yet to take anything and Jolena had very valuable things inside this room.

"Why would he look under the clock?" asked Sam. "Do you think he's looking for something in particular?"

"I don't know." Mathias took a step back and turned to the side, thus allowing the boy to walk past him.

"He's heading up the stairs," William called out as Owen pivoted and made a sudden right-hand turn.

Alex, along with Sam and William, simultaneously appeared at the top of the landing and awaited his ascent. Mathias followed close behind.

Sam rolled his eyes, his patience spent. "Enough of this nonsense. Perhaps one of us just ought to come out ask him what he's doing here," he said.

Alexander shrugged and turned to face his victim. "I'll do it." He approached Owen after he entered the first bedroom at the top of the stairs. As Owen stooped down to open dresser drawers, Alex put a hand on his shoulder, and leaned very close to his ear. "Why don't you go ahead and tell us why you're here. Perhaps an idea or two might surface that could aid your endeavor if you simply asked the question aloud," he whispered.

Owen sighed, shut the last of the dresser drawers, stood up, and took one final look around the room. "Where on earth would that woman stash a valuable letter?" he muttered, as he took a step backward and rubbed at his forehead. He glanced over at the clock on the bureau and then fixed his gaze on the window. "Sanders ain't gonna be happy if I can't find it."

"By all the saints—" Samuel gnashed his teeth and balled his fist. "Apparently that spineless coward is too terrified to come after the letter himself," he spat. "And thus has found a kindred soul to fetch it for him."

"I think we've gathered sufficient information lads," Mathias said. "So, I think it's time to let him know he's worn out his welcome." The moment Owen cleared the bedroom and stood in the hallway, Mathias slammed the door. Then, each door in the upstairs portion of the house followed in succession. One door after the other, banged shut, then flung open, before they each slammed shut again.

Startled by the frightening spectacle, Owen spun around in an obvious effort to beat a retreat down the stairs. Sam appeared in front of him, impeding his progress. The boy's eyes grew ever wider as he looked the ghostly apparition up and down. Mathias chuckled over the hideous expression Sam concocted for Owen's benefit.

The terrified lad drew in a deep breath, threw back his head, and bellowed at the top of his lungs. He headed for the opposite end of the hallway then and dashed toward it as if the devil himself chased after him.

Well, they weren't quite the devil, but—

William vacated his position to appear several feet in front of the boy. Owen skidded to a halt, raised both hands in front of his face, and whirled around. Once again, he made a mad dash for the landing. Mathias made the long hallway appear ever longer with each step he took. The boy's chest heaved with his relentless effort to escape the house. Finally, he stopped dead in his tracks and whipped his head from side to side. His eyes settled on the short hallway leading off the center and to the library. A small moan escaped his lips. He turned toward the unexplored corridor.

"Don't allow him to get inside the library," Mathias called out. "He doesn't need to know it's there."

William made his appearance just outside the doorway. He swung his rifle to shoulder height. Without hesitation, he aimed his weapon straight at Owen's head and fired. Owen jerked to the side, wiped the side of his face, and looked at his hand. Again, he screamed. William's ghostly bullet whizzed right passed his ear, and the smell of gunpowder filled his nostrils. The boy exhaled short gasps as he struggled for air. Owen squeezed his eyes shut for a brief moment, and then grabbed at the doorknob closest to his position. His gloved hand slipped right off the handle. Alex and William flew toward him while he frantically yanked off a glove. He grasped hold of the knob, then twisted and tugged at the thing to no avail.

For added effect, Mathias made the doors bulge out from their frames. Owen's shoulders slumped forward and while shaking his head, he inched backward, away from the sight. The doors creaked and moaned eerily under the strain as the wood expanded and contracted.

"Watch out, he's going to bolt," Sam called out.

Their guest alternately shrieked and cried as he staggered toward the stairway. Mathias moved off to the side to allow the descent, knowing Jed waited at the bottom with Dakota at his side.

Jedediah, standing with a tomahawk in each hand, let loose with one of his war cries. Owen stopped dead in his tracks. Dak rounded the corner and jumped right through Jed's ghostly form with teeth bared. The dog halted just inches away and all the while, he snarled and barked at the intruder. The kid dropped to his knees, rolled, and then bumped and twisted all the way down the stairway.

He landed at the bottom in a heap and then turned and looked back. Mathias, alongside the boys, appeared midway on the steps. With a skill honed by decades of experience, they slowly, so very, very slowly, descended the stairs toward the trespasser. They could hear the acceleration of his heartbeat with each step they took.

Jedediah patted the dog on his way down the steps. "That's a good boy, Dakota. You did a good job. Stay now."

Self-preservation prompted Owen to whirl away from them and make a break for the entryway door. Once again, he found himself tearing at the handle of a door that simply refused to open. "Let me out," he screamed pitifully, helplessly. "Please. Please, just let me out."

Mathias snorted his disgust and nodded at the others. "I think he's had enough, lads. Let's go ahead and let him out."

At long last, they allowed the door to give way. Yet, before Owen could make his escape, Sam slammed the door shut once again, sidled up next to him, and said, "I wouldn't think of ever coming back here if I were you— for any reason. Because next time you pay us a visit, you won't ever leave. You'll get to stay here forever and play with us. We'll have such fun—"

Owen squeezed his eyes shut against the voice that would sound like the rumble of distant thunder to his ears. At the same time, he turned the doorknob with ease. His eyes popped open in surprise. He jerked the door open and in one fluid motion, sprinted across the street.

"I think I'm going to follow him for a bit and see where he goes," Mathias said.

"I'm coming with you," replied Sam.

Owen ran straight through several harvested fields toward his home. The thick foliage slapped against his face and tore at his legs and arms. He paid them no heed. Several minutes later, his energy spent, he collapsed and rolled over onto his back. They could hear his pounding heart as he stared upward at the late morning sky. Several minutes passed before he regained a semblance of normalcy to his breathing. He placed his arm over his eyes, fumbled inside his pocket, and extracted his cell phone. His trembling fingers floundered several times before he successfully made his call.

Paul Sanders's muffled voice filtered through the phone, "Did you get it?" he asked.

"No. No, I didn't get it," Owen snarled back.

"Why are you calling me then? Where are you?" asked Paul.

"Where am I?" Owen breathed out a shaky laugh. He closed his eyes and rolled his head from side to side. "I'm in the middle of my neighbor's crops."

"Excuse me? I don't think I heard you right."

"There's no need to repeat myself," Owen snapped. "And you want to know something else? I'm actually enjoying the feel of slimy bugs and thorny weeds."

"What's wrong with you, man?" asked Paul. "You're not making any sense. Did you get inside the house or didn't you?"

"Oh yeah—I got in all right. You know, my aunt and uncle would die if they knew I broke into our neighbor's house with the intent of robbing her. I find it such a pity that I can't tell them. I mean, I could tell them a story that would top any they've shared to date about that creepy place, and they have some pretty wild tales of their own." His eyes glazed, Owen paused and heaved himself into a seated position. "That's it, isn't it? That's the real reason you didn't go in and get it yourself. Why you no good son of a—"

"I told you the real reason," Paul cut in.

"No—No, you didn't. You paid me a pittance and then served me up to the devil himself. You hoped I'd survive long enough to fetch your precious letter. Well, I did survive. Barely. No thanks to you. I'm outta here, dude, and I'm taking the money with me. I earned every dollar of it and then some for the hellish nightmare you put me through today. If you want that letter, you can go in there and get it yourself. Let's see how long you survive in a house full of demonic entities that don't appreciate visitors. Happy hunting." After letting out a string of curses, Owen shoved his phone back inside his pocket.

His legs trembled as he stood to his feet and took a deep breath. He wiped his nose with the back of his hand, brushed off his jeans, and headed homeward. Mathias saw no need to follow any farther.

"Although a bit brutal perhaps, do you think the boy's ordeal will have any impact on Sanders?" asked Samuel.

"I don't know. Owen didn't divulge any of the details as I had hoped," Mathias replied. "And you need to consider that Sanders's type usually allows their desires to overrule all sense of intellect, especially when they can get someone else to take the risks."

"You're right," Sam said. "I wonder then, if he'll try

to persuade someone else? Perhaps the next person won't care if Jolena is home or not."

Mathias clenched his fists at his side and shook his head over the very real possibility of such an occurrence. "Heaven help them both if he does."

"Indeed." Sam flashed a roguish grin as they turned toward home. "Though it's been awhile since we've last had the pleasure of something akin to this morning's entertainment, I find it comforting to discover we've not lost our ability for lack of use."

Chapter 17

The first snow of winter danced toward the ground, and formed a shimmering white blanket atop the landscape. Jo didn't have time to stop and enjoy the view, though. Not today. Instead, she wrapped her long coat close to her body in an effort to ward off the chill and hurried inside the mall. Brady O'Connor, the artist she hired to paint Mathias and the boys, called while she made the drive to the concert hall this morning. He said he had finished the painting, and she could pick it up at her convenience. She found it very difficult from that moment forward to concentrate on the upcoming Christmas concerts or anything else for that matter.

She hurried past the throng of shoppers and made her way inside the gallery. Several customers stood inside, yet the moment Brady spied her, he excused himself and made his way toward her. His smile charmed as they met near the entrance. The man, who seemed the living embodiment of Santa Claus, grasped both her hands with his own.

"Miss Michaelsson, as you might expect, I've anxiously awaited your arrival," he said. "Now, before we go any farther, I've a confession to make."

"A confession?" she repeated.

"Yes." He applied gentle pressure to her hands and said, "Before you see the painting, I need to tell you I didn't paint the scene we discussed. After careful consideration, I used my artistic license to fill the canvas with the portrait I saw in my mind's eye."

"Oh, I see." Jo took in a breath and nodded.

"Now, before you form an opinion, let me add this. If the painting doesn't please you, I'll not only give you the one I completed, but I will also paint the one you originally commissioned free of charge. And what's more, I guarantee I'll have it finished by Christmas Eve. What do you say to that?"

Jo returned his mischievous smile. She couldn't imagine him painting anything less than perfect. Several examples of that fact adorned the gallery walls. "You have yourself a deal, Mr. O'Connor. So, can I see it now?"

"A moment, if you please. I must also confess a love for theatrics, so would you kindly close your eyes until I unveil the painting? I'll let you know when it's time to open them. Don't worry, I'll lead the way," he said, nodding toward a large covered easel in the corner.

Jo dutifully closed her eyes and at once, he let go of one hand and then tugged her along with the other. "Let me know if I'm going to trip."

Brady chuckled. "I'm not going to let you fall. Now, recall with me for a moment the discussion we had about each of your Revolutionary War re-enactors. I did a little bit of research myself on Morgan's Rangers before I began the painting. Fascinating and admirable group of men. No wonder your little band of boys enjoy their hobby."

"Yeah—" Jo bit down on her lip to hide her smile. "No wonder."

"All right, here we are, but don't open your eyes just yet," said Brady. He positioned her, she assumed in front of the easel. "Take as much time as you need to study the scene before you say anything and then you can tell me what you think. Are we agreed?"

"I don't have a problem with that," Jo replied. A brief moment later, a soft rustling sound indicated the unveiling of her painting. Much to her surprise, along with the unveiling, several gasps of delight surrounded her. Then, applause thundered from the small group of people inside the gallery.

"Okay, now you may open them," Brady said.

Jo let out a small gasp of her own. A painting, much larger than the one she commissioned, stood before her and she just couldn't take her eyes off the portrait. When she first gave Brady the pictures, they discussed the possibility of putting the boys in a wooded setting around a campfire. Maybe position them in the relaxed stance for which the history books seemed fond of noting. Perhaps even have one of them leaning on his musket, even though their faces would reflect the full attention and respect given to their commanding officer.

"This—" Jo gestured toward the painting, and then placed her hand against her cheek. "This is just so much more than what I expected or hoped for." Unbidden, small rivulets of tears coursed down her cheeks.

The artist painted her boys inside a traditional eighteenth-century home without a single detail of the colonial home neglected. They appeared in various stages of readiness in preparation of an upcoming battle. Sam, geared up and ready to go made his way to the unseen door. He painted William in the act of retrieving his musket. Alexander checked his flintlock pistol. Jedediah stooped down to say goodbye to the ever-faithful dog at his side. How interesting that Brady created a big dog

194

with Dakota's same colors and similar markings.

The surprises didn't end there. Brady O'Connor included her in the painting as well. She wore a beautiful royal-blue-and-ivory-striped dress, with a royal-blue underskirt and bodice. The bodice featured ivory crisscross laces. He gave her an upswept hairdo with a few loose tendrils framing both sides of her face. The artist depicted Mathias with an arm around her waist, cuddling her close to his body. They smiled tenderly at each other in fond farewell. And to her delight, he painted Mathias with the grin she loved so much. In fact, other than their stance and clothing, the couple in the painting looked very similar to the couple in the photograph she left with him.

A tan-colored linen liner surrounded the painting and as a final addition, Brady included a dark-brown rustic-looking frame. That frame set the tone, mood, and colors to perfection. She dropped her gaze to the brass plaque, centered at the bottom of the frame. The oblong plaque contained the engraved names of her boys, dates of birth and death for each, and noted them as Morgan's Rangers. The artist simply entitled the painting, A Young Nation Calls.

"I take it you like it then?" asked Brady as his arm rested lightly across her shoulder.

"This painting is absolutely beautiful," Jo whispered in awe. "How in the world did you manage to come up with something like this?"

"The inspiration arose from the pictures you left with me. I think it obvious from those pictures, you and these fine gentlemen share a great and unique friendship," Brady said, pointing to Sam and William, then Alexander and Jedediah in turn. "And I found it equally obvious that a very deep love exists between you and our 'Mathias' character, though you failed to mention that fact. So, in spite of our first conversation, I found I couldn't paint this picture without all of you in it, no matter how hard I tried. Thus, this image was born and I just had to paint it."

In response to his observations, Jo found herself gazing objectively at the couple in Brady's painting. They did look very much in love with each other. But, surely, she didn't feel— No, she couldn't possibly have fallen in love with a—at least not in the sense that he—did she?

Of course, you love him, her heart shouted as if demanding a say in the matter. *You know you do—and you've known it for a long while now.* She found it difficult to swallow past the lump in her throat as the absolute knowledge filled and then like a raging fire, totally consumed her.

"The larger canvas is also my gift to you, for giving me such a wonderful experience. I can't remember the last time I enjoyed a project so much. Also, I want you to tell each of these fine men for me that never in my life, have I seen anyone portray a Revolutionary War soldier so convincingly. A person could almost believe they witnessed the Revolution for themselves."

"Yeah, almost." Jo breathed out a bit of laugh.

"So, Miss Michaelsson, what do you say? Shall I get started on the other scene we discussed or shall I not?" asked Brady.

Jo forced her gaze away from the painting to meet Brady's smile. "I should probably say yes, just so I can have two of your beautiful works of art hanging on my wall. But in all honesty, I have to admit, I'm very pleased with this one. Truly, you have exceeded all my expectations. Thank you, so very much."

"My pleasure." He gave her a hug and then added, "Well then, let me get my boys out here and we'll get this crated and loaded into your vehicle before you tempt me with painting a second."

During the drive home, Jo noted the brief clearing of the skies. In that small moment, she could see the full moon as it cast a magical glow over the fresh covering of snow. She didn't think on it long. Her mind centered on Mathias and her recent discovery.

Somewhere along the way, she fell deeply in love with Mathias McGregor. How and when it happened, she couldn't say. Maybe she loved him the moment their eyes met. Or, perhaps even before. Why did it take her so long to understand that fact? And now that she admitted it, what did she plan on doing with that knowledge?

Loving Mathias meant she would never know life with a man in the normal sense of the word. But would she trade away her love for Mathias in order to have a "normal" life with a man who breathed air and possessed a heartbeat? Would she trade that love for someone who could physically hold her? The ridiculous questions made her scoff. She could hardly stand the separation while she worked, for goodness sake.

The reason no one else captured her heart seemed obvious now. She waited her entire life to find Mathias. Yet, for whatever reason, the heavens withheld their appointed meeting until now.

None of the reasons really mattered nor did she feel any resentment. Nothing else mattered except that she loved him. Yet, as long as she drew breath, she could never reveal these feelings to him. Such a revelation might interfere with a growing need or desire he might have to leave this sphere. Despite her own wishes, she wouldn't want to hinder his choice.

****

Mathias sat back in the chair behind the desk and fastened his gaze on the framed picture of Jolena and her parents. They stood near a river, lush with trees in the background. Jolena positioned herself just behind them with the wind blowing freely through her hair. She placed a hand on each of their shoulders, and they all smiled happily for the camera. She looked so beautiful.

"It's all right to love her, you know," Sam said, as he appeared inside the library, seated askance in the leather chair across from the desk.

"Be it right or wrong, I'm afraid there's not much choice left in the matter, Sam," Mathias replied. "But in case you didn't notice, Jolena is a vibrant, *mortal* woman."

Samuel merely scoffed at the statement, shook his head, and sniffed. "Insignificant details. Mortality is naught but a fleeting thing. Here today, gone tomorrow. We've seen how quickly it comes and goes ourselves. And not only with our own mortal existence. Think of the generations of your own kin who lived out their entire lives from birth to death, right here in this house. Why, if not for calendars, newspapers, and now the television, we would have no idea the time or the century."

Sam did have a point. A total of five generations of McGregors lived in this house before the children of his great-great-great grandnephew sold the remaining property to outsiders in the year 1919. After that, the unwanted strangers who invaded their home vacated the premises with the change of seasons. They didn't allow any of them to stay for any length of time. Yet, as one looked at all of those events at once and together, they fell as a mere spit in the bucket of time.

"Jolena needs more than what I have to offer her. She should have the chance to find a husband and have children of her own someday—and grandchildren—maybe even great-grandchildren before she leaves mortality," Mathias said. "Live life the way one is intended to live it."

"Is that right?" A mischievous grin tugged at the corners of Sam's mouth. "So, what you're telling me then—is that you'd have absolutely no problem if some miscreant called upon Jolena and she got all dressed up, just for him. Just imagine how pretty she'd look each time he arrived on *your* doorstep, during *their* courtship. You want me believe it wouldn't bother you in the least to see him take her out of this house and have them gone for hours on end, perhaps to dance the night away or take a stroll underneath the stars. Any man in his enviable position, would take the opportunity to hold her very, very close, don't you think? And you, of course, would feel only pleasure after the end of such an evening. He'd return her safely home and while standing on *your* porch, draw her ever so tightly against *his* chest and pucker up for a series of long, good-night kisses that would surely rock the foundations of this—"

"I get your point," Mathias snapped.

Sam nodded, and gave him a wink as he smirked. "I think we both know the unfortunate man in question would surely suffer your wrath in one form or another."

Mathias shrugged in return. He didn't need to comment on the truthfulness of Sam's statement, especially after he placed so vivid a picture in his mind.

Chuckling over his response, or lack of it, Sam rose

to his feet. "Well, it's almost time for our movie to start. So, I'll head downstairs while you think on what I said. By the way, you just might want to find out for yourself how Jolena feels about all of this. The knowledge might surprise you."

Mathias understood what he meant. They didn't find it at all difficult to enter into the dreams of the sleeping and have conversations that reflected that person's personal desires and feelings. They acquired the ability early on after their deaths. Each of them, at various times, used the gift to visit their family members. In this way, they helped ease the grief of their passing. But, did he really want to know the extent of Jolena's feelings for him in return? Did he want to risk knowing she considered him naught but a friend?

Stepping out onto the veranda, Mathias looked out over the hill. He hoped to see the headlights of her car coming over the crest and through the falling snow. They expected her home much earlier. He worried over the delay and not just because of the weather. Surely, Paul Sanders had not given up his quest. A man like that wouldn't. He wouldn't find it surprising to discover he followed her at times, watching for another opportunity to seize Jacob's letter by any means imaginable. In fact, he almost expected it.

Despite his numerous offers, she refused the notion of an escort whenever she had to leave the premises. She said the idea of a "bodyguard" set her teeth on edge. When he tried to force the issue, he learned she had fine-tuned the ability to feel their presence, even when they hid themselves from her eyes. As she entered the car on that day of discovery, she turned around, looked directly into his eyes, and simply said, "Nice try, McGregor—"

Mathias shook his head in exasperation and muttered, "Saucy wench."

At that same moment, her car crested the hill and made its way toward the house. He vacated the library and appeared in the driveway to await her arrival. He had done so, ever since the night of Sanders's attack, despite all protests.

As expected, Mathias stood by the side of her car the minute she turned off the ignition. He looked relieved to see her. She looked down at her watch and noted the lateness of the hour. She should've called.

"You're late," he said as held the door while she exited the car with a shopping bag in the crook of her arm and her violin slung over her shoulder.

"I know. I'm so sorry. I should've let you know. But I just got caught up doing some Christmas shopping and then halfway home it started snowing again, so I slowed down a bit, for safety's sake." She walked to the rear of her car and opened her trunk. She didn't intend to leave her precious painting in the back of it.

She struggled with the large crate. The thing took up the entire space of her trunk and protruded into the dropped seat in the back of her car.

Mathias shook his head and waved her aside. "Allow me—"

"All right, thank you." She stood back while he extracted her parcel with an ease that still astonished her.

"What exactly do you have here, anyway?" he asked as they entered the house. "The thing has to measure at least four by five feet in height and width."

"That's none of your business, Mathias McGregor, and I'll thank you to stay out of my personal affairs," she said. Despite the bantered words, she was near to bursting with the desire to give the boys her gift the minute she walked through the door. Hopefully she would attain the patience and self-control to wait until Christmas.

"Well, go on and keep your secrets then," Mathias stated with mock indifference as they ascended the stairs. "I really don't care."

"I intend to keep all of my Christmas secrets and of course you care," she said before she turned the knob and opened her bedroom door. She pointed to the wall opposite her closet. "You can just slide it against the wall over there." After he completed the task, Jo put her shopping bag on the floor. She tucked her violin in the corner, then took off her coat and tossed it on the bed.

"Thank you again for your help," she said. Just as she turned, their eyes met and held. The intensity of his gaze said he considered something. Something important. "What is it?"

He shook his head, gave her *that* smile, and simply said, "Nothing, at all."

"Are you sure?"

"I'm sure," he replied. "Are you coming downstairs?"

"Yes." She nodded as she spared a final glance at the painting. "I'd like to talk to you all for just a minute, if I dare interrupt the movie, that is."

"We've seen the movie twice. I don't think anyone will mind. Is there something you need?"

"The Christmas concerts." She paused then and scrunched her shoulders. "We're doing several as you know, and I wondered if maybe you'd all like to attend one of the performances. As it so happens, one of them coincides with the date of your birth. So, I thought the concert could be my gift to you."

Chapter 18

A terrible case of the jitters took hold of Jolena the moment she finished fine-tuning her instrument. In fact, she couldn't remember being this nervous over having to perform in front of an audience since the tender age of thirteen. In all likelihood, she could lay the blame at Mathias McGregor's feet. She didn't realize having him in attendance at this concert would prove so unnerving. He'd listened to her play countless times before, but somehow in this setting, it seemed so much different from being at home.

Perhaps he made her feel this way because for the very first time in her presence, he changed the look of his clothes. He did it the instant they approached the entrance. The fact he would or even could change the appearance of his attire never once entered her mind. Yet, as the male patrons filtered in wearing suits, Mathias suddenly appeared in like manner. He didn't want to distract her while she played, he said. Yeah, whatever. He looked very handsome in his black, vested suit—*very* handsome. She found it difficult *not* to become distracted.

As the lights dimmed and the conductor stood ready with his baton, Mathias made his way to the front of the concert hall and stood off to the side. He couldn't have chosen a better position from which to observe the concert. However, his close proximity unnerved her even more.

Get a grip, Jo. She took a small breath and turned her attention toward the conductor. With a stroke of his baton, the joyous songs of Christmas filled the hall.

Yet, as the concert progressed, she found it difficult to keep her eyes off Mathias. The rest of the boys insisted he attend this concert alone and that decision now filled her with gratitude. Sam said by going alone, Mathias could enjoy his birthday gift without the interruptions and conversations they would surely have if they were all together. The rest of them, he said, would attend the following evening.

Finally, the time arrived for her solo performance. Jo vacated her seat and took her position at the forefront. She smoothed the non-existent wrinkles in her shimmering black gown and waited for her cue. Mathias winked and the small gesture left her feeling a bit weak in the knees. Once again, she refocused her attention. She would begin the set with "Away in a Manger," followed by her unique arrangement of "O Holy Night," the highly requested favorite of last year's audiences. For her grand finale, she chose to play a charming rendition of Mathias's favorite song as a special birthday gift to him. Those who filled the auditorium would hear "What Child is This," but Mathias would hear "Greensleeves." She took a deep breath and stepped forward.

****

Mathias retained possession of Jolena's gaze all throughout her flawless performance. She finished the first two pieces and then shifted her position in order to face him more directly. Although the program noted the title differently, she played his favorite song. The fact she remembered touched him, for he only mentioned it once during their first meeting. Her penetrating gaze and the

204

literal connection of their souls, said she played the song just for him.

At the end of her selections, the audience rose to their feet and applauded for several minutes in appreciation of her matchless talent. Yet, her gaze never once wandered away from his during the standing ovation. The wink he gave in response caused a pretty blush. She turned to her side and then swept her hand toward the entire membership of the orchestra. She looked out over the audience and gave them a smile. Another round of applause followed.

Much sooner than he anticipated or desired, the first concert he ever attended concluded. While Jolena packed away her violin and music, he scanned the crowd as the audience began leaving the hall. Quite by happenstance, his eyes fell upon Paul Sanders. The man rose from his seat, and for several long seconds, he stared in Jolena's direction. Did he come here by coincidence or did he come on purpose? A girl hung on his arm. That probably indicated he didn't aim to accost or follow Jolena tonight. But then again, his reasons for attending the concert didn't matter.

In a mere instant, he appeared beside the exit door Sanders now approached. The night Paul made his attack, Mathias made sure he caught a glimpse of him just before he and Sam rendered him unconscious. He had no way of knowing if the man remembered the encounter or not, but he would find out soon enough.

Mathias fixed his gaze on his target as Paul took one final look at Jolena before turning to leave. The man wore a contemplative expression and Mathias would give just about anything to know where his thoughts had taken him.

"Just what are you planning, Paul Sanders?" whispered Mathias. The smile Paul gave his woman held no affection. Therefore, he could only conclude his smug grin concerned Jolena in some way. Suddenly he wished Sam had accompanied him to this concert, for Sam could have followed him home. If they discovered where he lived, they could easily shadow his every step. For now, the opportunity escaped them.

Just then, Sanders met his gaze. His eyes widened in response and he drew in a sharp, audible breath. Ah, so he did remember his brief encounter with Jolena's enraged "neighbor." Mathias grinned when Paul grabbed hold of the woman and changed sides, creating a barrier between them as he and his lady exited.

After Paul rushed through the doorway, Mathias raised the man's anxiety a notch or two, simply by following him outside. He wondered then how quickly he could get Sanders to break a sweat on this cold December evening.

Mathias maintained just enough distance from the couple to keep Paul agitated. The fact that Sanders continued peering over his shoulder while he dogged his steps amused him. From all appearances, the man didn't know whether to grab his girlfriend and run for cover, or scream for help. Sanders settled on holding the girl close to his body, using her for whatever protection she might offer. Mathias shook his head in disgust as he disappeared from the coward's view once Paul faced forward. Then, as Sanders turned around once more, his annoyed girlfriend glanced over his shoulder in the direction of his gaze.

"What do you keep looking at?" she snapped, her irritation obvious in tone.

"I'm just checking the flow of traffic leaving the parking lot, sweetheart, that's all," Paul said as he mopped the sweat from off his brow.

Satisfied he accomplished his purpose, Mathias left Paul Sanders cowering behind his woman's skirts. He returned to the concert hall in search of Jolena. She stood in the center aisle with her back facing him. Directly in front of her, a multitude of people swarmed who craved her attention. Among them, stood the Parkers and Andersons along with their guests they sought to impress. In less than a heartbeat, he stood at her side.

"Once again, my dear, you had me in tears," Ellen gushed at that very moment. "You know, I've attended a lot of concerts in my time and enjoyed the talents of many master violinists, but you outshine them all."

"Yes, indeed," Gloria said. "You've given so much to this community, what with all your charity concerts and humanitarian efforts. I just wished we had a way to give something back to you."

"Well," Ellen cut in. "If Jo wants something we can give, she *knows* she has only to ask."

Mathias chuckled as he leaned close to Jolena's ear. "Do you think their guests are suitably impressed by their 'intimate friendship' with you?"

"Oh, I don't know about that," she said, answering him without really thinking.

"Oh, but it's true," Gloria replied. "You know we would love to do something for you, anytime and in any way we can."

"Except enter the domain of the gruesome ghosts," he teased.

Jolena bit down on her lip as she glanced down at the carpet. "Oh, well I—"

"Try it out," Mathias prodded. "Why don't you ask them if you can ride one of their horses? You have next week off. Go on, you know you've been dying to ride—if you'll pardon the expression."

"Hmm. Well, actually—" Jolena met Gloria's questioning gaze. "I do have rather a selfish request."

Gloria looked pleased as punch when she directed the comment her way. "Like I said—"

"You know, it feels like forever since I last had the opportunity to ride a horse, and a while back I happened across your pasture and saw all of your beautiful—"

"Anytime," Gloria and Douglas sang out in unison.

"I have several mounts you can choose from and they've all been itching for some exercise. I'm getting much too old to help them out these days." Douglas sighed and shrugged his shoulders. "So, it would make me happy to saddle one of them up for you, anytime you have the desire."

"I don't use a saddle," Jolena replied.

Douglas seemed surprised. "You don't?"

She shook her head as she clasped her hands together. "Never have. I just use a bridle and bareback pad, which I happen to own, so you needn't worry about tack."

"Brave girl," Gloria quipped.

"No, not really. It's just the way I prefer to ride," she said.

"Well, when would you like to come out?" asked Douglas.

"How about Wednesday morning?" Jolena's eyes lit up in sudden anticipation, and her eagerness made him smile.

"No problem." Douglas shot a bewildered glance at

Gloria after she elbowed his side.

Gloria cleared her throat. "Jo, dear, we have failed to introduce you to our guests—"

Mathias rolled his eyes as she proceeded to rattle off the name of each person. In all likelihood, Jolena would never see any of them again, so what difference did their names make? Nevertheless, she greeted each of them in turn as if delighted to do so. And then as Gloria's gaze rested on the last of the lot, he finally understood her motive and the pointed jab.

"This good-looking young man is Tyler Holden, the son of our favorite cousin," Gloria cooed, smiling in his direction. "I'm sure he could arrange his schedule to accompany you on that ride. After all, I don't think it wise to ride out all alone."

Mathias's eyes narrowed as Sam's long-winded speech about potential suitors crashed into his consciousness. "You already have a riding partner and therefore, do not require a nursemaid," he hissed.

Once again, Jolena bit down on her lip and briefly cast her eyes downward. "Well, I already have a companion who's very anxious to ride with me, and I don't want to inconvenience Tyler. But, I thank you for your kind offer anyway."

"Of course." Douglas nodded despite Gloria's exasperated sigh. "Does your friend need a mount as well?"

"No," Mathias growled. "Your 'friend' doesn't need a mount."

"No—" Jolena covered her smile with a feigned, quiet cough. "He has his own." She shot him a questioning glance and he nodded.

Mathias gloated for a brief moment over Gloria's

obvious disappointment.

Gloria tsked, and shook her head. Finally, she said, "Well, that's fine dear. We'll expect to see you, and your friend, Wednesday morning."

After they excused themselves so she could get on with her evening, Jolena turned to face him and said, "You really can't do that when people are around."

He shrugged innocently. "Do what?"

"Make me laugh with your little side comments when I'm surrounded. Do you want everyone to think I'm crazy?"

"No one would ever think you're crazy." Mathias paused then, and held her gaze. "You played beautifully tonight, Miss Michaelsson. I really enjoyed your concert. Thank you, for such a wonderful gift. I'll treasure it."

Jolena smiled over the praise. "You're welcome—anytime—and thank you, kind sir, for the compliment. And now, if you're ready, I think we can finally go home. I can't tell you how excited I am to go riding with you."

****

Wednesday morning didn't arrive nearly fast enough. Yet, now that she rode next to Mathias, on his ghostly black stallion, perhaps it arrived a little *too* soon. The first few hours passed in a whirlwind of continuous delight. They'd spent the greater portion of the early morning hours exploring the little known trails in the woods behind the Parkers' property and now, she desperately wished she had the power to make time stand still, for she wanted this day to last forever.

She glanced over at her companion and eyed the magnificent horse. He anticipated and then responded to his master's every command. What's more, her own mount, the beautiful chestnut Arabian named Lacy, seemed aware of his presence. She took it in her stride, though. In fact, the mare even flirted with the stallion a bit.

"I know I should cease being surprised about anything ghostly. But, it never once occurred to me the spirit of a horse would wander the earth. Is it a common thing?" she asked as she leaned away from the sweeping branches of a pine tree.

He shrugged as he gave Beadurinc's neck a pat. "That depends on what you mean by common. I've seen a great variety of animals in their spiritual form. I can't tell you why for sure. Perhaps they too, choose to remain on familiar ground near the things they love. As far as horses are concerned, many of them who die alongside their masters remain loyally at his side—or hers."

Her eyes flickered between Mathias and his gorgeous stallion. The way he phrased the comment made her wonder if he spoke from personal experience. He and the horse did seem very familiar with each other.

"You know," he said, "you might want to think about getting your own horse. As you know, we have a very fine barn that has withstood the test of time. And, you ride very well."

"Thank you and I've considered the possibility, actually," she replied. "Many times. But it wouldn't be fair to the horse. My free time is so limited and really, I don't have enough hours in the day to care for one properly right now. My dad taught me a long time ago, there is more to owning a horse than throwing it hay a couple of times a day. They need love and attention, just like any other pet. Since they're herd animals, the horse would need a companion, which would take even more time. Maybe one day, after I retire, I'll buy a couple of them, though."

"You? Retire? Really?" Mathias grinned as his brow lifted higher with each word he spoke.

"Who knows," she said. "Maybe one day my hands will be too arthritic to hold the bow, much less the violin, and the ailment will force me into retirement."

Mathias shook his head. "I doubt it. And speaking of your matchless talent, the lads really enjoyed their concert. They talked about it all night long, in fact."

"Did they?" The revelation made her smile. "Did the boys tell you they finally got to meet Carolyn? Well, they met her after a fashion, of course."

He grinned and nodded. "Yes. They said she enjoyed your performance almost as much as they did."

"That's Carolyn for you. From the moment I could hold a violin in my hand, she's ever been my biggest fan." Jo laughed as she considered the truth of that statement.

"Well, she has competition for that title now," he countered.

The expression on his face and in his eyes stole her ability to breathe properly. A heated blush colored her cheeks as she simply said, "Thank you." And then looking for a quick change in subject, she added, "Did Sam tell you about the woman in the green dress?"

"No, I don't believe so," he replied.

"Before the concert started, the boys roamed all over the place. If I didn't know better, I would swear they searched for someone or something in particular, instead of just wanting to explore," she said. "At one point they even looked a little disappointed, though I couldn't figure out why." She waved a hand in dismissal.

"Anyway, Sam stood at the back, near one of the

doors when a woman entered the auditorium with her hair piled haphazardly on top of her head. He just stared at the mess, with this look of total distaste and abhorrence. I think he even shuddered before he relieved the tangled knot of its glitzy clip. Her hair tumbled to her shoulders in disarray, much to her utter embarrassment and Sam's look of total satisfaction. I found it so funny. And then when I asked him about it later, he sniffed and said her hair looked like a nest for birds and that, of a certainty, his actions gave her escort a feeling of tremendous relief." Calling the scene to mind made her laugh all over again.

Mathias chuckled and nodded. "Sounds like Sam. He had no problem undoing a woman's hair. Especially if she wound the bun too tight—"

Jo glanced over at him as his voice trailed off. He reined in his horse, who nickered as if to alert, and then took in his surroundings. She found herself following his gaze.

The place was familiar to him, of course. Intimately familiar. However, Mathias didn't realize until this moment, he rode toward it. Not with the pleasant distraction Jolena presented. Normally, when he visited this place, he just appeared into it and then disappeared when the event ended.

"Mathias?" Jolena extended a hand and rested it very lightly atop his arm. "Are you all right?" The smile he gave her, didn't reassure her. He could see that much by expression alone.

"Please—tell me," she begged.

He briefly shook his head and once again, put something resembling a smile on his face. "Please don't worry, it's nothing, really."

"Oh, I see. You can't tell me." She dropped her gaze and withdrew her hand.

The notion hurt her. Yet, how to explain without making the situation worse? "This is the—uh, the place we—"

Her hand flew to her open mouth. He didn't have to tell her that he and the boys left their mortality behind in this very forest. She sat up a little higher and took in her environment from each possible direction. He could see she now envisioned the story he shared, by horrified expression alone.

"Oh, I'm so sorry, Mathias, I didn't know." Her eyes begged for forgiveness.

"Shh—there's no need to apologize. The place is not as traumatic as you seem to think or for the reasons you're imagining," he said.

He shook away the somber mood. He had no place for it on this outing, nor did he wish to discuss it any further. Days spent alone in Jolena's company seemed rare. He wouldn't waste these precious moments, thinking about things better left alone.

"Come on." He cocked his head to the side. "I'll show you the area Sam and I grew up before we built our current house. The place sits just over this hill. The way my mother tells the story, Sam introduced himself to me, well before we could walk—by hitting me over the head with a rock. I returned the favor in kind. We've remained the best of friends ever after."

Jolena appeared grateful for the change in subject and for the return of his playful mood and she joined him in his laughter. They didn't need to spend this glorious day with any unhappy memories.

"Sounds like something Sam would do," she said.

Chapter 19

"I really love your house, Jo," Carolyn said as her gaze roved over each detail of every room they visited. "On my way over I considered giving you an apology for taking so long to come here and see it in its finished state. But, now I'm glad I waited until you put the Christmas decorations out. I feel like I'm in the middle of the North Pole and Santa will come walking in any minute."

"Thanks." Jo beamed as she clasped her hands together. She had a lot of fun putting them out this year, mostly because the boys enjoyed the activity just as much as she did, and they helped in every way possible. In fact, they even helped decorate the tree by placing the topmost decorations and setting the angel on the treetop. Then, without any assistance from her, they put up a dazzling display of outside lights. She would never forget the spectacle as long as she lived.

"I know you've collected Christmas decorations your entire adult life, but still, I just didn't know you had so many." Carolyn picked up an antique Santa Claus for closer inspection and gently set it down beside Johann Andries clock in the sitting room.

"Well, this is the first time I've had a house large enough to display them all at the same time," Jo replied. "Now, come on, I've got some cookies and stuff in the family room, and I want to give you my gift, which you're not allowed to open until Christmas day. Do you hear me, Kay-Kay? Christmas. Day.''

Carolyn laughed as she followed her into the room where a cozy fire awaited them. "Don't be such a spoil sport, brat," she said as Jo retrieved a beautifully wrapped gift from underneath her tree. In turn, Kay retrieved a present, just as enticing from her bag.

Jo held the gift aloft. "Promise me," she demanded.

"Oh, whatever." Carolyn shook her head as she sat down in the chair opposite the sofa. "I can't believe you'd wrap my gift as nice as this and then expect me to wait. You should've used old newspaper and duct tape. Okay. I promise." As they exchanged gifts, she added, "I know I don't have to extract the same promise from you. We'll be lucky if you get the thing open by midnight."

"Don't pout, Kay." Jo put her present under the tree before handing Carolyn a glass of warm apple cider and a sugar cookie. "You know I'm going to love it no matter what time I open it."

"Yes, you will," she replied as she wiped a stray crumb from the corner of her mouth. "But it doesn't help when I call you at the crack of dawn to talk about my gifts when you haven't opened any of yours."

"Look at it this way," she said as she sat down on the sofa. "Instead of having one exciting conversation, we get to have two."

"I suppose." She nibbled a little more at her cookie, looked it over carefully, and nodded. "This is really good. What did you do different?"

"Added a few tablespoons of sour cream." Jo looked up as the boys filtered into the room, and she smiled her pleasure. "Now tell me, how are things progressing between you and Ray Brennan?"

Carolyn sputtered as crumbs flew out of her mouth in

every direction. She wiped them away and said, "How many times do I have to tell you we are nothing more than friends and colleagues? You would think by now you'd be off that kick. Nothing is progressing nor will it ever progress. I feel no attraction to him, whatsoever, I assure you."

"Methinks she doth protest too much," Jo teased. "Oh come on, Kay, I really think you ought to pursue the obvious, here. The man is attractive, and you have a lot in common. Besides, you need to get out once in a while—"

"Pul-eeze—" She shook her head and snorted. "Beside, look at who's talking. Shall I mention the fact that you haven't had a date in heaven knows how long?"

Jo shot a glance toward Mathias. He gazed at her as if awaiting her response to the accusation. "All right, all right, you win. No more jokes about Ray. So, tell me about work instead. What kind of projects are you working on now?" The innocent question caused a troubled expression to flicker across Kay's features.

"Oh, well—" Carolyn pursed her lips as she waved a hand of dismissal.

"No." Jo stopped her. "What's wrong? Did something happen at work?"

Carolyn's eyes widened before they dropped to the floor. She looked guilty.

Sam swore underneath his breath. "Sanders, I bet."

Mathias made his way to the sofa and sat next to Jo's side. "Ask her what happened."

"It's Paul Sanders, isn't it," Jo said.

Carolyn let go of the breath she unknowingly held. Her shoulders wilted as she nodded. "I was going to tell you, I swear, just not now. I didn't want anything to ruin the first Christmas in your house."

"I promise you, nothing will ruin it," Jo replied. "Unless he hurt you. He didn't, did he?"

"No." Carolyn shook her head and dismissed her concern with a wave of her hand. "You don't need to go in that direction. As far as he knows, I remain unaware of his actions."

"Tell me what happened." Jo placed her empty glass on the table and gave Kay her undivided attention.

"Well, the night I attended your concert, I got a text from Ray right before it ended. I didn't call him back until after I headed out to my car," she said. "He apologized for calling so late, but asked if I could meet him at the lab. The artifacts from his Anasazi dig site in New Mexico arrived. He said they'd be much safer with me than in his garage overnight. So, of course, I said yes. I arrived about ten minutes ahead of him and got the lab unlocked. I turned on the lights, booted up the computer, you know, that sort of thing. Finally, he drove into the parking lot, and I hurried out to meet him. He got out of his truck and told me I'd probably need to get my largest cart. He collected a great many things this season."

"He usually does," Jo said.

Carolyn nodded and then cleared her throat. "Before I could go inside to get it though, Paul emerged from the passenger door. I wished you could've seen the show he put on, Jo. He really exaggerated a limp when he walked toward me. After he grimaced, he said he didn't think he could help very much getting everything unloaded and inside. He pointed to the wrong foot, if you can believe that. He said he suffered a sprain when he stumbled into a pothole while they loaded the artifacts into the truck."

"You're kidding."

"No, and the charade was so obvious. I couldn't

imagine Ray buying into it. But then, he knows nothing about the letter, or his attack on you, so he probably didn't look for it," she said.

"Anyway, I think he created his so-called injury to keep me outside and busy while he searched my office. Therefore, since he wanted in so badly, I aided his effort. At least that way I didn't have to worry about him coming back later, breaking into the building and damaging my lab or office in his quest to find the letter."

"Smart," Jo said, repeating Mathias's sentiment aloud.

"So, I told him he could wait inside my office where he'd find it more comfortable. You should've seen his smug little smile. It almost made me gag. He jumped at the offer. I had my computer on and logged into the system. I'm sure the moment he discovered that, he sang out a halleluiah, because I couldn't have made his task any easier. Of course, he had no way of knowing he would find nothing during his desperate search. I stayed outside just as long as I could possibly stretch it, to give him the time to do a thorough search." Carolyn scrunched her shoulders together.

"About halfway through, he rushed down the hallway and peeked at us through the window. I don't think it occurred to him that we could see him. Ray even made a derisive comment. Anyway, I still 'fussed' over the artifacts, so he darted toward my office once more— funny. The man probably wanted to see how much time he had left to search."

"Did he seem disappointed when he left?" asked Jo.

"Oh, yes. He looked very disappointed." Carolyn picked up her glass, looked down at the contents, and swirled the cider around in circles. "But he also looked determined. I don't know what that means. You should probably stay on your guard, Jo. He might try to come back here, since he got nothing from me. Do you have an alarm system?"

As a series of threats to Paul Sanders life and limbs reverberated throughout the room, Jo simply nodded to keep the laughter from spilling forth. "Don't worry. I happen to have the best available."

They continued their visit for another hour, leaving the threat of Paul Sanders behind. Then, as the shadows of early afternoon fell through the windows, Carolyn glanced at her watch.

"I've got to go before the plane takes off without me." She looked over at Jo and said, "But I really hate leaving you here all alone."

"I won't be alone, I promise," Jo replied. "Just make sure you give your mom and dad a kiss for me. Give hugs to all of your siblings, and give my love to everyone else. Except Jared, you can just punch him in the arm. I'm sure he's done something to deserve it."

Carolyn laughed as she rose to her feet and hoisted her bag over her shoulder. "No doubt about that. In fact, my little brother deserves far more than he gets. Now, are you sure that you're not going to sit here all by yourself on Christmas Eve? Swear it, Jo."

"I swear." Jo crossed her heart. "Some friends of mine—who live here in this community—are celebrating the holiday with me."

Shortly after Carolyn's departure, Sam clapped his hands and said, "Well, let's get this show on the road. We're wasting precious holiday hours."

"I'll second the motion. Movies first?" asked Alex

"Movies first," said Mathias. "Come on, Jolena, you

can tend to the dishes later; there aren't that many of them to worry about right now."

Jed ambled over to the shelf and selected the movies they saved for this occasion. Without undue effort, he slipped *It's a Wonderful Life* into the player. *A Christmas Story* followed, which made her ghostly companions snicker and hoot with laughter. However, the dialogue between Scrooge and the ghosts of *A Christmas Carol* tickled them more.

"I really enjoyed watching all of those movies and I vote to make them part of our annual Christmas traditions hereafter," William said as Jo scooped the movies from off the table.

"Hear, hear." Alexander raised his pewter mug high and the others followed suit. "However, I think I enjoyed *A Christmas Carol* the best."

"Well, why wouldn't you," Jo teased as she put the movies back on the shelf. "That movie has the scariest ghosts in it."

"If you call that scary. Nonetheless, I especially liked the part where Marley walked through the door and Ebenezer Scrooge, quaking with dread, asks the ghost what he wants and Marley simply says *much*." William shot his companions a wicked grin. "Too bad we didn't think of that, ourselves."

"It certainly would've added to some of our mischief a time or two," Sam replied. "Who would ever think that such a simple word would cause the living so much apprehension?"

"I can't believe you guys." Jo shook her head ever so slightly. "Pray tell, did you have nothing better to do with your time than plot terrifying ways to rid yourself of unwanted guests?"

"'Guest' is hardly the proper word for them, Jolena," Jedediah said. "I swear they were nothing more than a bunch of beetle-headed interlopers, the lot of them."

Jo laughed over Jed's description of all the former homeowners. "Well then, I feel really special the 'fearsome five' made me feel so welcome and allowed me to stay."

"We allowed you to stay because you are special." Mathias gave her a wink and playfully tugged on a lock of her hair.

The look he gave her when he made the comment melted her from head to toe, and she found it almost impossible to concentrate on the rest of their activities thereafter. Still, she somehow made it through all of the games they chose to play which included the most hilarious round of Classic Clue she ever had the pleasure of participating in. The boys didn't just state their whodunit theories. They completely acted them out.

They shot, beat, stabbed, and hung each other repeatedly in their quest to solve each case, and while in complete costume, no less. She played as Miss Scarlet, Mathias as Colonel Mustard, and Sam played Professor Plum. Jedediah provided a rip-roaring Mrs. White, Alexander chose a haughty Mrs. Peacock, and William wanted to play a very frumpy Mr. Green.

Then when the games finally ended, Jo read them her favorite Christmas Eve poem, "'Twas the Night before Christmas," followed by the reading of the nativity story, which traditionally ended the Michaelsson Christmas Eve festivities and now ended theirs.

Then, before she climbed into bed, she informed Mathias he would have to spend his night somewhere other than the library. She told him she wanted her

Christmas present to remain a secret and no one could go into the room until invited to do so.

After securing his promise they would do as she asked, she snuck the painting into the library and placed it on the outermost wall above the settee. She then covered the face and edges with colorful Christmas wrapping and some large ribbons and bows, to make it easy for them to unwrap. Excitement overtook her as she stood back and examined her handiwork. She could hardly wait for morning to come.

She found it nigh on impossible to fall asleep. Exhilaration and anticipation settled into her being as she climbed into bed and the feeling reminded her so much of her childhood Christmases when she anxiously awaited her visit from Santa Claus.

Yet, somewhere during the night, she must've fallen asleep because all at once she found herself waking to the sound of some of the more lively Christmas carols. They originated from her stereo, down in the family room. The songs got louder and louder as the minutes ticked by. Finally, when she could no longer stand to hear one more rousing chorus of "Jingle Bells," she opened her bedroom door. "Okay, boys, I'm awake. I'll be down in just a minute," she called out.

Dakota shot past her and as he ran down the stairs, she added, "While you're waiting, would one of you let Dak out for me and give him that big ham bone in the refrigerator? It's his Christmas present." She donned her white jogging suit with royal blue trim before she raced down the stairs where the boys all waited, with broad smiles on their faces.

"Merry Christmas, Jolena!" they bellowed in almost perfect unison.

"Merry Christmas, to all of you," she sang out.

"Since you woke up so late, I think you'd better get started on those presents," Alexander said pointing to the gifts she received from her family and friends. "You might not get through them today if you don't."

"She might not get through them anyway," Jedediah said.

"Don't be absurd." She flung a lock of hair behind her shoulder. "First of all, it's not late. And second, if I choose, I can have that stack unwrapped in under fifteen minutes, I guarantee it."

"You're on," bellowed Sam. "Let's see, it's now nine o'clock so you have until quarter after the hour."

"No, wait—I want you guys to open your present first. So, I need you to gather in the library, if you please."

Despite their protests, it didn't take much coaxing to get them upstairs. Then, once they entered the library, she motioned them toward the desk, turned her computer on, and activated the slide show she prepared some time ago.

"Before you open your Christmas present from me, I need you to see this slide show first, because it will explain my gift. Nancy took the pictures you're going to see when she and her family visited." Jo winked at Mathias then turned her screen around where everyone could see it and selected the start key. She fastened her gaze on each of the boys in turn so she could drink in their priceless expressions while their images flashed across the screen.

"Why, we look no different than anyone else in these photos," Sam murmured as he kept his gaze fixed on the screen.

"But how is such a thing possible?" asked William as

he finally turned around to face her.

"I really don't know." Jo shrugged and said, "Believe me; I didn't question my good fortune, either. I'm just grateful to have them."

Feeling a bit self-conscious, Jo shot a glance at Mathias, wanting to give some kind of warning to the scene Brady painted. She cleared her throat. "I'm not going to insult anyone's intelligence by pretending you don't know this is a painting," she said gesturing toward it. "However, the idea for this particular painting originated from the pictures you see on my computer. I took these photos to an artist in the mall. He studied them for a few days, and then painted the scene *his* mind created."

She walked to the other end of the room, pointed to their gift and said, "So, Merry Christmas to all of you, and whenever you're ready?"

Alexander grinned as he faced his companions. "All right lads, on the count of three, then?"

"Three," Sam hollered out and amidst their laughter, the wrapping floated toward the floor. Total silence followed the rustle of the paper's gentle landing.

Chapter 20

After the silence, their expressions of joyous excitement and surprise filled the room. At once, they surrounded her and each in turn, gave her an exuberant ghostly hug and a feathery light kiss on the cheek. Their reaction to the painting pleased her no end. Mathias seemed especially delighted with the way the artist portrayed him—with her. She found herself blushing and smiling all at the same time.

"Thank you, Jolena," Mathias said, as at last, he turned away from the painting. "I think I can speak for all of us when I say you couldn't have found a better gift to give us. We'll forever cherish it."

Another round of rousing "Hear, hear" followed his statement. She smiled and said, "I'm glad you all like it."

"Like it?" Alex shook his head. "We love it, Jolena."

"That we do, and I know we would all love to remain here all day and enjoy our wondrous gift. At least, I know I would," Sam said as he winked at the boys. "But, I think it only fair Jolena now has a turn to open the presents that await her downstairs. The task will only take her fifteen minutes, or so she says. Then, once she's finished, we can all come back up here. Maybe we can try some of that eggnog the TV commercials keep going on about and see if it's as good as they say."

"What?" she asked, "Not happy with your ghostly ale?" Amidst their laughter, they vacated the room and headed toward the stairs.

Minutes later, she sat cross-legged on the family room floor with her gifts piled haphazardly in front of her. She glanced up at the clock and swept a hand toward it, drawing their attention to the time. "All right, are you ready for this?" She rubbed her hands back and forth, expelled a deep breath, and grabbed the first package in front of her.

As they cheered her on, she rapidly opened each present, held it up for their inspection, and called out the name of the person who gave it. She paused only once to say, "This goes against the grain, you know. Carolyn would be proud—astounded, but proud." Exactly fourteen minutes and forty-three seconds later, she finished the task and raised her arm triumphantly upward.

"I told you, I could do it." She beamed as she took in each of their faces. "And you were all so worried."

Mathias fixed his gaze to the clock, paused for several seconds, and then shook his head. "Nope, the way I see it, your fifteen minutes have come and gone. You haven't finished, so you lose the contest and therefore, must pay the price."

"What are you talking about?" Jo's mouth dropped as she stared at her companions "You can plainly see I have them all opened."

"Looks to me as if you have one more present under the tree," Sam said as he pointed it out.

Jo turned her gaze in the direction he indicated. Another gift lay hidden beneath the branches. She inched forward, took hold of the corded handle, and placed the dark green bag atop her lap. "I don't remember seeing this one before."

"I hope you don't mind, but we helped ourselves to

one of your gift bags," Mathias said. "We needed a place to put our gifts to you and the bag seemed most convenient, since we haven't quite figured out how to wrap with boxes and those silly ribbons and bows like you do."

Jo drew in a sharp breath as she gazed at each of them in turn. Pleased expressions looked back. She had no idea they would think to give her a gift or even that they could. The gesture overwhelmed her and made it very difficult to stifle her tears.

"Now without looking, you have to extract one item at a time," Mathias said. "When you have the gift in your hand, we'll tell you who it's from."

The small lump in her throat swelled and Jo's hand shook just a bit as she grasped something made of wood, about the size of her hand. She drew it out of the bag and gazed at the detailed carving of a hawk in flight.

"Merry Christmas, Jolena," Alex said as he took a step forward. "I used to whittle a bit in my time, taking my inspiration with what surrounded me. If I remember correctly, I made that one there a bit before the war. I know it's not much, but—"

"How can you say that?" Her eyes filled with unshed tears as she covered her mouth. "This is a beautiful work of art, Alex. The carving would rival anything I've seen in any art gallery, and it will look so perfect next to Johann's clock on the mantel. Thank you, so very much. You have no idea what this means to me."

"Well, go on," he replied, looking a bit embarrassed over her praise. "You've got more."

Once again, she dropped her hand into the bag and this time she could feel something soft. She closed her hand around it and withdrew the object from the sack. A small leather pouch with an intricate shell and feather work design lay in her open hand. After gently stroking the glassy shells, she peeked inside and found more shells, each unique in color and shape. She found braided hair from the mane or tail of a horse, intertwined with colorful strips of leather and some beautiful feathers. Dried berries and a mixture of crushed herbs, which smelled as sweet as any perfume, supplied a colorful nest for the braids and shells.

"Merry Christmas, Jolena," said Jedediah. "That there's called a spirit pouch. One of the finest maidens of the Lenni-Lenape I ever had the pleasure of knowing made it for me. She gave it to me as a parting gift and told me it carried great magic. I'd like you to have that magic now."

"Oh, Jedediah—I feel honored you would give this gift to me." Jo shook her head as she sniffed and dabbed at the first tear that meandered down her cheek. "Thank you."

Then as she looked into the anxious faces of the other boys, she dipped into the bag again. This time her fingers wrapped around a small piece of round metal. As she tugged the object upward, she could feel another like piece, attached to it. Once she cleared the bag, she opened her hand. She held two identical buttons, in pristine condition, about an inch in diameter, with the words Continental Army engraved around the outside edge. Inside the etching appeared the number one followed by a period, followed by the letter B. Centered beneath those, a perfectly engraved letter P.

"Merry Christmas." William gave her a nod and winked in affection. "A long time ago, those buttons were taken off my military coat. They signify the Pennsylvania

First Battalion. They're still in good shape because we didn't stay with them very long and trust me, my mother kept everything. Anyway, I wanted you to have something that once belonged to me, and I know how much you like things from the period."

"Oh, William, I'm going to display these and my spirit pouch, on the shelf next to the painting of George Washington. They'll look so perfect there. Thank you so very much," Jo said as she used the back of her hand to wipe away another wayward tear.

"Only two left to go, Jolena," Mathias said, urging her on.

This time as she searched the bag, her hand closed around the final item. She lifted the small porcelain box out of the bag with great care. The elegant trinket box featured gold painted arches that intersected each other. At the bottom of each intersection, a dainty blue forget-me-not added decoration to the underglaze.

"Merry Christmas, dear friend," Sam said. "Just a little something to express my gratitude for all the joy you've given us."

Though difficult, she swallowed past the lump in her throat. "This is so lovely, Sam and so delicate." She shook her head as she nibbled a bit on her lip. "Thank you."

"My pleasure," Sam replied and then pointed to the box. "You still have one final gift inside the box, lass."

Jo fixed her gaze to Mathias's as she opened the lid. She withdrew a small teardrop opal-and-sapphire pendant attached to a delicate silver chain. With trembling fingers, she put the antique necklace on, vowing to make it part of her wardrobe each day, from this moment onward.

"Merry Christmas, Jolena," Mathias said.

"This is the most exquisite necklace I've ever seen. Thank you, Mathias," she whispered, as she picked up the pendant for a closer look. Then after placing the rest of her gifts back inside the bag, she clutched the handle, rose to her feet, and tenderly kissed him on his cheek. All the while, she made every effort not to go through his form. Then turning to her other boys, she kissed them in like manner.

She stood back then, and took them all in at once. "To say I'm overwhelmed is a huge understatement of what I feel right now. Thank you all, so very, very much for your gifts. I'll treasure each one all the days of my life. And just so you all know, you have made this the best Christmas I've ever had, and I've had some pretty good ones."

"Oh, I don't know." Mathias shrugged and shot the boys a quick glance. "It's still a little early for you to make such a statement. You did lose the bet and therefore, you still have to pay the price."

Jo stood open-mouthed, with one hand at her brow while clutching her gift bag with the other. "But I don't recall even making it a bet, much less one with consequences. I merely said I could have my gifts open in under fifteen minutes."

"But you guaranteed it, which is one in the same," Mathias glibly stated. "Are you going to renege?"

"I can't believe you're making this such a big deal." She huffed out a breath. "Okay, let's get this done right now. What is the consequence for my tardiness?"

"Hmm, it needs to be something out of the ordinary—" Mathias looked over at Sam. "Got any ideas?"

"Well, let's see." He turned and gazed out the

window. "It is Christmas, after all. We needn't be brutish. So, something simple, I'd say."

"And we don't want it to take a whole lot of time, either," Alex muttered. "I want to get back upstairs and take a second look at our painting and I'd like to see those photographs again."

"How about she fetches Dakota without calling him?" Jedediah suggested. "We really shouldn't leave him out there in the snow. His coat will get all wet and natty."

"Perfect." Mathias gazed at her and winked.

"Fine." She turned around, placed her gift bag atop the table, walked out of the family room, and into the kitchen.

"You might want to get your jacket," William called after her.

"I won't need one," she tossed back.

Although she couldn't see them, the boys followed close behind. She opened the door and peeked all around looking for her dog. Oh, that's right. Jed gave him the ham bone. She stepped through the snow, and made her way to his doghouse. No Dakota. She turned around and almost ran into Mathias.

"Not fair, when you gave him that bone to devour," she chided.

Mathias merely shrugged. She sighed, but just then, she could hear Dakota barking. She shifted her gaze in the direction of the sound and spied the barn just up ahead. Perhaps he wanted to warm up a bit. She made all haste to the open doors, and all the while, wished she had taken the time to get her jacket.

She found all her ghostly companions waiting for her inside, grinning from ear to ear. She narrowed her eyes as she turned her head to the side. "What's going on? None of this makes any sense whatsoever. What are you all up to?"

Without saying a word, they stepped aside so she could see the stall behind them.

Both of her hands flew upward and cupping them around her nose and mouth, she stifled a cry of surprise. Lacy, wearing a big red bow on her royal-blue halter, nickered to her. Stunned, she looked over at Mathias.

"One final gift, Jolena." He winked as he extended a hand in invitation.

"But how? You—I can't believe you did this for me." Once again, she found herself wiping away tears she couldn't control as she made her way to his side. He placed a hand about her waist and turned her toward the stall.

Sam chuckled as he shifted his gaze from her to Mathias. "Believe me, my dear, when Mathias has a will to do something, he finds a way to accomplish it."

Mathias escorted her to the stall that housed her horse. *Her* horse. As she stood in front of the gate, her arms encircled the mare's neck. Lacy responded by curving her head around Jo's shoulders.

Mathias smiled his pleasure as they renewed their acquaintance. They bonded the moment Jolena spied her in Parker's pasture the day they visited the cemetery. Jolena had to have her, that's all there was to it. The task didn't prove all that difficult to achieve. He noted Parker's collection of antique farm equipment and offered to trade him his nephew's old cast-iron plow for the horse.

They made the deal from across the fence while he sat atop Beadurinc, thereby escaping the obligatory handshake. In accordance with their agreement, he placed the plow on Parker's doorstep two nights earlier, citing a logical need to drop it off while they slept. In turn, Parker arranged to have the mare delivered late last night so that it would remain a surprise.

"Oh, Mathias!" Jolena sniffed as she raked her fingers through the luxurious mane. "She's so beautiful. I still can't believe you did this for me."

"And," Mathias said, "If you look around, you'll see she isn't alone. She has Beadurinc for company as well as a few others you've yet to meet."

Jolena's eyes widened as she caught sight of his black stallion in the stall next to Lacy. Four other horses joined them in stalls of their own.

"You needn't worry, Jolena," Jedediah said. "We all look after them. She'll be taken good care of whenever you're gone or don't have the time or inclination to do it yourself."

Mathias placed a hand on her shoulder. "Did I cover all of your concerns?"

"All of them," she whispered. "Thank you, you couldn't have given me anything more perfect than the gifts you have all given."

They spent the remainder of the day going between the barn and the library. All the while, he and the boys entertained her with personal stories and experiences from Christmases past. Then, when at last they all grew quiet, she retrieved her violin.

"I know you've all waited so patiently," she said as she adjusted the strings. "But it took a while to find some of this music and then I wanted to memorize each piece and play it perfectly for you." She nestled her violin against her shoulder, and smiled first at Jedediah. "This one is for you, dear Jedediah."

Jedediah grinned, as she launched into "Sally in Our Alley," the song he requested, the first day they met. By the time she arrived at the chorus, he opened his mouth wide and chimed in with arms swinging to the tempo. He sang the song with such enthusiasm, the rest of them joined in the singing as well.

Next, she played "Bonny Farday" for William, "Early One Morning" for Alex and then "The Little Turtle Dove" for Sam. Finally, she ended the music fest with "A Soldier and a Sailor," played especially for him. She laughed aloud as they shouted out the final words to the song.

****

She shook her head, wiped at a tear and sniffed. "Forgive me, I need a moment to gather each wondrous moment of these past two days and tuck them safely away in my heart. You have all made it so special. Thank you all so much. I just wished it didn't have to end—" The statement pleased him far more than she realized.

Much later that night, Mathias stood in front of the remarkable painting. He would forever cherish this exceptional gift. How interesting that they wanted to make this Christmas holiday season special for her, when it fact, she made it so for them.

Jolena would probably have laughed if she caught sight of them going through their personal boxes of collected treasures to select the perfect gift for her. Boxes they stashed behind an original false wall built into the attic and which had remained hidden for centuries. They hoped for that look of astonished delight, and she didn't disappoint them in any way.

And now at the end of this unforgettable Christmas

day, perhaps he might give them both one more gift to share. At least he hoped so. He made his way into her bedroom and sat in the rocking chair next to her bed. Then, after taking hold of her hand while she deeply slumbered, he quietly entered her dreams.

****

Jo sat atop a large rock, with her arms wrapped loosely about her knees. She cast her gaze upon the roll of the ocean waves that crashed intermittently against her bare feet. With eyes closed, she lifted her chin so the light gentle breeze could caress her face. She took a deep breath and filled her lungs with the scent of sea brine. At the same time, she delighted in the songs of the seagulls as they chattered high above the ocean. The place seemed very familiar to her, and yet she had never been here before. As she took in the view, her hand wrapped instinctively around her beloved pendant, and she smiled with contentment.

"I hoped I might find you here," he said.

Jo turned toward the sound of his voice. Mathias extended his hand in silent invitation. He no longer wore his backwoods mountain clothing. Instead, he wore a form-fitting navy-blue T-shirt. His faded blue jeans skimmed the gently lapping waves that bathed his bare feet. At once, she took hold of the offered hand and gasped as its warmth and strength closed over her own.

"Mathias—" Stunned, she gazed at his hand while he assisted her to her feet. "I can *feel* you. Your hand—it's as if you—as if you're *alive*. How is such a thing possible?"

Mathias brushed a hand through her wind-blown hair. A touch of humor entered his eyes. "Didn't you know? Every now and again, when the moment warrants, all things are possible."

"Then I would have this moment with you last forever," she whispered.

"Forever is a very long time, Jolena Leigh Michaelsson. I can attest to that," he said. "Are you so sure that's what you want?"

She placed her free hand against his chest and fused her gaze to his. "I should think that every now and again, when a moment like this presents itself—forever is not nearly long enough."

Mathias gave her hand a gentle squeeze as his eyes filled with the same joy that enveloped her heart. "Then we'll have to make certain each of these moments we share last as long as possible."

Their leisurely walk along the beach stretched on and on for what seemed like hours. They talked about anything and everything. They filled the moments with playful laughter, quiet companionship, and serious conversation. Then, as can only happen in dreams, Jo suddenly found the darkness of evening encompassing them. She and Mathias, now elegantly dressed, danced together on an outdoor dance floor, lit solely by a luminous full moon and the brilliance of the stars. No other couple took advantage of this beautiful area, so they alone danced to the music of "Greensleeves" as it wafted out the open double doors of the main dance floor. "You look exceptionally beautiful this evening, Jolena. I must confess it truly surprises me someone hasn't whisked you away and made you his wife by now. Although I'm sure countless numbers have tried."

Jolena tilted her head to the side as she considered his statement. "I suppose there may have been one or two along the way."

"Did you find them all so very distasteful then?" he asked.

They looked at each other for several long moments. Mathias appeared to hold his breath while awaiting her answer. The intensity of the expression on his face, replaced the playful banter of a moment ago. She lowered her gaze and took a deep breath as the now familiar heat rose up from her belly and filled her being.

"Distasteful? No. It's just that—"

She struggled with putting her feelings into words. Yet, how could she form a coherent sentence when he held her so close? She stopped dancing then and looked into his warm brown eyes. She met the force of his gaze with boldness. At this moment, he wanted her to drop the last barrier that remained between them. He wanted absolute truth, with nothing held back. She could see the need in his eyes. Here, in this place, she could answer that need without hesitation or reservation.

"The truth is, none of them were you, Mathias," she whispered, her voice full of emotion. "No one on this earth, past, present, or future, could ever take the place you already have in my heart. Didn't you know? Haven't you guessed? You are the man I have waited my whole life to find."

With no words to express his joy, Mathias gently cupped her face in his hands and lowered his lips to hers. The searing kiss that followed spoke of all the love and passion he had kept hidden away—until now. For here, nestled away in this dream, he didn't need to withhold his feelings.

"I have waited for you all of mine. I love you Jolena Leigh Michaelsson, from the very depths of my soul. No matter what comes, no matter what happens in the future, somewhere in your heart, you must *always* remember that," he whispered against the softness of her lips.

"And I love you, Mathias. I don't know quite how to explain this, but—I have the strangest feeling that I have always loved you."

The declaration amazed him. He had no time to consider its meaning, for she brushed her mouth against his, seeking another kiss. He wasted no time in complying with the desire.

Finally, after several kisses that expressed the deep love he carried within his heart, he stepped back just enough to gaze into her eyes. "You might have confessed your feelings a bit earlier you know and eased some of my uncertainty."

Jolena gently traced the lines of his jaw with her fingers. "I wouldn't ever want you to doubt the love I feel for you. But surely you must understand that I couldn't tell you."

"Why not?" he asked as he gathered her closer to the warmth of his body. He gloried in the feel of her in his arms, and he wished this dream didn't have to end so soon. Yet, the dawn approached.

"Because I don't ever want you to feel that you have to stay with me," she answered.

"Stay with you?" Understanding eluded him.

"Stay with me, here," she replied. "Carolyn told me once that love can make a spirit feel bound to the person who loves him. That spirit doesn't feel free to leave this sphere for fear of breaking the person's heart. If the time should ever come—should it become your desire to leave this existence and join your loved ones, then I wouldn't want you to feel obligated to remain with me, just so my heart wouldn't break."

Mathias shook his head and gathered her closer still. "There will never come a time I would desire to leave you, Jolena, nor could I, even if you should ask it of me. If that day should ever come, I would hide away in the shadows, and simply watch over you until you took your last breath," he whispered huskily as he drew close to her lips once more. "I can promise you that—"

Chapter 21

Jo sighed and tossed her pen atop the desk next to the huge stack of mail she willfully neglected during the holidays. The tedious chore needed doing, yet she had no desire to tackle it today. Her hand sought her pendant as her mind drifted to the incredible dream she experienced Christmas night, now two weeks past. Again.

She'd never had one quite like it before and even now, she could recall it in glorious, vivid detail. Perhaps she recalled it so clearly, because in an effort not to forget it, she continued to relive it, and probably more often than she should. But, how could she help it? The dream gave her absolute knowledge as to the strength of his arms when he held her, to experience the feelings he inspired when he well and thoroughly kissed her. The dream gave her total understanding of what it meant to possess the love of Mathias McGregor, and it proved a fierce and powerful thing. She glanced up and found Mathias watching her with an intensity that made her blush.

"A penny for your thoughts?" he asked.

Jo let out a bit of a laugh. "I'm afraid that kind of information would cost you much more than a penny, sir." She retrieved her discarded pen and held the pile of mail aloft, hoping to shift his focus off her wayward thoughts and onto a much safer topic.

"Just look at all of this mail. Sorting through it will

take most of the morning I'm sure. Yet, I suppose it's the price I must pay for such willful neglect."

"Well, if you can wade through it this morning, perhaps we can go for a ride this afternoon," he said.

"You're on, McGregor. That's all the incentive I need." She tossed him a smile as she replaced the stack of mail, and began sifting through it, one piece at a time. Finally, she arrived at the large envelope near the bottom. She picked it up and as she studied the return address, she gasped.

"Look, Mathias. This package is from the Pennsylvania Genealogical Society. I wonder how long this sat here on the desk collecting dust." She shook her head as she picked up her letter opener and cut through the seal. "I suppose I should've tackled this job a bit sooner."

Mathias rounded the desk and stood just behind her as she all but yanked the contents out of the envelope. The information for Joshua Porter lay on top. She hurried through the pages but found no evidence of military service during the War.

"They have included an early plat map which shows the area of Joshua's property," she said, pointing to the highlighted area on the map. "And they've included all of his tax records, which ended in 1778."

While Mathias studiously looked over the map, the other boys popped inside the room and gathered around the desk.

"Look at that," Sam said, pointing to the area bordering near Valley Creek. "I didn't realize his property extended this far north."

"I didn't either," Mathias replied. "What else did they send us?"

"Besides the tax records, they have included some of his church records. We have the christening dates of his children, dates of communion, and things like that. On this piece of paper, they're noting the marriage to his wife, the church, the minister, and the witnesses. And let's see—" Jo took one page at a time and thoroughly looked over it. "They have sent genealogical records for some of his children and grandchildren, as well."

"You said his tax records ended in 1778?" asked Mathias. He rubbed a hand back and forth against his mouth. "Did he sell his property to someone else or did he die that same year?"

"I don't know. Let me look through this stuff again. They didn't include a probate record of any kind with this package or anything else to do with his death," Jo murmured. "But I don't think he sold the property, either. The 1779 through 1800 tax years shows someone named John Porter as paying the taxes on the property without transfer of ownership. Do you recognize the name?"

"John is Joshua's son," Samuel replied. "Fine lad—"

"They documented all of the cemetery records for the family on this page," Jo said as she perused the list. "They have recorded here a Jane Porter, 'beloved wife of Joshua,' but Joshua himself is not buried next to her. That's odd, and he doesn't show up anywhere else, either. Hmm—"

"Well, Jane is the name of his wife," Mathias stated as he began pacing the room. "Is there anything else of importance?"

"Just some odds and ends," Jo said. "Actually, as far as I can tell, there's nothing here that really helps us in our quest. Nothing mentions military service of any kind or anything else connecting him to the war."

"Unless we just can't see the forest for all the trees," Mathias added. "What about the records for Matthew?"

Jo picked up the stack of papers dealing with the Joshua Porter family, placed them inside a new file folder, and put it off to the side for later consideration. She then turned her attention to the information they received concerning Brewster.

"Again, they've included the plat map, which details the property he owned." She placed it on the edge of her desk, and then turned it toward the boys so they could study it for themselves. "The piece of property isn't very large, is it? However, I guess a blacksmith doesn't need much land."

"No, those few acres served him well enough," said Sam.

"How very unusual—" Jo looked up from the page and fastened her gaze on Mathias. "You're not going to believe this, but all of his personal tax records end in the year 1778, as well. Do you think it's just a coincidence or—"

"Possible, but certainly not probable. I think something is going on here." Mathias shot his companions a brief glance. "We just have to figure it out. What else do we have on the man?"

"The Genealogical Society sent us the records of some of his descendants, church records, and cemetery records." Jo ran a finger down the list of names included on the cemetery list. "I find a Sarah Brewster, wife of Matthew, but Matthew is not beside her, nor does he show up in any other cemetery they've included in this package. What does this mean? Where do you suppose these men are buried then?"

Alexander furrowed his brows and shrugged. "Where

is the connection to all of this? For all intense and purposes, each man disappeared in 1778, leaving no trace as to their fate."

"I don't know," Mathias replied. "Did they send us anything dealing with military service that might give us a clue?"

"I have one muster roll, which says he served with the Pennsylvania 4th Battalion during a short period of time in 1776 and once again for about two months in 1777, but nothing more. He doesn't appear on any of the muster rolls during the year 1778 either, so he couldn't have died in the service."

Mathias shrugged. "Well lads, what do you make of all of this? Anyone have any ideas?"

"We have two men, mentioned in your cousin's journal in the year 1778. All three men interacted with each other. And then without explanation, all three men disappear the same year," Sam said, summing up the evidence. "We're missing the vital piece or pieces of information. We can't tie it together without that piece."

"Well, now we know the full length of Joshua's property, perhaps we can find remnants of what we're looking for there," William said. "After looking at this map, it'll take us some time to search his property methodically."

"Understood," said Mathias. "Perhaps we can go out and begin traversing the entire property at night. Jedediah can lead the search. At the same time, one of us needs to remain behind. We can't forget Paul Sanders is still a threat, not only to this house, but to Jolena as well."

"Of course," Sam replied. "That goes without saying."

Jo's sudden gasp of delight interrupted their

conversation and Mathias turned to meet her gaze. She smiled in triumph as she held up a single sheet of paper and waved it in front of them.

"What did you find?" asked Mathias.

"This," she began, "comes from a biographical chapter, written in one of the Fairfield County history books of Ohio. Most every state and county in the Union has something similar. The author fills the pages with information about the notable residents. This particular entry deals with Matthew Brewster's grandson, a man by the name of Orrin Brewster. The author gives the details of his life and his children, of course, but then there's this passage, listen," she said as her eyes returned to the highlighted entry on the page.

"'Orrin's paternal grandfather, Matthew Brewster, is of English extraction, arriving in this Country in the year 1769, where he soon traded his previous occupation of tinker, for the more practical occupation of blacksmith. His exceptional skills in iron works, noted far and wide for high quality and workmanship, abound to this day. Thus, he remained in great demand throughout the region during his lifetime. Orrin followed in his footsteps—'"

She placed the paper down at the edge of the desk, where the boys could read it in full for themselves. "I think this passage reveals that Matthew Brewster is our source for the tinker we seek. So, do any of you have any ideas for the toy part?"

Mathias resumed his restless pacing. "What would one label as a toy, belonging to a tinker or a blacksmith?" he asked.

"Tools come readily to mind or perhaps even his forge," Samuel said.

"Matthew did indeed possess a talent for metal

works," Alex added. "I've seen some of the results of that myself. Just what if Washington assigned him to make spears for the patriots? Remember the letter Jolena read us from the book, the one where he said he ordered more spears for the defense against the British cavalry?"

"That's a very good possibility, Alex," Mathias said.

"Or perhaps they asked him to build something to house or carry the acquired weapons," William suggested.

"That's a good possibility as well," said Sam. "I remember one time General Washington said we needed a more effective way to utilize the spears. What if he or Thomas envisioned a cart that would not only efficiently carry the spears wherever needed on the battlefield, but also make it, so we could use them to greater advantage?"

"Let's speculate just for a moment, my cousin provided the wealth for the materials," Mathias said. "Joshua, of course, held enough property to secretly house a forge. Matthew is the likely choice to make the weapons or carts, maybe even both. But, what information would give the English cause to capture and execute Thomas? An act which caused Jacob Weidmann, a man obviously involved with this secrecy, to have the entire operation relocated elsewhere in the midst of a scheduled convoy?"

"What if the English found out about it, as Jacob feared?" asked Jedediah. "What if they discovered both Matthew and Joshua in the act of building it and then executed them both as well? Perhaps that's the reason these men disappeared from the records of history, all at about the same time."

"The English might even have had a spy of their own working within," Alexander said. "He could've exposed the entire operation before they even had the chance to utilize it."

"I think Jacob, being privy to the most secret doings of the English, would've known if they had any spies, Alex," Mathias replied. "The fact they intended to relocate their operation indicates the English didn't know anything about it, at least up until the night before our death. Perhaps a group of Redcoats just happened across Thomas in a place they deemed suspicious. Once they searched him, they might've found something that made them wary."

"And as we all know, it took naught but a suspicion for them to execute someone on the spot," Sam said. "Well, I for one am not going to rest until I find out."

Sam's last comment drew Jo's attention and she found herself staring wide-eyed in his direction. Her heart dropped somewhere into the pit of her stomach. *He didn't plan to rest until he found out.* He couldn't *rest* until he found out? All at once, Carolyn's words, casually spoken so many months ago, flooded her mind. Some spirits, she said, remained earth bound, *until* they concluded their unfinished business. Only then, did they feel free to leave their earthly existence.

Her boys fought and died in the service of their country in a failed attempt to deliver a crucial message to General Washington. Although they couldn't possibly give the message to the man now, nor would the knowledge of its contents change history, would the unraveling of that mystery give them a feeling of resolve? If they found success in learning all of the details associated with Jacob Weidmann's last letter, would they feel free to leave? More importantly, would they *choose* to leave?

As she considered their absence, her heart lurched in a moment of intense pain and sorrow. Almost the same sorrow that crushed her heart when she learned of her parents passing. *You made a commitment to these men, Jolena*, she sternly reminded herself. That commitment included doing everything in her power to help them in their quest, no matter the cost to her heart. No matter the cost—

"Jolena?" Samuel called.

Jo looked up. Everyone gazed at her as if awaiting a response to something Samuel must have said. "I'm sorry. Did you say something?"

"I just wanted to know if we've received anything back from Scotland on the sale of Thomas's property," he said.

"Oh. No, not unless—well, let me see if we have anything here." Jo picked up the remainder of the mail and looked at each piece. She shook her head. "Sorry, we haven't gotten anything back from them yet. Hopefully it will come soon, though."

"What if it turns out Thomas didn't sell any of his property at all?" asked Alex. "That still wouldn't prove or disprove anything, really. Just because Thomas possessed the wealth, doesn't mean he used any of it for this particular project. His involvement could stem from something else entirely."

"That's true, Alex," Mathias replied. "We need to remember Thomas had a brilliant mind. It's just as plausible for him to have come up with a unique design for the cart or the spears or whatever else the patriots needed to win the war."

"Still," Samuel reminded them, "nothing we've discussed would come cheap. I still believe a source of wealth had to fund it."

"And that could have come from a thousand different places as easily as it could've come from just one," William replied.

"Agreed," said Mathias. "I say we just start with Joshua's property and build on what we find there. Right now, anything else is pointless."

That night, Jo found it difficult to find sleep. Despite her exhilarating ride with Mathias this afternoon, or perhaps because of it, her mind wouldn't quiet long enough for sleep to overtake her. The mystery of her grandfather's last letter rested within an inch of full discovery. And then what? Would her boys leave all at once or would they leave one by one? Would some of them go immediately and some of them choose to stay for a while? Would any of them consider waiting until the final beat of her heart? What about Mathias? Would he choose to wait?

"There will never come a time I would desire to leave you, Jolena, nor could I, even if you should ask it of me. If that day should ever come, I would hide away in the shadows and simply watch over you until you took your last breath," he had said. "I can promise you that—"

She would give away everything she owned, or would ever hope to own, if that promise occurred somewhere other than within a dream.

Chapter 22

Jo turned into her driveway as the sun dipped below the horizon. Just as she expected, Mathias stood at the side of her door as she parked and then exited the car. The way he looked at her just now, and every day since Christmas, made her heart beat a little faster. What changed? Did the painting have anything to do with that expression? Or maybe, because of all the moments they shared during their frequent rides together, he might've fallen—

"Did you finish up the film score today as the conductor hoped?" he asked.

"Yes, finally, after all this time. Or at least we're finished until the director asks for the next set of changes." She shook her head and sighed as she took hold of her bag, hefted it onto her shoulder, and then grabbed her violin case before he shut the door.

"Soon he'll run out of time to make any more alterations," Mathias said.

Jo nodded as they made their way toward the porch steps. "Yep, and I think he's just about there. In fact, I think the film premiere is in less than three months," she said as she stopped long enough to empty the mailbox. After she cleaned it out, she glanced down at the letter on top, looked up at Mathias and smiled. She turned the letter toward him. "From the genealogist at the Scottish archives."

"Let's get the thing opened, and see what it says," he said as he opened the door and waved her into the family room.

She put her bag on the table and her violin inside the stand before walking into the room. Then just as she stood in front of the sofa, the phone rang. She shrugged out of her jacket, and picked up the receiver. "Speaking." She glanced once again at the letter from Scotland. "Oh. Hello, Mr. Clark, of course I remember you. How could I not? You were so very helpful when we—when I visited the Pennsylvania archives several months ago."

"Not as helpful as I should have been," Wilford Clark replied. "I don't know why it didn't occur to me that rather than tinkers toy, *stoys* was plausible as an abbreviation for Stoystown, Pennsylvania, and tinker a surname. But at least your colleague figured that part out."

Jo tossed her jacket on the back of the armchair across from the sofa as she held Mathias's gaze. "My colleague?"

"Yes," Wilford said. "I gathered some books that cited the surnames McCree, McCrae, and McBean as he requested, but he left the building before I could return them to his table. Therefore, I didn't get his name, and that's why I'm calling you."

"Oh, I see. Well, I'm trying to think which of my colleagues might've visited you today. Would you have spoken with the sandy haired blond who wears the silver-framed glasses?" She peeked over at Mathias. The tender expression he wore earlier disappeared, as the deadly Ranger resurfaced. The expression made her shiver. She sat down on the sofa and placed the letter on her lap. Mathias took a seat beside her.

"Yes, that's him," Wilford replied. "He spent almost the entire day doing his research and by late afternoon, he looked a bit frazzled. So, I offered to help. When he showed me what he discovered on Thomas Taenker in Stoystown, I recalled the hours you spent here."

Jo and Mathias looked at each other. "Um, did he happen to say why his research included the surnames you just mentioned?"

"Well, I asked him that question myself, since your research focused on the surname McGregor. He said something about the difficulty of interpreting the handwriting and he needed to consider the possibility the name might be something other than McGregor."

"Yes, the name is difficult to read. Did he tell you what he found on this Thomas Taenker in Stoystown?" she asked.

"No, he didn't say much, other than he seemed confident of his facts. He said Thomas Taenker served during the Revolutionary War and that many of his descendants used the surname Tinker," Wilford replied. "So you see you weren't far off initially."

"I wonder why he left without waiting to see the books." Jo made the comment to Mathias, but Wilford answered anyway.

"I can't say for sure, other than he suddenly asked if we carried the history of property deeds. I told him no, those records would be found on the county level," he said.

"Really?" she asked. "Did he want the history of Taenker's property?"

"I'm not sure. We weren't talking about Taenker at the time. Let's see. Oh yes, I believe he made the comment after we discussed the alternate names for

McGregor."

Jo's heart skipped a beat. She swallowed with a bit of difficulty and said, "Well, this is all very good news. I'm so happy you called me."

"No problem," he said. "I just wanted to let you both know the titles of the books he asked to see are written down on your card. Any employee should be able to retrieve them if either of you would like to come back in and take a look at what they have to offer."

"Thank you very much, Mr. Clark. I'll pass your message on to my colleague," she said. "You've gone beyond the call of duty, and I appreciate the time you took out of your busy day to get in touch with me."

"You're welcome, Miss Michaelsson. If I can be of further assistance, please don't hesitate to ask," he replied.

Sam popped in just as Jo hung up the phone. He glanced at Mathias, then at her and then back to Mathias.

"What's going on?" he asked.

"Sanders again," Mathias spat.

Sam sighed and shook his head. "What's he up to now?"

"I just received a call from the curator at the Pennsylvania archives," Jo said. "He called to tell me that one of my colleagues visited the building to do additional research on tinker's toy and offered his congratulations for finally figuring out the words referenced Stoystown, Pennsylvania."

"What does all of that mean?" Just as Sam asked the question, the rest of the boys stood behind him, awaiting the answer.

"It means," growled Mathias, "he remembers just enough of Jacob's letter to try and solve the puzzle himself. The curator said Sanders found a man by the name of Thomas Taneker who lived very near Stoystown, Pennsylvania, during the latter part of the eighteenth century. Sanders believes tinker's toy references that man and that place."

"He's also looking for someone named McCree or McCrae," Jo added. "Although Paul is trying to find the subject of our letter, I'd say he is on the wrong track."

"That doesn't matter," Mathias snapped. "What matters, is he's still looking with a portion of the clues and that puts you in even more danger, especially now he knows the name McGregor."

"How would looking in the wrong place possibly put me in any danger? I think it's a good thing he's off on some wild goose chase. You need to remember, Stoystown is in Somerset County. His search will take him quite a distance from here and from me," she argued.

"Yes, but when he discovers he's wrong, he'll have to come back to the original source. He'll believe you found the letter here and he'll wonder what else you might be hiding." Mathias shook his head and placed a hand on top her shoulder. "I'm so sorry, Jolena. We shouldn't have involved you in any of this."

"Don't be ridiculous," she said. "I wouldn't have had it any other way. Besides, I really don't think I'm in any danger, and even if I were, I have five of the best bodyguards on this earth. I know without doubt, you wouldn't allow anything bad to happen to me. You've already proven as much. Now enough of all of this nonsense. We have more important things to discuss, like this letter for instance."

She picked up the envelope from off her lap and slid her finger through the flap. After removing the single page from the envelope, she unfolded it, tossed her unused check to the side, and read the two brief paragraphs they sent in reply. She lifted a helpless hand and shook her head in disappointment.

"I'm sorry." She put the letter on the table so they could all read it themselves before she leaned back against the cushions. "There really isn't much to it. The genealogist said Thomas McGregor is a very common name in Scotland and that he would need more definitive information in order to check the land records for the specific Thomas McGregor we're researching."

"Right now that particular knowledge doesn't matter anyway," Mathias said. "We know Thomas is somehow involved and that's enough for the moment. I think our best course of action is to continue looking for the location he referenced in his journal. I think once we find the place, the next clue will present itself."

"You're right," Sam said. "Finding the location is the most vital thing we can do at present. Whether or not he sold property in Scotland doesn't solve anything."

"No, but it's still a piece of the puzzle," Alex said. "And we will need all of the pieces eventually if we're to understand the message in full."

Jo stood up then, stuffed the letter back inside its envelope, and tossed it on the table. "Well, if you'll all excuse me, I'm going to go up and have a shower."

After Jolena left the room and climbed the stairs, Mathias turned to the lads and said, "We must never leave Jolena alone in this house again. Paul Sanders will come back. It's no longer a matter of *if* but *when* and *how.* Especially since the curator from the Pennsylvania Archives supplied him with the McGregor name. If he's checking the property deeds, his research will return him to this house."

"I agree," Sam replied. "That man has a crazy look in his eye. I don't think he'll let a mere woman stop him from getting what he wants."

"Don't worry," Jedediah said. "He'll never get close enough to hurt her."

Mathias elected to remain behind while the rest of the boys began the survey of Joshua's property. He popped upstairs and into the library to keep a better eye on Jolena. Despite all their assurances, some things existed over which they held no power. And what if Paul Sanders made his attack during working hours?

That disturbing possibility gave way to a decision. She might not like it, could guarantee she wouldn't, but from this moment forward, he would not allow her to leave this house unless he accompanied her. The ringing of the telephone interrupted his thoughts. He glanced over at the clock and noting the hour, couldn't imagine who would call this late. After two rings, it stopped. Jolena must've answered the thing in her bedroom.

Without giving the call another thought, he ambled toward the painting. He never tired of looking at it. As he took in the lovely image of Jolena, he found himself considering another visit to her dreams. Enough time passed since the first to avoid suspicion, and he ached to hold her again.

"Mathias?" Jo called out as she burst into the library with a look of excitement etched across her features. Her blue eyes danced with anticipation. "You're not going to believe this."

"Believe what?"

"I hope you have your passport up to date because we're going to Glasgow, Scotland." Her voice quivered with excitement.

"Glasgow? What are you talking about?"

"Did you hear the phone ring just now? My Scottish counterparts have had this grand music festival in the works for well over a year now. I won't bore you with all the details, but they're going to put on several sold-out concerts over the course of a ten-day period.

"Unfortunately, the featured violinist they booked canceled at the very last minute for medical reasons. They said he needs to have some surgery and it's serious enough they can't wait until after the concerts are over. So, they asked me to take his place. Of course, I immediately said yes. Although it is possible I could've screamed my acceptance," she added as she tossed him an impish smile. "Did you, by chance, hear me do such a thing?"

Even though Mathias chuckled as he approached her, it took a few minutes to understand everything she said. "So, when is this music festival taking place?"

"We're going to leave in about three weeks and we'll remain in Scotland for a little over two, maybe a bit longer if I have anything to say about it. I've never had the opportunity to stay there for more than a day or two at any given time, and I would really like the chance to see the country.

"But, can you believe it? Do you understand this means we're going to have the opportunity to look for Thomas's land records ourselves? We'll have plenty of free time while we're there and I'm sure we can discover every detail concerning his property, from the moment he took possession of it, until the day of his death. Finally, one way or the other, we'll have that piece of our puzzle."

"Then I guess I'd better go and check that passport,"

he replied, at once matching her enthusiasm. If nothing else, this trip would take her far enough away from Paul that he couldn't touch her. At least for the duration of the journey. "Exactly what is a passport, anyway?"

Chapter 23

"Oh, stewardess?" the woman at the end of Jo's row called out. "I really need to change to another seat. I'm still freezing half to death, and this blanket doesn't seem to help at all. Look, I can literally see my breath."

The flight attendant rubbed both arms with her hands during the woman's exaggerated performance. "I'm sorry. You're right. I can feel it too." She looked up at the vent. "I can't imagine what the problem is. But, the plane does have several empty seats. Take any one of them you wish."

She turned her gaze to the man in the middle. "Would you like another seat as well, sir?" she asked

"Yes, please, if you don't mind," he answered.

As the passengers got up and walked toward the front of the plane, Jo tracked their progress.

"What about you, ma'am," she asked. "Would you like to find another seat?"

"No, thank you," Jo answered. "I'm fine right here."

"Are you sure you don't want me to get you another blanket then?" she asked.

"That isn't necessary," Jo replied, not really needing the first one. "Really, I'm fine."

"Well, if you should find it otherwise, just let me know," she said.

"Thank you. I will." A slight smile appeared on Jo's lips as the woman retreated down the aisle. Mathias and

Sam wasted no time in taking the recently vacated seats.

"That took longer than I expected," Mathias said. "Good thing the other lads elected to stay home. We might've aroused the lady's suspicions if we had to clear out another whole row."

Jo's fingers played against her lips to mask her amusement as well as her comments. "Still, I wished they would have come with us. I think they would've had fun," she whispered.

"Ah, you know them." Sam waved a hand in dismissal. "They assign a great deal of importance to searching every particle of Joshua's property. Besides, if every one of us evacuated the premises, who would look over Dakota and Lacy properly? Not to mention, with Sanders on the prowl, we don't need to leave the homestead unattended."

"You're probably right." Jo took a breath and turned to look out the window. An endless ocean lay before her and the sight worried her. What if it turned out the boys couldn't travel as far away as Scotland? What would happen if they discovered a barrier they couldn't cross? Could they find their way back home? Would some other sphere hold them captive?

"I don't know about this, Mathias," she murmured behind her hand.

"You don't know about what?" he asked.

"About this trip. What if you guys can't get all the way to Scotland?"

"You needn't worry, we'll be fine, Jolena," Mathias replied. "If I didn't think we could make it there and back, I wouldn't have come. Besides, as you know, I've looked forward to this trip, and not just because of our search."

Jo's mind traveled to all of their carefully planned activities. She spent the weeks before departure, scheduling something for every spare moment she had. They would research Thomas McGregor's land records first, but she also wanted to see as many museums, castles, and historic sites as they could possibly fit into her schedule. Some of them even included the ancestral lands of the McGregor and Fraser clans. Mathias and Sam both seemed excited over the prospect.

Nonetheless, something about the way Mathias looked at her during his last comment made her blush. Well, that and the fact he curled his hand on top of hers. "Just the same," she said. "Let me know if you suddenly feel something is wrong and maybe we can figure out—"

"Hush, Jolena," said Samuel, cutting off the last of her words. "Nothing is going to happen, I promise. Stop fretting. Just settle down and enjoy the trip. We intend to."

Jo let go of an anxious breath, dropped her hand, and laid it on her lap.

Sam looked past her then, to gaze out the window. "Just look at that ocean isn't she something? You know, I always wanted to sail at least once during my lifetime. I never got the chance, but I suppose flying over it is just as good."

She settled a little more comfortably into her seat and took in the view Sam mentioned. Her boys reassured her well enough and they did look as if they enjoyed the experience of this flight. A slight smile emerged as she recalled their marvel over the hustle and bustle of the busy, crowded airport. Of course, they just *had* to explore the complexity of the cockpit and the expressions they wore as the jet taxied down the runway and took off, she'd forever hold in memory. The long hours of the flight passed pleasantly enough, even though they kept all conversations to a minimum.

Within hours of their landing, they found themselves inside a quaint little two-bedroom cottage. The man in charge of the concerts gave Jo the use of it for the duration of her stay. A cozy fire roared in the large stone fireplace and the kitchen larder contained enough food to feed an entire army. The scent of a mouth-watering stew simmered on the stove, all courtesy of a lovely woman by the name of Agnes Galbraith.

Her husband, Timothy, picked them up at the airport and escorted them here to his "wee guest cottage" in the glen. He was certain she'd find it more comfortable than some musty old hotel in Glasgow, he had said.

As she opened her mouth to thank them, they halted her progress with raised hands and a firm shake of their heads. They insisted she did them the tremendous favor by agreeing to come all the way from America to perform in their concerts and on such short notice. Her humble lodgings couldn't even begin to repay the favor, they said.

"If you find oot yer a needin' anythin', dinnae hesitate tae call," Timothy said in his charming Scottish brogue.

"Thank you so much for everything and I will," Jo said in return. "You'll especially hear from me if I get lost."

Agnes laughed and nodded. "'Tis an easy thing to do, to be sure. Th' car haes one o' those computerized talkin' maps, so that shuid help you oot some. If you kin figure oot hoo tae use th' thing, tha' is. They stull mystify me, A'm afeart."

"Well, hopefully I can figure it out. More than likely my biggest problem will come in remembering to drive on the left hand side of the road."

"Jist gie yerself an extra thirty minutes to git tae th' concert hall," Timothy said while giving her a friendly wink. "You micht find oot you need it. So—if yer settled in then, Ah guess we'll see you day after tomoorow."

After they left her to herself, Jo set her laptop computer on the kitchen table. She promised the boys remaining at home she would send them an e-mail the minute they arrived. They learned how to use the e-mail program just as quickly as they did everything else. Mathias insisted on it, because should Paul rear his head, he wanted to know immediately.

"Hang on just a minute," she said as she began typing her message. "I'm sending the boys a quick note to let them know we arrived. We don't want them to have to worry for lack of hearing from us."

"Make sure you tell them for me, they really missed out on our grandest adventure to date," Sam said. "And, as a personal favor, lay it on really thick."

"Don't forget to add it only promises to get better, now that we're here," Mathias added.

Jo tsked and shook her head. "You guys are so mean. Here the other boys have made this huge sacrifice. They stayed home to watch over things just so you could come and have—"

"Sacrifice, nothing." Mathias chuckled. "Despite the remoteness of the possibility, they feared getting stuck out over the ocean somewhere and not have the ability to find their way home."

Jo's heart dropped as he made the confession. "But you said if you didn't think you could make it all the way here, you wouldn't have come."

Mathias shrugged and shot a conspiratorial glance at Sam. "Nothing ventured, nothing gained, isn't that what they say? And as it turned out, the risk didn't exist."

"Now there's no need to give us that look of recrimination, lass," Sam said. "We're here safe and sound, and we'll get home the same way."

"Let's hope," Jo retorted as she picked up her luggage, and made her way into the first bedroom. After she hung up her dresses and put away her clothing, she turned on the shower faucets, in anticipation of a nice hot shower.

Sometime later, after sampling the stew and tidying up the kitchen, Jo curled up in the large overstuffed chair in front of the fireplace. She discovered a book in her bedroom bookcase detailing the history of the Scottish clans and turned to the pages dealing with Clan McGregor. She laughed when the first reference to the clan defined them as troublemakers, born with a "natural unruliness." As she kept reading the history, if the author used reliable sources, she could see where he might consider the statement factual. The remark made her wonder, though—

"Mathias," she began in feigned seriousness. "Would you say the men who comprised Morgan's Rangers descended mostly from the Scots?"

"Oh, I don't know about that," Mathias replied. "Colonel Morgan commanded hundreds of men and most of those men were naught but acquaintances. However, I'm certain some of them must've had some Scottish blood flowing through their veins. Why do you ask?"

Jo shrugged, and lifted a hand to cover her traitorous mouth. "Oh, it's just this reference here to the 'natural born unruliness' of your trouble-making ancestral clansman. The description kind of fits with what the books said about the Rangers, that's all."

Mathias, along with Sam, laughed outright over her comment and she hurried through the following pages looking for additional evidence to boost the claim.

"What else does it say about the McGregor clan?" Mathias sat in the chair next to hers and leaned toward her. "You've managed to pique my interest."

"Well, let's see here." The abhorrent words put a knot in her stomach. "Did you know that in the year 1603, King James signed an edict which allowed anyone who desired it, the authority to kill anyone with the name McGregor? They didn't need just cause, either. Simply having the name was enough. The king sought the annihilation of your entire clan."

Jo looked up from the book and met Mathias's gaze. "The chapter goes on to say they hunted down and slaughtered hundreds of McGregors. They forced those who survived to change their name or flee to the safety of Ireland, along with other political outcasts of Scotland. And the women had either to change their name or wear a brand in their foreheads."

Mathias nodded as he toyed with his clasped fingers. "Yes, my family was aware of that part of our family's history, though we rarely talked about. My great grand uncle, the Reverend James McGregor, supplied the means to transport hundreds of Scotsmen from the shores of Ireland to the Colonies in the year 1718. My grandfather, Angus McGregor, sailed with him, thus these men became the first in my family to step foot on American soil."

"Did you know your grandfather?" she asked,

thinking about all the tales he could've spun that would have fascinated a young boy.

"He died before I was born," Mathias replied, offering no more than that.

"Well, I'm glad they decided to come," Jo said as she lifted her eyes from the page to meet his gaze.

"I am too," Mathias whispered.

The look he gave her quite easily stole her breath and at once, she returned to the book, hoping he didn't notice. "Well, thankfully, they officially repealed the law in the year 1774. But they shouldn't have sanctioned it in the first place."

"No, they shouldn't have. But you must remember when speaking about the character of the Scots, the McGregors hardly took the prize for unruly, natural-born troublemaking," said Sam. "At least, that's what I've been told. I, myself, wouldn't know anything about the subject at all."

Leave it to Sam to make her laugh. As she continued through the pages, she found and then related the stories of their more notable clansmen, their acts of bravery, strength, leadership, and the places they held in Scottish history. Mathias and Sam inherited these very same qualities from their forebears.

Of course, imagining them dressed in a fringed leather "mountain man" kilt while they attended their duties, proved somewhat amusing to her psyche. That night her mind concocted all sorts of strange dreams, featuring the boys dressed in such manner. Because of those dreams, she welcomed the alarm clock with open arms though her body protested the hour. She got out of bed and donned the long-sleeved white T-shirt and jeans she laid out the night before. After she dressed, she headed for the kitchen to get some breakfast.

"Good morning, Mathias, Sam. Did you both sleep well?" she teased when she found them in the kitchen, looking at her laptop screen.

"Who could sleep with all of that snoring going on in the bedroom?" countered Sam. "With that racket going on, I popped outside looking for a bear, thinking surely one roamed the premises. Couldn't find a thing, though. That led me to believe we didn't have a bear at all."

Jo just laughed while she poured herself a bowl of cereal. And then as she sat at the table to eat, she said, "I think as soon as I'm finished with my breakfast, we'll head to the Scottish archives in Edinburgh. After all, I really have no idea how long it's going to take us to find what we're looking for, so we should get an early start." She nodded at the computer then as she swallowed the bite in her mouth. "Did we get anything from the boys?"

"Nope, not yet," Sam said. "They're probably too busy kicking themselves for staying home."

"Or" Mathias added, "perhaps they're still out to Joshua's, looking for another clue."

"Well, hopefully, we can help them by finding something here," she said.

Four hours later, Jo glanced down at her watch. She yawned and stretched a bit before turning her attention to the record book in front of her. How many such books had they looked through so far with nothing to show for it? She sat there staring at the large file of notes she compiled into her laptop in the hope that something, anything, might jump out at her. Jo propped her arm on the table and rested her chin atop her closed hand. She must've looked lost because at that very moment, one of the curators approached her.

"Is thare somethin' Ah kin hulp you with?" he asked.

He listened attentively to her explanation. "Weel, Ah wuid think if yer Thomas McGregor sauld any o' his property in Scootlund, he wuid huv done so in person. Would you happen to knoo if he made any trips here, an' if so, th' approximate dates he made thaim? Perhaps yer lookin' at the wrong time."

Why didn't she think of that? "Actually, he did make a few trips here. I don't have the dates with me, but let me make a phone call, and I'll see if I can get them." For whatever reason, it never occurred to her to take notes from Thomas's journal.

Despite several tries, she couldn't get a connection from her cell phone at her present location. She glanced down at her laptop, hoping against hope one of the boys could hear her computer at home. A musical bell sounded when an e-mail arrived. She typed the request.

I need someone to look through Thomas's journal and find the dates he visited Scotland. And I need them as fast as you can get them to me. Jo.

For the next several minutes the man, who introduced himself as Ronald Murray, made friendly conversation with her while she waited for a reply. She introduced herself in turn, and from the highly publicized concerts, he recognized her name. Knowing the master violinist from America sat at his table, he doubled his efforts in trying to help her find Thomas McGregor's land records. He even began going through some of the records himself. A short while later, she received an answer from William.

First recorded trip March 17 1773 second trip August 23 1775 hope I got it fast enough for you. William.

After showing Mr. Murray the dates, he retrieved the volumes she needed. She read each of the entries. Much to her disappointment, she didn't find the name McGregor in the March/April 1773 volumes. She turned to the second volume and found a single reference to the surname, only it didn't name Thomas.

"This entry has a McGregor, but it is for a Catherine Campbell McGregor and not a Thomas." She pointed to the entry so Mathias and Sam could see it too.

Ronald nodded in agreement, shrugged and said, "So it is—"

"That's it. Catherine Campbell is Thomas's wife," Mathias whispered. "Perhaps the land is part of her inheritance or something along those lines."

Jo looked up at Ronald and said, "Yes, but that's the name of Thomas McGregor's wife." She found it a little difficult to talk to a ghost and a mortal person at the same time. "I believe this information is exactly what we— what I'm looking for."

"Och, that's guid news," Ronald replied, his satisfaction obvious. "Alloo me, if you wull—"

Jo waited, as he looked the document over and then pointed to the barely legible name at the bottom.

"Thomas McGregor sauld this laund, so noted here, to Archibald Campbell oan th' twenty-ninth day of August in th' year 1775, an' fur whit, they considered in those days, a guidly sum. Ah shuid think this property wis either a portion o' her inheritance or given as part o' her dowry. Then Ah wuid theorize, she an' her huisband sauld it back, to a brither perhaps, or some other relative who may huv been feelin' a wee bit generoos. Lit me make you a copy o' this transaction fur yer records, Miss Michaelsson. A'll be richt back."

"Well, that solves that part of the puzzle," Sam said with a satisfied expression on his face.

"And introduces another," Mathias said. "What did he do with the proceeds from the sale? The probate record made no mention of such a sum."

Jo could only shrug in response as Mr. Murray once again approached her table.

"Ah hud anither thooght if ye'r interested," Ronald said as he handed her the copy of the record. "Mony times oor eighteenth or nineteenth century colonial visitors purchased things while they wur here. Och, they wuid buy pieces o' furniture, linens, dinnerware, gowns, an' th' like. A ship's manifest micht reveal if yer Thomas McGregor purchased somethin' nice fur his wife or family. These things flesh oot a family history an' add mair than jist names an' dates. Shall Ah tak' a look an' see whit Ah can fin' fur you?"

One hour later, Jo and the boys exited the building. They remained quiet as they got inside the car and during most of the return drive to the cottage. The day supplied them with an answer they had sought for months and the knowledge of their discovery thrilled them no end. But it also managed to open up a completely new set of questions.

"Tell me, Mathias," Samuel finally said as he fixed his gaze out the window. "What in the blazes would your cousin want with seven tons of iron castings, smelted in county Argyll?"

Chapter 24

They discussed the mystery over the next several days. E-mails flew back and forth across the continents so everyone could share their ideas. But then again, Jo's rehearsal schedule precluded them from doing much of anything else. One thing remained certain: Thomas couldn't have transported actual cannon or gun parts. No captain would allow such cargo on board their ship, even though many Scottish sympathizers to the American cause would've looked the other way. However, at that particular time in history, no one wanted to risk the wrath of the English Crown, least of all the Scots.

"We may never know for sure why Thomas shipped so much iron to the Colonies, Sam," Mathias said when it seemed they discussed every conceivable notion at least half a dozen times already. "But I think we can conclude whatever its purpose, he intended to use it toward the war effort, and for now, that's enough."

"We are agreed on that issue," Sam said. "Still, you have to admit that seven tons of iron could be melted down and recast into—"

"Just about anything," Jo finished as she adjusted the mirror inside the car. "Come on, guys. Let's put the iron on the backburner, and just enjoy the day. Lest you forgot, this is one of the few days we have to spend in its entirety and do as we please."

Mathias bowed his apologies. "You're right, of

course, and I promise we won't mention the subject again today. So, where are we going first?"

"The museum that houses the works of James Watt. We talked about that before leaving home as you might recall. I think we'll go there first and then head off to some of the castles on our list. I really don't know how many of them we'll have time to see today, because I don't know how long each of them will take to explore. From my own experiences, one can spend anywhere from a few minutes to a few hours depending upon what's available and open to the public."

In a little less than an hour, they arrived at the museum and as advertised, they displayed many of James Watt's marvelous accomplishments and inventions. Among other things, the exhibit included the improvements he made to various musical instruments. This portion of the exhibit, especially intrigued Jo and she pointed out the differences between the versions. Several of Watts's early conceptual drawings, as well as his plans for the steam engine pump sat near the display of the famous Boulton-Watt steam engine. All of these things, along with his portrait, surrounded a life-sized statue of the man.

"I can see why your cousin spoke so highly of James Watt," Jo whispered as she gazed at the statue, which appeared to stare right back. "I wonder if during any of their scholarly conversations, Thomas ever suspected James would become so famous and so well loved among the Scottish people, especially given his troubled beginnings."

"Probably not," Mathias replied. "In all likelihood Thomas considered himself in the company of a kindred soul as they exchanged knowledge and ideas."

"Well, it's a shame James didn't live long enough to see some of his ideas come to full fruition," she said. "Perhaps some of the things he and Thomas talked about are right here on display."

Just as she made the comment, they arrived at the end of the exhibit. "Is there anything else you want to see before we leave?" she asked.

"No, I think we've seen just about everything the museum has to offer," Mathias said. "So, we're ready to go whenever you are."

Once inside the car, Jo looked at the long list of castles. In all reality, they couldn't see them all on this trip and she wanted to make sure they made the best of all possible choices. She should call Agnes Galbraith. The woman spent her entire life in this region, and could give the best advice.

"Just a minute," Jo said as she retrieved her cell phone. "I'm going to call Agnes and see which of these castles, she'd recommend first."

When at last she ended the call, Mathias turned toward her and said, "We were privy to a lot of uh-huhs and okays accompanied by a very long pause during your conversation. Did dear old Agnes have trouble advising us as to which castle held the greatest interest?"

"No, not really." Jolena picked up the notepad and studied the directions Agnes supplied her with and then turned left at the next intersection. "If you had taken the time to listen to everything we said, instead of prattling on about the iron, you would know we're going to see a castle that isn't listed on any of the castle touring guides."

"We're not?" asked Sam.

"Nope." Jo paused and flashed a smile. "We're not."

Mathias gazed pointedly in her direction, waiting for

her to reveal the remainder of her conversation. When she didn't, he finally said, "Are you going to share the destination with us, or are you not?"

Jo laughed and turned to meet his gaze. "No surprises for you, huh? Well then, if you must know, Agnes told me about a privately owned castle off the beaten path. She put me on hold for a few minutes and called Laird MacNaughton, the man who owns it. He's a very good friend of hers and is a great fan of the orchestra as well. That always helps get one into places they otherwise can't go.

"Anyway, he gave us his permission to explore the place on our own and told me where to find the keys to his kingdom. A caretaker lives on the property, but he said he'd give him a call and alert him to our arrival. He's going to tell him not to bother me unless I seek him out. Agnes said it would take us at least a half an hour to get there. So relax, and enjoy the beautiful scenery."

It took more like forty minutes but as Jo got out of the car, retrieved the keys, and opened the gates, she marveled over the structure. This castle rivaled, and even exceeded, any castle in any country she'd seen to date. Some of the stones on the turrets and towers were missing as one might expect, and the laird told her to proceed with caution once she entered the structure. He said portions of the upper level flooring had become a bit unstable.

Still, as Jo nudged through the weathered doors and entered the great hall, she envisioned what the thirteenth-century castle looked like, right after its completion. She expected to find the inside empty. Instead, remnants of furnishings met her gaze. Long medieval-style tables and benches sat perpendicular to the door. Antique chests in varying shapes and sizes sat abandoned on the left side of the room, and a few tattered tapestries still hung forlornly on some of the walls.

"Want to take a look upstairs?" she asked, turning an excited gaze toward Mathias.

He chuckled over her enthusiasm, swept a hand toward the spiral staircase, and said, "After you."

As she ascended the narrow steps to the second floor, she turned to the right and opened the first set of thick wooden doors off the roomy hallway. She glanced over at Mathias and Sam who remained close enough to keep her in sight, but investigated other points of interest to them.

"I'll be just in here," she informed them, as she turned the latch and entered the room.

A gasp of delight accompanied the discovery of the small castle chapel. Behind the altar, she beheld a beautiful stained glass window, still intact. The scene depicted one of the saints, though she couldn't tell which one. The cupboard that once held the sacramental wine now housed cobwebs, spiders, and the remains of their various dinners. A thick layer of dust covered the floors and weathered pews.

After exploring every nook and cranny of the chapel, she closed the doors behind her, and then went looking for Mathias and Sam. During her search, she peeked in each of the rooms she passed. She didn't find much to look at. Most of the rooms lay empty, with tiny pieces of crumbling rock strewn across the floor.

Just as she entered the main hallway, Mathias appeared on the stairway leading to the next level. He held his hand out in invitation and smiled broadly.

"Come with me, Jolena, I want to share something with you," he said. "Don't worry, I won't let you fall."

Jo remained close to his side as they ascended the winding stone stairway. The stairs led to the turret and then Mathias took her over to one of the crenels. This particular opening allowed her to see miles of countryside. She looked out over acres of grassy fields. Beyond those fields, she could see thick forests, rivers, and streams. The scene looked like something straight out of a fairy tale and oh, how she wanted to explore it.

"This view is so beautiful, Mathias," she said as her gaze meandered over the scenic panorama. "Just imagine all of the celebrations, the tournaments, and the hunts that must've taken place on those grassy fields."

Her mind conjured images of jousting knights, heralds, lords, and ladies dressed in their finery. She could even imagine one of those ladies, standing exactly where she stood right now and as she gazed out over these very same fields, she sought for the first sign of her brave knight's return.

"Actually, several bloody battles took place out there," Mathias said with a reverence to his tone. "You're looking at a place where countless men lost their lives in defense of their family, their clan, and this castle."

Jo turned away from the sight to meet his gaze. "How could you know that?"

"Because Sir Cailen just shared a brief history of this castle with us," Mathias said. He made contact with the spirit the moment Jolena stepped inside the chapel.

The fourteenth-century knight clamored down the stairway with his sword drawn, intent on defending his home from unwanted intruders. Much like they themselves had done, many times over, minus the swords. The knight seemed somewhat surprised to discover the invaders were naught but spirits themselves, and had escorted a mortal woman from across the sea. The notion apparently intrigued him.

"She's nae afeart o' ye?" he had asked, seemingly mystified by the very idea of such a thing.

"Not in the least," Sam replied. "In fact, I count her among my dearest of friends."

The knight simply shrugged and then asked them about their country, the time from whence they originated, and about the wars in which they fought. They in turn questioned him in like manner. Shortly thereafter, Mathias sought out Jolena. He wanted to show her the countryside from the vantage point of the tower and he'd not been disappointed in her reaction.

"Sir Cailen?" Jo met Mathias's steady gaze.

Sir Cailen, who stood just off to the side, witnessed the entire exchange between them. The moment Jolena repeated his name; the knight appeared to her view. Mathias smiled inwardly over her reaction to the unfolding spectacle.

"Mah lady," he said as he bowed ever so slightly.

Jo just stared as he, in turn, took his time looking her over as well. Without any reservation whatsoever, she accepted the reality of ghosts. She lived with five of them. But right now, not two feet away from her, stood a very handsome knight in full shining armor. Well, maybe his armor didn't exactly shine and he actually wore chain mail and leather. Nonetheless, she gazed at an honest-to-goodness knight who lived centuries before her time.

She finally managed a slight nod of her head in return greeting, and hoped she didn't allow too much time to pass before she did so. She swallowed past the lump in her throat and said, "Sir Cailen, I'm honored to meet you." The statement must've sufficed, as just a hint of a smile tugged at the corners of his mouth. Relief filled her in the instant.

"Ye huv come to see th' castle, aye?" he asked.

"Yes, but only with your permission, of course," she held her breath as she waited his reply. The ghostly knight looked pretty fierce—

"Perhaps ye wuid lik' me to show ye aboot then?" he asked as he stepped toward her.

"If you don't mind, I'd love to see your castle." She smiled at him and then, as if an everyday occurrence, Sir Cailen placed his hand under her elbow. Together they strolled down the stairway as he began the story of this castle. His ancient Scottish brogue immediately charmed her.

The tales her attractive escort spun as he took her through each room of the structure fascinated her no end. He showed her the solar where former lords and their ladies slept and described in vivid detail what those rooms once looked like. The ghostly knight took her inside the treasury room and to the great hall where the king knighted him and his men for their acts of valor. She explored the kitchen and a room he called the gallery, where musicians often played during the feasts. He even led her through hidden passageways that hadn't seen a human foot in centuries. The last several owners, he informed her, didn't even know they existed.

Finally, he took her outside to the bailey and then beyond the outer walls to where the garrison conducted their training exercises. Right there and right then, Jo witnessed a most spectacular and unforgettable sight. In an instant before her eyes, there appeared a very large number of medieval knights. They engaged in swordplay, and they seemed just as deadly serious about the activity as did Mathias and her boys when they conducted their own training exercises back home. The age of the knights tugged at her heart. She would say many of them never lived to see their twenty-first year. So many young lives cut down in the prime of their lives—

In awed silence, she assumed the role of spectator, until at last the brawny knights turned to face her. They acknowledged her presence with nods and bows before they slowly faded away. Her host had nothing left to show them, so she turned toward him and smiled her gratitude.

"Thank you so much, Sir Cailen," she said. "You've given me a most memorable experience. I'm so very pleased to have made your acquaintance and learn the history of your wonderful home. I'll never forget you or this day, not ever."

The knight beamed as he placed an arm lightly around her shoulders. "'Twas mah pleasure, Jolena Michaelsson, an' ye'll fin' a welcome shuid ye e'er wish to return."

Mathias shook his head ever so slightly. The knight certainly didn't need to keep touching her, nor did he need to keep looking at her the way he looked at her, either. Therefore, he extended his arm toward the knight, forcing the issue. Sir Cailen dropped his arm from around Jolena's shoulder, took the offered hand, and shook it.

"Thank you," Mathias said, "we found it a pleasure."

Sir Cailen bowed in return. "Ah dinnae ken it afore, Mathias o' Clan McGregor, but 'tis clear noo, why ye've fallen fur the wee lass. Shuid she become a fixture in thes castle, 'tis verra possible Ah micht fall fur her mahself."

Mathias shrugged and said, "Well, you needn't worry. She isn't staying in Scotland long enough for you to get attached."

The knight met Mathias's comment with uproarious laughter. Jolena looked at him questioningly, for the brief conversation passed silently between them. Mathias simply winked and cocked his head toward the door.

Though she looked bewildered, Jolena thanked Sir Cailen once again as Mathias escorted her back to the outer gates. He shut and locked the gates before returning the castle keys to their hiding place. Once he entered the car, Jolena took hold of her cell phone and while placing her call, gave him a smile.

Jolena promised Laird MacNaughton she would call the minute she finished exploring, and let him know she hadn't injured herself. The Scottish laird answered the phone on the second ring. Mathias could hear the anxiety in his tone of voice.

"Hello, Miss Michaelsson. Ah tak' it yer all richt, then?" he asked.

"I'm fine and I'd like to thank you so very much, for such an enjoyable afternoon. Your castle is just amazing, and I enjoyed myself far more than you realize," she said.

"An' nothin' untoward happened while you poked aboot th' place?" he asked her.

"Nothing at all, and I believe I explored every inch of the castle as well as the grounds. I can only hope you'll enjoy the concerts as much as I enjoyed my visit."

Mathias listened as the Scottish laird released a sigh of relief. "A'm happy to hear it. You see moost people wha' visit th' castle report frightenin' experiences, at th' haunds of ghoostly knights."

Jolena locked her gaze with his and a broad smile emerged as Laird MacNaughton made his final comment. They could do naught but laugh in return.

Chapter 25

Jo strolled out the door of the charming little cottage, gazed up at the brilliance of the stars, closed her eyes, and filled her lungs with a deep breath of crisp Highland air. She wouldn't have this same opportunity again. At least not during this trip. Come the morning, she and her boys would head back to the airport and fly home. She followed the cobblestone walk down to the stone fence and sat down on the thick ledge.

"Seems as though you're a little bit sad about leaving here, Jolena," Mathias said as he appeared near the fence.

"I suppose I am, just a little," she confessed as she shifted her body a little more toward him. "But I've also missed the other boys, being at home, and taking our rides together. So in a way I'm ready to leave. Still, having you and Sam here with me made all the difference in this trip, I think," she added.

"Well, if it gives you any comfort, I'm sure Timothy and Agnes will insist on having you as a frequent guest. We'll come back again, I'm sure, and if our hosts have anything to say about it, we'll return often," he said as he sat down beside her.

Jo let out a small laugh and nodded. "Agnes and Timothy are so cute. I don't think they could've treated royalty any better than what they have treated me. Actually, the entire orchestra pampered me something awful. All the fuss made me just a bit uncomfortable, though."

"Any fool can see you've won the hearts of the Scottish people with your talent. But such is inevitable," Mathias replied. "Whether you choose to believe it or not, something magical always happens when you pick up your violin. For those who hear it, they find it quite an experience, as all your audiences have attested."

Jo tilted her head to the side as she considered the compliment. "Thank you, Mathias. I'm glad you think so."

"It isn't a matter of thinking," Mathias lightly grazed her cheek with his fingers. "It's a matter of knowing."

Jo briefly lowered her gaze, in the hopes he didn't see the blush, caused by his simple touch and tone. She looked for a change in subject. "So, did you and Sam enjoy your visit?"

"We did," Mathias replied. "I didn't think I would ever see the home of my ancestors, or ancient castles filled with a bunch of rowdy knights still hanging about the place."

Jo laughed as she recalled her experience with those unruly knights. "I didn't either. Still, I have to admit, I found meeting Sir Cailen quite a shock. Yet, I wouldn't have missed the chance for the world. I found it enthralling to hear about life in the fourteenth century from someone who actually lived it."

"An interesting tale, from an interesting escort," he said.

She breathed out a sigh. Interesting yes, but the handsome knight didn't hold a candle to the Pennsylvania Ranger who held possession of her heart. How she wished she could tell him that. Mathias gazed at her then as if he wondered where her mind had taken her. Better to change the subject now, before he asked. She glanced up at the stars for a moment before she returned his gaze.

"Mathias, I've been meaning to thank you for coming here with me despite the risk you took in doing so. Having you here meant a great deal to me," she said.

"I think the greater risk would have come in remaining at home," he said. "So you needn't thank me."

Jo could feel the butterflies take flight simply because of the way he looked at her while he spoke. And she wondered at that moment, what it would feel like if he leaned over and kissed her—really kissed her. She shook her head to clear away the impossibility of the notion and rose to her feet.

"Well, I suppose I better go in and try to get some sleep. The day will start early enough, and I want to make sure I'm packed and ready when Agnes and Timothy arrive."

"Good night then and sweet dreams," he said as she made her way back inside the cottage. In truth, he meant what he said. He hoped her dreams this night would be sweet indeed.

Sam's sudden appearance on the walkway outside the cottage drew his attention. That Sam wanted to come along on this trip, pleased Mathias to no end. Then again, it wouldn't have happened any other way. Sam, ever loyal, and ever at his side, never allowed him to take risks alone.

"I'll get back about sunrise," Sam said as he turned south toward the small village in the distance. "As I mentioned earlier, I want to say goodbye to the lads at the pub and thank them for their fine hospitality."

Mathias chuckled and raised a brow. "You forgot to mention the lovely Rosalie. Surely you want to bid her farewell too?" He referred to the lovely nineteenth-century barmaid. From what Sam told him, she seemed quite captivated by the appearance of the eighteenth-century American spirit who visited her pub.

Sam merely laughed in return and winked. "Well, we just can't go home without so much as a by-your-leave, can we now?" And with that, he disappeared.

Not that Mathias minded his absence. For just as he hoped, a short while later Jolena fell into a deep, restful slumber. He entered her room, took hold of her hand, and lifted it to his lips.

"Where would you like to go tonight, my love?" he whispered and waited for the images in her subconscious to manifest themselves.

****

Jo waited eagerly on the green grassy fields outside of Laird MacNaughton's castle. Mathias rode swiftly toward her on a beautiful stallion that gleamed in the sunlight. Somewhere during his exhilarating ride, his hair loosened from its queue. He looked very handsome as he approached her. He flashed a grin as he reined his mount to a halt.

Then, he stretched his hand out toward her and said, "Come with me, Jolena, I want to share something with you."

In one fluid motion, she found herself sitting behind him on the large horse. The stallion danced his impatience. "Where are we going?" She wrapped her arms around his waist and adjusted her seat.

Mathias grinned anew and said, "Wait and see."

He turned his mount in the direction of the forest and urged him into a flat-out gallop. Jo smiled with delight as Mathias continued his wild run through the fields. Shortly thereafter, they found a path that took them over an ancient bridge, and inside the wooded terrain, where they had to slow their pace. They rode until the tall, ancient trees became so thick, the horse couldn't move forward without undue hardship. He helped her down then and after dismounting himself, left the horse to graze freely on the luscious grass.

Mathias took hold of her hand and gave a nod to the right. "This way."

Jo marveled over the beauty within this woodland. She desperately wanted to explore it the day she and Mathias stood on the turret and looked out over it. But they just didn't have the time to indulge the whim.

The sound of rushing water grew ever louder while they strolled hand in hand toward a river. Just as she conjured the image of what it might look like, they suddenly stood beside it. "Look, Mathias." She pointed at the rocky bottom. "See how clear the water is."

"That it is, but come now, just a little bit farther." He tugged on her hand and stepped into the dense vegetation. Then, just before they arrived at their final destination, he stopped. "Now close your eyes, Jolena."

Jo complied with his request and with one arm firmly around her waist; he led her up a small incline. As she climbed to the top, she could hear the roar of rushing water. Mathias stood just behind her then and wrapped her in a protective embrace.

"All right," he said. "You can look now."

Jo stood very near the edge of the river, and as she opened her eyes, she beheld one of the most enchanting waterfalls she'd ever seen. The water splashed and played along the stones as it stair-stepped its way down the mountain. Water fell between the lush trees and then crashed into the river below and she gasped in delight.

"I'm so glad I got the chance to see this before we left Scotland," she murmured.

Then once she could drag her eyes away from the mesmerizing scene, she turned around. She ran her fingers through the length of his hair and she gloried in the feel of it. In turn, he drew her close against his chest and tilted her chin upward. "Thank you," she whispered.

He joined his lips to hers and after several heart-stirring kisses, he took a small step back, and gazed into her eyes. A look of regret filled the warm brown depths. "The heavens have played naught but a cruel joke on us, Jolena, my love, dividing our lives by the centuries that have kept us apart."

Jo released a sigh as she shook her head. "No, Mathias. The heavens are never intentionally cruel. I believe each person is born to the time and place he or she is most needed. In the beginning, our nation struggled for each breath of life she took. She needed men such as you. Men with strength, courage, and the skills you possess to make her independent and free. Your life, the valiant deeds you accomplished, the risks you took, and the impact you had while you lived, is more important than what you could possibly imagine. Someday you'll know this for yourself, but *I* know it now."

"Such high praise for an ordinary man, and I'm not sure I deserve it. But, even if half of what you say is true, why couldn't you have lived during my time and shared your life with me there?" he asked.

"What? And leave me a young widow, alone and defenseless?" she said in an attempt to tease him out of his present mood.

"I suppose you have a valid point." He cuddled her

closer to his chest and for a moment, rested his chin lightly atop her head.

She snuggled against him. "I don't know all of the answers, Mathias. Perhaps I'm needed here and now, to do nothing more than play my violin for someone who needs to hear it," she said as she searched his eyes. "I love you so much, and I know I'll have forever to love you. So this short life, even if it lasted a hundred more years, doesn't really matter, does it?"

"Are you promising me forever, Jolena Leigh Michaelsson?" he asked as his lips grazed lightly across hers.

"If you want it," she said.

"Oh, I want it," he whispered as he gave the kiss that stole her breath and made her his.

Jo awakened to the feel of Mathias's lips still warm against hers, and whispered words of forever ringing in her ears. She rolled over and peeked through her lashes as the first light of dawn entered her bedroom. She cherished the dreams she had of Mathias. They made her feel as if she lived them. She remembered each one so vividly; she could relive them whenever she wished. All other dreams became vague, if not altogether lost upon awaking. Did that mean something?

All throughout the flight and the drive home from the airport, the dream never strayed far from her mind. At times, Mathias gazed at her with probing eyes as if wishing to discover the reason for her silence. What would he think if she told him? She scoffed inwardly. Yeah, right. She could never tell him such a thing. Though, at times, she would give anything, if she could.

Finally, after hours of travel, they arrived home. Jo expected to see William, Alex, and Jed all standing beside the car as she turned off the ignition, but no one rushed out to greet them. They entered the house and found it empty. Not even Dakota made his presence known. She dropped her luggage by the stairway and turned to face Mathias.

"Where would all of them have gone in the middle of the afternoon?" she asked.

"I don't know. Maybe they're still out looking for our unknown location and feel it safe enough for all of them to leave at one time," he replied. "Especially now we know we're looking for a place large enough to house seven tons of Scottish iron."

"I guess that makes sense. All right, while we're waiting for their return, I'll just run upstairs and unpack my things," she said as she retrieved her bags from off the floor. "It should only take me a few minutes."

Once she had everything where it belonged, she picked up her camera bag and walked into the library. Mathias and Sam stood talking near her desk, but fell silent once she entered the room. "Let me guess," she said as she rolled her eyes heavenward. "You're talking about the iron again."

"Iron?" Sam appeared confused. "What iron?"

They both assumed an innocent expression, but just couldn't quite make it believable. Jo shook her head and laughed. "Oh, whatever." She opened the bag and withdrew her camera. "I think I'll go ahead and download all our pictures. The boys seemed anxious to see them."

The process took about ten minutes. Once she completed the file, she started the revolving slide show. Mathias and Sam joined her behind the desk to watch. Amidst the laughter and recalled memories the photos invoked, the unmistakable sound of Dakota's neck chain chimed up the stairs.

With a smile on her face, she glanced up at both Mathias and Sam. "The boys are home."

Everyone converged into the library at the same moment. Jedediah, Alex, and William made their sudden appearance in the middle of the room. A split second later, Dak rushed through the open door. At once, he jumped up and rested his paws on either side of Jo's shoulders. He whimpered in excitement, and made every effort to lick her face in greeting.

Jo laughed over his exuberance and just managed to keep her face out of range while she stroked his fur. The wild wagging of his tail took hold of the book on top the end table and sent it flying half way across the room. All eyes followed the flight as the volume slammed down on the surface of the hardwood floor and skidded to a halt. Silence followed the thud.

"Jolena, I'm so sorry," William said, sounding contrite. "I should've put that away, but I just didn't think—"

Jo looked down at the scattered pages of Thomas McGregor's journal and then up at William's horror-stricken face. She waved a hand in dismissal.

"Don't worry about it, William. None of this is your fault. As you see, the fall didn't destroy any of the pages and we still have access to all of the same information we had before. Besides, I'm pretty sure Carolyn can fix it as good as new," she said.

She stooped down to pick up the pages that tore away from the binding, and then picked up the leather cover. She carried them over to the desk and placed the cover on top. After she arranged the pages, she opened the journal so she could put them back inside. But as she did so, she suddenly stopped and stared. The outermost endleaf had broken away from inside the back cover when the journal hit the floor, and the very act uncovered something.

"What is that?" asked Mathias as he leaned over her shoulder for a better look.

"I'm not sure." She used just the tips of her fingernails to extract the folded linen paper from out of its hiding place. The page didn't feel brittle in her hand as her grandfather's letter had. "I'm going to try to open it."

"Careful, lass," Sam cautioned.

Jo nodded and with slow, careful advances, opened the document. She took in a breath and then looked from Sam to Mathias to gauge their reaction.

"These drawings are very similar to the steam engine sketches, designed by James Watt," said Sam.

"I'd say they are almost identical. What does that say there in the corner, Jolena? Can you make it out?" asked Mathias, pointing to the smudged and faded writing.

"Let me get my magnifying glass, maybe we can see it a bit better." Jo retrieved the instrument from her desk drawer. She held it a few inches above the writing. "Well, I can see the words 'steam engine' and what looks like 'simple modifications' right here. We have some arrow indicators with notations that I can't quite make out. But I have no idea what all of this means." She looked up and met Mathias's gaze.

"That's probably because we're missing page two," Sam said in jest as he nudged Mathias with his elbow.

"Wait a minute Sam, maybe you're right about that," Mathias replied. "Jolena, check the other side of the journal and see."

After finding her pocketknife, Jo carefully lifted the

edges off the front cover. She smiled then, looked up at Mathias, and said, "You're right."

Once again, she extracted a large piece of linen paper, folded flat inside. The room remained deathly quiet as she opened the sheet in its entirety and placed it before their view.

"Tinker's toy," Mathias said in marked amazement, "we found it at last. And it's been right here all this time."

Chapter 26

Everyone in the room crowded around the various drawings Thomas McGregor sketched over two centuries earlier. In all likelihood, he shared these very drawings with Matthew Brewster and Joshua Porter soon after he finished them. Thomas took the idea of James's steam engine, and turned it into something the patriots could use to further their cause. He designed the steam engine to power small paddleboats. The boats, loaded with gunpowder, would target the ships used by the English Navy and sink them once the gunpowder exploded.

Thomas's detailed drawings showed how this would work. Mathias deduced that with Thomas's guidance, Matthew built the boilers to power the engines, as well as the engines themselves. Hence, the need for the large amount of iron purchased in Scotland. They intended to have someone guide the boats toward the English Naval vessels and once they got close enough, they would light the fuse to the powder. After the operator lit the fuse, he would abandon the boat and head for safety. The engine would thrust the paddleboats steadily into the ships and then according to plan, the powder would blow at the same time they hit their targeted destination.

"Just like a torpedo," Jo murmured. "An absolutely brilliant plan for the time period."

"We could've used such boats as these," Mathias added. "Just months before our deaths, the English managed to choke off most our supplies with their blockades. The blockade-runners couldn't always find a successful way to get the supplies through. Something like this, that could've destroyed part of their fleet, might have made the Redcoats consider revising that plan. Especially if we destroyed enough of their ships."

"I wonder why they never tried it," Jo mused aloud. "Something like this would've been in all the history books, even if it failed. Just like the first crude submarines used during the Revolutionary and Civil Wars, and as we learned at the museum, the steam engine itself didn't find success until several years after the war ended."

"Yes, but remember all three men involved with this project either disappeared or died the same year. Perhaps the reason for that is because they never finished and thus never put the plan into motion," Mathias said.

"Well, if that's the case, then the entire operation is still out there, waiting for us to find it," Alex replied with a touch of excitement to his tone. "I say we continue our search. Something made of iron would stand the test of time, and I would like to know just how far they got with the thing."

After the boys agreed with the sentiment, Sam added, "You know, I think we've conducted our searches in the wrong places, lads. If you take a close look at these drawings, and from what we learned at the museum in Scotland, water is a crucial element. They would need a large supply not only while they built the thing, but they would also need it to test the design."

"That means they wouldn't work *inside* the borders of Joshua's property. More likely, our unknown location is *outside* his land and close to the creek itself. Yet, it's near enough to his property that he would know of its existence," William said.

"I think you're right," Jedediah said. "They would look for a spot, partially hidden. A place most people wouldn't give a second glance."

"You could find such a spot, Jedediah," Alex said. "All we need do is look for it."

Sam nodded his agreement. "I think it best to revert to our predawn searches. Not too many people are out and about that time of the morning."

"Then it's settled. We'll begin the search right after nightfall," Jedediah replied.

Once they firmed up their plans, the conversation turned to Scotland. Mathias and Sam drew the boys' attention to the photos, still playing on the computer. While they looked them over and asked their questions, Jo tackled the pile of accumulated mail, which sat atop her desk. However, the light blinking on her answering machine demanded her attention too. Perhaps she should clear that out first.

"Oh, that reminds me," Alex said as he followed her gaze. "Carolyn Taylor has left several messages for you on the phone over the past few days. She seems excited about something and she wants you to call."

Mathias looked up from the pictures. "Perhaps it has something to do with Sanders. Maybe you ought to call and find out what she wants," he said.

Jo nodded, picked up the phone, and placed the call. Carolyn answered on the first ring.

"Hey, Kay-Kay, sounds like you've been trying to get a hold of me. What's up?"

"Yes I have, and I'm so glad you're finally home, Jo. I couldn't remember when you said you'd get back, so don't get upset that I didn't call your cell. I just didn't want to take the chance of interrupting you in the middle of a concert or during one of your planned outings. But, you are never, ever going to believe this," Carolyn sang out.

"Believe what?" Jo could tell from the tone of voice that something excited her beyond measure.

"I'm engaged!" she all but screamed the words into the phone. "Can you believe it? Me, of all people. We're getting married next month. May fifteenth, to be precise, so I hope your schedule is clear for that day. If not, you're just going to have to find a way to clear it. After all, I can't get married without you standing next to me."

Jo shook her head and laughed. "That's a pretty good announcement, Carolyn, especially since you've neglected to tell me you were even dating someone seriously."

"I know, I know and I'm so sorry about that," she said. "But it all happened so fast. As you know Ray and I started out as just good friends and then suddenly it was as if we both knew that—"

"Wait—Ray Brennan?" Jo's mouth fell open as she stared down at the phone. "You're going to marry Ray Brennan of all people? The man you had absolutely no interest in?"

"Yes. I know you told me I ought to pursue the obvious, but so many things needed consideration and then— Oh, I don't even know where to begin. We need to find a time to get together so I can share every single detail with you. And don't forget you promised while still in the sand box, you would stand as my maid of honor."

"Always the bridesmaid and never the bride," Jo teased. Just as she made the jest she caught sight of

Mathias's gaze, and it seemed as if—

No. His expression didn't *seem*, at all. He *looked* at her *exactly* the same way he did at the waterfall in her dream, and it left her feeling very short of breath. A heated blush slowly rose into her cheeks.

"Jo, did you hear me?" asked Carolyn.

"Hmm? Oh, sorry, what did you say?" Right now, she found it very difficult to focus.

"I said I'm well aware you just got home. I also know this is very short notice, but we would really like you to come to New Jersey for our engagement celebration. Ray's parents are throwing us a party over the weekend. I really need *my* best friend there with me. So, will you come, please? Their place is just beautiful and their backyard opens right up into this lovely little beach that will remind you so much of one of the beaches back home. I know you're going to love it."

Jo leaned back in her chair and sighed. "You know I can't tell you no. So, just e-mail me the directions and all of the tedious little details, and I'll be there with bells on my toes."

After she hung up the phone, Jo looked at each of her boys in turn and sighed. "All right, who wants to play my bodyguard this weekend? I just may need one," she muttered more to herself than to anyone else.

****

No one disputed his claim to accompany Jolena to Carolyn's party. In fact, it didn't even need discussion. As they got into her car Friday afternoon and began the drive to New Jersey, he said, "How long do you think it will take us to get there?"

Jolena laughed and spared him a quick glance as she merged onto the freeway. "You know, I used to get in trouble for asking that question when I was a kid. Of course, according to my parents, we asked it about every five minutes or so. The funny thing is I don't remember it that way. I remember waiting *hours* in between whining out the question."

Mathias chuckled as he rested his elbow atop the console. "Seems it remained a common question throughout the centuries then. We used to ask it whenever my parents dragged us to visit some of our neighboring friends or relatives."

"Really?" A breath of quiet laughter accompanied the question. "How far away did they live?"

"Oh, we had them stretched out anywhere between say, a couple of miles to about ten, which by carriage or wagon took a while. Especially if you were the one jostled around in the rear, or if you walked."

"I don't think anyone would even consider walking that distance, now. Our modern conveniences have made us lazy, I think."

About two hours later, they arrived at their destination. Jolena looked down at her watch, tossed him an impish smile as she opened her car door, and said, "Oh, and by the way? I think it will take us a couple of hours to get there."

Mathias laughed as he exited the car. He didn't have time to reply as Carolyn rushed toward them, leaving her beau stranded on the porch.

"Well, let me see it." Jolena demanded after receiving Carolyn's exuberant hug.

The woman dutifully extended her left hand so Jolena could see her ring. "Isn't it just gorgeous?" Carolyn asked.

"Yes it is, and I'm so happy for you," she replied as

she then took hold of both her hands and gave them a gentle squeeze.

"Jo!" Ray wore a broad smile as he approached her. "We're so glad you could make it. I know having you here means a great deal to Carolyn and therefore, it means a great deal to me as well. Thank you so much for coming."

"I wouldn't have missed this party for anything," Jolena said as she accepted his friendly peck on the cheek. At that same moment, she turned her head, shot him a glance, and rolled her eyes. Mathias chuckled in response.

During the exchange of pleasantries, he spotted a familiar car, rolling down the road at a snail's pace. His eyes narrowed. Paul Sanders must've received an invitation to this party as well. Perhaps he could reverse that invitation. In keeping with his mortal ruse, he popped over to the porch and while walking down the steps, he projected himself just to Sanders. Their eyes met the moment Paul approached the house. The man's face took on an expression of panic.

"Hey, there's Paul," said Ray as he lifted a hand and waved.

Jolena and Carolyn shot each other a glance before they cast their gaze in the direction of the approaching car. Paul reversed his course, screeched the tires as he rolled back, turned in the opposite direction, and then raced off. Seconds later, Ray's cell phone rang.

Mathias didn't care what lies the man spouted, as long as he kept going. Jolena gave him a questioning look and he winked in return. "Not to worry," he whispered.

She breezed through the weekend without a whole lot of difficulty, once the single men Ray and Carolyn invited for her benefit understood her disinterest. Of course, some of his whispered suggestions might have helped her out of her dilemma. And along the way, Carolyn managed to divulge all the particulars concerning her relationship with Ray. The shared details amused him somewhat and left him wondering if all females engaged in such practices. In a few short hours, at the close of breakfast, the celebration would officially end. Shortly thereafter, they would leave to go home. They both looked forward to the journey.

****

Jolena had arisen early, so they could take a walk on the beach and explore it a bit before the morning meal. The activities of the past few days had precluded her from wandering very far from the backyard and she said that she really wanted to see the area. After kicking off her shoes, they strolled down the deserted beach.

"Do you always walk barefoot in the sand?" he asked as he ambled alongside her.

"Every chance I get," she replied. "I used to do it all the time growing up. Mom and Dad took us to the beach whenever they could back then. Sometimes we'd take along picnic lunches and just spend the whole day doing whatever pleased us. The entire Michaelsson clan carries an inherent love of the ocean or any large body of water for that matter. My dad loved to fish. However, since he preferred fresh-water fish, we'd usually go to the lakes or rivers whenever he wanted to indulge the whim."

"Is that what you were doing in the picture you have on your desk?" he asked.

Soft laughter accompanied a nod. "Yep. Dad caught a big one that day. You can probably see from the expression on his face, just how proud he is of—"

Mathias looked up from the sandy beach when she stopped mid-sentence. She focused on something off to her right. Her smile faded. A look of total confusion took its place.

He followed the direction of her gaze. Understanding dawned, even if a bit tardy. He willed Jolena to this very beach Christmas night while she dreamed. From all the changes that had transpired over the centuries, he didn't recognize it himself until this moment. Nevertheless, the distinctive rock she stared at remained intact, albeit, a little more worn with time since he last visited this place.

He and the lads spent a fortnight very near this area on one of their covert assignments for Colonel Morgan. During the early morning hours, he would come out here and walk the beach. He recalled standing on that rock while he took a few personal moments to watch the rising of the sun and change of the tides.

Jo made an abrupt turn, approached the familiar rock, and lowered herself onto the stone. Just as she did in her dream. She inched her feet into the sand as the morning waves rolled gently over her toes. The seagulls chattered overhead and she could smell the brine of the ocean carried on the gentle breeze. Her fingers wrapped around her pendant. She turned and found Mathias gazing at her with an intensity she could feel.

"Hey, Jo," Carolyn called out. "Looks like you found this magnificent place all by yourself."

The sound of Kay's unexpected voice broke the spell that bound her to Mathias. She turned away from his gaze and shook her head. "Found *it*?" she asked as Carolyn approached.

"Yes. I intended to drag you out here before you left. Don't you think it looks just like that private beach we used for senior grad night?"

Jo took another quick look around, released the breath she unknowingly held and nodded. "You know, it really does. Except, of course, this beach is much smaller, the rocks are much larger, and the surrounding trees are far different," she teased.

"Oh come on, Jo. You usually have a much better imagination for things like this. Look at that rocky face over there. And, you have to admit it twists and turns in very much the same way as that beach back home did," she said in defense of her argument.

"I'll have to give you that one," Jo said. "The beach does do that."

"And Billy broke his foot that night, jumping all of two feet off that stupid rock. Do you remember? What a nerd," Carolyn said as she nibbled at her lip and shook her head.

Several hours later, just as they crested the hill heading for home, Mathias turned toward her and raised a brow. "Billy Byrd is a nerd? Please explain, Miss Michaelsson. Exactly what is a nerd?"

His bewildered expression made Jo laugh. "Oh come on now, Mathias. Surely, someone said the word in a movie or TV show you've all seen. It's a very common term used today."

Mathias shrugged and said, "I'm not sure I recall it."

"Okay." Jo touched the tip of her tongue to the top of her lip as she sought to explain. "Well, I guess it can mean different things, depending on how it's used. But in Billy's case, it means a boy who's trying to impress all the girls by doing some stupid stunts. In particular, bouncing up and down on a two-foot rock in order to gain more altitude. Then hurtling himself into an ocean that should've been at least ten feet deep, instead of merely twenty inches before he found a rather sharp rock at the bottom to cushion his fall. The dork had to wear a cast on his foot for the longest time." She shook her head and laughed as she recalled the memory of that incident.

"Dork?" he asked.

"Along the same lines as nerd." She shot him a glance as she slowed the car to make her final turn and once again, he looked at her the way she remembered in her dreams. The intensity of that expression made her feel very weak in the knees.

This morning's experience convinced her that somehow and in some way, Mathias shared the knowledge of and perhaps even participated in the dream she experienced on that beach. She was well acquainted with that shore, every detail of it. Therefore, it couldn't have been something her mind conjured from something as ridiculous as senior grad night, could it?

Yes, similarities existed in those two beaches, but the differences far exceeded the similarities. If only she had the chance to walk farther down and around the next bend, she could've known with certainty. But Carolyn and Ray's unexpected interruption precluded her from exploring the notion and she couldn't just come right out and ask Mathias.

Nothing in his demeanor suggested he recognized the beach. But how could he? How often did he get to New Jersey during his lifetime anyway? At least, not without being shot at.

Still, the feeling that somehow he was involved with the dream continued to plague her and refused to go away despite all efforts to banish it. In fact, little else occupied her mind throughout the remainder of the day.

She carried those same thoughts with her as she climbed into bed that night, snuggled deep into her covers and prayed that sleep would silence her troubled thoughts.

Chapter 27

Jolena struggled to make sense of the conflicting logic her mind presented her obstinate heart. Mathias saw it in her eyes all throughout the day. He almost told her there on the beach, would've told her, if Carolyn hadn't interrupted them. His own desires and selfishness would've superseded all else at that moment, just as it had with the men at Carolyn's party. He never gave them the chance to win her heart.

Yet, she deserved such a chance, didn't she? But, even if she did find someone else, could he stand by and watch their love blossom? Could he find a measure of contentment knowing she found the happiness life intended her to find? Could he really let her go? The conjured images of another man holding her, loving her, caused a moment of rage, and intense pain. He closed his eyes against it.

"Mathias," Sam called out as he strode into the library from the outside wall. "Jedediah found it."

"Where?" Mathias asked as the other lads barged into the room behind him.

"Very near to where Valley Creek *used* to run its course, about a half mile or so from where Porter's old barn once stood. Just as we deduced after seeing the drawings, the place isn't on his property at all," Sam said. "Jedediah found some rubble which masks the entrance to an old abandoned coal mine. The place hides behind some overgrown branches and vegetation now. Nonetheless, we walked through the rock to see what we could find. Once we got to the other side of the stony wall, we had no doubt but that we found the place of operation. An unfortunate cave-in sealed the entrance about the time we met our deaths. We know that, Mathias, because the remains of Matthew and Joshua are still inside."

"Does it look as if the Redcoats are responsible for their deaths?" asked Mathias.

"No, the English never stepped foot inside the place. We believe their entire operation remains intact. The iron, the forge, the tools, everything is still inside. And gauging by Thomas's drawings, four of the boilers are complete. Even some of the engines look close to the drawings in their finished state. I'm certain if the Brits discovered the site they would've cleaned it out and made use of it themselves. If not the invention, then at least the iron."

"Did you see any other bodies inside the mine beside those belonging to Matt and Josh?" Just as Mathias finished the question, Jolena stood in front of the library doorway. She still fussed with the ties of her robe. From the look of her tousled hair, it appeared she received very little sleep, if she got any at all.

"Is everything all right, Jolena?" he asked.

Jo caught and held his gaze as he asked the question. She found it difficult to sleep while the battle raged between heart and mind. One way or the other, she had to know about the dreams. She slipped out of bed intent on asking Mathias outright about his involvement. If he admitted taking part, then she needed to know if they truly reflected his feelings. At least she would finally get her answers and if nothing else, the knowledge would give her peace of mind. Her heart pounded with both anxiety and anticipation. As she took hold of the handle, she held her breath and turned the knob. Yet, just as she entered the room, Mathias said something about "bodies."

Her gaze wandered about the room then as she took in the expressions each face presented. "You found Matthew and Joshua," she said.

Sam cast a brief glance at his feet and nodded. Then as he lifted his gaze to meet with hers he said, "A short while ago, right before dawn. I just finished telling Mathias about the discovery. And Mathias, to answer your question, I'm sure no one else occupied the mine when the entrance sealed shut. We found no evidence of anyone else."

"What are we going to do about them?" asked Jo.

"There's nothing anyone can do," Alexander replied. "The entrance has at least a foot of hard rock, solidly packed in front of it. The important thing is we found it. A mystery spanning two centuries is finally solved."

Mathias nodded as he began to pace. "We now know that at the very least, General Washington, Jacob, Thomas, Matthew, and Joshua conceived a plan to aid the patriots. The bold and daring plan might've worked if given the chance. We'll never know why the British executed Thomas. The possibility exists they simply found him at the wrong place, at the wrong time, carrying something that made them suspicious. They needed no other excuse than that.

"Nevertheless, his execution set off a chain of events. Jacob Weidmann learned of Thomas's death through the British officers who used his home as their base of operation. Because of my cousin's execution, those involved needed to relocate the operation elsewhere to ensure secrecy. Matthew and Joshua took on that task. Unfortunately, the mine entrance gave way, sealing them both and the entire operation inside. Meanwhile, Jacob wrote his letter to General Washington, notifying him of current events.

"As fate would have it, a trusted servant of the Weidmann household betrayed Jacob's trust. He alerted the British army of the meeting I had with Elisabeth. A British company in turn conducted a search for me. They successfully ended our mission to retrieve the letter and get it into the hands of George Washington. At the same time, Peddelton must take responsibility for the death of Jacob Weidmann. General Washington probably never learned what happened to the men involved or to the plan itself. Without Thomas or his drawings, they couldn't recreate it."

"But we just can't leave those men in there, Mathias. It's just not right," Jo said. "They might not have worn a uniform or served in a battalion at the time of their death, but they died for their country the same as all of you did. At the very least, they deserve a proper and decent burial. They deserve to come home."

They gazed at each other for several long moments. Then his expression softened. "How would you suggest we get them out, Jolena? We can try, but I don't believe we possess the ability to maneuver solidified rock. Even if we could, how would we explain it to those who'd witness the occurrence? Valley Creek has many visitors now and on a daily basis as I'm sure you know."

"I don't know." A deep sigh escaped as Jo sat down feeling dejected. Each idea that engulfed her mind held an obvious flaw and needed discarding. Yet, she couldn't allow Matthew and Joshua to remain entombed in such a place.

"Let me see if I can go back in there and find another way out," Jedediah volunteered. "The Lenni-Lenape taught me there are many ways to advance through the mountains. Perhaps I can find one that connects to the mine tunnels."

"Don't you think if another way presented itself, Matt and Josh would've used it?" asked Alexander.

"Not necessarily, not if the cave-in killed them outright or if they remained so focused on the main exit, they spent their last breath trying to heave those rocks, instead of looking for another way out," Jedediah replied.

"Jolena," Mathias said as he knelt down and brushed the tangled hair away from her face. "If Jed can find another way to get inside, it means you're going to have to go in there yourself. We'll accompany you, of course. But I know of no other way to explain the discovery to the proper authorities. This also means you'll see everything inside the mine that still exists, including the remains of Matthew and Joshua. Are you really up to all of that?"

"Mathias, if any one of your bodies rested inside that place, I would fight heaven and earth to get you out. I don't think I should do any less for Matthew Brewster and Joshua Porter. All of you were part of the same mission, even if you didn't know it at the time."

"All right then," Mathias said. He looked up at Jed and gave him a nod. "Go ahead and take some of the boys and see what you can find."

Jed, along with Alexander and William, disappeared from the room. She could only pray they could find another way inside the mine. Matthew and Joshua deserved no less than a decent burial. Yet, at the same time, the notion brought her to another.

"Mathias, did you all receive a proper burial?" She never asked the question before, not even when they visited the Weidmann family cemetery. But what if no one ever found them out there in the woods?

He nodded, giving her the assurance she sought. "We did and not too far from here, actually. Our bodies rest at the old Lutheran cemetery just west of here. Would you like me to take you to the graveyard and show you sometime? You could pay your respects," he teased, in an obvious effort to lighten her somber mood.

"Are all of you together?" she asked.

"Yes, we're all together, 'as in life, so as in death,' I believe the minister said at our collective funeral," he replied. "The church is gone now, but the cemetery remains and is well looked after."

"Then, someday I would like to see it," she said. Just not right now. Not when the vivid images of his death that early June morning so long ago, still filled her with so much anguish.

The day passed at a snail's pace. Every moment she expected the boys to return. Yet, the hours ticked by, one tedious minute at a time. Mathias and Sam did their best to keep her occupied.

Nevertheless, time and again, she found herself wondering if they could accomplish such a lofty goal. Even if they did find a way to transport the bodies out of the abandoned mind, how could she explain it without mentioning Mathias and the boys? Her desire to protect them from public scrutiny far outweighed her desire to see Matthew Brewster and Joshua Porter properly buried. If it became necessary, she would leave the men where they were.

The wait seemed nigh on unbearable and she looked around for something with which to occupy herself. Perhaps she could make a file of evidence to submit to the authorities. She took one of the copies of Jacob Weidmann's letter to George Washington and placed it in a newly created file folder. Copies of the loose pages from Thomas McGregor's journal dealing with the project, and copies of the drawings found inside the back and front endleaf, soon followed. She also made copies of the pictures she took in Scotland of the James Watt exhibit and in the cemetery. Then, along with the information from the Pennsylvania Genealogical Society, placed that evidence inside the file. With nothing more to add, she placed the file on top the desk. She glanced up at the clock. Two minutes to nine and they had yet to hear from the boys.

Just then, Dakota lifted his head in full alert. She glanced over in the direction of his excited gaze. Jedediah plowed through the wall just seconds ahead of the others. He wore a victorious smile.

"I think we found a way to get you inside, Jolena," he said. "But you're going to need a shovel and maybe even a small pick to make some of the passages wide enough for you to pass through."

Jo rose to her feet and started for the doorway. "That won't pose a problem. I'll get some tools together and we can get out of here right now."

Mathias stepped in front of her, impeding her progress. "Wait. Just wait, Jolena. You didn't get much sleep last night. You've endured a long and trying day. The last thing you need to do is go running off through the mountain right now. Please, for me, go to bed. Try to get some sleep and we'll all go at first light."

Worry and concern filled his eyes as he spoke, and she just couldn't deny his request. "All right, at least let me get everything ready tonight. I don't want any unnecessary delay come the morning. Jedediah, how long do you think it will take us to get there?"

"I would think if the digging is easy enough, we should get you there in about an hour, maybe an hour and a half. It could take much longer, though," he warned.

"Then I'll plan on four maybe five hours to get there and back. I'll need to take along some water, a few protein bars, fruit, and of course, I need to take my flashlight. I better take fresh batteries just in case, and I'm going to need my camera as well. We need to take pictures of the find and add them to the file."

Even though Mathias wanted her to get some sleep, she found herself waking every couple of hours throughout the night. In truth, she really wanted to get this task done and over with. Finally, at about five a.m., Mathias knocked on her door. About twenty minutes later, they packed the car and then headed for the mine. Once they arrived at a specific area near Valley Creek, she parked her car and followed Jedediah as he led them along the fertile path of a dried-up riverbank. Finally, he halted their steps.

"This is the original entrance to the mine, right here," Jedediah said as he pointed out the differences of color and texture on either side of the mountain's rocky face.

Jo broke away some of the foliage so she could get a better look. The debris could also mark the exact point of entry to the other side for Carolyn and Ray's benefit. During the drive, Mathias suggested she call them with her discovery as soon as they returned home. Their credentials made them the obvious choice to take over the site, and Jolena could trust them to carry out her wishes. She concurred.

"All right now, this way," Jedediah said.

They continued their journey to the other side of the mountain. Jedediah soon stopped and said, "Follow me straight in through this opening, right here. I promise you, it's bigger than it looks."

The left side of the rock protruded a bit and then overlapped an opening she didn't even see at first. She passed through it, and then extracted her flashlight.

"Mathias?" she called out anxiously, when she couldn't locate him in the dim light.

"Right behind you, love," he whispered.

So intent on following Jedediah's lead, it took a few minutes for the endearment to sink into her consciousness. She wondered then, if he even truly said it. *Not now, Jolena,* she told herself. *Don't think of it now, lest you lose your concentration.* Just as she took her next step, her boot slid on a pile of loose rocks and she slipped backward, thus proving her point. Nonetheless, Mathias kept her from pitching backward.

"Thank you," she murmured and in return, he gave her waist a gentle squeeze.

"Okay, Jolena, this is where you might have to dig a little bit, but be very careful," Jedediah said as he pointed to another, obscure passageway.

She nodded. In order to pass through the opening comfortably, she needed to make it larger. She retrieved the small hand pick from her backpack. With a few gentle strokes, the rocky dirt gave way. Dust filled her nostrils and in between the dull thuds, she coughed and sputtered until at last, she could ease her body through the opening.

Once she crawled through the hole, she found herself in a more open area. The tunnel continued its twists and turns. Twice more she needed to dig in order to pass to the other side. At times, her leg muscles ached and burned with the effort to climb. Several times along the way, Mathias insisted she stop for a rest and some water. She found she needed both.

"We're almost there," Jedediah said. "Are you all right?"

"Yes, I'm fine. I think I'm looking forward to the return trip, though. After all, the passageways are already dug and most of the time, we'll travel downhill, am I right?"

"Right you are," Jedediah said. "Now, Jolena, just around this corner is the connection to the tunnel that takes us to the bodies of Matthew and Joshua. Prepare yourself for what you're about to see, all right? Remember we're all here with you."

Jo nodded and as Jedediah made the turn, she followed him through the corridor. After a few more turns, he led her into the cave. She found her composure slipping a bit as she gazed down on the remains of the two missing men. Mathias placed a comforting arm around her waist and she wanted so much to wrap herself in his arms in return.

Jo took a deep breath and then dropped to her knees beside the two men, lost to history for well over two hundred years. She envisioned the torment and grief their families suffered as they waited—endlessly waited for a husband, a father, who one day, never returned home. What a difficult thing to endure.

Finally, she stood up, retrieved her camera from out of her backpack, and took the required pictures proving her discovery. The pictures would offer indisputable proof she left everything in the condition she found it. The boys waited patiently for her to finish the task.

As Jolena focused on the bodies of Matthew and Joshua, Mathias turned her around to face him. He tilted her chin upward to meet his gaze. She didn't know these men, but she grieved their loss just the same. "It's all right, love, I'm sure they found their peace a long time ago," he murmured.

Mathias looked over her shoulder just as Paul Sanders rounded the corner. The man entered the main part of the mine like some crazed madman. His arm rose up and without a shred of conscience or hesitation, aimed his pistol straight at Jolena's head. At that point, several things happened almost simultaneously.

Mathias yelled for Sam who stood the closest to Paul. Sam, followed closely by the others, rushed toward Sanders. Despite their speed, they arrived too late. They grabbed hold of him just as he fired the weapon. Yet the force of their impact threw his aim off his intended target and sent the bullet spiraling upward.

While his men bolted toward Paul, Mathias took hold of Jolena and yanked her to the ground to avoid the projectile. Scant seconds later, a burst of fire belched flames in every direction at once. A deafening roar followed. The blast rumbled and shook throughout the mountain. Clouds of dust and falling rock spewed forth inside the cave. Mathias could do naught but watch in horror as the single blast from Paul Sanders's weapon, set off an explosion formulated from centuries of noxious coal dust. The discharge resulted in another cave-in, sealing Jolena inside.

Chapter 28

Instinct drove Mathias to cover Jolena's body with his, but it served no real purpose. Several large rocks battered, and then covered a portion of her body. Using the force of his anger, he sent the offending stones flying toward the wall. They smashed against it, and fell to the ground in crumbling pieces. He brushed the long strands of hair from off her face and inspected her from head to toe, looking for any outward sign of injury.

"Jolena," he whispered. "Jolena, can you hear me. Please—"

She didn't respond to his voice. He could see from the slight rise of her chest that she still breathed. Right now, he would ask no more than that. She still lived and he would fight against any force in heaven or hell to keep her that way. He looked up and found the boys working to chuck the rocks that blocked the passageway. The air inside this chamber wouldn't last, despite the small gap at the top of the rubble. A gap which merely served to prolong the inevitable.

"We've got to get some help," Mathias said. "We can't shift all the rocks in time to save her life."

Sam turned around to face him and with a look of determination on his face said, "Tell me what you want me to do."

"E-mail," William suggested, coming toward them. "What if we send an e-mail to that friend of hers? We can write it so she'll think Jolena penned it. We'll tell her she needs to come straight away and see what she found. Once she hears the details, I'm sure she'll come."

"Yes, we could do that, but what if she doesn't read it soon enough to do us any good?" asked Alexander.

"We'll have to see to it that she *does* read it in time. The only other alternative is to explain the situation to her *personally*," Sam declared through clenched teeth. "Either way, I don't care."

"We may have to go look for her," Jedediah warned. "And then we'll need to make sure she comes out here quickly and finds the right place. I think the best option is to look for someone who's already outside and aware of the ruckus."

"Which is highly unlikely this time of morning," William pointed out. "Still, we'll give it a once-over."

Mathias looked at each of his men and nodded. "Do whatever you have to do. Jolena can't survive in here very long. Just—hurry, Sam, please. I'll stay with her."

At once, the boys gathered in front of the main entrance to the mine. Then, in unison as if they already discussed it, they attempted to take down the wall, using the combined force of their will. The wall didn't so much as rattle in return.

Sam shook his head. "We tried, lads. I think the best thing we can do now is to get that e-mail sent if no one is out there to help us. William, I'll put you in charge of that if we find it the only alternative. Alexander, you'll come with me to Carolyn's lab. We'll see if she's there. Jedediah, you need to make a trail for her to follow once she arrives. We'll meet back here as soon as we have each completed our assignments. And Mathias, take good care of her while we're gone. I can promise you, we'll hurry."

Mathias nodded and as they disappeared, he turned his attention to making Jolena just as comfortable as he could. He had no way of knowing if she sustained internal injuries, so he didn't shift her body very far. For now, he could see to her needs—he could wait—and for the first time since his death, he could pray. Some time later, she finally stirred.

"Mathias—" The moment Jo lifted her shoulders, unbearable pain beset her, and she halted all progress. She didn't know for sure just where she lay. She coughed. Her throat burned and as her hand traveled toward her aching head, she suddenly remembered. They found Matthew and Joshua. And she—

"I'm right here by your side," he whispered.

"What happened?" she asked. The chamber spun around in vicious circles and her head hurt so bad it made her nauseous.

"The bullet from Paul Sanders's gun caused a portion of the ceiling to collapse," he said.

Jo recalled the events though a thick cloudy haze. She remembered Mathias shouting Sam's name, and then—and then she looked over and peered into the darkness. A man stood in the shadows. She couldn't see him clearly. But she did see a gun in his hand. Why did he have a gun?

"The lads have gone to get help. They're going to send an e-mail to Carolyn and tell her you found something important she needs to see. They'll tell her you want her to come right away."

She managed a small smile over the revelation. "Then she'll come." Her eyes closed of their own volition. A semblance of peace settled over her being.

She allowed herself to give in to the tranquility.

"Hang on, Jolena, just a while longer, my love—you must hang on, a little while longer."

****

Time passed, but she didn't how much time. Jo could hear Mathias's voice through the fog in her mind. She loved his voice and he said something—it sounded so important. Her eyes didn't want to open, yet they must. She dug down deep inside and found the strength to make them obey. Dutifully her eyelids fluttered and at last, she gazed into his face. A powerful love shone from his eyes. Just like in her dreams. She could see it. His love gave her the courage to speak. She caressed his jaw, and traced its outline with her fingers. Interesting, she could actually feel it this time—even the stubble. Perhaps she dreamed again.

"Mathias," her voice sounded hoarse. Why?

"Yes?" He took hold of her hand then, only to discover he could actually feel it as if he still lived. Warmth radiated from her fingers as they twined around his own. Lord in heaven, what did that mean?

"I've had a series of dreams—about you and me," she whispered.

He nodded. "Yes."

"You know about them, don't you," she said the words as if stating fact, rather than asking him a question.

"Yes." Without releasing her gaze, he drew her hand to his lips and kissed it gently.

"We're they real?"

"Oh, they were real, my love," he replied.

"All of them?"

"All of them—in their entirety. Each word, each embrace, each kiss." Mathias let go of her hand and

319

stroked her cheek with the back of his fingers. He could see the great effort it cost her to speak.

"Did you mean what you said?" she asked.

"Every word," he replied.

A smile of contentment touched her lips as she closed her eyes.

Mathias gathered her into his arms and cradled her close to his chest. He could still feel her warmth against his body and he could feel every breath she took. Each breath seemed a little shallower than the one before. She kept falling in and out of consciousness and he could do naught but witness her life ebb away, inch by precious inch. He never remembered feeling this helpless in his entire existence.

"Jolena—Jolena, I need you to stay here with me, my love. Please, please don't go—"

****

Dreams meandered into her mind—strange dreams. She didn't know quite what to make of them, nor could she recall them right now. Too much effort to remember. Mathias seemed worried. She could hear it in his voice, but she didn't understand what he said. Thirsty—she wanted something to drink. Her throat burned. She sensed something cool against her lips then. Mathias urged her to drink. He gave her water. Did she ask for it? It didn't matter. The liquid cooled and refreshed her throat. She took a little bit more and then opened her eyes.

"Mathias—"

He tilted her chin upward. "It's about time you woke up, sleepyhead. How are you feeling?"

"Like I'm slipping away," she replied. "To…somewhere…else." The words tumbled out in response to his question, but she didn't know exactly what she meant when she said them.

"No," Mathias said as he cuddled her even closer to his body. "I need you to stay here, with me. You promised. I'm supposed to watch you get old and crotchety remember? You can't go back on that promise. I won't let you."

"You…could just…come away with me…we could go off together…and stay together…forever…just like my parents," she whispered. "You don't have…to stay here. I think maybe, it's…not so bad on the other side."

"I know. We've had this discussion before and when the time is right, we'll walk through the light together, hand in hand, I promise. But not right now, Jolena," Mathias said as he shifted her body more toward him so he could look into her eyes. "Not now. You need to finish what you've begun. We need to take Matthew and Joshua out of here, remember? You don't want them forgotten. What about all of the places we want to see and all of the things we want to do together. Please, Jolena—"

Jo suddenly tightened her grip around his fingers. Her body trembled of its own volition. "I love you, Mathias McGregor, firstborn son of…Adam and Tamar Davies McGregor…I think, I think I always have," she said as suddenly, she drifted away. While she drifted weightlessly toward—something, she could see in panoramic vision, almost every detail of her life, even before it began.

Someone escorted her toward some kind of portal—a portal made of white marble and trimmed in gold. The most amazing garden filled with trees, bushes, flowers, and clear blue water surrounded the beautiful structure. Excitement filled her as she approached it. Her escort told her not to forget her violin or Mathias. What a strange thing to say. How could she ever forget either?

In a millisecond, her entire life passed before her eyes, her family, childhood, Carolyn, her teenage years, the college years, and the death of her parents. She revisited her struggles to make a place for herself in the music world, the friends she made, and the men she dated. The concerts, the places she traveled, finding her house, meeting her boys, and most especially, Mathias. Each precious moment she spent in his company, she relived.

Then as the memories ebbed, she suddenly found herself bathed in a brilliant light that sang to her soul. The enchanting beam encompassed every particle of her being, giving her a tremendous sense of love, peace, and serenity. She wanted nothing more than to touch it, to feel it, to experience it. But not without Mathias. Never without Mathias. As she turned around, away from the light she could no longer see him or even feel his presence. Darkness ruled outside the light and it frightened her. Panic set in. Where did he go? She needed him more than she needed anything else. Even the light paled in comparison.

"Mathias?" she called out. "Mathias!"

****

Jolena's heart raced at an alarming rate. He could feel it beat against his chest and he could see she struggled for each breath she took. Helplessness overtook him, and as he clutched her body tightly against his, he bowed his head—and wept.

"I'm afraid she's dying, Mathias. She's now in the process of crossing over. Such is the reason you can feel her, and in turn, she can feel you."

Mathias looked up at the ethereal being. The man

stood near the entrance of the cave. He'd seen him before, many times throughout the centuries. His presence didn't surprise him now. He shook his head. "No, not like this. You mustn't allow it."

"Despite what you think, this is not your fault," he said.

"Yes, it is." Mathias looked down at Jolena's beautiful face, now so very pale. He stroked her hair. "I should never have asked her help. I shouldn't have involved her. None of this would've happened if we didn't go after the details of Jacob's letter. And really, what difference did any of it make in the end?"

"She held the key to all your questions. Such was destined from the beginning. You now know the reason you sacrificed your life for your country," he replied. "Surely this knowledge has great personal worth."

"Not if it means she needs to sacrifice her life in return," Mathias said.

"I don't understand." His visitor folded his arms against his chest. "She's right you know. I don't see why you can't cross the threshold with her. You'll find it a most amazing experience. What's more, she'll remain at your side for all time in a place void of sorrow and pain."

"Not yet," Mathias argued. "Not in this way. She has only just begun her life. Jolena is still so young, and she has so much left to give—so much to share with the world."

"Share?" He shook his head as if understanding eluded him. "Share what? Are you speaking of her life or her talent?"

"Both," Mathias replied.

"She won't share her life with anyone but you. How can she? She now knows how much you love her, and she loves you just as much in return. She's happier than you can possibly imagine. No one can question the depth of your feelings for each other. Therefore, as long as she's in love with a ghost, she may as well come home," he said.

Voices echoed throughout the maze of hallways. Jo could hear Mathias speaking to someone, but she couldn't find either him or his companion. No matter which way she twisted or turned, she couldn't get any closer to the sound of his voice.

"You can't let her die, please—"

"Don't be silly, Mathias," she silently whispered. "I'm not dying."

"I'm willing—"

Willing? What did he mean by that? She turned a corner and found yet another hallway.

"—if you'll just—"

Jo stopped dead in her tracks. She could hear the raw emotion in the sound of his voice. Something caused Mathias intense pain and anguish. She needed to stop it somehow.

"Mathias," she called out. "Mathias?"

"—love her enough—"

"You know I do— But I can't—"

"—let her go—"

The voice she didn't recognize interfered with her ability to locate Mathias. "Please!" she screamed out the word as she turned a complete circle, all the while keeping her gaze focused upward where the voices originated.

"—sacrifice—"

"Please," Jo whispered the word as a single teardrop fell down her cheek.

"—allow me time—"

Nothing mattered at this moment, but finding Mathias. Something terrible happened. Jo could feel it. She no longer cared about the light or the visions she wanted to share with him, she just wanted *him*—

At that moment, the sound of gurgling water, tumbling forth from a fountain, entered her ears. She turned toward the sound, only to discover an immense hallway. A huge door, twice the size of any she'd ever seen before, stood at the end of it. Somehow, she needed to get to the door and taste the water that lay beyond it.

"—June—"

"—Done—"

How long did it take her to reach the elegant white door in a place where time didn't exist? The voices and echoes fell silent as she took hold of the large golden doorknob, yet it didn't diminish her need to find Mathias. She turned the knob all the way to the right, and opened the door with ease. The luscious fountain lay just outside and she drank deeply from it. The more she drank, the stronger she felt.

Without warning or logic, Jo found herself walking alone inside Laird MacNaughton's castle. She tried so hard to find Mathias, but after checking through each of the rooms, the hallways and inside the bailey, she still couldn't find him. Then it occurred to her—perhaps he waited for her up in the tower. She raced up the stairs, calling his name. But again, she found herself alone. She stepped toward the crenel they shared not so very long ago. Then, looking out over the vastness of the green fields and the beauty of the enchanting forest just beyond it, she suddenly remembered.

Mathias called to her then, and it was as if he called to her from a very great distance away. He wanted her to come to him. He waited for her now, just as he waited for her ever since the day he entered mortality. Joy filled her soul as she hurried toward the sound of his magnificent voice.

Mathias stood by the waterfall. She ran straight into his waiting arms and at once, he gathered her close and began kissing her tenderly, gently. In response, her arms encircled his neck, holding him closer still. She wanted nothing more than for his kisses to go on forever. His lips caressed her cheek as he whispered her name against her ear. She shivered with delight.

Jo slowly opened her eyes, and found Mathias kissed her in truth. She could feel the warmth of his lips against hers, just as she could feel them when she dreamed. He drew back and grinned. She could see the joy in his gaze. Yet at the same time, another emotion revealed itself, something she couldn't quite name. In fact, she shied away from it. She didn't *want* to name it.

"You called me to our waterfall," she murmured.

"I hoped you'd notice," he replied, as his lips grazed against the corner of her mouth.

"Is it a real place?" she asked while her fingertips brushed through his hair.

"Yes, it is." He drew slightly away so he could hold her gaze. "And I want to go back to Scotland—soon, and show it to you so you can see it for yourself. I want you to hear me tell you, without benefit of dreams, just how much I love you, how much I've always loved you. How much I *will always* love you. Promise me you will come, so I can do that. Promise me—"

She managed a feeble smile. "I promise—"

Mathias sought her lips once more, to seal the bargain.

Chapter 29

Jolena rested comfortably in his arms now, and her struggle to breathe eased significantly. She didn't look quite as pale as she did earlier, either. Mathias had no doubt that she would regain her full strength and vitality. The knowledge gave him a measure of comfort, despite the intensity of pain and the cost that accompanied it.

"Mission accomplished. They're here," Sam said as he burst through the rock. "Jed is leading them in now, and they noticed Sanders's car parked close to Jo's."

Mathias turned his head toward the sound of the voices on the other side of the mountain and listened.

"I don't know. According to Jo's directions, the entrance should be right here. Do you see anything?" he could hear Ray ask. His question filled Mathias with relief.

"No, but if she said it's here, then it's here somewhere," Carolyn said.

"Look behind you and you'll see the indentation in the rock, just look behind you," Jedediah whispered the suggestion.

"In here, Ray. Look. She must've gone in here through this opening," Carolyn said. "Do you think Paul followed her in?"

Alexander appeared next to Sam. "Jed is going to take them around to the front. He said we could get her out quicker this way. Sanders caused a lot more damage on the other side, so it will take them significantly longer to dig through if we use that route."

At that moment, from the other side of the mountain, Jedediah coughed and sputtered as if exhausted and then he said, "Did you hear it too?"

"Hear what?" asked Ray, sounding perplexed.

"That explosion. Something happened in there a while ago, man. Dust and dirt flew everywhere. I think someone is in there, because when I jogged along the trail on the other side of the hill someone screamed. The sound was followed by gunfire or maybe even some kind of an explosion—or something."

"Oh no, Jo! Ray, please," Carolyn's voice held panic.

"Did you go in?" asked Ray.

"As far as I could, but, it looks like a cave-in and it's really, really dark the farther in you go. And I can tell you, it goes in quite a ways," he replied, sounding anxious.

"Show us your exact location when all the commotion started," Ray said.

"Who are you calling?" he could hear Carolyn asked now.

"I know someone who has a tractor. He doesn't live far from here. If Jo is in there, we have to get her out quickly," Ray answered. "I'm also calling 9-1-1."

A short while later, Mathias noted the sounds of heavy equipment as the vehicles approached the mine entrance. Once the tractor began digging, a host of people gathered around the area. Soon, every emergency vehicle known to man converged onto the scene.

The lads continued going back and forth, offering suggestions to the rescuers. All the while, Mathias never relinquished his hold on Jolena. Not when he could still feel her in his arms, and not when he needed to take advantage of every precious moment at her side.

The teeth of the tractor bucket scraped along the rocky wall and with each bucket of debris, they inched closer to Jolena's rescue. He leaned down and placed a kiss on her forehead. "Not long now, my love," he said.

Thirty minutes later, the tractor broke through. Mathias could see the crowd of people who stood waiting to enter. Ray and Carolyn huddled together as they waited and discussed Jo's findings.

"If it's everything Jo thinks it is, then it's the most important discovery about the Revolutionary War in this century," Ray said now.

"That pales in significance when it comes to Jo's life, Ray," Carolyn shot back, clearly annoyed.

"That goes without saying," Ray replied in a tone of appeasement.

Mathias agreed. Once they extracted most of the rubble from the entrance, the paramedics squeezed inside. He could do naught but watch as they took Jolena out of his arms, and place her on the gurney. They gave her a cursory exam and checked her vital signs. Unable to wait any longer, Carolyn rushed to her side and took hold of her hand.

"Jo—Jo darling, can you hear me?" She looked up at one of the paramedics when Jolena remained unresponsive. Tears formed in her eyes. "Will she be all right? Her hands are like ice and she's so pale."

The man gave her a pat. "We'll do our best. It might help us if you can answer a few quick questions, though. To begin with, do you know if she is allergic to anything?"

While Carolyn answered questions, Ray inspected

the mine. As he scanned the area, he spied Jo's backpack and her digital camera on the ground. He walked over, picked up the camera, dusted it off, and began going through the photos. They pleased him well enough, and that in turn, would please Jolena.

"Excuse me, Professor Brennan. We're going to have to ask you and Dr. Taylor to wait outside while we remove the rock from the other side. We're aware of the importance of what lies within this chamber. However, we need to get to the other victim. I can promise you, we'll try not to disturb anything, least of all the remains of these men."

"Is Sanders still alive?" he asked.

"For the moment," the paramedic answered.

Once the paramedics had Jolena hooked up to a thing they called "IV" they covered her with blankets and rolled her out to the ambulance. Mathias rode along on the way to the hospital, as did Carolyn. Ray stayed behind to protect the site and watch over the bodies of Matthew and Joshua. The act would please Jolena.

Twenty-four hours later, Jo approached full awareness. She didn't know her present location, but remained aware that Mathias and the boys stood at her side. Part of her wanted to open her eyes and greet them, but exhaustion prevented it. Perhaps she could rest a bit longer and think about all the wondrous things she and Mathias shared in the mine.

In truth, they all transpired, for she could still feel the strength of Mathias's hand as he held her own. Bits and pieces of her experience seemed hazy. She remembered two voices, one belonged to Mathias and one to someone she didn't know. Maybe she made it up, because nothing they said made any real sense. Of course, they probably wouldn't, dreams never did.

The light—she remembered the amazing light, and the hallway and the door. Mathias also admitted knowing about her dreams. She smiled inwardly as she recalled their conversation, his tender, gentle kisses, and the castle in Scotland. Mathias wanted to take her there and she recalled a sense of urgency as he made the request.

Distant voices grew louder, and she turned away from her castle in Scotland as she tried to make sense of the words. One of them said something about "Miss Michaelsson" and "not yet." A door opened, closed, and then footsteps approached ever nearer her bed. Finally, she made the effort and opened her eyes. Mathias received the first of her smiles. He squeezed her hand in return. She took a deep breath and looked over at her doctor.

"Well, it's nice to see you're finally awake, Jo. Care to tell me what you were doing inside that old coal mine which resulted in two cracked ribs, a multitude of contusions, and a pretty severe concussion?" he said as he raised a brow in question.

Jo shot a quick glance at Mathias who simply shrugged. "I don't know, I guess I was feeling a little adventurous," she said as the doctor sat down beside her. When they finished their visit, the doctor asked if she could handle a few visitors.

"Dr. Taylor and her fiancé are waiting outside. They've hovered like a couple of hungry scavengers circling the carcass," he said.

Jo let out a bit of a quiet laughter and nodded. "That sounds like Carolyn, all right."

Moments later, Carolyn rushed through the door, over to her bedside, and took firm hold of her hand.

Debbie Peterson

"You scared me half to death, Jo," she scolded. "Don't you *ever* do anything like that to me again, do you hear me?"

"You needn't worry," she replied. "I think I've had my fill of derring-do for a while."

Carolyn released her hand, sat in the chair the doctor vacated, scooted it closer to the bed, and said, "I'm sorry, but we weren't able to get the file on top your desk, as you asked. The door to your library is locked, and we couldn't find the key."

Confusion set in. She didn't have a lock on the library door, and how did they know about the file?

"When we e-mailed Carolyn, we gave her detailed information about what she would find in the mine," William said. "We also mentioned you had all of your documented evidence dealing with the discovery in a file waiting for her on top your desk. The e-mailed letter asked her to come immediately to the location where she could see everything for herself. We also mentioned you wanted her to take over, once she got there, hoping such a statement would make her come quickly."

"But I couldn't let her come into the library this morning, Jolena," Jedediah added. "I needed to let her see me in order to show them the entrance. If I allowed her to see the painting she would recognize me, and we didn't want to chance having to answer the questions which would surely arise after that."

"That's all right, Carolyn," Jo said after hearing their incredible explanation. "I'll get the file for you when I get out of here."

"The whole thing is so unbelievable," Carolyn said. "I mean, I can't believe you set off to discover the meaning of your grandfather's letter all by yourself. How

332

on earth did you figure it out?"

"I didn't do it by myself, Kay-Kay," Jo murmured as she closed her eyes. "I had a whole team of experts helping me every step of the way."

Mathias chuckled. "I think you have that backwards, my love."

A smile tugged on the corners of Jo's mouth as she drifted away toward Laird MacNaughton's castle, where Mathias waited by a waterfall—

"Aw," she could just barely hear Carolyn whisper. "Poor little thing has gone back to sleep. Well, that's okay. We'll just let her rest now and she can fill us in all of the details when she's better."

****

Four days later, Carolyn whisked her out of the hospital and escorted her home. Once they exited the car, she led her down the walkway, holding tightly to her waist. A difficult thing at best since Mathias had his arm around the other side.

"Careful now," Kay said, "we're almost at the steps."

"You're holding on to me like I'm a ninety-year-old woman," Jo grumbled. "And I can clearly see the steps and am quite able to take myself up them."

Carolyn sighed and shook her head. "Yes, but the doctor said you might suffer through some dizzy spells, due to the concussion and could fall quite easily. Therefore, I'm *not* going to let you walk unassisted."

"Might, Kay-Kay, *might* is the keyword here. If I needed a nursemaid, I would've let Nancy come and hover over me," she said, as she turned toward Mathias and rolled her eyes. Mathias chuckled in response.

"Don't be such a grouch. The only reason she conceded on that issue, is because I promised I would stay with you for a few days," she replied. "Besides, I don't want you to think of me as your nursemaid. I have an ulterior motive, you know. I'm your best friend and I have only a few short weeks to plan the perfect wedding, and you, my dear are going to help me finish all the details."

True to her word, they spent the next several days discussing bridesmaids, dresses, flowers, decorations, photographs, and food. In fact, if Carolyn showed her even so much as one more cake design, she'd throw up for sure.

"There," said Carolyn as she hung up the phone. "I think I've made my last order. We've completed everything we can possibly do for now. Can you believe it? We're done until it's time for the dress fittings."

Jo applauded. "And it's about time, too. I'll give you this much, though. You've taught me that elaborate weddings are not worth the effort. If I ever get married, you can better well believe, I'll elope."

Just as the words left her mouth, she glanced over at Mathias. A look of pain briefly marred his features. Surely, he didn't think she actually meant she wanted to get married. He couldn't think it—

The sound of the doorbell stole her attention. Carolyn got up from the sofa and hurried to answer it. Moments later, Ray greeted his future bride. Then, as they entered the family room, Ray extended his arms toward her.

"Good morning, Jo. How's my favorite patient today?" he asked and then leaned over to kiss her cheek.

"Absolutely fabulous now that we have the wedding chores complete," she said.

Ray turned toward Carolyn with a look of delighted

surprise. "All done?"

"Yep," Carolyn said with an ear-to-ear grin. "See what two girls can do when they put their mind to it?"

"Jo, you're a lifesaver." Ray winked as he shoved a hand inside his pocket. "You got me out of a whole lot of trouble, and I'm forever beholden to you."

Jo waved a hand. "Think nothing of it. It's the least I could do since I robbed you of your intended for almost an entire week. How are you holding up without her?"

"I've had plenty of things to keep me busy," he said as he sat in the chair, opposite them. "In fact, one of those reasons is why I showed up much earlier than expected today. I need to discuss something with you."

Carolyn raised a brow. "Really? What's up?"

He glanced at Carolyn before turning his attention to Jo. "Your discovery has garnered world-wide attention, Jo. As you know it's been all over the news every day since the um—accident. Anyway, the Smithsonian is going to display all of the artifacts found in the mine. They want to make the 'Tinker's Toy' exhibit a really grand affair."

Carolyn's mouth dropped. "That's great news, Ray."

"Yes, it is," he continued. "They would also like to display your grandfather's letter and as many of Jacob's personal artifacts that you're willing to share. Hopefully, they said, all of them. They've prepared a contract for you. The agreement states that should you ask for the return of any or all of the items, or should they no longer wish to display them—which is highly unlikely— everything will revert to the Michaelsson Family Trust. And what's more, they're prepared to pay you quite handsomely. They are willing to pay a great deal more, for complete ownership of the letter."

Jo looked over at Mathias and the boys. They looked pleased with the arrangement and nodded their agreement. The Smithsonian could keep all of her grandfather's artifacts well preserved and safe from theft. Not to mention, she could place the proceeds in a separate account, giving the boys access to the funds, so they didn't feel the need to trade away their things if they wanted to buy something—like a horse, for insistence.

"I don't have a problem with that," she said. "Letter, included."

"Excellent choice." Ray withdrew his cell phone from his pocket. "I'll call and let them know. Oh, and before I forget, I want to tell you that the descendants of Matthew and Joshua have come forward to claim their remains. They're having them buried at Arlington. The media will cover that event, as well."

"That's very good news," Jo said as she connected her gaze to Mathias's. "They deserve no less."

"And Jo." Ray placed a gentle hand on top of hers. "I just want to let you know before you see it on the news—Paul Sanders can never threaten you again. You're safe."

Jo shook her head. "But, I still don't understand how he learned about the mine in the first place."

Ray and Carolyn exchanged glances. Carolyn nodded as if granting permission and he said, "Well, several months ago, Paul hired a private investigator to follow you. He called the authorities right after the news broadcasted the attempt Paul made on your life. He said he had no idea Paul meant you any harm. You see, Paul hired him once before to track his ex-wife and he believed this a similar circumstance. Once he led Sanders to the opening at the back of the mountain, Paul paid him off and dismissed him. It is my understanding that he fully cooperated with the authorities."

"Oh, I see," she said.

Later that afternoon, Carolyn finally made ready to leave. As Ray picked up the last of her bags, she said, "My wedding is coming up sooner than you realize. I'm leaving you alone against my better judgment. Don't disappoint me by doing something foolish that will keep you from attending."

"Don't worry," Jo said as she ushered them out the door. "Nothing can keep me from holding you steady on your big day. I know you. You're going to need all the assistance you can get."

****

Several weeks later, she did manage to keep Carolyn on her feet—several times throughout the day, in fact. Mathias bore it all with patience and good humor. Despite her stress, Carolyn looked beautiful, and the wedding service culminated without incident.

Following the ceremony, they entered the reception hall, lavishly decorated in several shades of blue, and trimmed in white. She dutifully stood next to Carolyn in the bridal line while they greeted the many guests. Cameras clicked incessantly and she posed for so many pictures, Carolyn would need to number them in volumes. Then, when at last the time arrived to throw the bridal bouquet, Jo made certain that Carolyn's niece caught it, even though Kay threw it straight to her.

The bridal dance followed, after which several couples joined them on the dance floor. Jo took that moment to get a glass of ice water. As she stood next to the table, she caught sight of Carolyn's great-aunt hobbling toward her with the aid of her cane. She had a gentle smile on her face and—a smidgen of pity. This sweet old lady, now in her eighties, seemed a part of her and Carolyn's life for as long as she could remember. They both loved her dearly.

"How are you doing tonight, Jolena?" she asked in a voice that quivered with age.

"I'm wonderful, Aunt Helen. How are you? I haven't seen you for such a long while, and I've missed you," Jo replied and then leaned down to kiss her affectionately on the cheek.

"Oh, I can't complain. I can still get around on my own accord and no one has put me in a home just yet, so I suppose all is well for the moment," she said.

"Aunt Helen," Jo said in mock sternness. "You know very well, not a single soul in your family would allow you to go to a nursing home. After all, why should a nursing staff have all of the fun?"

Helen laughed and nodded. She pivoted a bit then, so she could look Jo fully in the eye. "Tell me, sweetheart. Are you seeing anyone seriously right now?"

Jo shook her head, knowing her question related to someone who actually breathed. "No, no I'm not."

"Are you even dating at all?" she asked.

"Nope, not for quite some time now." Jo smiled. Helen asked the question each time they met. The adorable woman meant well, and Jo found she simply couldn't take offense.

Helen paused for a moment then, as if to choose her words. "Well, you know Jolena, I've come to realize, not all of us are meant to find our soul mate during mortality, and that knowledge gives me a measure of comfort on my lonelier days.

"You must remember, we've suffered through so many terrible wars throughout the centuries, and so many wonderful young men lost their lives in defense of their homes and countries. I wouldn't hesitate to say they numbered in the millions. I firmly believe they need someone to love, too. Perhaps the man destined for you died during one of those wars, and is waiting for you on the other side." She patted Jo's hand, which rested on the table.

"Actually, Aunt Helen, you're right. Mine died during the Revolutionary War, June 16th, 1778, right here in Pennsylvania." Jo took another sip of her water as she maintained eye contact. Perhaps the little devil inside prompted the admission, but she just couldn't help herself. She allowed herself a smile as she took in the woman's shocked expression. Nevertheless, Aunt Helen wouldn't repeat the statement to a living soul.

Caught up in the fun of the moment, Mathias manifested his form to Aunt Helen. With a possessive hand around Jolena's waist, he gave the woman a nod and flashed a grin. Her mouth dropped, as she looked him over from head to toe. He gave her a really good look too. Once she couldn't possibly dismiss his presence as mere imagination, he winked and faded away.

"Oh, it looks like I have one more picture to pose for," Jo said as she pointed a finger at Carolyn who frantically motioned her toward the wedding party. "Perhaps we'll have another chance to chat later?"

"Not if I have anything to say about it," Mathias whispered. He'd wanted to get Jolena all to himself for a while now. She looked exceptionally beautiful in the gown she wore tonight. The shade of blue she wore matched the color of her eyes to perfection and as the only adornment to the dress she wore the pendant he gave her for Christmas.

His lovely lady smiled and then hurried away to get the last of the pictures over with. She seemed just as anxious to spend the remainder of her evening with him. While the camera snapped, he approached the leader of the small orchestra that provided the music. He leaned close to his ear and whispered his request. Once the photographer declared the session complete, Mathias made his way to Jolena's side. On a whim, he changed into a black tuxedo. Her mouth opened in surprise, and then curved into a dazzling smile.

Mathias offered his hand and said, "After all this nonsense, it looks as if you could use a bit of fresh air, shall we?"

He tucked her hand into the crook of his arm, led her through the open doors and outside. The floor, decorated with scores of flowers and lights, remained empty. The feat took a great deal of effort on his part. While Jolena performed her duties as maid of honor, he visited each guest and made that very suggestion. They all complied.

He wanted to make this evening just as perfect for her as he possibly could. Despite his earlier request inside the mine, she found it impossible to return to Scotland any before the end part of June, too late to do him any good. But his disappointment didn't matter. He really didn't need the forest or the waterfall behind the castle to tell her how very much he loved her.

"Care to dance the night away with me, my love?" he asked as the first strains of "Greensleeves" wafted out of the reception hall. Her instant look of surprise mingled with delight made his efforts all worthwhile.

"I would love to dance with you." The miracle of the mine had yet to evaporate completely. She could still feel a trace of Mathias's body when he held her.

Humor filled his eyes as he fused his gaze to hers. "You look exceptionally lovely this evening, Jolena. I must confess it truly surprises me that someone hasn't whisked you away and made you his wife by now. Although, I'm sure countless numbers have tried."

She giggled, but at the same time, managed a shrug. "I suppose there may have been one or two along the way."

"Did you find them all so very distasteful then?"

A breath of laughter escaped as she dropped her head close to his chest. "No, Mathias, no one on this earth, past, present or future, could ever take the place you already have in my heart. Didn't you know? Haven't you guessed? You're the man I've waited my whole life to find."

He held her all the tighter. "And I have waited for you all of mine. I love you Jolena Leigh Michaelsson, from the very depths of my soul. No matter what comes—no matter what happens in the future, somewhere in your heart, you must *always* remember that," he whispered.

The intensity, with which he spoke the words, drew Jo's gaze upward. Something entered his eyes then that—

The desire to understand the expression abruptly ended as Mathias lowered his lips to hers. As they touched, an exquisite electrical shock filled her entire being, beginning somewhere in the pit of her stomach. The current spewed forth in fluid warmth, which would rival any volcano eruption known to mankind. The heat encompassed her soul in every direction at once. Not even in her dreams did she experience such a tender, passionate kiss. She held completely still so the kiss could linger for as long as he willed it so.

Finally, he broke free and captured her gaze. She shook her head in wonder. "Oh, Mathias, I never believed that I could feel such—" She stopped as if searching for words.

He chuckled softly. "Just shut up, Jolena, we can talk later," he said as he once again sought her lips.

He didn't need to ask her twice.

Chapter 30

"Could I talk to you for a minute, Jolena? I don't mean to interrupt you, but it's getting late, and I need to talk to you before you go to bed," Jedediah said.

"Of course. I just finished practicing, anyway." Jo could see from his expression alone that he needed to tell her something important. Something he found difficult to say. She put her violin away and sat down in one of the leather chairs. "Why don't you sit beside me?" She patted the empty chair.

Jedediah simply nodded and sat down. He lifted a hand to his mouth and gave it a rub. Dakota inched forward and looked up expectantly. He stroked the dog's head and neck.

"Jolena, I want to thank you for everything you've done for me, and most especially for your help in solving our final mission. You put so much time and effort into helping us and you risked your life in order to get it done. You've given so much of yourself from the moment you entered this house and never once asked for anything in return. This house is bright and cheerful again, and you've made us feel as if we're all part of your family."

"You *are* part of my family, Jedediah. And because we're family, you don't have to thank me for anything." Jo stopped short as Jed held up a hand to halt her words.

"Yes, I do—because you see—because this is my last opportunity to do so, at least for a while, that is."

She could see he had trouble meeting her gaze, and it alarmed her. "Your last opportunity?" Jo shook her head. "I don't know what you mean."

Finally, Jedediah looked up and met her gaze head on. "Never once in my life, have I run away from anything because of the difficulty of the task, and I don't want to start now. So, I'll just come right out and say what I have to say."

Jo placed her hand lightly on top of his. "You know you can tell me anything, Jedediah. I'll understand, I promise."

"Thank you, because I'm going to need your understanding. I've come to tell you... You see, I think I'm going to go ahead and take that next step. I'm...I'm finally ready to let go of my life here and get on with whatever comes next." He paused and peered into her eyes as if gauging her reaction.

At once Jo's throat constricted while a lump formed and the formation of tears stung her eyes. The day she dreaded finally arrived. Common sense told her the boys shouldn't remain earthbound indefinitely, and she didn't want them to stay behind once she met her demise. But did he have to go right now? She found she could only nod in response to his words.

"The spirit pouch I gave you for Christmas," he said. "I never did give you all of the details surrounding it, and I would like to share a little bit more about that with you now. The girl, Runs-Like-a-Deer, as her people called her, gave me the pouch. After she converted to Christianity, my father gave her the name of Rachel. She's very pretty, Jolena, just like you. And just like you, she's gentle and kind to everyone she meets. To this day, she keeps a special place in my heart. I've never said this to anyone else, but I think—I think maybe I might've married her, if she didn't die of the yellow fever, and of course, if I didn't die myself.

"I'm telling you this because ever since I gave you the pouch, I've seen her from time to time. I think it's because I finally let go of the past and faced myself forward. Every now and again, I look up, and I can see her gazing at me with this beautiful smile. She beckons me to join her, and I want to go where she is. I didn't consider it before, because we needed to solve the details of our final mission. We wanted to know and to understand what we left undone and whether or not dying for it mattered.

"The mystery is solved now and I've begun to think—well, Mathias has you, and he won't need me around as much anymore. I don't know what's there on the other side, and I don't know if once you cross over, you can ever come back to say hello. But if I can come back from time to time—then I will, I promise.

"However, if for some reason I can't, please know, Jolena, I will always keep you in my thoughts and the love for you in my heart until such time as we meet again," he said.

Tears streamed down Jo's cheeks. She couldn't stop them. "When do you think—you might go?" she asked passed the lump in her throat.

"Soon," he said, nodding more as if to himself than to her. "My next opportunity is coming up in a while, and when it comes, I need to take it."

"I love you, Jed, and—and even though I'll miss you, please know, I wish you all the happiness with Rachel—" Jo presented a small smile through her tears."

Sensing she needed some time to reconcile his

unexpected announcement, Jed kissed her on the cheek and disappeared. She remained in the chair long after he vacated the room. The tears continued falling as she considered everything he said, many times over. What did he mean by "the next opportunity"? For whatever reason, she concluded that a ghost could leave at will. Yet, he said it would come in "a while." How much time encompassed a while? As she extended a hand toward the box of tissue, the desk calendar caught her eye. Her hand hung mid-air as she locked onto the date. June fifteenth screamed at her from off the page as if trying to grasp her attention. Come tomorrow morning, Mathias and her boys would pass the anniversary of their death.

That knowledge triggered a memory of something she read long ago. She read it on one of the many ghostly Web sites Carolyn sent her shortly after she met Mathias. One particular site presented theories about the various types of haunting. She got up from her seat, circled behind the desk, sat down, and turned on the computer. Minutes later, she opened her bookmarked file of ghost sites.

"Come on, Jo," she murmured as she scrolled down the alphabetical list of names. "Which one is it?" Finding the right one took forever, but finally, she found the one she sought. She spied the button marked *Residual Haunting* and clicked.

"We define 'Residual Haunting' as photographic scenes from the past. Scenes that play repeatedly, nothing deviating from the original occurrence. The ghosts are not aware of any changes to the location or the presence of mortals. There are those who believe such a haunting is an imprint in time, or for lack of a better explanation, 'films' left hanging in the very place and atmosphere in

which they occurred. These traumatic events play repeatedly, most often on the anniversary of its occurrence though evidence also suggests they can occur more frequently.

Recent findings propose an alternative theory for such occurrences. It is believed by some in the paranormal field of science, ghosts who have chosen to remain behind, are given yet another opportunity to escape this earthly sphere, once the event of their death is replayed in full on the anniversary it transpired. That they are, in fact, aware of their surroundings and everyone in it, be they mortal or spirit. In a sense, they exist in two planes, simultaneously. They can see their environment as it was and as it is. Yet, they focus on the former. Evidence reveals that—"

"Are you all right?" asked Mathias, as he suddenly appeared, standing at her side.

Jo jumped at the sound of his voice and immediately turned off the screen. Yet, as she turned and gazed into his eyes, she could see his concern. She bit down on her lips and shook her head.

As she vacated her seat, she folded her arms against her chest and walked toward the painting. She stopped in front of the settee and absorbed every detail of the scene Brady O'Connor painted.

Come tomorrow, Jedediah would leave her with precious memories, a few amazing pictures, his treasured spirit pouch, and this painting. Sadness washed over her anew.

"I just didn't expect it." She wiped away the tears with the palm of her hand. "I'm sorry. I know this is silly. I'm happy, truly happy Jedediah is reuniting with the woman he loves. He deserves to find happiness with

Rachel. Yet, I'm going to miss having him around." She sniffed. At once Mathias stood behind her. She could feel him.

"I know," he said.

He wrapped his arms around her and drew her close to his heart. And it occurred to her then that she could feel him as she did inside the mine. She wouldn't question the gift, for right now she needed the comfort he offered. After a moment, he led her to the settee, and once they sat down, he settled her against his chest. Comfort and warmth enveloped her as her thoughts wandered to Jedediah and the experience he would have come the morning.

As a thousand questions tangled themselves up inside her mind she finally said, "I have so many things I need to ask and I've yet to tell you everything that happened inside the mine. I have questions about that incident and I hope you can answer some of them for me as perhaps you experienced something similar."

A very long silence followed the request, and just as she drew away to discover the reason, he kissed the top of her head.

"It's very late, Jolena. You can hardly keep your eyes open now. Why don't we wait until the morning? Perhaps we can go for a ride and we'll talk about everything you want to talk about then, all right?"

Jo's eyelids grew heavier as each second ticked off the clock. Mathias's suggestion seemed reasonable enough, and she nodded in agreement. She could ask him about his reluctance to answer her questions tomorrow. "Okay, just don't keep me waiting—"

Once in bed, dreams overtook all sense of logic and reason. Strange dreams. She walked outside in the darkness of night, in her pajamas and barefoot, heading toward the barn. Nothing seemed more important at that moment, than brushing Lacy. But why, she couldn't say. She stopped at the barn doors and picked up her grooming bag before going inside. Lacy nickered in greeting. She scooped up a handful of oats and let her eat them from her hand. Afterward, she took hold of the brush.

"Hello, sweetheart," she said, as she began grooming her coat. Lacy nuzzled her head against her chest in return. Suddenly then and without warning, William and Alex appeared in the stall next to Lacy's. She couldn't imagine why they would do such a bizarre thing. Why did they choose to appear in Beadurinc's stall? And—where did Beadurinc go?

"Oh! You scared me there for a minute. What are you doing out here? Did you come looking for me?" she asked as she looked from one to the other.

They shot each other a look of dread. Once again, she could feel her throat tighten in anticipation of their words. She lowered her hand, yet still clung to the brush she held.

"I have to tell you, that for all the world, you look just like Jedediah did when he told me goodbye," she said.

William cast his eyes downward and nodded. "We're finding it's not an easy thing to say, nor an easy decision to make," he admitted. "In point of fact, we've just now made the decision, or we would've told you in person, just as Jedediah did. But the time for that is past, I'm afraid."

A sorrowful smile tugged at Alexander's mouth as he placed a hand against her cheek. "You see, dear friend, here of late we've come to feel we've accomplished all we need to accomplish. We've seen everything we need to see. There's no longer a reason or purpose for us to remain on this side."

"You know, since you've graced this household with your presence, we haven't even had the desire to do any serious haunting. So what's left for a self-respecting ghost to do, huh?" asked William, in a sweet attempt to tease.

Jo nodded because she understood their feelings on the matter. Although she tried very hard not to cry, the tears fell anyway.

"Seriously, Jolena," William said as he brushed away the first of her tears. "We wouldn't have arrived at this moment, if not for you. We can't thank you enough for giving us this sense of freedom. At long last, we're ready to join our families and take on whatever comes next."

First Jedediah, now William, and Alex. Did Sam lurk somewhere in the shadows waiting to pounce? If so, her heart just might break.

Escape!

The word swirled around inside her mind.

Run away—

"Jolena—"

They called to her repeatedly, but she needed to escape this pain—run away from it. How could she bear it? All at once, she clung to Lacy's neck and without aid of bridle or bareback pad, raced for the hills, clinging to her mane. The hills morphed into the beach she shared with Mathias and she turned her mount toward the curve, knowing he'd be there. Right now, she needed him. She needed his arms around her. She needed his strength and his comfort. Nothing else mattered.

He stood waiting for her by the rock. As she approached him, she slid off Lacy's back and ran toward him. At once, he gathered her into his arms, and she clung to him with all the fierceness she could muster.

"Mathias," she cried. "Everyone is leaving me, and it just hurts."

"I know, shh—don't cry," he whispered into her ear. "I promise you, everything is going to be all right, you'll see." His lips crashed down on hers. Within those kisses, she sensed not only the power of his love, but also a feeling of—of—*desperation!* And then, as he drew away, she stepped back. That same desperation filled his eyes. The now familiar look of intense pain and suffering marred his features. What did that mean? She struggled to make sense of it.

Understanding arrived very slowly. No, her heart screamed. No, surely not. He wouldn't leave her. He wouldn't. He promised. She shook her head as her hands flew to her face, covering her mouth. A pitiful wail escaped her lips. She squeezed her eyes shut.

"No! You promised," she choked out the words as the tears began anew. "You promised to stay with me forever. Oh, you promised…"

"Circumstances beyond my control negated that promise," he murmured as his arms encircled her waist, needing to feel her in his arms, needing to feel her body close to his one last time. She backed away from his embrace and shook her head. "Circumstances? What circumstances would nullify your promise? I need you, Mathias. Don't you understand? I love you so much it hurts, and if you leave me, you'll leave behind a pain that will never go away. Not ever."

Mathias cursed under his breath and then shook his

351

head. "No, you'll find someone else, and you'll love him and he'll love you. How could he help it?" His hand grazed the length of her cheek. "You're so very beautiful, inside and out. He'll be so lucky to have you and to share your life. Together you'll raise a houseful of kids and all the while, you'll play your violin for those who need to hear it. You'll live life as intended."

"You're wrong." She shook her head and lifted her chin in defiance. "I will never love anyone but you. You can't force that to happen just because you say so. Yes, you can leave me, but I will never give my heart to anyone else. Don't you understand? You have already filled every corner of my heart and every particle of my soul. There's no room, or desire for anyone else. If you leave me, you'll leave only a mere shadow in your wake, and I'll live out the rest of my days in pain and sorrow. The music inside my soul *will* die!"

He caught her into his arms and despite her struggle to free herself, he held her there until she finally gave in and buried her face against his chest. His eyes closed in anguish as she sobbed. How he wished he didn't have to leave her.

"No, you won't, because I won't leave you suffering. Listen to me now, Jolena," he crooned into her ear. "When you wake up, you won't remember any of the dreams we've shared. You won't remember anything that will give you pain. You'll only remember the deep and abiding friendship of five ghosts, whom, through your tireless efforts, you gave peace and contentment after centuries of torment."

She shook her head. "No."

"I love you, Jolena Leigh Michaelsson, I've always loved you, and I will continue to love you for all time.

When you cross the portal, leaving your mortality behind you, many, many years from now, should you find you still love me as much as you do this moment, I'll be waiting for you. I promise," he vowed.

He couldn't bear the pained expression in her eyes. Yet, he couldn't deny himself one final kiss either. He poured all his love and all of his passion into the kiss. She returned it in kind. And though he wished it could continue, he could feel the all-too familiar draw of his past taking him back through the centuries. A draw over which he had no control.

"I have to go now," he murmured. "I'll see you on the other side, my love. Somewhere, deep down inside, remember that I love you."

Despair consumed her as Mathias faded from her view. His pain etched itself into her heart and settled beside her own. "No, Mathias," she whispered with steely resolve when she could no longer see him. "You hold no power to make me forget. I will never forget—not ever."

The words echoed in her mind as her eyelids fluttered open. Despite the intensity of the pain it caused, she committed this last dream to memory by reliving it many times over in the darkness of her bedroom. Yet, merely memorizing each moment didn't seem good enough.

She tossed back the covers and slid out of bed. Dakota whimpered as he rose to his feet and followed her out of the room. Together, they made their way into the library. The house had an empty, eerie feeling. She ignored it. Right now, she needed to record each experience, so she would have them in her possession all the days of her life. Despite Mathias's wishes, she would never allow herself to forget. She would create a journal of memories. All of her feelings, all of the dreams, her daily interactions, the wondrous moments inside the mine chamber—

She gasped as a wave of disjointed images stormed into her consciousness. The mine!

Suddenly, those little wisps of memory spread like liquid silver inside her mind. They filled every crack and crevice of the missing pieces. Before she walked through that magnificent door and over to the fountain, she could hear Mathias's voice. He talked to someone. His words didn't make sense at the time. What exactly did he say? Let's see, she remembered him saying, "You can't let her die, please—I'm willing—if you'll just—you know I do—but I can't—allow me time—done—"

And the other voice said, "Love her enough—let her go—sacrifice—June—"

Jo drew in a breath as pieces of the mystery fell neatly into place. Mathias made a deal with someone in the mine. Whom? His guardian angel—hers—the angel of death? Did it matter? That man, whoever he was, allowed her life to continue, but only if Mathias loved her enough to let her go in return. To sacrifice his desire to remain with her, so she could live life in the normal sense of the word.

No wonder he so desperately wanted to return to Scotland by the end of May. Their clock relentlessly ticked off the minutes they could share the moment she left the chamber. She could see now that he strived to fill each of those moments with an amazing array of beautiful memories.

Yet he made those memories for his own benefit, for he desired to leave her with none of them. Just so she wouldn't grieve…

She placed her elbows on the desk, buried her head in her hands, and through a flood of tears, gave in to her sorrow. She sobbed as intense pain wracked her body while her bleeding heart ripped into a thousand tiny pieces.

Chapter 31

Then, a sudden rebellion overtook her grief. Mathias made a deal with someone. Perhaps she could make one herself. Just what would the possessor of the unknown voice think about that? Surely, she had a say in all of this. How dare they map out her life without asking her opinion or consent! How dare they act as if they had the right to control her decisions— Somehow, she needed to get to the forest and, and—

And do what, Jolena? the voice inside her head mocked.

What made her think she could change anything at all? She glanced at her computer. The article—she didn't finish reading the article. Perhaps she could find the help she needed if she finished reading it.

She activated the screen button. Since she didn't shut the computer down last night, it remained right where she left it. She placed her focus on the final paragraph.

"Recent findings propose an alternative theory for such occurrences. It is believed by some in the paranormal field of science, ghosts who have chosen to remain behind are given yet another opportunity, each year, to escape this earthly sphere once the event of their death is replayed in full on the anniversary it transpired. That they are, in fact, aware of their surroundings and everyone in it, be they mortal or spirit. In a sense, they exist in two planes, simultaneously. They can see their

environment as it was and as it is. Yet, they focus on the former. Evidence reveals that mortals, who are sensitive to ghosts, can break the vicious cycle by intervening before the moment of death occurs. Click on the following links to read supporting case studies, which detail—"

Jo glanced at the clock. Mathias told her he met with Elisabeth Weidmann about daybreak. Once her grandmother gave him the note, he gathered the boys and raced toward her grandfather's home. She didn't have time to read case studies, not if she wanted to intervene *before* the moment of his death. But how? The question nagged at her as she hurried into her bedroom, threw on a pair of jeans and a T-shirt. She didn't have time for shoes. Dakota followed close at her heels as she raced barefoot down the stairs, and out the back door. In her haste, she left it wide open.

Lacy snorted and fussed inside her stall as she continually called out to Beadurinc and her other stall mates who didn't answer. The barn stood empty, save the mare Mathias gave her. She grabbed her bridle and tossed it over the horse's head. Her hands shook as she fed the chinstrap through the buckle. The task took twice as long as it should.

"Not now, Jo," she berated herself. "We don't have time for butter fingers."

Finally, she swung up on the horse's back, ignoring the bareback pad altogether. "Come on, Lace, we've got to go and get our guys." Moments later, she raced for the trail that would take her to the place of Mathias's death. A sense of urgency accompanied the ride. Dakota understood, and kept up with the pace of her horse.

How she wished she had the time to read those case studies. She didn't know what to do once she got there.

Just how did one go about "intervening" in the death of a ghost, who by definition is already dead? Should she ask the soldiers to put their weapons down and go back from whence they originated? What if she couldn't find the exact place again or what if she couldn't see Mathias once she arrived? And the question that cut the deepest, what if she arrived too late?

No. She refused to consider that possibility. She had to arrive on time. She just had to. With a gentle pressure of her heels, she urged her mare ever faster. Fifteen minutes later, she arrived in front of Lacy's former home. The herd of horses inside the fenced pasture recognized her as they approached. Lacy answered their calls. And then suddenly, an idea formed in her mind. An absurd idea, but a great idea if it worked.

She turned the reins to the right and led Lacy over to the gate. Dakota tilted his head and gazed into her eyes. She patted Lacy on the neck, and said, "I'm going to need you both. We're going to herd those horses straight into the English army. Whatever you do, don't let me down." She leaned down, flipped the latch, and swung the gate open.

Jo rode through the gateway and turned sharply to the right. She needed to get behind the horses just as fast as she could. Once she positioned herself, she drew the reins upward and began twirling them in large circles above her head. All the while, she whistled and shouted commands behind the startled horses. The combined sounds made them panic and at once, the herd tore out of the gate. She raced past them then and with the help of Dakota's continuous barks, turned the horses toward the mountains. The dog understood her directions, and perhaps he sensed something more.

Several times, he turned his head, his ears forward as if something caught his attention. Did he hear the sounds of the English soldiers as they approached? Because if he did, that meant they had yet to confront Mathias and her boys. She leaned forward and encouraged her horse. "Hurry, Lacy! We have to hurry—"

Time—How much of it did she have left? Did she follow the correct path? She could only hope she did, as she relentlessly drove the horses toward the forest. Dakota could now hear something else. He skidded to a halt and adjusted the direction of his gaze. Yet, with the ruckus made from stampeding horses, she could hear nothing but the thunderous sound of hooves as they pounded against the ground. "Please," she said aloud, "Please help me get there in time."

Just then, an unexpected voice rang out. "I've a mind to take the lot of them to hell with us, Mathias, starting with that one, right there."

Jo gasped as Sam's voice fearlessly roared out the threat. She could almost see his intimidating look of deadly calm. Shots rang out as she broke through the small clearing. She rode straight through them hoping the act would supply the needed interference. Yet, the vast number of English Redcoats caused her a moment of panic. As the horses trampled through the area, several of the soldiers dissipated underneath the hooves of the horses. Dakota ran straight for Jedediah, stopping long enough to lunge at one of the soldiers who threatened him with bayonet. The man vanished.

She hurried around to the front of the herd to turn them around. Seeing the need, Dakota joined her, nipping at the heels of those who disobeyed her orders. Seconds later, the horses turned around and hastened back through the clearing, heading for home. The bewildered English soldiers that remained appeared unsure of themselves and their purpose. One by one, they disappeared, leaving only her boys—and they looked just as stunned as the group of English soldiers. Her Rangers dismounted then and walked toward her, clearly puzzled, but she only had eyes for Mathias.

She slid off Lacy, suddenly unsure of what to do next. Could one walk into a film from the past? For that matter, which time and place held them at this moment, now or then? It seemed as if they approached her, but did they see her or did they see the light? Suddenly, Mathias quickened his pace, stepping ahead of the others and extended his arms wide open in invitation. He seemed surprised, relieved, and delighted all at the same time.

She raced into his arms and clung to him because she could feel his arms as they wrapped around her—not flesh and bone, yet somehow far more solid than spirit. She discovered she could rest her head against his chest without penetrating his form. "Mathias— Please, please, don't go. Not without me," she cried.

"Jolena," he whispered against her hair. Then, he took a small step back and cupped her face with his hands. He fused his gaze with hers. "What are you doing here? I don't—"

"I'm so sorry about the disruption, but I had to stop this event," she murmured as her gaze briefly swept over the woodland. "I couldn't let you go without a fight. Especially since nobody bothered to ask my opinion on the matter. I hope I didn't mess things up for the boys. I didn't mean to if I did, but—"

"What are you talking about?" he asked.

"I overheard the two of you talking inside the mine

chamber. I didn't figure it all out until this morning, but I found this article on the ghost Web site and it said a mortal could intervene and I needed to try, I had to try—because—well, because I can't live without—"

Mathias stopped her incoherent babble, and she did babble, with a most exhilarating kiss. That connection filled her with delectable warmth from head to toe. Finally, he broke away and weaved his fingers through the length of her tangled, wind-blown hair.

"Now, my love, let's try this once again and this time from the top."

"Come, Mathias, it's not that difficult to understand. I believe Jolena is protesting our arrangement."

She and Mathias turned toward the sound of the unexpected voice. The same voice, in fact, that talked to Mathias inside the mine. For lack of a better description, the man—glowed. The glow didn't come from around him. His entire being radiated the light from within his body. Surely, he couldn't be the gruesome angel of death she always pictured in her mind. But just who or what—

Mathias gave the man a respectful nod as he clutched her just a little tighter. "Grandfather—"

"Grandfather?" Her mouth fell open as she looked from one McGregor to the other.

"Angus McGregor," Mathias clarified.

"Indeed," he responded as he strolled toward them. "And I've been trying to corral this scalawag for over two centuries. I almost had him this time."

Jolena stepped in front of Mathias in a desire to keep him away from the ethereal being. "No, please. You can't take him. He's my very life—the very reason for my existence. If you're taking him, then you have to take me too."

Debbie Peterson

Angus chuckled as he folded his arms against his chest. "I can see that. So, what to do? Hmm. He wants her to stay put and live out the length of her life and she's willing to go beyond to remain at his side." He rubbed his hand against his white beard as if considering the dilemma. His gaze traveled back and forth between them.

The hands of the eternal clock paused and time, quite literally, stood still. How she arrived at this absolute knowledge, she didn't know. She held her breath waiting for his decision, because he had a say in the matter. In fact, he had the *only* say in the matter.

Angus turned around to face the other boys. "It's my understanding that you three"—pointing to Jed, William and Alex in turn—"are of a mind to come home. I assume this is still your wish?"

Each of them nodded while sparing her a glance. "Good, good. You have family anxiously awaiting your arrival. And Alexander, Charity is growing a bit impatient with you, I might add."

"Sam?" he asked, amid the chuckles.

Sam gazed steadily into Angus's eyes for several moments and then grinned. "Absolutely not. Unlike William and Alex, I haven't accomplished everything I want to accomplish, and I haven't seen everything I want to see. I believe I'll stay put, if it's all the same to you, sir."

"Ever loyal, Samuel. Good man. You've earned my respect." Angus bowed slightly before he gave his full attention to Mathias and Jolena.

"Well, since my grandson is as strong willed as any McGregor I've ever known, and believe me, I've known my fair share of them, I guess all that's left is to let him stay around and wait for you." He smiled at Jolena and winked. "Your parents send their love, lass."

Jo finally let go of her breath and smiled, first at Mathias's grandfather, who surely must be his guardian angel, or hers, or both, and then at Mathias, who returned it in kind. She could both see and feel his joy. He took her hand and held it tightly. And then suddenly, it seemed as if the clouds parted to allow the light of the sun to shine down upon the clearing, except one could see nothing but blue skies all around. This light didn't come from the sun.

Nevertheless, Jolena recognized its brilliance the moment it appeared. She beheld its magnificent glory once before and she would again, but not right now and thankfully, neither would Mathias.

Jedediah stepped toward her first. "Jolena, I meant what I said earlier. I'll keep you in my heart, until such time as we meet again." He leaned forward and kissed her gently on the cheek. He then turned to Sam, who stood next to Jo.

"Be sure to give your folks my best regards—mine too, if you see them," Sam said.

"You can be sure I will." Jedediah smiled as he offered his hand.

Sam ignored the hand and yanked him into a hearty embrace. "We'll be there soon enough, lad."

"And I'll be watching for you," Jedediah said as he turned to face Mathias.

Mathias let go of Jolena's hand in order to embrace his young friend as well. "Scout out a nice piece of land for us, Jedediah," he said. "We'll all want to remain together, once we're all together again."

Jedediah smiled broadly, as he saluted his friend. "Yes, sir, and Mathias, thanks for everything. I want you to know, I found it a pleasure and an honor serving beside you. I'm proud to call you my friend."

"Likewise," Mathias replied.

"I'll miss you, all of you," Jedediah said as he stepped back and gave Dakota one last pat on the head. He turned around then, mounted his horse, and urged him toward the light, but just before he entered it, he turned back. He had the most joyous expression on his face as if what lay ahead of him held an unimaginable glory and he said, "I'll be seeing you."

As he disappeared into the light, Alexander and William shared a private goodbye with Mathias and Sam. She had no wish to intrude. Part of her celebrated the fact that Mathias and Sam would remain at her side. Yet part of her sorrowed for the loss of three very dear friends. She couldn't stop the tears from welling up in her eyes as William and Alex approached her.

"We don't want you grieving for us, either," William ordered as he wiped away the tears. "We want the rest of your life filled with one happy adventure after another. And we want you to remember all of the good times and all of the laughter we've shared. I want you to recall, every day of your life, just how ridiculous Alex looked as he portrayed Mrs. Peacock, and what a sight Jedediah made in that frilly pink apron he conjured."

Jolena managed a laugh as she called the hilarious scene to mind.

Alexander gave her a kiss and said, "I'm glad I hung around for a couple of centuries, Jolena. I surely wouldn't have wanted to miss the chance of forging an eternal friendship with you."

"Nor would I," William added.

"I love you both, very much. Remember that during this time of separation." Jolena sniffed. "And, take very good care of yourselves."

Sam retrieved their mounts and handed over the reins. Both William and Alex chose to walk into the light with their horses following close behind. And just like Jedediah, they both turned back before they entered and smiled.

"Until we meet again." William saluted Mathias and Sam, and then blew her a kiss.

"We'll be waiting," Alex added. "You can count on that."

With a final nod, they too, were gone. Moments later, the brilliant light receded until it disappeared from sight altogether.

Only then did Angus McGregor approach her. "You've a gate to close, Jolena Michaelsson, before the owner discovers your mischief, and I need a private moment with the boys."

His words filled Jo with alarm. She exchanged a quick glance with Mathias. Why would Angus ask her to leave? She didn't want to go unless Mathias accompanied her.

"Don't worry. He'll be along by and by. You've got my word on that," Angus reassured her as he extended his hand toward Lacy, and then as if she understood the unspoken command, Lacy sidled over and stood next to her.

She swung up on her back and Angus handed her the reins. Despite her reluctance, he had dismissed her and surely, one could not butt heads with an angel. So, as time once again resumed, she turned Lacy toward home with only Dakota to accompany her. When she finally arrived at the pasture, all of the horses quietly grazed as if they'd never left. She wandered over to the gate, nudged the topmost bar with her foot, and shut it tight. Then, she leaned over and latched it.

Once she arrived home, she put Lacy out in the small pasture, traversed the property toward the house and the door she left wide open. She shut it behind her, ambled into the family room, sat down, and waited for Mathias with all the patience her restless heart could muster.

In fact, she waited all day, pacing between the family room, sitting room, and library. She wandered out to the barn several times, hoping to see Beadurinc in his stall, but it remained empty. Each hour that ticked by, the waiting became more difficult to endure. Did something happen to prevent Mathias and Sam from returning? What did Angus McGregor mean when he said, "by and by?" To an angel, time meant nothing.

Somewhere along the way she fell fast asleep on the sofa, the morning sun streaming into the windows woke her. She sat upright. The house still felt empty. She could hear Lacy as she continued calling for Beadurinc and her other ghostly companions.

"Mathias?" she called out. Funny, she could hear the desperation in her voice. Jo toyed with the idea of riding back to the forest. She couldn't compel herself to do it, because without doubt, she'd find the woodland empty. The day passed at a snail's pace, despite intense rehearsals at the concert hall and so did the night that followed. She found she couldn't concentrate on any one thing for any amount of time. Come the dawn she wanted to release the torrent of tears she'd held inward and just as she gave in to despair, Carolyn burst through her front door and called out to her.

"Come on, Jo. You have to come with me, right now. We have an emergency." She skidded to a halt and looked her over. "Good heavens, girl, you look awful. What happened? What's wrong? Wait—never mind that right now. We'll talk later. Have you had a shower yet this morning? Never mind answering that, either. Get upstairs and get yourself cleaned up. And for heaven's sake, hurry!" she commanded.

"Why? What's going on?" asked Jo as she wiped away the tears and stood to her feet.

"We don't have time for explanations, just hurry. Make yourself beautiful and put on something nice, I don't want you to embarrass me," she said as she dragged her up the stairs.

About an hour later, they were in the car and heading toward the freeway. The shower did make her feel better and this unexpected outing gave her the diversion she needed. Hopefully when she returned home, Mathias would be there waiting—*hopefully*.

"Where are we going?" she asked.

"New Jersey," Carolyn said as she shot a glance in her rear-view mirror.

"Why?" she asked.

Carolyn put a trembling hand to her mouth, squeezed her eyes shut, and shook her head. "I can't talk about it right now. Please. Can we talk about something else? Anything else?"

Carolyn looked terribly upset. She could only hope something hadn't happened to Ray. Two hours later, they turned into the Brennan's driveway. Jo's heart dropped into her stomach. Parked cars filled both sides of the road. Had something happened to one of Ray's parents?

Carolyn flew out of the car and Jo followed suit. They walked up the sidewalk and into the house in silence. Jo just didn't know what to say. Carolyn led her into the kitchen and opened the sliding glass door.

"I'm sorry for all of the drama." She sniffed as she dabbed the corner of her eye. "I need to gather a few things. I'll meet you outside in a few minutes and explain everything. Could you wait for me by the beach? You know the one."

Jo took a deep breath, kicked off her shoes, left them on the patio, and headed for the ocean. A gentle breeze caressed her face, and the scent of the brine filled her lungs. The gulls chattered above her as they played with the windy currents high above her. The day seemed so perfect, she found herself dreading what Carolyn might say that would surely ruin it.

And then as she rounded the bend, she cast her gaze on Mathias. She stopped dead in her tracks. He looked so handsome and somehow, different in a way she couldn't quite pinpoint. He wore a pair of black jeans and a white, long-sleeved dress shirt rolled to the elbows, with the first two buttons left undone. His hair blew freely in the wind. He gave her a smile as he extended his arms toward her. She forgot to question his knowledge as to her whereabouts since she didn't know about the trip herself. The answer didn't matter. Not right now, anyway.

All that mattered is that he stood not thirty feet in front of her and he wanted to hold her. Her exuberance propelled her forward. Once close enough, he drew her into a crushing embrace. Her eyes widened in shocked surprise as she gazed into his eyes. She could feel the warmth of his hard muscled chest beneath her fingers as well as the beating of his heart.

"Mathias!" she breathed out. "What—how did—I don't—"

Mathias didn't want to answer questions. Not right

now. He just wanted to kiss her—really kiss her for the first time as a mortal man, and he wasted no time in giving in to that desire.

Jolena melted into his arms and returned each of his very thorough kisses with some of her own. Her kisses released a tidal wave of emotion and feelings he had held in check far too long. A thousand questions needed answering. Yet, they could all wait for a better time—a much better time.

Mathias shook his head as he finally forced himself to put a little distance between them. He locked his gaze with hers and said, "I believe you once said something about eloping? You did mean that, did you not?" he whispered in one ragged breath.

Jo started laughing. "Are you asking me to marry you, Mathias McGregor?"

"If you'll have me," he whispered and as his lips grazed across hers, he added, "and the sooner the better, for both our sakes."

Chapter 32

"Oh, for crying out loud," griped Carolyn as she happened upon the scene. "Can't the two of you wait until the 'I dos' have been said?"

Jo blushed as she looked over at Carolyn and the entourage, which followed. Ray, his parents, a minister and Sam. He looked just as mortal as Mathias did. Tagging along behind the group, strolled several of their friends. Her lips parted as she gazed into each of their smiling faces and finally understood the reason for their presence. She looked down at her clothes, suddenly grateful she had chosen her brand-new white eyelet summer dress, trimmed in organza lace.

No, wait a minute. Carolyn chose it. She laid it out on the bed while she showered and along with the dress, she selected her diamond earrings and dressy white sandals. She raised a brow as she turned to face her.

"I presume this is the emergency you had me so worried about, Kay-Kay?" she quizzed.

"Of course, that much should now be obvious. Mathias would surely have had a coronary if I didn't get you out here right away. So, an emergency it was. And by the way, you have some explaining to do yourself, missy. You could've knocked me over with a feather when he showed up at my lab with all his requests, which sounded more like demands if you ask me—

"Nevertheless, I don't think your guy here knows

what it takes to get a wedding together, even a very simple one. The favors I had to call in and the strings I had to pull to get you a marriage license on the sly, which you can't forget to sign or it will be my head. You know, it's a darn good thing I know all the right people or—"

"I'm sorry—" Mathias cut in. "Do you think this conversation and all your complaints and explanations can wait until I've made this woman mine?"

Carolyn rolled her eyes. "If you insist. But one would think you'd allow me just a little more time after you ran me so ragged these last couple of days," she grumbled as she dug around inside her large bag. She withdrew an exquisite band of flowers, made up of pink and white rose buds mixed with baby's breath. She weaved them through Jolena's hair. Once she finished the task, she adjusted the lacy cap sleeves of her dress, drawing them a little off her shoulders, then handed her a bridal bouquet that matched the flowers in her hair. With a critical eye, she stood back to survey the results. All the while Ray took pictures of the unfolding scene.

"Oh no, Jo! You kicked your shoes off again? You can't get married bare foot," wailed Carolyn.

"Oh yes, she can," Mathias asserted, as he tugged her toward the decorated arbor. Once they stood in front of it, he looked at the minister and said, "Now, if you'd be so kind as to make this woman my wife, sir?"

Tears slid down Jo's cheeks as she listened to the words that bound her to Mathias. He refused to allow the minister to use the words, "until death do us part," instead asked him to say "for all time," and those were the words to which they agreed. To seal the deal, Sam, acting as best man handed Mathias a ring. He slipped on her finger, an intricately etched platinum ring with small sapphires and diamonds adorning the band. The ring was a perfect match for her pendant. She looked over at Carolyn who smiled knowingly, and she in turn, handed her a matching band for Mathias, minus the gems.

When told to kiss the bride, Mathias hastened to comply. Jo's toes curled into the sand as he gave a singular kiss that promised forever.

Then, an exaggerated clearing of the throat, provided by Sam, ended the lengthy kiss. Everyone rushed forward to congratulate them. Sam just about crushed the breath right out of her once he took his turn.

Jo shook her head as tears formed and just as she opened her mouth, Sam held a finger to her lips. "The long version will have to wait. Suffice it to say we took a quick trip back in time since we were halfway there already, collected our bodies before the English had a chance to ruin them beyond repair, and then visited a fountain of water before our return. I believe you are aware of such a fountain?"

"Oh, yes, I am. And Sam? Thank you so very much for staying," she whispered.

Sam winked. "Not to worry. I'd not have it any other way. Mathias and I entered this world almost simultaneously, and I daresay we'll *all* leave it the same way."

"The horses?" she asked.

"They're all in the barn. We couldn't very well leave them behind, now could we? Now if you'll excuse me, I promised to act as escort for that lovely little lass over there," he said, cocking his head a little to the right.

Jo glanced at the woman in question. She returned his smile, kissed him lightly on the cheek, and whispered, "You know, Emily would be a good match for you,

Sam."

"Think so?"

"Most definitely."

Sam merely laughed in return.

Carolyn waited until last to offer her congratulations. She hugged her close and whispered. "You look absolutely beautiful, my dear. And we're going to lunch very soon, so you can tell me all about how you and Mathias found each other. I mean, that man is drop-dead gorgeous."

Jo laughed and briefly lowered her gaze. "Yes, I know—"

"All right, everybody," Carolyn yelled out when she turned around to face the small group. "We've got mounds of food in the kitchen and a cake that needs slicing by a groom and his bride."

Several hours later, as the celebration of their wedding finally wound down, Mathias withdrew a very old pocket watch and looked pointedly at the time. Carolyn sighed and tossed him a key from off the shelf. The scene made Jo laugh.

"There's a little beach house just down the way from where you said your vows," Kay said. "If you keep walking, you'll see it. There's a wedding wreath on the door. Enjoy. I'll pick you both up at ten a.m. tomorrow to take you to the airport. Don't worry, Jo, you're already packed." She ushered them to the sliding glass door in the kitchen.

Once she shut the door and they were a good distance away, Jo gazed at Mathias and said, "Airport?"

He grinned as he took her hand and strolled past the arbor. "In continuation of the many miracles which have transpired, I finagled a couple of tickets to Scotland. The

Galbraiths seemed exceptionally pleased to allow us the use of their cottage for our honeymoon."

Jo released a sigh and smiled. "Well, as I recall, you're supposed to take me to a certain waterfall, hidden away in an enchanted forest, not far from a fairytale castle."

"We've a promise to keep inside that very forest, you, and me." Mathias winked as he turned her around and gathered her into his arms. They stopped just shy of the beach house door. "However, I'm not about to take you anywhere near MacNaughton's castle or Sir Cailen again. I'm afraid we'd find ourselves engaged in an eternal duel for your affections, if I were so daft as to take you back there."

"Oh, Mathias," Jo whispered as she brushed her fingers through his hair and grazed her lips tantalizingly against his. "I promise—I absolutely promise, I'm going to *love* you every minute of every day, always and forever—"

Mathias flashed a wicked smile. A pretty blush followed. "Is that right?" Once he unlocked and opened the door, he swept up her into his arms and as his lips played against her own, he whispered, "Then come, my love, let's not keep forever waiting—"

A word about the author...

Debbie has a soft spot for fairy tales, the joy of falling in love, and happily-ever-after endings. She incorporates these aspects into all of the paranormal stories she writes.

When she is not busy conjuring her latest novel, she spends time with the beloved members of her very large family. She also pursues her interests in family history and all things ancient and historic.

Thank you for purchasing
this publication of The Wild Rose Press, Inc.
For other wonderful stories of romance,
please visit our on-line bookstore at
www.thewildrosepress.com.

For questions or more information
contact us at
info@thewildrosepress.com.

The Wild Rose Press, Inc.
www.thewildrosepress.com

To visit with authors of
The Wild Rose Press, Inc.
join our yahoo loop at
http://groups.yahoo.com/group/thewildrosepress/

www.ingramcontent.com/pod-product-compliance
Lightning Source LLC
Chambersburg PA
CBHW071646260626
47170CB00001B/258